THE LOVER

Helene Flood

THE LOVER

Translated from the Norwegian
by Alison McCullough

MACLEHOSE PRESS
QUERCUS · LONDON

First published in the Norwegian language as *Elskeren*
by H. Aschehoug & Co, Oslo, in 2020
First published in Great Britain in 2022 by

MacLehose Press
An imprint of Quercus Editions Ltd
Carmelite House
50 Victoria Embankment
London EC4Y 0DZ

An Hachette UK company

This translation has been published with the financial support of NORLA

A CIP catalogue record for this book is available from the British Library.

ISBN (HB) 978 1 52940 611 5
ISBN (TPB) 9781 5 2940 612 2
ISBN (Ebook) 978 1 52940 614 6

10 9 8 7 6 5 4 3 2 1

Typeset by Jouve (UK), Milton Keynes
Printed and bound in Great Britain by Clays Ltd, Elcograf S.p.A.

Papers used by Quercus are from well-managed forests and other responsible sources.

And the shark he has his teeth and
There they are for all to see.

And Macheath he has his knife but
No-one knows where it may be.

Bertolt Brecht, *The Threepenny Opera*

PART I

I promise I won't disturb you

You asked me about when I met Jørgen. Would you believe me if I said I don't remember? It must have been some occasion in the garden, or on the stairs, or by the entrance to the house, but I have no memory of it. My son was born just after we moved in, and he was premature. There were so many hospital appointments, so many things to worry about. I'm not saying this to be evasive – I mean it. I quite simply don't recall.

But I remember the first time I saw him. It must have been the beginning of July, the year we moved in. I'm able to date this so precisely because it was just a few days after Åsmund and I got the keys to the new apartment, a warm summer evening when we were sitting around at home back in our old flat, and I just couldn't help myself. Simply had to get up and go see the new place, where our new lives would soon begin.

They were sitting out on the patio in the garden when I arrived. You know how the path to the entrance goes straight past it? I looked over at them as I walked by, ready to greet them, but they were eating and paid me no attention. They were five in total, obviously good friends. I came alone, heavily pregnant, huge, and I'd been walking quickly, so I was dripping with sweat. And I didn't know them. I let myself into the building.

Inside, the apartment was empty. The previous

owners had taken all their belongings with them, but their smell still hung in the air. It didn't smell of us there, you know? When we closed on the apartment it felt as if we had bought our way into a certain life-style. Or into a certain social segment. As if we were now just that tiny bit finer than we had been, simply because we owned this place – at this address. But now that it was no longer tastefully furnished, now that my steps echoed between empty walls punctured with holes left by nails, I felt unsure. I can't explain it any other way than this: I felt as if I was playing dress-up in shoes that were far too big for me.

In the kitchen I went over to the window and looked out at the patio and the people sitting out there, though I didn't open it, despite the heat. I don't know. Perhaps I didn't want to intrude. It looked as if they had just finished eating; a few wine bottles on the table. They were chatting, and I could hear their voices through the closed windows – not what they said, but their tone. They were discussing something or other, fairly intensely, or so it seemed, but the mood was good. Occasionally they broke out into laughter, all five of them. Three men and two women. One of the men I recognised – he was a film-maker who had made a controversial documentary a few years back, about what I couldn't remember. Refugee policy or integra-tion, something like that. Quite a bit was written about it in the papers. There was something about one of the women, too – I had the feeling I'd seen her on TV. At one of the table's long sides sat a man and a woman who were obviously a couple. His arm was slung along the back of her chair, and on one of the occasions when everybody laughed she turned towards him, smiling, and wiped something from his cheek. A little later he moved his arm, setting his hand on her lower back as she was leaning across the table to say something. Her hair was long, a deep shade of red, gathered into a thick, elaborate braid that travelled the length of her spine; when she bent forward to speak, it slid off to one side. Her husband – the man sitting next to her – gently put it back. She turned to face him, aware that he had touched her, and continued to speak as she smiled at him. Perhaps she was telling the others about something they had experienced together.

He was sitting with his back to me in a way that made it difficult to see his face, but when he turned in a certain direction, I could see it. He was good-looking, with curly hair that had started to grey. He had prominent cheekbones and a big, charming smile that he clearly used often. I guessed that he was probably in his mid-forties, approaching fifty, perhaps.

That was Jørgen. That was the first time I saw him.

Since they didn't appear to have noticed me, I just stood there and watched them, these five friends discussing important matters around a dinner table, one summer evening in a garden in Kastanjesvingen.

Then the woman with the braid got up. She took an empty serving platter from the table and made her way over to the paved path that leads to the front door. Halfway down the path she caught sight of me – and no wonder, really. I was standing right in front of the window. Not even trying to hide the fact that I was watching; I was so captivated by them that it hadn't even occurred to me that I ought to move. She stopped, looking at me. I raised my hand and waved.

She just stood there. She didn't wave back, and nor did she smile at me – though she didn't look put out, either. She seemed almost neutral, standing stock-still and considering me. It lasted only a moment, and then she walked on. From where I was standing, I heard her open the front door to the stairwell. I hurried away from the window, fretting at having been caught staring so openly. Felt it deep in my stomach – that I had acted inappropriately, and so felt ashamed.

FIRST SATURDAY

The trees around me are deciduous, with huge crowns and strong branches. Nothing like the spruce forest that bordered the house where I grew up, and yet I know, in the way dreamers do, that I'm in the forest of my childhood. I know it well, understand how easy it is to disappear in it. You stick to the well-worn paths. But then you take a detour, following the sound of a deer or a glimpse of a lush blueberry patch a little off the trail, and when you turn back, everything has changed. Trees in all directions, dark and silent, layer upon layer. None of them look like the trees I know.

In the dream, I'm searching for someone. At first, I don't know who it is I'm looking for, but then I realise – it's my children. Lukas, I shout, breaking into a run. Emma! Before me, the forest opens out into a clearing. It isn't large, maybe five metres across, but the sun slips between the leaves and it's light and warm, fresh grass covering the ground. I stop. It's beautiful here, but my throat tightens. Without me fully understanding why, I am certain that something terrible has happened.

Out in the living room the air is still filled with the morning cold. I quietly close the bedroom door behind me, not wanting to wake the others. The room is unfamiliar in the flat dawn light. Perhaps the nightmare has yet to release its grip on my body, because the furniture seems huge and severe; the bookcase looks closed and secretive, and the coffee table is uncharacteristically tidy. My bare feet soak up the chill from the parquet. In the hallway I find my slippers, stuff my feet into them and go out into the kitchen.

It's surprisingly tidy in here, too. Åsmund and I shared a bottle of wine last night while we watched a film, a fairly mediocre one, although perhaps it got going eventually – I was tired and went to bed halfway through. Åsmund must have tidied up. The red symbol on the dishwasher tells me that it's finished its cycle, so for once he must have remembered to put it on before he came to bed.

I lean against the kitchen counter. This room is the major selling point of our apartment. This was where they took the photograph that filled the front cover of the brochure we were given when we attended the viewing. The kitchen is large and light-filled, and while the rest of our windows face either the overgrown hillside behind the house or the apartment complex next door, those in the kitchen look out on the garden. In order to make full use of the light, the architect who designed the house at some point in the 1950s made this wall a single long row of windows. We've positioned the kitchen table in front of them, and when we sit there, we can see the small garden in its entirety – the patio with its garden furniture, the barren apple tree, the stand for the mailboxes and the white wooden fence. Beyond it is Kastanjesvingen, a little cul-de-sac that ends in a turning circle forty metres or so past our gate. On the other side of the road are detached houses – some of them from the same period as this one, which has been split into four apartments, and some of them newer. Behind them is the hill known as Bakkehaugen, which separates us from the city centre, and although I can't see it from the kitchen window, I get a warm glow just from knowing that it's there, behind the hill. That this is where we live, in this quiet cul-de-sac, but with the city so close we can almost touch it.

I take a seat at the table. Sit quiet as a mouse, listening. Is he awake up there? Is he moving around, can I hear him? But no, it's too early, I know that. I'm probably the only person awake in the entire building. Still, it isn't completely silent. The soundproofing isn't good enough – you can hear even the lightest of breezes, the chestnut tree whipping its branches against the living-room window, the creaking of joists and timber whenever a neighbour moves.

Still sleepy, I stretch my body. I slept so heavily last night – I didn't even hear Lukas when he came into our room. Waking blind and afraid from my nightmare, I flicked open my eyes and saw his dishevelled head, his little hand beside mine. Tiny fingers with dirt under the nails; a green plaster around an invisible wound on his index finger. I felt so relieved, surfacing from the dream – he was there, everything was fine. I brushed his fringe aside. When had he come in?

Across the street, I see Hoffmo emerge from his brown-painted house. He stands on his front step and looks around, like a petty king surveying his kingdom. Then he sets his hands on either side of his big stomach and stretches, rolling his hips first one way and then the other, his belly quivering in front of him. He'll be heading out for a run, because that's what he's like – over seventy and still running twice a week, whatever the weather. His blue tracksuit with its white stripe down each leg is a relic of the seventies and makes his silhouette even more comical, but there's something about Hoffmo – a kind of natural authority – that stops people laughing at him. The two of us get along well.

"Done any running lately?" he tends to shout over his fence whenever he sees me. "Exercise is good for the brain, you know, Prytz. Healthy body, healthy mind."

We address each other by our surnames – it's a kind of joke. I watch as he bends forward and touches the ground. He's not doing too badly on the flexibility front, I think, for a man of his age and his size. He straightens up, stretches, ready to run. I lift a hand and wave to him from my window, but he doesn't see me.

*

I can hear him even before he reaches the kitchen, his tiny, quick feet slapping against the floor. Lukas grabs hold of me and clambers up into my lap, leaning his head against my shoulder and closing his eyes. He could easily fall asleep there, I know – he can sleep anywhere. Part of me would like that, to just sit here in peace and quiet with a sleeping child on my lap.

"Lukas," I say. "Did you come into our bedroom all by yourself last night?"

He opens his eyes, looks up at me.

"Yes," he says, but hesitantly – like it's a question: Yes? Did I?

"I didn't hear you," I say.

This he doesn't deign to answer. He sets his head back against my shoulder and closes his eyes. I breathe deeply, listening for signs of life in the apartment above. Lukas opens his eyes again.

"Mamma," he says. "Can we find my big tyrannosaurus?"

I stand up to see Hoffmo jogging down his drive with short, light steps. As he reaches his gate and opens it, he catches sight of me, raises a hand and waves. I lift my own to give him a kind of military salute for his efforts and see him chuckle, his laughter rumbling through his big body.

After breakfast we dress and get ourselves ready for the day, which is going to be a hectic one. The plans were made long ago – all we have to do is follow them. This is the way every weekend will be now, right up until December. Sometimes I feel like we're rats on a wheel, we hurry from one appointment to the next in an uphill struggle that never ends. A few years ago I dreamed of renting out the apartment, taking all our savings and buying four plane tickets to Vietnam. Settling there and running a little hotel on the beach. Living life in the now and having time for each other, for the kids. Watching the days come and go – not racing to beat the clock, to make it to activities on time, to get everything done before diving into bed and recharging our batteries so we can do it all over again the next day, but able to really check in with ourselves. To live authentically, in touch with nature. I no longer think this way. On the beach in Vietnam we'd have other problems. We'd worry about whether our hotel was bringing in enough money; the guests would be dissatisfied with this, that and the other; there would be floods or drought; the plumbing would be old and the cost of replacing it too great, and so on.

Åsmund digs out a T-shirt from the pile in the corner. I make the bed as I tell him about my dream. I no longer remember the details – I was looking for something, I was afraid. I must have been dead to the world, I say, because when Lukas came and got into bed with us, I didn't even wake up.

"We ought to start weaning him off that," Åsmund says, fastening the strap of his watch around his wrist. "He's old enough to sleep alone."

"He's only four," I say.

"Emma slept all the way through in her own bed when she was four," Åsmund continues. "And all the sleeping during the day, Rikke – he needs to stop that. He's too big to need a mid-morning nap."

"Yeah, well," I say, not wanting to discuss it any further.

Lukas is my miracle baby – he was born almost two months premature. We were moving into this apartment when he arrived; I was in the process of unpacking cups and plates from boxes when the biting pain in my belly and back took hold. Åsmund was off somewhere picking up new furniture, Emma was with her grandmother, and I stood there before the empty kitchen cabinets, thinking: Have I overdone it with all the lifting and carrying? Have I overexerted myself? Maybe I should sit down for a minute?

When I finally left for the hospital, it was almost too late. I called Åsmund as I waited for the taxi; he jumped straight in the car and only just made it. The baby was taken from me the moment he was born – he had to be tested, measured, weighed, time was of the essence, and some information must have been lost in all the urgency, or perhaps I was so groggy after the birth that I didn't quite catch it, because I wasn't sure if everything was alright – was he alive, or not? They disappeared with him, and I turned to Åsmund and said:

"Are we parents again?"

Åsmund was crying – it's how he is, he can't help it, the tears just leak out of him at weddings and christenings. Then a doctor came in, her brow wrinkled and her lips pursed. I saw all this and thought: The baby is dead. Felt the terror first as a punch to the gut before it spread to my arms and legs, possessing my body. The doctor wasn't aware of this, and nor was Åsmund, but in the seconds it took for her to tell us that everything looked fine – the baby was small but strong, there would be a lot of tests and we might require follow-ups at the hospital going forward, but there was every reason to believe that everything was going to be okay – in those seconds I was certain that I'd lost him. It was a reality for me. And when I realised that I hadn't lost him after all, or in all likelihood hadn't lost him, at least, the relief was so great that all the rest of it – the risk of asthma and ADHD and problematic lung infections – was immaterial to me. I've returned to that moment again and again. I still do. My miracle baby. In some true sense, he's a bonus. I really did lose him. But I got him back.

"Okay, I'm ready," Åsmund says.

He's wearing a Lycra cycling suit, which is black with fluorescent yellow go-faster stripes. While I take Emma to her school play rehearsal and then go for coffee with my sister, he's going to take Lukas and ride out to Bærum to visit a friend. On the e-bike, of course, but he's dressed as if for a training session. He's gained a bit of weight in recent years. There's nothing unusual about it, it's just how it is. His friends have put on weight, too. Something happened in their mid-thirties. It left physical traces.

"What is it?" he asks.

"What?"

"You're looking at me?"

I smile.

"The Lycra," I say.

"Oh, that," he says. "Too tight? Is it embarrassing?"

"No, no. Very professional."

He winks at me.

"Tour de Tåsen, baby," he says, and goes out into the living room.

I can hear him out there, lifting Lukas into the air and roaring. Lukas laughs. My conscience stabs me in the gut, sharp and painful. There he goes – the father of my children. The man I have promised to love and honour. I quickly finish making the bed, then pick up the dirty clothes from the floor. Up in Jørgen's place, it's still completely silent.

"But at any rate," Lea's mother says to Saga's mum, "it's incredibly unpleasant, the whole thing."

"Ugh," Saga's mother says with a frown.

I'm standing with my back against a pillar beside the fabric-covered gymnastics ladder, listening to them as I consider the stage. It's empty, for the moment. The actors – if they can be called that – are shuffling between the front row of seats and the back room, where two mothers from the costume group are taking their measurements. I was back there just now, hoping to talk to Emma, but she was standing with a group of friends and didn't want to acknowledge me. One of the girls was being measured, and one of the costume mothers, armed with a measuring tape and safety pins, had said to her, now let's see, what size do you take? The girl had turned red and mumbled something in a low voice; Emma and the two other friends had laughed. I had looked over at my daughter. She's tall and slim, without so much as a hint of womanly curves – the way they are, these kids – but the friend having her measurements taken has already filled out a little at the chest and hips. With nothing else to do back there, I returned to the hall.

The mothers I can overhear are from the school activities group. I haven't really got to know them yet. Saga is one of Emma's new friends, and her mother is a journalist for one of the big newspapers, I see her photograph next to articles from time to time. Not so long ago she wrote a somewhat personal piece about body image pressure, and how quickly girls grow up these days. Lea's mother is a stay-at-home mum – apparently by choice, because she has a master's degree from a prestigious university in the UK. When school started in August, she and her husband invited all the girls in the year over to their house. They live in a villa, high up the hillside in Tåsen. I went there to collect Emma and tried not to be impressed by the huge house, the neatly cultivated front garden.

"From what I've heard, the poor cat was almost turned inside out," she says, this housewife with the master's degree. "Its innards were spread all over, and the rest of it – the skin and bones, from what I gather – were strung up on the wrought-iron fence."

"Just *awful*," the other mother says.

"The boy who found it was only young, poor thing. Just ten or eleven, I think. And the poor twin girls who owned the cat – well, apparently they're devastated. They're in the same class as my youngest – their mother said she had to keep them home from school for a couple of days. You know how they are, they get so attached to pets at that age, and it's one thing if they disappear or die of natural causes, but when they're killed like that . . ."

"Poor kids," says Saga's mum.

I lean my head back against the pillar. I will not be dragged into this. I will just let it lie.

By now the young actors have arranged themselves onstage, ready to begin. Emma and her friends are standing in a cluster on the right, and on the sofa at centre stage sits the ninth grader playing Mack the Knife, along with a couple of other boys in leading roles. The director is speaking to them from the front row, explaining how he wants them to approach the scene. The girls aren't paying attention. Emma says something, but I'm standing too far away to hear what. The four friends around her laugh in unison. There's something affected about it, I think. As if they're laughing on cue, without thinking about whether what they've just heard is funny or not.

"And you know," the housewife says, "it isn't the first time it's happened, either."

"No, exactly," says Saga's mother. "There were the incidents this spring, too."

"Yes!" the housewife says. "First they found one in Godalsparken, and then in a garden in lower Tåsen. He hung it from a tree, you know – with a noose and everything, as if from a gallows. Luckily, it was an adult who found it."

"Well, that's the worst thing about all this, isn't it?" Saga's mother agrees. "How it's affecting the children."

"Of course – they might be traumatised," the housewife says.

They're quiet for a moment. As if savouring the seriousness of the situation, allowing the unease to build up.

Down in the front row the director has finished speaking with the boys. He doesn't go over to the girls, just shouts at them: "Remember to stay present, okay?" He's a fairly young man, tall and thin, with thick, dark-brown hair and the kind of horn-rimmed glasses men in their twenties wear when they want to let everyone know how creative they are. Apparently, the school employed him just before the summer. He introduced himself at the parents' meeting in August – his name is Gard. He's a recent graduate, and he wants to work with young people because he believes that it's precisely at this point in life that one is most open to impulses and ideas. He wants to introduce his students to world literature. Their first play would be *The Threepenny Opera* by Bertolt Brecht – nobody could accuse him of not aiming high enough. Drama is just an optional subject, but Gard argued his case well and managed to borrow a few hours' rehearsal time from the German, Norwegian and music teachers. This arrangement brought about a surge in recruits, and Emma, who had never shown much interest in the theatre, applied for a part when she realised she would get to spend her time standing around onstage instead of conjugating German verbs.

"Are we ready?" Gard shouts, running a hand through his thick fringe. "Yes – this is where the music will come in, but since Merete isn't here today, we'll have to do it without. I'll just mark it – one, two and *ta-ram-tam-tam-tam*."

He has an impressively deep voice for someone with such an ungainly appearance. Still, his humming is no replacement for Merete's deep, suggestive piano chords, which usually attend the scene. The housewife appears to agree:

"Is Merete not here?"

"She's taken Filippa on a camping trip, apparently," Saga's mother says. "And you know, Jørgen isn't very interested in the theatre."

"A camping trip?" says the housewife, raising an eyebrow. "When there's a rehearsal?"

Don't the rest of us *also* have things we'd rather be doing on a Saturday, that eyebrow says. Do we *really* want to be standing here in this sports hall that still smells of sweat, even now that the stage curtains have been hung along the walls? Don't *we* have cabins that need to be closed for the summer or opened for the winter, don't *we* have gardens to tend to, houses to maintain, skis that need to be prepped well before the season begins?

I say nothing. Emma is going back to Saga's house after the rehearsal because I'm going to grab a coffee with my sister. I'm about to sneak out in an hour. I really am no better than that.

In the front row sits Nina Sparre, the deputy head teacher and our neighbour across the hall. I can see her small head with its close-cropped hair nodding quickly up and down, as if her neck were a coiled spring. What is she doing here, I wonder – why is she spending her Saturdays attending these rehearsals? Presumably she's here on behalf of the school administration. She stretches her skinny bird's neck, and even though I can only see the back of her head, I can imagine how she's scrutinising her surroundings with eyes that dart from one person to the next, as if she prides herself on ensuring no detail evades her.

"Ugh, I just can't stop thinking about those cats," Saga's mother says. Then she turns to address me: "Wasn't one of them found down by your place, Rikke?"

"No," I say quickly. "No, it was in Hauges vei. Quite far down, too."

She nods. The stay-at-home mum gives me a sceptical look. In my opinion the neighbourhood has taken these incidents – the cats that have been found killed – far too seriously. Of course it sends a shiver down your spine, and I understand that it affects people, but this collective panic is way out of proportion. All this casual throwing around of big words like *evil, traumatising, criminal activity*. The police have even been called.

"You know," says the housewife, "it could happen anywhere in Tåsen. Once this kind of psycho gets going, nobody in the neighbourhood is safe."

Both their faces are deeply creased with concern.

"I mean, who knows what goes on in the head of a person who would do something like that?" Saga's mother whispers.

I can no longer bite my tongue.

"But isn't all the speculation getting a bit out of hand, too?" I ask. They look at me.

"Of course, people are afraid when something like this happens in the local community," I say. "But then, in some ways it ends up being depicted as worse than it really is."

"That animal was tortured," the housewife says, a touch defensively. "And no cat falls onto a wrought-iron fence like that – the police said so themselves."

"I'm sure it looked terrible," I say. "But this talk of – what did you call it? – this *evil* at the root of it all, is a bit much, don't you think? I wouldn't be surprised if it was just some kids who found a dead cat and decided to have a bit of fun."

This last part I try to say cheerfully, as if to lift the mood, but I can hear that I'm way off the mark. I'm being too brusque, too pompous, writing off what they have to say and discrediting their fears. I'm right, of course – or at least, I think I am. But I don't express myself in the right way – make a mess of it. They consider me. This will be remembered. I take a breath, wanting to say more, but before I get that far a dad in worn jeans appears, a glue gun stuffed into his belt.

"The pizzas are here," he says.

The housewife slings her handbag over her shoulder and follows him out. Her gym leggings seem sprayed on to her body; she's nothing but skin and bone.

It turns out my sister can't meet up after all. I lean my back against the pillar as I read her text message. Something important has come up, she has to sort it out. Beside me stands Saga's mother, immersed in the contents of her own phone. We've agreed that Emma will go home with Saga after the rehearsal. Åsmund and Lukas won't be back for several hours. I'll have the apartment to myself.

And Jørgen will be alone upstairs. He messaged me yesterday morning to tell me that Merete and Filippa will be gone until Sunday and that he'll be home all weekend, writing. There was a hint of an invitation in his words, but I ignored it. Good luck with the writing, was all I wrote in reply. Left it at that.

Up onstage, Peachum pulls the proverbial strings and gets Mack the Knife arrested. The director has already lectured the kids on the moral aspects of the play, I've heard him at several rehearsals: Mack the Knife commits terrible misdeeds without the others so much as batting an eye, but when he seduces Peachum's daughter Polly — which is perfectly legal — Peachum declares that Mack the Knife must die. Can we understand Peachum's indignation, with Mack the Knife being the person he is, the director asked rhetorically — or does he become the play's villain when he snitches on Mack the Knife, in effect sentencing him to death? So far the young actors haven't had very much to say about this — they're more concerned with the costumes and who's going to snog who onstage.

The girls have stepped down to sit in the audience. Emma fixes her hair with quick, practised hand movements — there's something grown-up about this gesture, I think, something feminine. Her hair is blonde, like mine. People often tell us that we look alike. I see her cast a glance over her shoulder. Maybe she's looking for me, because her gaze slides across the pillar I'm standing against and meets mine. I smile at her. Something moves in her face, the slightest admission that she has seen me. Then she turns back around, and all I can see is her neck, taut and strong, her blonde hair wound into a knot above it.

"I'm not a criminal," says Peachum from the stage, affecting a high-pitched, unpleasant tone – it sends a shudder through me. "I'm just a poor man, Brown."

This is the scene in which Peachum justifies his betrayal, and the boy playing the part can really act. There's movement in the second row; Emma and one of her friends are giggling. Onstage, Peachum quickly turns in their direction. Maybe he thinks they're laughing at him. The director shouts cut.

"Now they'll have to do it all *again*," Saga's mother sighs in my direction.

"Looks like it," I answer, hoping this means that amiability has been re-established between us.

I won't send Jørgen a message. That's what I'm thinking. No, I'll spend these hours I now have at my disposal on myself. Go for a walk, perhaps. Read a book. I'm looking forward to it already as I stand there, shifting my weight from one foot to the other. Can I go now, or is it too early? How would it look?

"Yes," the director says. "Now it's actually time for Filippa's song, but, well, she's not here, so I'm not sure whether it's worth bothering with this scene today."

There is some discussion up at the front. Nina Sparre leans forward and says something to the director; he nods sceptically at what she says. Peachum grins out into the hall – at someone standing behind me, is the impression I get – and when I turn my head, I see Simen Sparre making some gesture in the direction of the stage.

"Hi," I say.

Simen shifts his gaze to me, smiles amiably and says hello.

"Back to visit your old stomping ground?"

He completed his final year at Bakkehaugen last year; he now attends a sixth-form college in the city.

"I'm helping out with the play," he says. "Rigging up the lights and the sound system, that sort of thing."

He's a rather attractive boy, I think, although he hasn't reached his full potential just yet, and probably isn't the most popular in his class. He's still wearing awkward khaki trousers, and he has acne and an uneven shave. But he's a late bloomer. Give him a few years and the girls will be flocking to him.

"That's nice," I say. "A favour for Nina?"

He turns to face the stage and, with a hint of defensiveness in his voice, says:

"I'm getting paid for it."

For a minute or two we stand wordlessly beside each other, looking up at the stage. Simen is possibly assessing the lighting, or perhaps waiting to be given something to do. Up at the front his mother is still deep in conversation with the patient director, but Simen isn't looking at her – it's as if he doesn't even know her. When I see them together, in the garden or in the stairwell or on the street, he's often silent, it strikes me, while Nina is always talkative. His father runs a kind of staffing agency, if I've understood correctly. He earns big money and is loud and burly, and on occasion says rude things under the guise of *speaking one's mind* and *saying it as it is.* Simen is seventeen, and – perhaps as an act of rebellion against his father – he's exquisitely polite.

Just as Nina seems to have said all she wanted to say, and the director shouts something to the students on the stage, Simen sticks his hands in his pockets, says goodbye, and crosses the floor. Peachum watches him disappear between the two stage curtains that cover the exit. I let thirty seconds pass before I pick up my jacket and turn to Saga's mother.

"I have to dash off now," I say. "Could you maybe send Emma home around six?"

There's a light on in the kitchen up in Jørgen's apartment. I stop outside the main door to the house and let my gaze slide over the facade, as if I'm just surveying my home, not looking for him. There is something archly Norwegian about this building, as if it is the bearer of real values: equal opportunities, growth, freedom and progress. Built in the 1950s, it oozes social democratic housing policies and post-war optimism. Since then, neo-liberalism has swept through the neighbourhood, and the apartments in our building and all the other converted houses have been expanded to include the loft above or cellar below; they've been done up and improved in the most exclusive fashion, but they still look frugal and modest when viewed from the outside, an earlier time's moderation a flattering mask that conceals the excesses within. I take a deep breath. The garden is empty. The windows are dark – most of the building's occupants must be out. And yet there's a light on in Jørgen's place. Not that this means anything.

The front door that opens on to the stairwell is large and modern, in sharp contrast to the building's modest exterior. They put it in just a year ago, and the board of the housing cooperative, led by the enterprising Nina, went for a coal-black colossus with a hardwood veneer.

"It looks as if it belongs in a high-security prison," I said to Åsmund when it was being installed.

Åsmund, who in a moment of weakness had let Nina pressure him into taking a role on the board, simply shrugged.

"You know, she decided right there and then, the moment it was presented at the board meeting," he said. "Surely it's a good thing? It's *very* secure, apparently."

Where this collective paranoia came from I have no idea, because this was before the neighbourhood's cats began to disappear. The modern door has no keyhole, and has to be opened using a keypad. Each apartment has its own unique code, which is to be changed at regular intervals – how regular would of course be up to each individual household, Nina told me when she collared me on the stairs one Tuesday afternoon, but she and Svein would be changing theirs once a month.

"That's the best thing, Rikke," she said. "Make it a habit. The first of every month. Put it in your calendar."

Åsmund and I still haven't changed the code, and as I enter it now, it's the same one we decided on when the door was first installed a year ago. 1812. The date of our first kiss. That's how sentimental we are. Or at least how sentimental Åsmund is – he submitted the form specifying the code we wanted.

Inside, the stairwell is empty and silent. On the noticeboard beside the front door hangs the list of communal tasks that need to be completed this autumn. Nina pinned it up a few weeks ago – and it's extensive. Fences need painting, roots pulling up; the lawn needs to be weeded and stones cleared away. *There's lots that needs doing*, it says at the bottom, *but if we all pitch in, it'll be child's play!* She's even thrown a smiley face on the end for good measure. I haven't signed up for anything, and neither has Åsmund. I walk past the noticeboard and let myself into our apartment. Lean my back against the door frame. The others won't be home for several hours. It smells of family life – food and jackets and a hint of rubbish long overdue being taken out. The hours lie open before me.

*

I don't sit down. The book I'm currently reading is on the coffee table in the living room, and in the kitchen the newspaper still lies open from this morning, but I can't settle. I think about tidying up a bit, making an effort for my family.

Above me there is complete silence. Not a sound. Isn't that a little strange? The light was on, and he said he'd be home. It's ten past one in the afternoon. I'm not going to send a message to check if he's there. And I'm certainly not going to ask whether he still wants me to drop by. The dirty dishes from breakfast are still on the kitchen counter; I decide to put them in the dishwasher. The milk on the breakfast cereal has congealed; the grains have swollen during the hours they've sat there, and turned into porridge. I scrape out the half empty bowls, one after the other. Anyway, what Jørgen does is none of my business. When the scraped-clean bowls are all in the dishwasher, I look around. The place is actually fairly tidy. Perhaps I could just as well go take a walk.

I manage to resist for half an hour before I message him. I feel a little ashamed as I type the words, because I knew that I was going to do it all along, of course I did, it was obvious the moment my sister cancelled, and there's something so depressing about this act I've put on for myself – the tidying up, the book I told myself I might read.

Jørgen doesn't answer. It doesn't even look like he's read the message.

I empty out the children's backpacks from yesterday – Åsmund said he'd do it, but he's forgotten. I put their shoes in the hallway, together in their inevitable couplings, the one no good without the other. I gather up Lukas's toys. Now there really is nothing to do, and my phone is just as silent.

But he *is* home. The light is on. Perhaps he's so engrossed in his work that he's forgotten time and space – it's happened before. Maybe it hasn't occurred to him to check his phone.

Of course, I could just go up there. Simply knock on the door and say hi. Ask whether he still has time, as he told me he would in the message he sent me yesterday. I don't *have* to wait for him to answer – that's what's so good about being neighbours. Encouraged by this idea I straighten the cushions on the sofa, put the iPad away, and flick through the letters on the chest of drawers in the hallway. He still hasn't answered. It's been an hour, and we don't exactly have all the time in the world either, so I leave the apartment and go upstairs.

On the upstairs landing there are two doors, one to Merete and Jørgen's apartment and one to Saman and Jamila's. On Merete and Jørgen's doormat are the words THIS IS A GREEN HOME. A brass plate engraved with the name TANGEN has been screwed to the door. Now that I'm here, I hesitate. Am I being overbearing? Is this too much, too intrusive? This is the downside of being neighbours – and we've spoken about it, Jørgen and I. The need for space. The need for discretion. It's not just us who are neighbours. Our families are, too.

I'm on the verge of withdrawing, of going back down to my own apartment. I look back down the stairs, at the window where they make a U-turn. That would probably be wise. It might even let me feel that I'd been good, that I'd resisted temptation – coming so far, but then leaving well alone. But on the other hand . . . I hesitate. Stand there, ready to go either way. It's so thrilling, that feeling you get when you've decided to do something wrong. Weightless and fluid – the sense that anything could happen. My encounters with Jørgen happen somewhere outside the rat race. He has the ability to suspend time, to take me out of what feels like an inevitable progression: you have children, they grow, you take care of them, they transition from nursery to school, you plan holidays, your finances, they start secondary school, you save for your pension and think about what you want out of life, they go to sixth-form college, you worry about whether they're going to come home at night, you wonder what will become of them, they move out, you tell your partner that it's also nice to have a bit more space, you support them financially, try to hold on to them as they try to pull away, and then you're old, it won't be long till you retire – if you've saved up enough, that is – and then working life is over, your children have children, and you make all these plans, you travel, go on cabin trips with friends, look after the grandchildren, as if all these plans are life itself, as if the idea is to tick off as many things as possible before you die or end up in a nursing home. Oh, I know, I know – this is an oversimplification, a caricature. There are moments of happiness, of course. Sunsets on the veranda with a glass of white wine, the children asleep on Christmas Eve, or the everyday joy of seeing the chestnut tree down at the end of the road covered in yellow and orange leaves as you cycle home from work one day in early autumn. But even these moments are marked by the time that is passing, nothing but breathless attempts to stop and be present and catch your breath. With Jørgen, this unending, inevitable chain is temporarily broken. We meet on the outside. And who can resist making time disappear, even if only for a moment?

I knock on the door, my knuckles striking the wood. It's silent inside the apartment. I wait, listening for his footsteps. Maybe it's taking him a moment to pull himself away – he's in the middle of a thought, he has to rouse himself from it to come to the door. I give him time. But nothing. I knock again – hard, heavy raps. Wait. Still nothing; only silence.

Is he out? But the light. And he said that he'd be here today. *I'll be alone up here all weekend*, he wrote, *if you find you do have time after all*. I stand there. What do I do now? I hadn't expected this. I turn back towards the stairs. I suppose I'd better go back down to my own apartment, then; let the opportunity pass.

On the landing windowsill there's a small flowerpot with a painted-leaf begonia in it. An especially hardy begonia, it seems, because despite receiving scant attention it's hanging on, making it through the cold winters and dry, hot summers. Everybody in the building knows that down there, beneath the plastic inner pot at the bottom of the ceramic decorative one, lies a key to Jørgen and

Merete's apartment. We've all watered plants for them, brought in their post, checked something or other for them while they've been away. What if Jørgen is sitting there with his headphones on? I can just imagine him in his study, lost in thought in front of his computer, concentrating deeply on whatever he's doing – as is so often the case. Miles away, watching YouTube videos, perhaps – of Taliban soldiers, or lectures in recent Afghan history from Harvard or Oxford, talks by the world's leading experts streamed right here, to Jørgen's computer in Kastanjesvingen. It would be hard to hear someone knocking over the headphones. Even more difficult over the voice of professor such-and-such with a PhD in geopolitics.

I feel under the flowerpot and find the key. It isn't on a key ring, there's no decoration attached to it. It's all alone, a lonely piece of metal in a ceramic plant pot. I squeeze it hard in my hand – it's damp from the soil – and then I go back up the stairs, to Jørgen's door. Insert the key into the lock and turn it. The door floats open, and I go in.

Inside, the apartment is quiet. It smells clean, alongside some other faint but clear fragrance, something pleasant. The way the forest smells after the rain. I stand in the hallway and look into the living room. See Merete's shiny grand piano, its lid open as if gaping at something. The sofa with its cream woollen fabric, the bookshelf made from tropical hardwood. The door to the study is closed. That must be where he is, but I stop. My feet refuse to budge from the hallway floor. My gut tells me that something isn't right.

The living room is empty – it looks abandoned, somehow. It's almost sinister how clean and tidy it is. All I have to do is open my mouth, call out to Jørgen. Just lift a foot and walk into the room; go over to the door to his study and open it. But I don't move. This faint hint of something in the air. My breathing is quick and shallow. My gaze jumps here and there, from the neatly arranged sofa cushions to the rug that lies there on the floor without a wrinkle, to a strip of light from the kitchen that falls across the living room wall. To the closed door to the study. Something in here is dangerous. I can't put my finger on it, I don't know what it is, all I know is I have to get out, get away, but I'm unable to move. One second passes, then two, and I just stand there breathing hard, looking from one thing to the next, sniffing the air. Then I tug myself free. Take the two steps out of the apartment in one and slam the door behind me. Try to keep my hand steady enough to get the key in and lock the door; it takes a few attempts before I manage it. I try to calm my breathing, tell myself there's nothing to be afraid of, I'm getting myself all worked up over nothing. I put the key in my pocket and am about to turn and hurry down the stairs when I hear the sound of a throat being cleared behind me.

In the doorway opposite stands Saman.

"Hi," he says.

"Hi," I say, my voice weak, nothing but air.

He looks at me, and I try to pull myself together. Swallow several times. What will he believe? I'm panting as if I've been running. He might have seen me come out and lock the door, too – no, I don't think so, but I can't rule it out, and at the very least he's seen that I'm here, while Jørgen is home alone. I clear my own throat a couple of times, attempting to regain my composure.

"I was just," I say – I'm still shaking, my hands, my voice – it's so hard to think. "I just wanted to borrow something. Eggs. I'm baking, and we've run out. I should have checked, but I didn't think . . ."

I've forgotten to breathe, and now I draw in air as I swallow – it catches in my throat. I cough once, twice, and swallow again.

". . . didn't think of it before I started," I say. "So I was just wondering if I could borrow some. But there was nobody home."

Saman nods.

"Merete's away, apparently," he says.

Clearly everybody knows – that's how things are around here. Go out for an evening, and the next day the neighbours ask if you had a good time out on the town. Sometimes it's nice. Others it's suffocating.

"I can see whether we have any," says Saman, turning around. "Just a minute."

He disappears into the apartment leaving the front door ajar, enabling me to peek into his clean, minimalistic space, so modern and stripped down that Jamila could have taken her photographs in there, had she wanted to. I push the key further into my pocket. It's so small it can't be seen through my jeans, but I tug my sweater down over it anyway.

Saman returns with two brown eggs, one in each hand.

"Here," he says.

He passes them to me, and I take them, trying to keep my hands steady. The eggs are cold and round against my palms.

Down in my apartment I sit at the kitchen table. Ten minutes later I hear steps out on the stairs, and from the rhythm of them, quick and precise, I know it's Saman. After I hear the front door slam, I let seven minutes pass. Then I go out into the stairwell, up onto the landing, and stop in front of the begonia. As I let the key slip gently into the pot, I look out the window, towards the slope next to the house where nothing happens, where the bushes grow wild because nobody bothers to prune them or rake up the dead leaves. Propped against the wall is a ladder. Maybe someone's decided to wash the green algae from the cladding or noticed a wasps' nest up in the eaves. Were anyone to see me, standing here like this at the window, it would probably look as if I'm considering the ladder, thinking that someone ought to put it back in the shed before it rusts. By the time I go back downstairs to my own apartment, I've almost stopped shaking.

Åsmund comes home at around four-thirty, still wearing his helmet, a slight sheen to his forehead.

"Hey, hey!" he shouts, his voice filling the entire apartment.

I've been looking forward to having them back after the eerie disquiet upstairs, which the passing hours have only partly served to dampen. But now Åsmund is here it seems too much – he's so loud. I force a smile, thrown off balance, though I don't know why, because there's no reason for it. There's nothing I can point to as a trigger for my discomfort in the apartment upstairs. It's ridiculous. I have to pull myself together. Maybe I drank too much coffee at the rehearsal, or perhaps it is the damn cats after all.

They began disappearing just after Christmas. Cats do that, it's nothing new, but suddenly three were missing at the same time. Then one more, and yet another. Almost six months passed before the first one was found, and a few weeks later the next one turned up, hanging from a noose in a garden down a side road a little south of Kastanjesvingen. A few more months passed, and while further cats disappeared, no more were found. Until a couple of weeks ago, when Garfield – a Norwegian Forest cat belonging to a family down in the garden city area – was discovered impaled on the fence surrounding the Bakkehaugen farm estate. Talk in the neighbourhood has bubbled and seethed since the first cat was found, fuelled by each subsequent finding. You hear people talking about it on the street, in the supermarket, in their gardens. Everybody has something to contribute: a theory about the motive, or what it means, an observation – whether first-hand or second – to add to the collective narrative, and the loudest among these myriad voices is Hoffmo's.

A few weeks ago, just after the second cat was found, he rang Nina Sparre's doorbell with the intention of getting his concerns off his chest. His sonorous voice boomed through the stairwell – Åsmund and I could hear it all the way inside our apartment: *This is too much, Nina – you should have taken action on this long ago, why has nothing been done?* Nina, chairman of the board of the housing cooperative and self-appointed first protector of the neighbourhood, responded as best she could:

"But surely most important is what *the police* intend to do, not to mention the *urban environment agency.* And pets and domestic animals are also the responsibility of the *local municipality*, and in the first instance the ball is of course in their court at – you know – municipal level."

"The police?" Hoffmo snorted. "They're not going to do a damn thing. What are *we* going to do, Nina?"

"Well, I've asked that anyone who has seen anything go to the authorities," said Nina self-importantly. "It's for them to deal with now."

Hoffmo snorted again. He's another of the neighbourhood's self-appointed protectors of the realm, and when it comes to doing his duty, the old man is no less dedicated than Nina Sparre. He spent his entire working life in the Norwegian Armed Forces. It must be almost ten years since he retired, but it seems time has in no way diminished his compulsion to act when danger threatens. The danger, in this case, is likely kids trying to act tough, but to hear Hoffmo speak you'd think a hostile government was rattling its sabres.

A few years ago, not long after Åsmund and I moved in, the neighbourhood had been plagued by vandalism. Nothing especially crude or extensive, just a few graffiti tags here and there, but Hoffmo, true to form, took this as an affront. When the police failed to regard these offences with what Hoffmo deemed the necessary seriousness, he took matters into his own hands. He installed cheap little surveillance cameras in the playground and along the hedges of Kastanjesvingen, set up a tripwire around his house and patrolled the neighbourhood in the evenings. His campaign wasn't particularly successful. Half the cameras were stolen or destroyed, his wife was the only person to be caught by the tripwire, and all that came out of his nightly patrols was a detailed overview of which of the good citizens of Kastanjesvingen came home the latest and the most intoxicated. The police were decidedly uninterested in the results of Hoffmo's campaign, and when word got out that he had been secretly filming the neighbourhood, Hoffmo found himself on the receiving end of the wrath of a lawyer who lived at the end of the road. You can't just set up cameras and film people on municipal land, the lawyer said, that's against the law. The argument that followed would have been a prolonged one had Fru Hoffmo not had serious words with her husband, which resulted in Hoffmo reluctantly agreeing to let sleeping dogs lie and to offer up a half-hearted hint of an apology.

"You have to make sacrifices for the sake of domestic peace, you know, Prytz," he had mumbled when I asked, but otherwise Hoffmo had precious little to say about his campaign and subsequent retreat after the event. It seemed he was almost a little embarrassed by the whole thing.

But the neighbourhood watch campaign was trying for Nina, who felt it was her responsibility to ensure that everything was proceeding as it should in Kastanjesvingen. There's a gap in the insulation between our apartment and that of the Sparre family, and if we open the kitchen cabinet that hides the boiler, we can hear what's going on in their kitchen as if it were happening in ours. This isn't something we do often, but on one of the days after Hoffmo had forced out his apology I opened the cupboard door almost at random and heard Nina rabbiting on at her husband. She was relieved, I could tell, that a sense of harmony had once again settled over the neighbourhood. She said it over and over again. What she said to Svein when the first dead cat turned up, I have no idea, but she did manage to convince the police to come up to Tåsen. They took photographs before clearing away the cat's corpse and speaking with a few neighbours. Perhaps Nina argued her case well, or maybe they just thought humouring her was the easiest way to get rid of her.

"The police coming out for dead cats," I said to Åsmund later in the evening, after I'd seen two policemen taking photos at one of the crime scenes. "I've seen it all now."

"I can understand why people feel afraid though, Rikke," Åsmund said.

At the housing cooperative board meeting, people had started to cry. Åsmund let himself be swayed – he thinks I'm cynical. I think he's being soft, but I know that I'm alone in viewing the matter this way, so I keep my opinion to myself. I let it slip at the rehearsal today, and I'm regretting it already.

Why does it irritate me so much? That's a question I don't have an answer to. My sharpness towards the other mothers surprised me. Am I afraid after all? Have I simply failed to notice it? Is that why I felt such a strong sense of unease just now, up in Jørgen's apartment? Was that what woke me earlier today, disturbing my dreams and ripping me from sleep at six in the morning?

Jørgen still hasn't answered my message. It doesn't even look like he's seen it. Upstairs, it's still completely silent.

Lukas is curled up on the sofa, ready for his regular afternoon dose of children's TV. I've just picked up the remote to give it to him when Åsmund shouts from the kitchen:

"Rikke? Why are there two eggs on the counter in here?"

I stop, freezing there in the middle of the room with the remote control in my hand, and think: Damn, I forgot about the eggs. How diligent I've been, even standing there on the landing and looking out of the window for a little while after I put the key back in the plant pot so any onlooker would just think I was considering whether or not we could compost the garden waste on the slope – it was all so well thought-through. But I forgot the eggs. I can't believe it.

"I just borrowed them from Saman," I say, my voice strained. "I thought I might bake some muffins."

I tap the remote, pressing the wrong button and putting on the BBC instead; Lukas makes a whining sound of complaint. Behind me I hear Åsmund coming out into the living room.

"We have eggs in the fridge," he says.

"Oh, we do?" I say, still pressing the remote control and trying to remember which button is the right one. "I didn't see any."

Standing there with my back to him, I take a deep breath, down into my belly, and finally find the right button. A cartoon in fun, vivid colours appears on the screen. Behind me, Åsmund gives a little laugh.

"Okay . . . So did you bake any muffins?"

"No," I say.

I set the remote on the table and turn to face him. He's leaning against the door frame. He's showered after his bike ride, and his hair is wet and smooth against his skull.

"I changed my mind," I say. "It seemed like such a hassle – I don't know."

"Okay, I'll have them, then. We should probably use them, since they've been out of the fridge."

I turn to the four-year-old on the sofa, pass a hand through his messy hair. He twists away from me, his eyes glued to the screen.

"Sure," I say. "Yes, you eat them."

Åsmund pushes himself up from the door frame and heads into the kitchen again.

"It's a shame you decided not to bother," he says over his shoulder. "I think I've earned a muffin after that bike ride."

On the other hand, I remember the first time I was in their apartment very well. I remember how the scent of it overwhelmed me, it was so pure, so unobtrusive. While our place stank of sick and food and various faint, undesirable odours – bodies, breath, nappies – the air in their apartment was delectable. As if no living or breathing or sweating or digesting took place up there, as if all the humanness had been removed. I remember standing there in their living room and thinking: How on earth do they manage it?

Merete had invited us up. There had been talk of it every now and then over the course of the year we had lived in Kastanjesvingen. *We'll have to have dinner together some time*, we had said to each other – *we have to get to know each other better.* Nevertheless, it had taken us a year. Åsmund and I had Lukas, and there were all the sleepless nights, not to mention doctor's appointments and hospital visits and tests for one thing and another. He was now eleven months old, and this was the first time since he was born that we'd been out together during the evening. When we knocked on the door, I was wearing the baby monitor on a cord around my neck. Åsmund had laughed and said that the floors were so thin we likely wouldn't need it.

I don't know what it was like for you when you entered their apartment for the first time – I'm sure you had more important things to think about than the interior decor. But I was filled with a kind of reverence, as if I had walked into a gallery. The art on the walls. Books about Renaissance painting and modern photography, side by side with professor so-and-so's account of the conflict in Kashmir, the Weimar Republic, or the political ideas that enabled the Russian Revolution. In the corner by the entrance to the kitchen stood a huge black grand piano, polished to such a shine that you could see yourself in it. I didn't dare touch it for fear that my fingers would leave greasy prints on its surface. The lid was closed over the keys, but I imagined them, the white and the black lying ready beneath it; I envisaged Merete's strong, slim fingers manipulating them. All in all, it was an uncommonly beautiful instrument. I couldn't believe that something so exceptional could be standing in a living room identical to our own.

I mentioned this to Merete when we sat down at the table. Jørgen sat opposite me, sporting a soft linen shirt with a couple of buttons open at the neck, more elegant than Åsmund, who was still wearing the crumpled shirt he had worn to work. There was white wine in our glasses, and we ate risotto with scallops and lobster tail.

"It's a Steinway," she said. "Not the very best, but more than good enough for my use. I bought it back when I played concerts – I needed it then."

"You don't play concerts anymore?" Åsmund asked.

Merete was silent, and for a moment our chewing was all that could be heard, the sound of four adults devouring their food. Then she told us that when she first met Jørgen she was performing a lot, and – if she could be so bold – had a promising career ahead of her. She was young, of course, but on the way up. She worked all the time. Travelled a lot.

"It's an exhausting life," she said. "Not easy to combine with having a family. When we decided we wanted children, it became necessary to make some changes."

Merete had been forced to choose between family life and the career she had dreamed of for years. When she was twenty-one, being a concert pianist had seemed so thrilling, but it's also desperately hard work, and certainly not as glamorous as you imagine it to be when you're a schoolgirl and your piano teacher tells you that the sky's the limit. When it came down to it, the choice had been an easy one to make.

"The real shame," Merete said, "is that there aren't very many ways to be a pianist that are family-friendly. I teach a few students, play for a couple of choirs. Every now and then I'm offered more high-profile jobs, but – well. I gave it all up, for the most part."

She laughed.

"And that's fine by me. Honestly. I've never regretted it."

Jørgen, who hadn't said a word as Merete related her story, turned to me.

"And what do you do, Rikke?" he asked.

"I work at a research institute," I said. "I'm currently leading a project about the cognitive and emotional impulses behind consumer behaviour."

He leaned forward.

"I see. And what impulses are we talking about?"

"Well," I said, a little hesitant, as if I didn't quite trust that his interest was genuine. "Guilt, for one thing."

"Guilt?"

"Yes. I'm interested in the points of intersection between attitudes and behaviour. The way we often regard something as morally right, and yet do its diametrical opposite. I might think of myself as a good person who cares about the environment, for example, but if I go on a shopping trip to New York for a long weekend, there's a contradiction, right? The idea is that if you act in a way that you know is harmful to the environment while also viewing yourself as an environmentally conscious person, then it will be quite normal to experience guilt."

"Like climate shame?"

"Not exactly. Shame and guilt are different emotions, with different functions. Guilt motivates us to repair what we've damaged – shame motivates us to hide it."

Jørgen smiled. One of his front teeth was slightly crooked, leaving a tiny gap between them that gave his smile the appearance of something wily, something astute. When he focused his attention on me, as he did then, it was as if he was inviting me into a warm, friendly bubble that was his alone. Inside it, there was space for thoughts and ideas, the time and willingness to play with hypotheses, to pick them up and turn them in your hands and see where they might lead.

"We propose that guilt carries the seed of change within it," I said. "That if people feel guilty about something, they'll also be motivated to remedy it. The first step is to establish the connections. We're sending out questionnaires to four thousand people. Later, we might be able to perform experiments, too."

There was a chinking of plates – they clattered against each other as Merete stacked them. The baby monitor on the table lit up bright orange; it crackled, and I jumped. Åsmund put his hand on my arm.

"It's nothing, Rikke," he said. "Relax. We'll hear it if he starts to cry."

I smiled at Jørgen and withdrew my arm from beneath Åsmund's hand.

"And you?" Jørgen asked Åsmund. "You work in the public sector, is that right?"

"Yep," Åsmund said. "IT support at the Directorate for Education and Training."

He thumped his chest. It was a gesture I'd never seen him make before, and it made him reminiscent of an ape. Merete set a stack of dessert bowls in front of Jørgen. They exchanged a glance, Merete raising her eyebrows meaningfully at her husband. With languid movements, Jørgen picked up the bowls and handed them out.

"And so what does an IT man in the Directorate for Education and Training do?" Jørgen asked.

Åsmund began to speak. He offered up far too much detail, but at least he knew his job inside out and could give good answers to Jørgen's questions. Merete set a cake on the table.

"It's called a mud cake," she said. "I got the recipe from one of my friends from Philadelphia. It looks a little strange, but it's supposed to. Rikke, would you like to take the first slice?"

I took the cake server.

"It looks lovely," I said.

Merete smiled flatly. There was something in her face, as if she was elsewhere, no longer paying attention. Perhaps they had been arguing just before we arrived, or maybe she was just tired. As I reached out to cut myself a piece of the cake, Lukas whimpered over the baby monitor. I dropped the cake server and got up before Åsmund could put his hand on my arm again.

"Excuse me," I said, and walked out of the kitchen, past that glossy sneer of a piano and into the hallway.

Feet shoved hastily into my shoes, I hurried down the creaking stairs and let myself into our apartment. Sensed the sour smell of sick and nappies and leftovers, but the scent of children, too, beneath it all, a sign that a family lives here. In the bedroom, Lukas was standing in his cot, his little hands gripping the bars. He stared at me, two tears running down his cheeks. I picked him up and pressed him to me, feeling that I could finally breathe now that I was holding his body against mine.

When he had fallen asleep again, I walked slowly back upstairs. I let myself in, as quietly as I could. Or at least, that's how I remember it, even though I can't think of a reason why I should have entered the apartment that way. Perhaps I was looking to eavesdrop. As I took off my shoes, I could hear them talking in the kitchen. It was Åsmund who was speaking.

"It was completely crazy," he said. "I understand that now, I mean, when I think about it after all this time, I just can't believe the idea even occurred to us. But you know what young men are like. They have to act tough, and things can get a little out of hand. It's scary to think about it, actually, now that I have a son. We could have been killed. But at the time, I didn't think of it like that at all, I just wanted to see how far my buddy and I would be able to skid. It's a miracle things didn't turn out much worse. The car swerved off the road and smashed through the crash barrier, and the only thing that stopped it from rolling down a twenty-metre slope was a couple of trees at the side of the road. One of them cut through the car like it was butter. Half a metre further and it would have killed the guy in the back seat. The door on my side was torn up by the crash barrier and pushed into the car – I have a huge scar along my thigh where it hit me. I lost quite a lot of blood and damaged a few nerves – I still have reduced sensitivity in the tissue around the scar – but it's not exactly something that inhibits me in my day-to-day life."

Here, he laughed. Neither of the others laughed with him, as far as I could tell.

"I also ended up with a fractured thigh bone where the door slammed into me. I was in hospital for a week and had a cast for several months. Off school for six weeks, too – I had to catch up on some classes the following year."

"Oh my God," I heard Merete say. "That sounds so dangerous."

I leaned against the wall in their hallway and closed my eyes. I knew where he was going with this.

"Rikke and I had been together for two years at the time," he said. "I remember how furious she was when she visited me in hospital. She gave me such a rollicking."

He laughed a little.

"She called me an idiot. And that's precisely what I was, too. How could you do something so stupid, she said; there was nothing I could say to that. She left, and I was certain that I'd lost her."

There was silence. I imagined him giving them a serious look, or maybe he was so moved by his own story that he had to swallow a few times before he could continue. Jørgen cleared his throat and said, in a voice that was either sympathetic or ironic, I couldn't quite decide:

"But you hadn't, of course."

Åsmund ignored the interruption.

"She was eighteen years old," he said. "She could have left me right there and then. Maybe she should have – I wouldn't have blamed her. But she stayed with me. Drove me to my appointments with the physiotherapist during my rehabilitation. Drove me everywhere, seeing as I lost my licence for two years."

Silence again, apart from a faint rattling of crockery. Perhaps someone was cutting a slice of cake, or maybe Merete had started to clear the table.

"I've never forgotten that," Åsmund said. "The love she showed me. Right there, in the hospital, I knew that she was the one. We didn't tie the knot until six years later, but I knew that I was going to marry her. That we'd be together."

There was the sound of chuckling; Jørgen said that it was a nice story. Merete said it was good that everything worked out well in the end, and would anyone like coffee? Åsmund said yes, please. I could just imagine him, a blissful smile on his face, so satisfied with his story and the importance he ascribed to it. I stood there, leaning against the hallway wall, wishing the floor would open up and swallow me whole.

FIRST SUNDAY

We're aware of the blue lights even before we turn onto Kastanjesvingen. They flash against the walls of the large houses that sit above the slope behind our house, illuminating them in a flickering blue, as if at a disco. Completely silent, and yet screaming.

"Crikey," Åsmund says. "Has something happened?"

"Maybe it's the fire brigade," I say, leaning towards the dashboard and trying to catch sight of the source of the flashing lights as Åsmund brakes to take the sharp bend that leads to our little road.

We're coming home late. Lukas should already be in bed, and it's quiet in the back seat. The plan was for Åsmund's mother to serve us an early dinner so we could be home well before bedtime, but I realised as soon as we got there that it wasn't going to happen. It's nothing new, she's constantly dragging out the time. *But do you have to go already,* she says whenever I try to prepare to leave, *can't you just stay a little longer, you've hardly tasted your pretzels.* I say that it's starting to get late, signalling to Åsmund with my eyes, but he pretends not to see. He has a soft spot for her, his poor little mamma. Since his father died she's called us every single time she needs something, speaking with the same coquettish voice she used to use on her husband: *Åsmund, my tax return is due, and you know how terrible I am with numbers, I just can't get my head around it, would you mind coming over and taking a look at it for me?* Åsmund goes to her and spends an afternoon on her tax return while she clucks around and mollycoddles him, serving him coffee and offering him cake. Lavishing him with praise – what would she do without him? – and he smiles proudly and eats the cake or the sweet buns or whatever it is she's baked as his reward this time. They're telling each other something with this exchange of services and baked goods, and if I ever seem as if I might be criticising this communication between them, Åsmund is offended. Do I not understand that these are acts of love? That this is the kind of thing you do for the people you care about? So I leave them to it. Do my best to get him to leave when we've said we're going to leave; grin and bear it when he ignores me. Although I'm not above letting out an exasperated sigh in the car on the way home – *well, here we are, heading back far too late once again.*

The drive has therefore mostly passed in demonstrative silence, but as we exited the ring road, Åsmund suddenly turned to me.

"You look lovely today," he said, putting his hand on my thigh and smiling.

His unexpected amiability still hangs in the air as we drive up in the direction of the blue lights.

"What's that, Mamma?" Lukas says from the back seat.

He's usually beside himself with excitement whenever he sees an emergency vehicle, but he seems to have picked up on our unease.

"I'm sure it's just a faulty fire alarm," I say.

"Maybe it's another cat," says Emma, and I say her name sharply, not wanting her to upset Lukas, who so far hasn't heard the stories because we've managed to shield him from them.

Once we're past the chestnut tree we see the first police car, pulled up at the side of the road with its flashing blue lights on. Just after it stands another, and beside our gate a third.

"Is it our house?" I ask.

"I don't know," Åsmund says, also leaning forward. "I think so."

Then we say nothing more. The car glides slowly up to the gate and stops beside one of the two police cars that are parked there, their sirens off and blue lights on. The lights are so insistent in their intensity, and the fact that they are soundless only serves to make them more alarming. Beyond the three police cars stands an ambulance, also silent with its blue lights flashing against the night sky. We just sit there, staring at our house. None of us says anything.

A uniformed policeman comes towards us between the cars. He walks slowly – there's nothing in his body language to indicate an ongoing crisis, nothing that expresses urgency. Åsmund lowers the window on his side, and the policeman bends down, leaning towards us.

"Yes?" he says.

"Hello," Åsmund says. "We live here."

"Has something happened?" I ask, leaning over the handbrake. The policeman clears his throat.

"Someone has been found dead in the house."

Each and every one of us feels the weight of this sentence. *Someone has been found dead*. Said as if referring to a complete stranger who has collapsed in our garden, but that isn't it – I know that already. This is something that concerns us. As I sit there, with my upper body leaning over towards Åsmund on the driver's side, I have a clear view of the building. Our apartment is dark, as is Saman and Jamila's. But the lights are on in Nina and Svein's place, and in Jørgen and Merete's.

"Really?" Åsmund says.

"Yes, unfortunately," the policeman says.

He has one of those square, unshaven jaws; he looks robust and a little rough around the edges, like a policeman from an American film.

"Where?" I ask. "Where was the person found?"

But I already know. The lack of footsteps upstairs all weekend. The unanswered text message, the door that failed to open. The shudder that had run through me when I stood in the hallway.

"The apartment on the top floor, to the right," the policeman says.

Åsmund turns to face me. His eyes are wide, as if he can't believe this is happening. Something closes around my throat, making it hard to breathe, just like in the dream where I was looking for my children. I sit completely still and feel the weight of all this: it will be impossible to remain unaffected by what we've just been told. This is something that will leave its mark on all of us.

And then Lukas begins to cry.

We stay outside, standing on the lawn. Lukas is in Åsmund's arms, his face pressed against his father's neck. I stand next to Emma. We look up at the house, past the long row of kitchen windows belonging to our own apartment, fixing our gazes on the row above. People are walking about inside, we can see their shadows. Every now and then a figure appears in one of the kitchen windows up there. They're visible mostly as silhouettes, but as they move away from the glass we catch the occasional glimpse of the pale blue of their uniform shirts. I reach out an arm, try to pull Emma towards me. She bends closer, reluctantly at first, but then she settles her entire weight against me, leaning into me in the same way that her little brother is leaning against Åsmund, and lets me hold her.

In the window of the ground floor apartment next to ours, Nina Sparre comes into view. Her silhouette is unmistakable. The thin shoulders, the small body – short, but with an evident strength to it – and the hair, short and spiky, cut in a style that she would call modern, but which in reality is anything but. The nose long and aristocratic, the chin so small that it almost disappears into her neck. She looks out. The garden and the road must be quite a sight from her perspective, all the luminous police cars, all the people. It looks as if she sees us. She doesn't wave, and nor do we, because I'm not quite sure how I would manage it, and then she disappears from the window.

"This is . . ." Åsmund says.

"Yes," I say.

Lukas gives the occasional sniffle. The sounds he makes are for the most part smothered against Åsmund's neck, so I'm not sure whether he's still crying or if he has stopped. I tighten my arm around Emma, pressing her to me.

The front door opens, and out comes Nina, in a targeted march towards us. It occurs to me that I rarely see such resolve in her steps. Not that she's all fired up – her face is of course arranged into an appropriately creased and serious expression – but there's an energy about her that she doesn't usually have.

She comes to me first and hugs me, pulling me to her, so I can smell her sharp perfume more intensely than I ever have before. She rocks me back and forth three times before she releases me, but she continues to hold my shoulders – sort of pushes me away from her as if to study me. She peers up into my face and says, "Oh, Rikke," as if I'm a child to her. I don't know what to say. Nothing has sunk in just yet. All this feels so fleeting, as if it's just a particularly vivid fantasy, or a nightmare. Blink twice, and it will be gone. The garden will be there as before. The blue lights, the people, the whole sound- less, intense situation will dissolve into nothingness.

Nina shakes her head.

"No, oh dear me, no," she says. "This is just awful. That's what I said to Svein, too. I can't believe it. I quite simply cannot believe it."

"Yes," I say.

I can't believe it, either – to the extent that I'm not even able to say as much. But contrary to Nina's words it seems she *can* believe it, since she's speaking so effortlessly about it. She lets me go and moves on to Åsmund. Hugs him, more lightly than she hugged me, since he has the sobbing boy on his arm, and then it's Emma's turn.

"And now you, oh, dear little Emma," Nina says.

She sighs deeply as she strokes Emma's hair. Emma looks at her.

"Where is Filippa?" she asks.

It's the first thing I've heard her say since the policeman planted that ominous seed of a sentence in our car: *Someone has been found dead.*

"As far as I understand," Nina says, looking up into the air as if she has to concentrate to pull together the countless pieces of information she possesses, "she's off with Merete somewhere or other. They haven't come home yet. Although of course they've been informed."

Nina shakes her head.

"No, oh dear me, no," she says again. "That poor child. It's just terrible."

"Is it . . ." I start, but then I say nothing further.

She looks up at me, her eyes are alert – she's ready. There's nothing she would rather do than help out, answer questions. But I don't want to ask. I don't want to know, at least not from her, and not here, on the lawn, with my family.

But then Åsmund asks anyway:

"Do they know who it is?"

"Oh," says Nina, looking up, compiling her information again. "They're not saying anything yet, I mean, they *can't*, can they? But surely there's no doubt that it's Jørgen?"

The words hit me like a boot to the chest, and it is only this emotionless, uncomprehending state I assume must be shock that prevents me from collapsing to the ground. Instead, I breathe out, quickly and audibly, as if somebody really has kicked me. Nina looks at me.

"Yes," she says sympathetically. "It's just dreadful. Svein and I were just sitting around in the living room when the police arrived."

None of us says anything in reply to this. We look up at the house. Nina turns and looks the same way.

"And here, in our building," she says. "That's what's so incomprehensible. This neighbourhood is such a safe one. We've lived here for fifteen years, Svein and I, and nothing even close to this has ever happened before."

The hole in my chest is aching. It feels as if it isn't entirely possible to breathe. After a slight delay I feel the panic coming, and I want to get inside, away from Nina, away from my family, too. I just want to be by myself when the full weight of this hits me. But it doesn't seem possible to go in just yet, nobody has said that we can. And then the front door is pushed open again, and out comes a policeman. He sees us and begins to walk in our direction.

Information will be exchanged, I think, we'll have to say who we are, he'll have to inform us, and Nina – of course Nina will have to say who she is and what she's told us, and she'll want to check it against what the policeman says, whether she's right, whether all her conclusions are correct. So many words will be passed back and forth. Such an unbearably long time until I can sit down, alone, and allow the huge black wave that is thudding against the base of my throat to wash over me. And I don't know how long I'll be able to hold it back, how much my will has to offer in terms of resistance. I hope this will be over quickly, but I already know that it won't.

The policeman stops beside us. He looks nothing like his rugged colleague. His face is so young, so round and open, as if he's only just reached adulthood.

"Hi," he says, holding out a hand. "My name is Robin Pettersen, and I work for Oslo Police District."

His hand is large and white. It is stuck out towards me, and I'm just thinking I won't be able to take it when my body acts of its own accord, its autopilot lifting my hand and placing it in his.

"Rikke Prytz," I say.

My voice is cold and mechanical. It doesn't feel as if it comes from me, but nobody else seems to notice this. Robin Pettersen offers his hand to Åsmund and Nina, too; Nina informs him that he's already met her, she lives in the apartment down on the left. She points.

To my surprise, Robin Pettersen says in a bright, friendly voice that we can now go into our apartments.

"Somebody will come and speak with you in a little while," he says. "Do you plan to be home all evening?"

Åsmund and I nod in unison.

"Good," Robin Pettersen says. "Then you can just go on in and put the kids to bed and do what you would otherwise do. We'll be with you shortly."

He walks past us, down to the police cars at the gate, and we exchange glances. Åsmund's face looks haggard, too, and he says:

"Well, then. I suppose we'd better go in."

We heave our bodies into motion. Lukas lets out a sob. I take Emma's hand, which is cold and rough in mine.

I assumed it would take time to get Lukas off to sleep after all that's just happened, but after a single page of *In the Forest of Huckybucky* his eyelids slide closed. I've only just turned off the light when I hear his breathing change, becoming slow and rhythmical.

Still, I don't go back upstairs to the living room. Instead, I lie down with Lukas, in his bedroom in our converted cellar, listening to Åsmund's footsteps up there – maybe he's tidying up, carrying laundry to and from the bathroom. Emma is in her room – I heard her close her door, the next one along, as I was reading to Lukas – and since then it's been quiet. She's probably in there with her headphones on. I should go in to her, ask her how she's doing. Sit on the edge of her bed and listen to her. Say wise things about everything that's happened, things she can hold on to and think about later, when she's lying alone in bed and feeling afraid. But I don't think I can do it. Nor do I know what I'll manage to say to Åsmund. I'd rather be down here with Lukas, lying beside my sleeping child under the watchful gazes of all the dinosaurs exhibited in rows along the shelf on the bedroom wall, sorted by size and period, a parade of extinct species. I only want to go up once I can be sure how I'll react. So that I can avoid inadvertently bursting into tears in the middle of the kitchen, or something similar. Not that I think Åsmund suspects anything, he's not the type. He trusts me completely, and I know that I've taken advantage of it, his kindness, that unconditional trust. No, Åsmund won't suspect anything, even if I happen to shed a few tears, but it would still feel uncomfortable were he to see me like that, as if my tears might reveal something indecent. I'd rather not see him until I'm absolutely certain that I have control over the black wave. For the moment, it just laps at the hollow of my throat now and then. It hasn't yet threatened to crash over me as it did earlier, out on the lawn.

Lukas's dinosaurs are dark silhouettes against the wall. I try to stop thinking, to avoid drawing the inevitable conclusions. Jørgen did not simply collapse to the floor from some undetected but deadly physical defect, a veritable death sentence lying in wait in his body, ready to paralyse his brain or stop his heart. Not when there are two police cars by the gate, not when who knows how many police officers are walking back and forth up in his apartment, and when they're going to stop by to speak to us. But I can't get into it now, can't follow these conclusions, which will invariably lead to more questions. What happened up there, and where were we when it happened? Did he do something to himself, or is this something someone did to him? In a house like ours – with the thin walls that were all the builders of the fifties had to offer – how is it possible that some unmentionable violence has been committed on one floor while ordinary family life has continued to play out on the floor below? I don't want to follow these trains of thought – at least, not now. I count Lukas's breaths. Oh, to be a child and sleep so peacefully, while everything beyond our apartment has been turned upside down.

Only when I hear our doorbell upstairs do I leave the room. I kiss my boy on the forehead before I go, passing a hand over his tousled hair. I close the door gently behind me, then look over at Emma's door, which is closed; not a sound comes from her room. I feel a sharp pain in my chest. I should have gone in – I should have had that talk with her. That's what you do when you're a mother. Now it's too late. The police are at the door, and they want to speak to us. With heavy steps, I walk up the stairs with the gnawing feeling that I have failed her.

*

The youthful Robin Pettersen asks the questions; his colleague with the square jaw looks around our apartment as we speak. He stands at the row of kitchen windows for a long time, studying each of them individually, opening and closing them, fiddling with the hasps.

Robin Pettersen sits at the kitchen table. Åsmund and I sit opposite him. They were already in the kitchen when I came up. Åsmund offered the police officers coffee; Robin said no thank you, while Square Jaw and I answered yes please, and so here we sit. Åsmund and I with our cups of coffee, and Robin on the other side of the table without one.

"So," Robin says. "Can you tell me about the weekend?"

We look at each other.

"Pfft," says Åsmund. "I mean, what have we actually done?"

I clear my throat.

"Well, yesterday Emma had a school play rehearsal, so she and I were there. She goes to Bakkehaugen school."

"And I was with a friend in Bærum with Lukas," says Åsmund. "We were out for most of the day."

"Great," says Robin, flashing us a wide smile as if we're children who have just solved a difficult puzzle.

Åsmund smiles at me, proud at the acknowledgement he's received from the policeman, as if he's happy that we've completed our assigned task correctly. Square Jaw is rattling one of the windows.

"Times would be good," Robin says. "I mean, I understand that there's a limit to how accurately it's possible to remember, but to the best of your ability."

"The rehearsal started at ten o'clock," I say. "I was there until, let's see, around one. Then I was supposed to meet up with my sister, but she cancelled, so . . . Yes. I came home."

I avoid looking at Åsmund as I say this. I was home at one o'clock, spent several hours here alone. Presumably there's nothing suspicious about that. I live here. Surely I'm allowed to come back to my own home whenever I like?

"I think I left at around nine-thirty." Åsmund says, turning to look at me. "Wouldn't you say, Rikke? Around then?"

I nod. Now the window in the living room is being rattled – Square Jaw has made his way out there.

"I got to my friend's place at about, yeah, ten-ish. We have an e-bike."

It's almost touching, just how proud Åsmund seems as he says this. We bought the bike at the start of the summer. Jørgen and Merete's electric cargo bike had been stolen from right outside the house just a few months earlier, and I had pointed this out, but Åsmund was determined. Practical transport and exercise in one, he said. But with the bike doing all the work, surely the amount of exercise you'll get will be limited, I said. He had shrugged that off, too.

"And then I was home again at around . . . What would you say, Rikke? Around four?"

It now sounds as if Robin's colleague is slamming the living-room window, and he shouts to us:

"This window, do you usually keep it closed?"

"Yes," we answer in unison.

"Was it closed on Friday and Saturday?"

We look at each other.

"I think so," Åsmund says.

"Yes," I say. "We probably opened it for a little fresh air in the morning, but not for long. Twenty minutes, maybe. Everything was closed when we left."

The policeman seems to consider this. There is silence for a while, before the locking mechanism rattles again.

"And so how about Friday?" Robin asks.

"We were at work," Åsmund says. "I picked Lukas up from kindergarten and got home at around four-thirty. Emma was with a friend after school and came home at around five. Rikke came home at around, what, maybe five as well?"

"Later," I say. "Five-thirty."

"Right, five-thirty. And then we were home all evening. Ate some pizza, watched *Nytt på nytt* on TV. And then we watched a film once the kids were in bed – what was it called again?"

Robin smiles – of course it doesn't matter which film we saw – and I shrug, but Åsmund doesn't give up.

"Wasn't there something to do with breathing in the title?" he asks.

"I'm sure it's not that important, Åsmund," I say.

"And then how about today?" Robin asks.

"We were home this morning," I say. "We went to see Åsmund's mother in Bærum at around twelve-ish, so Lukas could take a nap there, if need be. When we got home you were already here, when would that have been, somewhere around seven?"

Robin's pen moves quickly across his notepad, taking down all the times in detail.

"When did you last see the Tangen family?" he asks.

"I bumped into Merete on the stairs on Friday morning," says Åsmund. "She was with Filippa. She said they were in the middle of packing. Apparently, they were going on a cabin trip or something."

"And you?" Robin asks me. I stare off into the distance, as if trying to remember, while I think of the text I received on Friday, in which Jørgen wrote that he would be home alone all weekend.

Our last contact – of course that's what they're asking about. It would be strange not to mention the message, almost unnatural. I should tell the police about it – and about the text I sent on Saturday, and how I received no reply. It could be important. But Åsmund is sitting beside me. If I mention the messages now, Robin will ask to see them. I'll have to fish my phone from my handbag, pull up the texts, and set the phone on the table for all three of them to see – Robin, Square Jaw and Åsmund. *I'll be home alone all weekend.* Was that what he wrote? Or was it more explicit? Regardless, it would be strange for him to tell me that. And what might I have answered?

And then I think: Robin asked about when we last saw them. *Saw* them. As in, when I last laid eyes on one of them. Technically, the message is irrelevant.

"I saw Jørgen in the stairwell one day last week," I say at last. "And then I bumped into Merete and her daughter in the supermarket at the Tåsen shopping centre . . . let's see, could it have been Wednesday?"

It's as easy as that. Robin makes a note, and Åsmund knows nothing. But, of course, the matter of the text message won't be resolved just like that – it will rear its head again. In fact, I ought to bring it up myself. Pull Robin or his colleague aside and tell them, before somebody finds it on Jørgen's phone. Speak to one of them privately, confess my sins. Not wanting to mention the text message in front of Åsmund would be understandable. Reprehensible, perhaps, but understandable all the same. And anyway, it's not a crime. Not in any legal sense, at least. I have to tell them – if not now, then later. I can find Robin's number online, call him from work. Tomorrow. Or another day. I presumably have a little time.

Robin's colleague has finished what he was doing in the living room. He examines the kitchen windows again, fingering the hasps once more. Robin puts down his pen. He looks at us in turn, and the expression on his round, childlike face is freighted with seriousness. It occurs to me that Robin Petterson is a man who becomes genuinely upset at bad news. He must find being a police officer quite difficult, I think.

"I'd also like to inform you of some of the facts," he says, his voice heavy. "The person who was found dead is a man, apparently aged somewhere between forty-five and fifty. He hasn't been identified yet, so I don't want to speculate as to who he is, but . . . well. I can confirm it's a man we're talking about here."

We understand what he's saying. And in a way, I already knew. Although, in another way, the whole thing has so far seemed rather theoretical. The black wave in my chest breaks against my palate, and a sob escapes me. Åsmund looks at me, but he doesn't put his hand on mine. I swallow and swallow, not wanting to release any further sobs, but now I can feel it again, I have to get out, it's about to overtake me, and I can't be here in my kitchen, observed by my husband, when the dam breaks.

The police officers want to look at the rest of our windows before they leave. Åsmund takes them into our bedroom. I find my gym bag in the hallway, go into the bathroom and change into my training clothes. I'm careful not to look at myself in the mirror, catching sight of myself only out of the corner of my eye, like a shadow. Under no circumstances do I want to meet my own gaze. I go back out into the hallway, find my running jacket, put it on and tie the laces of my trainers. They're all in the basement now, examining the window in the corridor down there, and I stick my head over the top of the stairs.

"I thought I might just go out for a run."

The three men turn around. Åsmund gives me an uncomprehending look.

"Now?"

"Yes."

I try to say it casually, and it strikes me then that Åsmund and Robin are quite similar. Åsmund doesn't have Robin's hairless child-likeness, but both of them have such open faces. Looking at them side by side, Robin could be Åsmund's little brother.

"I'm not sure that would be advisable at the moment," says Square Jaw.

I stand there with my arms hanging heavily at my sides. It looks strange, I realise, that I want to go running in the dark right now – it's not improbable that a crazed murderer is prowling the neighbourhood. What business do I have being out there, when I can seek comfort and support here at home with my husband? My throat feels tight and closed, the wave is about to crash over me, and I want nothing more than to be outside these four walls when I'm no longer able to restrain it. But I can't go against what the police are suggesting, either.

"Okay," I say.

I go back into the bathroom. In an unguarded moment I catch my face in the mirror and see just how worked up I look, my hair escaping its ponytail, my eyes wide and terrified. I turn on the shower to full. Water gushes out of the showerhead and pounds against the tiles, and I hope the noise is enough, hope it camouflages the noises I make as I collapse onto the bathroom floor, a towel pressed to my mouth, and cry hysterically.

Jørgen spoke willingly about his travels, and the riskier and more touch-and-go his experiences were, the more it delighted him to tell people about them. You almost got the impression that there was a kind of competition between his colleagues: who'd had the closest brush with death while out on assignment. In this context what happened on his first trip, when he was in his early twenties and could easily have been killed, wasn't all that spectacular, and yet it is this story that I remember best, because he told it so stiffly and unwillingly, without his usual raconteur's enthusiasm. In fact, I don't think he'd intended to tell me about it at all. We were in London, sitting in deep armchairs in a bar in Camden Town, each nursing a whiskey, because it had seemed the appropriate thing to order in that particular establishment. I spoke about a prize he had just won – it was fantastic, I thought – but Jørgen had looked so uncomfortable. And then, for no apparent reason, he told me this story. I remember how he seemed to brace himself before he began, and that he hardly looked at me as he spoke.

It started with him sitting in a car somewhere outside Sarajevo, with a Bosnian journalist he knew, and the journalist's wife. Exactly where they were going I didn't catch, if he even mentioned it at all, but at any rate the car they were in was a wreck. The engine had been hacking and spluttering on and off for the entire journey, and then it finally gave up the ghost in the middle of a road, far from town. They got out to assess the situation. The journalist cursed, because spare parts were hard to get hold of. They decided to look for a café where they could use the phone and call for help. The wife cast quick glances all around her as they walked, and Jørgen, wanting to keep her spirits up, said something along the lines of how he was sure everything would be fine. She looked at him, mumbled something. He asked her to repeat it. And she did: This area isn't safe.

They hadn't got very far when the bullets began to rain down. When it came to the part about the shooting, Jørgen's narrative became noticeably less detailed – he spoke to the glass he held in his hands and I said nothing, understanding that I shouldn't disturb him with questions, that this story would be as long or as short as he wished it to be. Without warning, he told me, there was a banging and cracking in the wall of the building behind them, and then they were in the thick of it. They instinctively threw themselves down behind a wrecked car at the side of the road. The married couple spoke frantically to one another in Bosnian, the wife gesticulating towards the rooftops. They could hear the shots being fired around them, but Jørgen assumed they had decent enough cover, and it seemed the snipers were moving away from them.

Then shots were fired from a nearby roof. The first whizzed past him, centimetres from his earlobe, and a deep, guttural sound rose from his throat. He lay flat, his heart against the asphalt. The car they were hiding behind was stripped so bare that it could shield one person at most, and Jørgen threw himself forward and crept under it. Something shifted in his gaze when he said this: there was only space for one, and he had shoved the others aside to save himself. Under the chassis he could hear the cracks and bangs of bullets hitting home; the journalist screamed in pain. Jørgen flattened himself against the tarmac, squeezing his hands into fists. He closed his eyes, certain that he was going to die.

This was where his story ended. That is, he also told me that they survived, all three of them – that the journalist was hit in the leg and helped to the hospital, but Jørgen hadn't stayed in touch with him and his wife and so had no idea how things had worked out for them later. But these details were presented more as extraneous facts – the story itself ended there, as he lay under the wrecked car, eyes closed and waiting for death. In the armchair in London, Jørgen looked up from his glass, and with the roguish half smile that was his trademark – the one that charmed his partners in conversation, but which often made me unsure whether he was serious or kidding around – he said:

"I've always believed that everything that comes after that incident is a bonus for me. I could have died, but I didn't. So now I think that no matter how I meet my end when it comes, I'll be satisfied. Y'know?"

I thought about Lukas, my own bonus, and said that I understood, although later I figured that I probably didn't. This was the only time we ever spoke about it, too – and straight afterwards, he suggested we go back to the hotel. I tried to get him to talk about it again once or twice back home in Oslo, but without ever refusing to answer my questions he always managed to steer the conversation on to something else. I thought about what I saw happen to his eyes, how something had seemed to flicker behind them when he told me about how he had protected himself at the expense of the others. What kind of understanding can he have drawn from that – what did he think it said about him? This reckoning with death, so intense and sudden, and in your early twenties – is life over now, is this all there was ever meant to be? – how did he relate to this later on? And now, as I lie in a foetal position on the bathroom floor and sob into a towel, I think about it – the fact that Jørgen, who was almost shot in broad daylight in Sarajevo in the nineties, believed that no matter how he died, he would die satisfied. And maybe some comfort can be found in this, or at least that's probably what I would have thought had someone told me about it, but that's not how it is, no, it's not how it is at all. Instead, it seems to make a mockery of what's happened. As if there was some darkness that settled over Jørgen as he lay there on the ground, a curse laid upon him for cheating death, which finally came to take him, here, in Tåsen – one of the safest places on earth – as he sat alone in his own home. And now I have to press the towel against my mouth to ensure that my crying will not be audible beyond the bathroom door. My body seems to be trying to turn itself inside out, shaking violently, as if plagued by something external. I have no control over it, and so I simply let it happen.

Afterwards, I undress and shower, still thinking about the story from Sarajevo. About just how many of his stories were like that, tiny glimpses of what happened, with no connection to what came before or after. Did he go back to a hotel room that evening, crawl under the duvet and cry? Did he tell anyone about it, a colleague he had dinner with, for example, or his boss or his mother over the phone? Now I'll never know.

By the time I've finished showering, the policemen have gone. Åsmund is sitting in front of the TV in the living room. I walk past him into the kitchen, as if I'm going to find myself something to eat, to avoid having to sit down next to him. He doesn't follow me. Outside, the police cars have turned off their lights. I turn my back to the dark garden, take out a loaf and some sandwich toppings, and make a start on buttering a slice of bread I don't want. As I eat it – because I have to, of course – I think about how I was up in Jørgen's place yesterday, the minute or two that I stood there in his apartment. And afterwards – how Saman came out onto the landing. Did he see me leaving Jørgen's apartment? Does he know that I was in there, or did he believe me when I said I had only knocked at the door to find nobody home? I push the thought away. I don't want to think about it, at least, not now. I mean, it looked as if he believed me. And after all, he gave me the eggs. I feel it in my gut all the same. If I'm wrong – if he saw me letting myself out of the apartment – then I have a problem.

That night, I dream that I've arranged to meet Jørgen. I'm trying to make my way upstairs, but things I have to do constantly keep cropping up, getting in my way. My phone rings – his name is on the display – and I pick it up and say: I'll be there soon, there's just a couple of things I have to do first. I don't wait for him to reply. When I finally knock at his door, nobody answers. I let myself in and stand in the middle of the living room. The room is empty. On the floor lies his phone. Otherwise, it's dark – I see nothing but the phone – but I know that there's somebody in there. That someone is hiding in a dark corner, watching me.

The hum of the bar had reached a level that made it hard to follow the conversation. My colleague leaned across the table to say something – something funny, was the impression I got, because she laughed even before she had finished speaking. The others grinned in expectation. Their smiles were somewhat looser than usual – they'd likely had quite a bit to drink. I leaned back in my chair. I'd had quite a bit to drink, too. A tired feeling crept up on me from somewhere behind my ear. Maybe I should start thinking about making my way home. I looked around, not following the conversation, happy just to watch the people at the bar. Lipsticked smiles; hands emerging from the cuffs of fine shirts to lift glasses. Long, dangly earrings that swayed when a head was turned; a well-maintained beard on a face that was stroked as its owner laughed.

He was standing at the bar, one arm propped against the counter as he spoke to another man. He was in the middle of telling some story, a small smile playing at the corner of his mouth – an indication that his yarn was about to take a surprising turn. The other man was standing with his back to me, so I couldn't see how Jørgen's words were being received. Then he caught sight of me. He stopped mid-sentence, or so it seemed, and changed gear. Smiled. Lifted a hand and waved. The man he was talking to turned around, and I saw that it was a famous author – I can tell you who it was, if you think it's important. The author nodded at me. Then they went back to their conversation. I laughed to myself – my colleagues were so deep in conversation they hadn't noticed. At one point, when I presumed the author must be speaking, Jørgen looked over at me and smiled again. Well, here we are, his smile seemed to say. As if it were the two of us, he and I, who were actually there together. Does that make sense? I don't know whether it's even possible to explain it. It wasn't as if we knew each other very well.

After a while I got up, excused myself to my colleagues, and went over to him.

"Hi," I said.

"Hi," said Jørgen.

He hugged me. He smelled clean, with the slightest hint of alcohol but no trace of cologne or aftershave. He was a good hugger. He gave hugs that were appropriately firm, and I felt the contours of his torso against mine.

He turned to the author.

"This is Rikke," he said. "We live together – but not like that."

The author laughed. I shook his hand and gave my name, even though Jørgen had already said it. The author told me his name, which of course I already knew, and it dawned on me that he had recently published a much-talked-about book, the kind of thing everyone who's anyone had read, but I hadn't. I wondered if I should say I had anyway. The author turned to face a man and a woman who were standing a little further down the bar, and Jørgen leaned towards me. With his mouth not far from my ear, he said:

"Fancy a glass of something?"

I considered his offer. The plan was to head home. I was tempted to stay, but it was already late, and Lukas tended to wake up in the middle of the night.

"I was actually just leaving," I said.

Jørgen smiled.

"Me too. It just takes me a little while to get away."

Neither of us made a move. He told me about a story that had been circulating in the media, concerning a politician who had been caught cheating on his taxes, and how one of the people Jørgen had had dinner with earlier in the evening was known for having publicly supported this politician. During dessert, he had delivered an impassioned speech about why it was acceptable to cheat on your taxes under the right circumstances. I laughed, feeling the need to offer something in response. An opinion, or an anecdote that complemented his – something to show that I, like him, was a person to be reckoned with, someone who keeps up with what's happening and sets current events in a sociopolitical context, who draws links from the planned economy to the glory days of the yuppies to Norwegian local government policy, all in a witty and natural way, as if I belonged to this landscape and felt at home in it. I couldn't think of anything.

"That's funny," I said, which, in the end, was all I had to contribute.

He took his jacket from the bar stool next to him. "I think I should be getting going now, too. Fancy some company for the journey home? We're going the same way, after all."

On the way to the bus stop he asked me questions. About the kids, and whether we were happy in Kastanjesvingen, about my research. About what I learned through the studies I ran, and what I planned to do with it. The paralysis I had felt in the bar still hadn't left me, this feeling that I had to be interesting. Not just smart in a bookish way, no, but smart in an *active* way, too, where you form opinions based on what you've read and observations you've made, and say things like *the political swing to the right we're currently seeing is understandable given the financial crisis; the right often does well after periods of economic downturn, perhaps because uncertainty and unrest make us more inclined to embrace the conservative idea of preserving what once was.* But I found it too difficult. Maybe I just wasn't smart enough, and at the very least, I was too tired. My responses were brief and dull. I listened to them as if I were walking alongside us, hearing how everything I said sounded so obvious. But at least I felt that I looked pretty good that evening.

But didn't I also think that Jørgen was asking me questions in order to reveal something about himself? To show me that he was a good listener, perhaps, or how deeply he cared about other people? I don't know, but I do know that the thought occurred to me every now and then, later, when I knew him better. I'm not sure what I think about it now. He was genuinely interested in people, but he was also keen for everyone to see just how good he was at getting others to speak.

We reached the bus stop. It was chilly out, the temperature somewhere between autumn and winter, too early or too late, right in the middle. Our breath was visible on the air, and we pulled our coats closer around us.

"Where did you grow up?" Jørgen asked.

"In Bærum," I said. "In Lommedalen, in the forest."

"Lommedalen," he said, and smiled, as if trying it out.

"And you?" I asked.

"Right in the heart of Oslo. I'm a city boy from Bolteløkka. Do you have siblings?"

"A sister. You?"

"A brother and a sister. Is she younger or older than you?"

I laughed. He wouldn't let me shift the focus on to him. I wasn't particularly interested in talking about my sister. Although plenty of people ask me about her, as I'm sure you can imagine. Not that I think he was fishing for information.

"Younger," I said, and then, also refusing to give up: "And yours?"

"An older brother and a younger sister. What are your parents called?"

"You want to know the names of my parents?"

This time he was the one who laughed.

"Now we're really getting to know each other, Rikke."

"Sure," I said. "Because there's absolutely no way you can truly know me without finding out what my parents are called."

He grinned at me, suddenly looking like a young boy. We fell quiet for a moment. Smiled at each other.

"You know, I've always wondered—" he said.

"The bus is coming!" someone shouted behind us.

We turned around to see a group of people in their early twenties running towards us, a boy first, then a girl, and another boy a little further behind. The boy at the back was wearing a Santa hat. And sure enough, down the road beside us came the bus. The guy who had shouted sprinted as fast as he could. The bus arrived before him, and Jørgen and I stepped aboard. Jørgen held his hand between the doors so they would make it.

As we stood next to each other, each grabbing on to a pole to keep our balance as the bus jerked away from the stop, I said:

"You were saying?"

"What?"

"You were saying you've always wondered about something."

"Was I?"

He shrugged. The bus took a turn, tilting, and thrust me towards him.

At home, in the stairwell, the mood between us was different. We had to speak in low voices so as not to wake anyone up, and I felt acutely aware that Nina and Svein might be able to hear us. I imagined Nina standing on the other side of the wall, her ear pressed against it.

"Are your family asleep?" he asked.

"I should hope so," I said, laughing quietly.

He made no reply to my laughter.

"And yours?" I asked.

"They're away," he said. "I'm all alone up there."

It hung in the air between us. The empty apartment upstairs, with its tasteful furniture, its expensive bottles of wine. The soft creamy-white sofa. All of it so accessible. Was that really what he was asking me?

"How nice," I said. "You can sleep in, stuff like that."

It felt as if I was steering us away from something dangerous.

"Yeah."

We stood there, still, for a couple of seconds. Was he waiting for me to say something?

"Thanks for the company, Rikke," he said, and leaned towards me.

The hug he gave me was lighter than the last one, his cheek scarcely brushing mine. But as he leaned towards me, I inhaled sharply.

He turned and went up the stairs.

"Sleep well," he said over his shoulder.

It was dark in the apartment when I let myself in. I closed the door behind me and leaned my back against it. Above me, I could hear him. He walked across the floor, into the kitchen. His steps were even. I stood there like that in the dark, my breathing shallow and hot. It felt as if every cell in my body was aglow.

MONDAY

The corridor outside my office buzzes with activity. My colleagues stop by the neighbouring offices to pass on messages before meetings, stride back and forth clutching printouts and cups of coffee. My head is heavy; I hardly slept last night. I sit in front of my computer, looking at the document I'm supposed to be reading to find something to say at the Monday meeting that's due to start in twenty minutes, while the words seem to slip away from me, as if entirely unfamiliar. My cubicle-sized office has glass walls, and I hide behind my computer screen as I rub my tired eyes. I went to check on Lukas several times during the night, opening his bedroom door with my heart pounding against my ribs, certain that something terrible would be waiting there behind it, but he slept peacefully through. Then I wandered around the apartment checking that the front door was locked, the safety chain was on, the window hasps were closed. I stopped outside Emma's door a couple of times, too – there's a fire door that leads from her bedroom out into the cellar, and I wanted to check that it was locked, but I hesitated. I wasn't sure whether I should, whether it would be some kind of violation – she's so grown-up now, and she's entitled to her privacy. But she's still my child, so at around four in the morning I opened the door, just a crack, and peeked into her teenage girl's room. Saw her sleeping, lying on her back, one hand up beside her face and her mouth half open, lost to the world.

Everything is so neat in there. She has posters on the walls – not of boys she likes, as I had at her age, but of girls in calculated poses, wearing expensive clothes. Her friends' rooms are decorated in the same way – there's something sad about it, that these young girls are more concerned with appearing attractive to others, rather than looking at what they like themselves. On the shelf above the bed stands a framed photograph of Emma and two of her friends. They're smiling, their arms around each other, free of the self-consciousness they so often exhibit in pictures, but then this one is a couple of years old. Beside the photo sits her teddy bear, which lay beside her every night until she was eight years old. I tiptoe inside and try the fire door, which is securely locked, then sneak back across the room again. I stop beside her bed. The hand and the lost expression – she's in dreamland now, and I can't reach her. On her bedside table is her script for *The Threepenny Opera*, and my old iPod, which she's borrowed because we don't want her to have a phone or tablet down here in her room. You're welcome to use them, we say – just not when you're alone. It's with a certain disappointment that I see she prefers old technology and solitude over an iPad and our company.

I was twenty-six when I found out that I was pregnant with her. I'd just been awarded a research fellowship that I badly wanted. The competition was fierce, but I'd been convincing at the interview, and I remember how invincible I'd felt – I was young, I was capable, I was a new type of woman, unfettered by the kinds of things that had held my mother's generation back. Then the murmuring suspicion had arisen: a missed period, feeling unusually tired – surely it couldn't be? While I waited to start my new position, I was working as a research assistant for a professor at the institute where I had studied for my master's degree, and one day, on my lunch break, I went to the pharmacy in Blindern and bought a pregnancy test. I did it in the toilets of the university library, terrified that someone would see me with the incriminating paper bag, and sat on the lid of the toilet with my legs drawn up as I waited the required two minutes. When I saw the result, I refused to believe it. I sat there in the cubicle, whispering to myself: no, no, no, no, no. I began to argue with a creator who, up until that point in my life, I had never believed in – dear God, I said, you have to help me. You have to sort this out. Get this thing out of me, as fast as fucking possible. You hear about people having miscarriages all the time, so come on, God. How about you take a little responsibility here?

When I told Åsmund I cried, my body wracked with heaving sobs. He said everything a modern young man should say – it's your choice, he said, and I'll support you no matter what.

"How can you say that?" I roared. I needed an opponent, somebody to scream at. "How can you put this all on me? This clump of cells is just as much yours as it is mine!"

"I can't decide what you should do with your body," he said.

"Why the fuck not?" I said. "So is this solely my responsibility now? Are you going to absolve yourself of all moral culpability, let me make the most difficult decision of my life all alone?"

I wanted to make him feel the despair I felt, needed to see the same desperation in him. He said:

"We've been together a long time. We love each other. We'll end up having a family sooner or later anyway. Maybe this wasn't what we'd planned right now, but why not?"

"What about my job?" I shouted.

"You'll get maternity leave."

I played every card I had. What about the holidays we had planned to go on, the round-the-world trip we had talked about, albeit in a completely non-committal way? What about our friends, who of course would dump us because from now on all we'd be able to think or care about would be nappies and pushchairs? What about my body, which would become flabby and fat and be destroyed forever after? What about our long Saturday mornings in bed?

And Åsmund answered me, statement by statement. We'd still be able to travel, we'd just have to plan a little differently. Of course we wouldn't lose our friends – and if any of them couldn't take this sort of change, well, then they weren't true friends anyway. I'd get my body back – it would be just as beautiful – and he would only love it even more after this. And the Saturday mornings in bed would continue – he promised. I looked at him in disbelief, seeing how the side of him that wanted this was pushing its way to the fore, and felt as if he was stabbing me in the back.

"I don't want it," I said. "I'm having an abortion."

"It's up to you," he said. He looked sad, and I hated him for taking sides, just as I had asked him to.

But when it came down to it, I couldn't do it. Because what would it do to us if I took this from him? When I asked him to make the choice for me, I also made it impossible to do the opposite of what he wanted and continue as before. And he had made some good points, too, I couldn't deny that. So I put off booking the appointment, and one day, when I was ten weeks along, and we were eating pizza in front of the TV in our flat, I said:

"Okay, fine. I'm keeping it."

He put his arms around me and didn't let go for a long time.

"But you can deal with most of the sleepless nights," I said. "Seventy-five per cent."

He promised. But back then we knew far too little to understand that such promises aren't worth the breath it takes to make them.

Now I'm feeling the night's repercussions. My head is heavy and fuzzy. As usual, the entire department will attend the Monday meeting – we discuss each other's projects, provide suggestions and challenge each other – and they're always so long, filled with so much humming and hawing. The document I've opened is an application for funding to appoint a new PhD candidate. I've been working on it for several weeks, but I can't seem to make sense of it.

Instead of reviewing the application, I surf the Internet, switching between the two windows, bringing up the document whenever

I hear footsteps so that nobody will see what I'm reading. I run my fingers through my hair. I'm so tired, I just can't do this. I so wish I could have got some sleep last night. I was tired then, too, but once I was lying there in bed my thoughts began to spin out of control. The text message from Jørgen. Saman's face when I turned and saw him in the doorway, that uncomfortable feeling of being caught red-handed. Jørgen's voice from the armchair in London, *everything that comes after that incident is a bonus*. The two eggs on the kitchen counter. The sinister atmosphere in Jørgen's apartment. It had been impossible to sleep.

Now, it seems it would be so easy. That all I have to do is lie down, and sleep will come. I consider rolling my jacket into a ball, putting it on the desk and settling my head on it as if it were a pillow. Would have done it, too, had the walls of my office not been glass.

On the website of one of the major newspapers the headline says DEATH IN TÅSEN. My body gives a start. Of course it had to come out – but still. Isn't it still confidential? I click the link. *At around 5 pm yesterday, police reported that a person has been found dead in an apartment in Tåsen. The police confirmed yesterday evening that the deceased is a man. The death is being regarded as suspicious.* That's all. The first two sentences contain nothing new to me, but they still seem raucous and loud as I read them – I almost have the urge to ask them to quieten down. The last one shocks me. *The death is being regarded as suspicious.* Our paper-thin walls; my family living and sleeping so close to all this. And what does "suspicious" imply?

That feeling in his apartment when I let myself in on Saturday. Why in all the world did I do that? What an invasive thing to do, to let yourself in uninvited – or, not uninvited, exactly, but not entirely invited, either. What the hell was I thinking? What made me tell myself that it was okay? And could it have been dangerous? I shift in my chair, sensing how cold my hands feel. Could somebody have been in the apartment while I was there? On the other side of the wall, behind the closed door I couldn't bring myself to cross the living room to open?

I can't find a comfortable sitting position, it's as if something is prickling or tingling or crawling no matter how I position my legs. I still haven't looked up Robin Pettersen's telephone number. I really ought to, sooner rather than later. I'm not so shocked by the ordeal that I don't understand that the longer it takes me to do this, the worse it will look. But then the thought twists my insides, because what will I say? To a police officer who seems so personally affected by bad news?

The door to my office opens, and I jump and whip around.

"Did I scare you?" my colleague asks.

"I was miles away," I say.

The newspaper article is open on the screen behind me. She could look at it, should she wish to, but she doesn't.

"Will you be presenting the funding application at the meeting?" she asks.

"Actually, I have a terrible headache," I say. "So I'm not sure. I might have to go home."

"Oh, I'm sorry," she says. "Stress?"

I pretend to consider this.

"Could be. Or lack of sleep. I don't know."

"Well, feel better soon," she says, and closes the door.

Once she's gone, I feel my shoulders relax, as if I'm afraid my guilty conscience is written all over my face. Obviously, the crime that's been committed is what's important here – whatever people might say about what I've done, murder is far worse. But it doesn't feel as if people will see it that way. People don't like to admit that guilt is something that can be shared in bite-sized pieces, with everyone receiving their allotted portion. Or that it's fluid. No, in this case, I'm guilty – if not of one thing, then of another. And I know that I should call Robin with his childlike face, know that I should tell him about the text message. And if I'm not prepared to take the chance that Saman didn't see me coming out of the apartment, I should at the very least explain that I went in there but came straight out again.

But then I hesitate. Maybe I should wait until I've got a better grip on myself. Who knows what I might end up saying in my current state?

My phone beeps, and I jump again – I'm so nervous, can't seem to sit still. Beside the text message icon is Jamila's name. *How's it going*, she writes. *I'm in complete shock, I can't believe it! Can we grab a coffee? I'm working from home today, come up whenever you like!* I read the message several times over. It seems ordinary enough, even though it's full of exclamation marks and emojis. Jamila's upset – she wants to meet up, wants to talk. This I can manage. I should go see her now, hear what she has to say. If Saman saw me leaving Jørgen and Merete's apartment, he must have mentioned it to her. Especially once he found out what happened. If we meet up, and Jamila says nothing about it, then maybe it's safe to assume Saman didn't see me. Maybe I can weave it into the conversation, mention the eggs I borrowed and see how she reacts. I should do it before I call the police. I send a message back to her: *Just on my way home, see you in half an hour.*

Before I go, I stop by the receptionist.

"I have such a pounding headache," I say.

"I have paracetamol?" she says. She's so young and sweet and helpful, already rummaging around in her handbag.

"Thanks, but I've already taken one," I lie. "Could you register a sick day in the system for me?"

In the years before we bought the apartment in Kastanjesvingen, Åsmund and I existed in a state of perpetual disagreement over where we were going to live. It crept into every conversation, all the silences at the dinner table, the tone we took with each other every time we carried heavy bags of shopping up the stairs to the tiny flat where we lived. Most of Åsmund's friends had moved back to Bærum when they had kids. They bought narrow terraced properties on housing developments squeezed between the forest and the T-banen, where the houses are like bird boxes, each with its own little fleck of garden in front of it, which the residents immediately fill with trampolines. They look like blue mushrooms, clinging to every available patch of green. The tiny gardens they fill to the brim with oversized gas barbecues and garden furniture; they buy big lawnmowers and snowblowers and spend their weekends weeding and raking, maintaining their homes.

"Would it really be that bad?" Åsmund asked. "Think of the kids."

We went to visit one of Åsmund's childhood friends and ate waffles out on their veranda. The friend and his wife couldn't praise the area enough, it was so *family-friendly*, close to the countryside but still on the T-banen, so they could take the train into the city whenever they liked. I asked them whether they ever still went out for dinner in town midweek, and they looked at each other and laughed, well, no, not very often, but that's because of the kids, although we could if we wanted to. Their daughters had taken Emma out to play on the trampoline, and we could see them from the veranda. The girls showed off all their tricks, bouncing up and down and turning around. Emma was leaning against the picket fence and watching them with an expression of utter indifference.

In the car on the way home, I said:

"I don't want to live in a box."

"And our flat isn't a box?" Åsmund asked, pulling out from one of the smaller side roads onto the main artery leading back to the city.

I thought about my mother-in-law, widowed no more than a year earlier, who lived in a large, impractical villa five minutes' drive from the terraced home of Åsmund's childhood friend we had just visited. I already knew what it would be like. The endless phone calls – sorry to disturb you, but you see, I need help with this, that and the other, and you know how useless I am with that kind of thing. Åsmund would come running, I could already hear him: poor little Mamma, of course we'll help you. Just the knowledge that she was so close would be like a dark cloud hanging over me. It would feel like she were constantly breathing down our necks. And since I couldn't say any of this to Åsmund, I said:

"I don't want to have to buy a robot lawnmower. I don't want to have to care about slugs destroying the garden, to have to get in the car to go anywhere or to end up spending every single evening at home on the sofa with Netflix because I can't be bothered to go all the way into the city."

"You're such a snob," Åsmund said. "I reserve the right to watch as much Netflix as I want."

We said nothing further after that. Emma sat in the back seat, looking out the window. She didn't say a word, either. I looked down at my belly. You couldn't see it through my clothes just yet, but when I was naked, the swelling there was obvious. Our flat only had two bedrooms. Or, if you wanted to get technical about it, it had only one, because Emma's room was so small that it would hardly meet the standards for a bedroom when we had the property valued. She was eight years old, and a bigger apartment was long overdue.

As we reached the city limits, Åsmund said:

"Fine. Not Bærum. I can't exactly force you, can I?"

Back home that evening, when Emma was in her box room and we were in our cramped living room watching TV, he said:

"But we do have to move, Rikke."

"I know," I said. "We'll find something."

This apartment became the answer to our dispute, which only grew more bitter in the months that followed the visit to Åsmund's friend in Bærum. My growing belly could no longer be hidden, but Åsmund wanted a garden, and everything we found that was central enough for me was too small and surrounded by too much concrete for him. Then the advert had appeared: an apartment with a converted cellar in a house divided into four flats in Tåsen. Too small and impractical for a family with greater means, but big enough for us and more suitable than where we currently lived, with three bedrooms and a shared garden. We went to the viewing, walking up from Sagene, crossing Voldsløkka and sauntering into Tåsen, between the houses with their lush gardens, until we reached the huge tree where Kastanjesvingen turns off Bakkehaugveien. The house was one of three that had been converted into apartments, situated one after the other, each with a garden around it and a steep slope behind. Inside the apartment, I forced my way between the hopeful couples who were looking around, clutching the brochures handed out by the estate agent, and went into the kitchen to stand before the windows. As I looked out into the garden, I thought: *This is where we're going to live.* I cast a glance at Åsmund, who nodded appreciatively. This was somewhere he could see himself, too. A garden. A quiet cul-de-sac. Peaceful, green. Still just fifteen minutes' walk down to Sagene; a quick cycle ride to work. The price was steep, but if we were willing to cut our outgoings a little, eat more cheaply and reduce our holiday budget, it would be possible. We looked at each other. We were willing.

Now two police cars are parked outside the house – I see them as I walk up Kastanjesvingen. They don't have their lights on, they're simply parked there, perfectly still. Just beside our gate stands a car with a TV station logo on its door. This tugs at something within me, but there's nothing threatening about it. In the driver's seat sits a man, engrossed in something on his phone. As I walk past and open the gate, he fails to notice me.

A police cordon has been established around the house. Just outside the tape a policewoman with a camera is crouching down on her haunches. She takes the occasional photograph – of what I'm not entirely sure, the grass and the soil, perhaps, or our cellar windows. The garden is otherwise unchanged. The grass is damp, and here and there the lawn is scattered with yellow leaves, still few as yet, but they provide an intimation of what inevitably will come.

I don't go into our apartment. I could drop off my bag before going up to see Jamila, but I'm reluctant. It would be so quiet in there. Instead, I go straight up to the first floor. Past Jørgen's door, which I don't look at. I turn my gaze towards Jamila's instead, and knock.

"I'll be right there," a voice shouts from inside – unnecessarily, as it turns out, since it takes less than five seconds for her to open the door.

"Rikke!"

Her voice, high and unfettered, is cast back by the walls of the hallway.

"It's so good to see you!"

Jamila always wears stiletto heels, so I'm used to standing eye to eye with her, but indoors she's barefoot and therefore ten centimetres shorter than usual. When she hugs me – which she does the moment she sees me, almost without waiting for me to open my arms – I look down at the top of her head, where the strands of thick black hair meet in the middle. She smells of shampoo, of freshly washed hair and elder blossom.

She releases me. Her eyes are shining.

"This is all just so awful," she says. "I hardly slept a wink last night."

She sets a hand on my arm and pulls me inside; I close the door behind me. She walks ahead of me, her footsteps quick, the soles of her feet slapping rapidly against the parquet. As she walks, she speaks – she's in a total state of shock, she tells me, can't believe that this is actually true. She and Saman had to go visit friends yesterday evening, she found being at home while the police were carrying on right next door far too stressful – not to mention the fact that *he was in there*.

"But they must have taken him away by now," she says. "Don't you think?"

I have no idea, but I nod all the same. We take a seat in the living room. Jamila sets a pot of coffee – which she obviously had ready and waiting – on the table, and slumps down onto the sofa opposite me. She's gathered her long black hair into a bun, and is wearing a T-shirt and a pair of jeans I'm willing to bet cost an arm and a leg, and which, in all their simplicity, make her look as if she might feature on some film star or fashion icon's Instagram.

"Can you *believe* it?" she asks. "Can you in any way *believe* that this is actually happening?"

Her eyes are bloodshot, I realise, and this surprises me. Of course I've seen her speak to Jørgen, but no more than is usual between neighbours, and without me entirely understanding where it came from I've always had the impression that she wasn't especially keen on him.

"I mean," she continues, "he was *murdered*. Here, Rikke. In our house. Right next door to us. Just on the other side of that wall."

She throws out her arm in a superfluous movement, pointing to the wall that separates their living room from that belonging to Jørgen and Merete.

94

"Maybe we were sitting right here watching TV, or asleep in our bed, while he was bleeding to death right next door," she says. "Ugh – it's so awful to think about."

She rubs the skin around her eyes, which is a touch greyer than usual. Restless, I shift my legs.

"Yes," I say. "Yes, of course, it's completely . . ."

"Poor Jørgen," she says. "I mean, it isn't as if we were close or anything, and there were certain things about him, but still. Killed in his own home."

For a moment there are tears in her eyes. She has such big eyes, so shiny I find it impossible to look away from them, with their long, curving lashes. Then the tears vanish again, as if of their own accord. She rubs an index finger adorned with pale pink nail polish under each eye, but it doesn't look as if there's any moisture to wipe away. Between my hands I turn the tiny coffee cup she's given me.

"But are they certain that he was murdered?" I ask. "I mean, do we know that for sure?"

She looks at me. It's as if she's struggling to understand what I'm saying. As if I'm presenting a hypothesis, and she's an academic supervisor attempting to determine if I'm simply careless or a total idiot.

"They reported it as *suspicious* in the newspaper," I continue. "But surely that can mean different things. It isn't necessarily a given that it was . . ."

I can't make myself say the word.

"You know," I say finally.

"Rikke," Jamila says. "He was slumped over his desk in a pool of blood."

The description roars through me. Jørgen, hunched over his work. A pool of blood. An image I find it impossible not to conjure up. Her words stick in my chest, and rage surges up from my stomach. Who the fuck is Jamila to create some gory drama out of all this?

95

"How do you know that?" I snap back at her, more sharply than I intend to.

She seems not to notice my tone.

"But don't you know?"

"Know what?"

For a few seconds she sits in uncharacteristic silence.

"I was the one who found him," she says.

Jamila had been sitting here in her apartment at her Mac, touching up some photographs – the cosy bit of the work, she calls it. She was listening to music and drinking tea, tinkering with the results of a photo shoot from earlier that week, when Merete had called. There was irritation in her voice, and a hissing all around her – she was in Skar, she said, in the forest deep in the valley. Along with her sister and Filippa she was standing in a deserted car park out there, waiting – Jørgen was supposed to come and pick them up at three o'clock, but it was twenty-five past and he still hadn't arrived; she couldn't get hold of him on the phone, either. Was Jamila at home, by any chance? Would she mind popping over and seeing whether he was there?

Yes, Jamila said, she was home. Of course she could pop over. She went out into the hallway in her stockinged feet and knocked on the door. Here she gives me a knowing glance, and says breathlessly:

"But nobody answered."

Jamila called Merete back and told her that Jørgen hadn't come to the door, and Merete sighed heavily and said, well wasn't that just typical, but thanks all the same. And then she asked whether it would be too much trouble for Jamila to let herself into the apartment. He sometimes listens to music, Merete said, or he watches lectures from God knows where on his computer with his headphones on and loses track of time. The key is in the flowerpot in the stairwell – you know where it is. Jamila said it was no trouble. She found the key and let herself in.

"It was so quiet inside," Jamila says. "So eerily quiet. There was something in the air – I don't know how to explain it."

I nod, knowing all too well what she means.

Jamila had looked around. The kitchen was empty, but the light was on. There was a plate in the sink that had traces of grease and sauce on it, which nobody had rinsed off. On the kitchen counter stood a dirty saucepan. Nobody had put it in the dishwasher. Jamila went back into the living room and saw that the door to the study was closed. She knows that it's probably the drama of what followed playing a trick on her in retrospect, she says to me, but as she approached the door, she felt as if she already knew. A sense of dread at having to push it open.

He was lying with his head resting on the keyboard. The computer screen was black. At first she thought he might have nodded off over his work, but then she saw the blood. Surprisingly red, she said. Of course, she had never seen such huge volumes of blood in real life before, only in films, but it was different from what she would have expected. A brighter shade of red. It felt as if she stood there for an eternity, just staring, as the knowledge of what she was looking at dawned on her. Like that feeling you have when you see a vase falling, Jamila says. You stand there and can see the accident, the thousands of pieces the vase will shatter into when it hits the floor – it feels as if it's happening in such slow motion that you have all the time in the world to act – and still you just stand there, unable to move, and watch it happen. Does that make sense?

I nod, and Jamila goes on:

"Then I screamed. Or at least, I think I did. What I mostly remember is that I ran out of the apartment. And that I cried."

She lowers her voice, and with a hint of wonder in her huge eyes, says:

"I'd never seen a dead person before."

Jørgen is one of those people who hardly sleeps. He can manage fine with six hours a night, often less, and likes to work while others are sleeping. Several times, during the nights we shared a hotel room, I was woken by the sound of his fingers clattering across the keyboard. But now Jamila is talking about a pool of blood, and this pool has contaminated all the other memories, those of Jørgen working in the hotel room in London as I lay there half asleep, watching him. And I suspect that this is how it will be now, that every image I have of him will soon be contaminated by this pool, until it's all that remains. Opposite me Jamila sits cross-legged on the pale-grey minimalistic sofa, waiting for me to say something. But I don't want to talk about it anymore, don't want to soil any more memories of him. I feel sick, but I mustn't show it. But Jamila is worked up, her bare foot tapping impatiently against the sofa cushion, and when I don't say anything, she sets her cup on the coffee table and leans over it, towards me.

"Who could have done this?" she says. "That's what bothers me. There must be something we've seen, something we've heard – after all, we live right next door."

"I don't know," I say, thinking of all the things I hope nobody has seen or heard. But Jamila doesn't hear my scepticism – she's brimming with initiative. According to her, it should be possible to figure this out. She wants to talk to the other neighbours, the ones she bumps into in the local shop or on the street. Maybe I can speak to the parents at the school, all the Tåsen mums I've told her about. Somebody must have seen something. And there are plenty of things people might be reluctant to mention to the police. Neighbourhood gossip, for instance. Little observations. People live on top of one another around here – you see things, it can't be helped. And so maybe people think that something they noticed is insignificant. Or perhaps they don't want to risk bothering the police with it. Maybe people don't want to seem gossipy, or to create problems for a neighbour. But to tell her, or me – well, that would be something else entirely.

"People in the neighbourhood like us, Rikke," she says. She takes my hand in hers and squeezes it with a surprising strength, her thin, bony hand gripping mine so hard that her rings cut into my fingers. "They trust us."

The headache I lied about at work has now crept up on me for real. The hand that Jamila is holding hurts, and I think: What is she actually suggesting? And why?

"Jamila," I say, pulling my hand away and feeling the ache in it as she lets go, "this is a police matter. I think it's best we stay well out of it."

"But we *can't* just stay well out of it," she says.

Her eyes are so wide that I can see the whites all the way around their irises. She stares at me. Don't I get it? We're implicated by the simple fact that we live so close to each other. This is about taking responsibility for the people around us, looking out for one another.

"Something evil lives in this neighbourhood, Rikke," she says. "You know this mystery with the dead cats? Well, that's what I've been thinking ever since I first heard about them. What would make people do something like that, other than pure evil?"

Yet again, I sigh. Here they are again, the blasted cats. And Jamila has a propensity for drama. More than a propensity. *Something evil lives in this neighbourhood.* She's allowed herself to be seduced by the novelty of it, she's so easily swept along. Doesn't realise just how worked up she is. And the terrible thing she experienced yesterday means that I can't say any of this to her.

I think about her husband out on the landing and the two eggs he gave me that ended up on our kitchen counter, reminding myself of the lie. I had planned to mention them to her, but now I'm not sure how to bring it up. And anyway, I don't want to draw attention to them, to risk a big deal being made out of it. I'm not entirely sure if I can trust her.

"It was so creepy, Rikke," she says as she shows me out. "Blood all over the keyboard. I've hardly slept."

And then I remember how young she is, not yet even thirty. I put an arm around her shoulders. She looks up at me, and for a moment I feel like a big sister.

"Try not to think about it," I say.

Out on the landing I stare at Jørgen's closed door. I've opened it so many times after sneaking up here in my stockinged feet as carefully as I can, painfully aware that every creak of the stairs can be heard in all four apartments. The lock behind me clicks, and I turn around. Jamila never usually locks her front door.

I have to pass Jørgen's door to go downstairs, and I move as if attempting to circumvent it, pressing myself against the banister rail opposite. A pool of blood. On many occasions I was excited as I tiptoed up here and made my way through that door, but at times it was something I did against my better judgement – especially towards the end. I might feel something akin to reluctance, accompanied by a desire to do the right thing, to heed the tiny weak voice that whispered: Leave it alone. Turn back. Think about the people waiting for you at home. Arguments that have little potency in the face of lust, though there were times I felt there wasn't much satisfaction to be found up there. Now the whole thing is indisputably over. I no longer have to think about it.

Once inside our apartment I lean my back against the front door. Do I not also feel a certain relief? He's gone. It's over – and this time, it's over for good. Is there not a hint of liberation in that? I'm done with him, there's nothing more to think about. I close my eyes. Try to breathe calmly, maintain control. Yes. If I'm being honest, there is also relief. But I can't possibly tell anyone – not ever. I shouldn't even think it. Jørgen's death is a tragedy, and that's all there is to it.

The policewoman with the camera is nowhere to be seen in the garden, she must be on the other side of the house now. It's completely silent up on the first floor. For the moment the police seem to have finished whatever they were doing up there, and Merete must be staying elsewhere, seeing as her home is a crime scene. Under ordinary circumstances she's often at home during the day; when I was on maternity leave, I would hear her. Her steps, soft and quick. I heard her students playing the grand piano, the notes that were hesitant or rushed, well played or piercing. Sometimes Merete would take over, and when she did I was never in any doubt that it was her I could hear – she has a particular self-confidence at the keys. Her notes flow effortlessly, strung together without error. She often plays when she's home alone – mostly the great composers, Debussy, Tchaikovsky, Bartók – although I once heard her playing David Bowie. She approached "Life on Mars?" as if it were a classical piece, and it made me smile. Lately, I've heard her practising for *The Threepenny Opera*, Kurt Weill's deep, suggestive chords coming through the walls of our shared building, albeit with an entirely different timbre than in the sports hall at Bakkehaugen. How Merete ended up being the play's pianist, I have no idea. Maybe she spoke to Gard at the parents' evening in August, and perhaps he invited her to take part after that. I can't imagine that she actively sought out the role herself. Something about her makes me think that she never asks for anything, that everything is offered to her and that it's her privilege to choose, yes please or no thank you.

Gard has been here on at least a couple of occasions. I saw him from the window once, and another time I bumped into him on the stairs. He had a huge pile of papers with him, sheet music, perhaps, or notes on the script. What the tone is like between the two of them, I have no idea. Merete, somewhat aloof and a professional to her core, discloses no antipathies, but I think I've seen something in her face at the odd weekend rehearsal when Gard has been going on about his interpretation of the play.

"Ultimately, the question is whether or not Mack the Knife is a bad person," he once said, "and if he is, is that his fault, or have his circumstances shaped him? And regardless: is it right that he should die for his sins? Is any crime so heinous that the perpetrator deserves to be put to death?"

Merete had sat there waiting for him to finish, an irreproachably neutral expression on her face, and yet I think I noticed a little twitch at the corner of her mouth, a not-so-subtle set to her brows, as if she was thinking, *God, what a Cub Scout leader.* But even if she was, nobody can accuse her of expressing it.

It's now over a month since the big *Threepenny Opera* controversy broke out following an email from a fired-up mother who had realised that her eighth-grade daughter would be playing a prostitute. In the script, her daughter's role was specifically designated as *whore*, which had caused the mother some distress. *What do we actually think about this*, she wrote, *is it really appropriate for a school production?* The parents' group had immediately moved into a state of high alert, and a landslide of emails was triggered. In the endless threads of electronic conversation, it was argued that the play was inappropriate, perhaps even harmful. Someone wrote that vulnerable teenage girls would have their sexuality put on display, as if for sale – and all under the auspices of the school, no less! Saga's mother composed a rousing appeal, including a link to her article about the pressures surrounding body image. Others were more restrained. *The Threepenny Opera* attempts to say something about the social conditions that provide especially fertile soil for evil, wrote a father who worked for a left-leaning think tank. And don't our privileged children need to learn about how poverty and marginalisation lay the foundations for criminality? A mother who holds an associate professorship at the university wrote that Brecht is, after all, one of the greats of world literature, and the fact that the play forces us to endure discomfort, just as all good literature does, was an argument *for* it being performed. These suggestions were met with little understanding – *do you genuinely find it unproblematic that girls as young as twelve are playing prostitutes?* one parent wrote – and with that, the more reticent members of the apologists began to argue more forcefully. Are we going to hide the hard realities of life from our children, someone wrote, while in many parts of the world children who haven't even hit puberty are being sold into marriage or sexual slavery? Are we going to put a gag on freedom of speech, asked Jørgen, who otherwise didn't seem to care very much about what happened at the school, but now threw himself into the debate. He, at least, was proud that his daughter would be playing Low-Dive Jenny, singing a song about how destructive it could be for a young woman to be abused by a pimp.

At this point, somebody brought school management in. Nina Sparre, who was both fired-up by the conflict and frightened by it, grabbed me in the stairwell at home and asked me what I thought about all the controversy surrounding the school play. What I thought? I replied by saying that I thought the whole thing had been blown up out of all proportion, and that it was neither as important to put on the play as certain individuals seemed to believe, nor so harmful as others insisted, and although I would never have admitted it to Jørgen, I was secretly relieved when the school put its foot down and decided that Brecht would be rewritten, meaning that Emma would no longer have to stand on stage and play a whore. Gard was upset, having allied himself with the parents who believed that the play should be performed in its original form, but when it came down to it, he was a pragmatic man, and therefore agreed to make the whores into dancers and to cut certain songs, including the "Pimp's Ballad", which Filippa Tangen was supposed to sing.

Merete never aired her opinion on the controversy. Of all the parents it was she who worked most closely with Gard, and it seems likely that he asked her opinion, but if she did offer him her support it was never given in public. She's a connoisseur, and has surprisingly refreshing taste considering her elegant appearance. Still, it wouldn't surprise me if she, like me, was a little relieved at the way things turned out. At the rehearsals that have taken place since the matter was resolved her posture has remained just as erect as it always was, but I can't remember having seen Gard here in Kastanjesvingen since the rewrite, so perhaps he felt that she'd betrayed him.

The car from the TV station is still parked at the edge of the road – I can see it from the kitchen window. The apple tree has lost its leaves, its branches stretching towards the sky; it could probably do with pruning. Last summer, Jørgen and I would sometimes sit on the bench below that tree, each with our own book. That was before everything between us began. But it seems like another bench now. It has something to do with the autumn, I think. It's about the autumn. Rather than the fact that Jørgen is now dead.

Jørgen is dead. It's so hard to grasp. Am I allowed to grieve? In a flash I find myself jealous of Jamila. *She* can cry over Jørgen, *she's* allowed. It's so uncomplicated for her, while I have to watch myself. I have to be sad, but not too sad – especially not in front of Åsmund. Poor Åsmund, who hasn't done anything wrong. There was nothing I could point to, he never drove me away. We went through a slightly difficult patch, perhaps, but even that wasn't that terrible. No more so than the kinds of things all couples experience. It was never about him.

When I was in my early twenties, I lived in a flatshare with my friends. They were single, all of them, and I sometimes envied their adventures. Every evening out on the town was an opportunity to meet someone. A new mouth to kiss, a body to undress. New stories told at the kitchen table the morning after. But the stories were often about what went wrong, men who didn't show up for dates, all the doubt and self-scrutiny – what had she done wrong? All the weird men, slightly crazy or self-obsessed, not to mention frightening, the ones who bordered on being downright dangerous. And on top of all this were all the awful break-ups, delivered via text message or a friend, or never delivered at all, the boyfriends who simply vanished. I listened to their stories; gave suggestions and offered my support. All while hiding my gratitude for the fact that I had Åsmund. Who answered my messages, who was ordinary and could be trusted, and whom I also loved. Would I ever consider leaving him for all this?

The dissatisfaction came and went in waves. At times, everything was great; at others, not so great. Sometimes I dreamed about meeting someone, anyone at all. A man without a face, without a past or future, someone to fuck in the reading room toilets or in an alley on the way home from a night out. I never acted on it. There were a couple of occasions when I could have done – nobody would have ever found out. I could have got the lust out of my system and gone home to Åsmund afterwards, continued our life together and never given it another thought. But I refrained. Surely there must be a line there, somewhere – cross it, and you can't go back. And, at the end of the day, I wasn't the type, so I always backed out before things went too far.

Åsmund is home when Lukas and I get back from kindergarten. He's in the kitchen, I can see him from the garden. The apartment smells of fried mincemeat and onions.

"Hi," I say from the hallway, my voice catching a little.

"Hi," he shouts back.

Cheerfully? No more so than usual, but this is precisely what squeezes my chest, the fact that Åsmund is his usual self. Lukas runs inside to find his toys in the living room. I go out into the kitchen and find Åsmund standing at the stove with his back to me. He hasn't heard my footsteps, doesn't know that I'm standing behind him, and I watch him for a few seconds as he reaches up to take something from a cupboard, peers down into the saucepan, uses a spatula to turn the meat in the frying pan. He hums as he works, or half hums – not any one tune in particular, just these sounds he makes. I remember this half humming from the mornings in the flatshare, when Åsmund had stayed the night and made everyone omelettes for breakfast. The girls showered him with praise. I pretended to shush them – don't flatter him too much, I said, he'll end up too big for his boots. But I enjoyed the envy of the others. I had something they wanted.

He turns around.

"Oh, hey," he says, surprised. "There you are."

"Yeah," I say.

"Is something the matter?"

"No."

He smiles at me, as if to cheer me up. Dear, kind Åsmund, who always wants life to be good for me. I know there have been times when this has irritated me, I've even told him as much – do you have to be so fucking nice to me all the time, do what you want for a change, you don't always have to be so damn considerate – but as I look at him now, I can't understand it. Is there any more powerful declaration of love than this: day after day, year after year, doing your best to make life better for someone else?

He looks at me, and I think he's about to say something about Jørgen – I can see that he's considering it from the way his brows twitch together. But then his forehead smoothes out, and he says:

"Are you looking at my arse?"

He turns again, wiggling it back and forth. Reluctantly, I laugh.

"Yeah, you caught me."

He smiles at me over his shoulder. His brown hair has faint flecks of grey at the temples. When I picture Åsmund, I always think he looks exactly the same as he did when he was twenty, but he's getting older, too.

"Feel free to look all you want," he says. "All this is yours."

My throat tightens unexpectedly, as if I have to cry, intensely and all at once. Without speaking I leave the kitchen and walk quickly through the living room, where Lukas is on his knees digging for something in his toy box, and go into the bathroom. I lock the door and stand at the sink, turning on the tap so that the sound of the running water will camouflage my sobs like last time, and then I wait, but nothing comes. I try, frowning, creating pressure in my forehead, miming the facial expression I make when I cry. Still nothing. Have I forgotten how?

I go back to the living room.

"Don't pull out all your toys, okay, Lukas?" I say half-heartedly.

It's already too late. He's emptied the box over his head, but I have to say something. Åsmund appears in the doorway.

"Really – is everything okay, Rikke?" he asks.

Is it? I have no idea.

The people upstairs seem to be multiplying. From the living room where we're watching TV, Åsmund and I can hear them tramping up the stairs. Every now and then somebody comes down, but that doesn't seem to happen as often. The car from the TV station has gone, but two others have appeared in its place, one from a tabloid newspaper and one from another TV channel. We're watching a series on Netflix. Åsmund is keen to switch to the news, but I don't want to.

"Are you sure?" he says. "They might show our house."

"Well, that's something I *definitely* don't want to see," I say, and Åsmund shrugs.

Lukas is asleep, and Emma is doing her own thing in her room. She's in a bad mood, has been silent and sulky all afternoon, hardly responding when spoken to. As a rule, she's more friendly towards Åsmund than she is towards me. When Åsmund gives himself fangs using his chopsticks, or plays his cutlery like drumsticks, she often laughs just as she did when she was small, a gleam of true joy in her eyes. She never does this with me. But then, perhaps I don't joke around so much, either. And I have no idea what she's doing down there in her bedroom. I half do and half don't want to ask.

When they really start stamping around, right above our heads, we look up.

"That seems a bit much," Åsmund says at one point, but otherwise we say nothing. It's as if they no longer concern us, as long as we don't talk about them. And why should they concern us, anyway – what happened up there surely has nothing to do with us – but it writhes within me all the same. Why did I have to go up there on Saturday? I still haven't spoken to the police about the text messages. I could have called them today when I got home from work, or after I had been to see Jamila. It makes no sense to have resisted contacting them to this extent. There's no logic to it.

We hear footsteps coming back down the stairs, not quite so thundering this time. Voices, too – not the words, but the sound of them. A man and a woman. They walk down the corridor outside our apartment, then knock at the door.

I jump up, as if I've been sitting here waiting for this – I haven't, but I'm ready as soon I hear the knocking, halfway across the room before it stops. Åsmund gives me a questioning look but says nothing, and as I make my way into the hallway to open the door something stirs in the pit of my stomach. My hand trembles as I reach for the lock.

Out in the corridor stands Robin, along with a woman. Robin is in uniform while the woman is not, but you can tell that she's a police officer and I recognise her immediately.

"Hi," Robin says to me. "Is now a good time for a quick chat?"

"Ingvild?" I ask, and a look of astonishment breaks through the woman's professional expression.

She stares at me in confusion – I've surprised her, and she seems to be the kind of person who is rarely surprised.

"It's Rikke," I say. "I'm a friend of Hege's – remember?"

And then she smiles. Warmly and broadly, even.

"Yes," she says. "Rikke. Now I remember you. Hi."

She holds out her hand. Had she not been here in an official capacity she might even have given me a hug – or at least it feels like that might have been the natural thing to do.

When we were twenty-two, my friend went through a brief lesbian phase, which was when Ingvild Fredly started to turn up at the flatshare. She was a police officer, wore a leather jacket and rode a motorcycle, and was in many ways the perfect stereotype of the kind of woman you're supposed to have a lesbian experience with, if you're only going to have one. Ingvild was thirty; Hege was twenty-two and agreed with every lover she took about absolutely everything. Whenever Ingvild offered an opinion, Hege would nod in approval, although I don't think Ingvild was the type to appreciate this kind of idol worship. Their relationship only lasted a couple of months, but during that time Ingvild often came over to our place. She sat at the kitchen table, drinking coffee in the mornings and beer in the evenings. She came from a tiny village up north, I seem to remember. She once told us about how the older boys used to give the teenage girls a ride home from parties on the condition that they sucked them off. I remember being shocked, and that Ingvild had said, fairly laconically, that it had at least given her a good reason to get herself a motorbike.

"How are things?" I ask her, as if we're meeting in an entirely different context – while paying someone a visit, or through friends we didn't know we had in common.

"Oh, you know," she says. "I'm fine. Working, keeping at it. And you?"

"Yeah," I say. "Good. This is where I live."

She peeks inside and smiles.

"And you have kids?"

"Two of them. A girl and a boy. Thirteen and four."

"Right," she says, giving a nod towards the folder she's holding in her hand, "I read that here."

We look at the folder, and it dawns on us both that we are not in fact meeting through a common acquaintance, that this situation demands something else of us. Our smiles disappear to be replaced by other expressions, hers professional, mine a little more reserved. It feels strange, as if our cheery, light conversation continues to float above the hallway. Robin casts a curious glance back and forth between us.

"I'm leading the investigation," Ingvild says, her voice suddenly deeper, more authoritative. "I'd like to talk to the two of you. May we come in?"

Once again, we sit at the kitchen table. Åsmund and I sit next to each other, with Ingvild and Robin on the opposite side. Ingvild clears her throat.

"Can you tell us a bit about the kind of relationship you have with your neighbours?" she says. "That is, how well do you know Jørgen and Merete Tangen?"

"Well," Åsmund says, looking at me. "What can we say to that? We don't know them that well, do we?"

My heart is pounding, hard and fast. But I have to take control here. Have to play the role of the average neighbour, as if we were talking about Saman and Jamila, or Nina and Svein.

"We're just ordinary neighbours," I say.

My voice carries. It's almost as if I believe the words myself.

"What does that mean?" Ingvild asks. "Did you go over to each other's apartments every now and then? Eat dinner together, go on holiday?"

"We eat together out on the patio every now and then, in the summer," I say. "We have a kind of neighbourhood party once a year, for everyone who lives in the building. And Merete invited me up for a glass of wine a couple of times. But other than that . . . we've only had dinner at their place once, haven't we?"

Åsmund nods.

"And that was a few years ago," I say.

Robin notes this down.

"And apart from that?" Ingvild asks.

I pretend to think.

"Our daughter is in the same class as theirs at Bakkehaugen secondary school. So, you know, there's parents' evenings, and . . ."

My throat is dry. I cough.

"And the theatre production they're working on at the moment. *The Threepenny Opera*. The opening night will be just before Christmas – our daughter is in it, as is theirs, and the parents help out. So . . ."

There must be invoices from the hotel stays. There must be information in his email inbox or at the hotels about how we've stayed in the same room.

"No trips, or anything like that?" Ingvild asks, as if prompted.

"No," I say, my voice light and breezy.

Have they found them already? Plane tickets, or the emails we wrote to each other, making our plans? Ingvild looks down at the notepad in front of her, and says:

"There was talk of a cabin trip. Some time towards the end of the summer, let's see, the twenty-fourth to the twenty-sixth of August? To Beitostølen?"

"Oh," Åsmund says, surprised. "The guys' trip?"

"Yes," Ingvild says.

Robin says:

"It appears to have been Jørgen Tangen, Saman Karimi, Svein Sparre and you? Is that correct?"

The air seeps slowly and soundlessly out of me.

"Yes, that's right," Åsmund says. "I don't remember the exact dates off the top of my head, but the four of us went, it may well have been at the end of August."

"Can you tell us about the trip?" Ingvild asks.

Åsmund looks at her, not comprehending. Then he looks at me, before looking back at her again.

"I'm not sure what there is to say, exactly. We drove up on the Friday after work, cooked some food, stuff like that. On the Saturday we went on a long hike, and then we went in the sauna – yes, they have one of those huge saunas there. It's Svein's cabin, he was the one who invited us. And well, then we had some dinner, a few beers. The next day we took another hike, a shorter one this time, cleaned the cabin and left. Jørgen drove up with Saman, and I got a lift with Svein."

Robin takes notes as Åsmund speaks, his pen rushing across the notepad. Åsmund gives the two officers a questioning look – was this what they wanted to know?

"So, that was that," he says. "I don't think there's much more to say about it. Unless . . . there was something in particular?"

"Was there a disagreement one evening?" Ingvild asks.

There's something efficient and businesslike in her tone. I wonder to what extent this is due to the evenings spent at the flatshare, our conversations over a beer and our friendly chat at the door just now – I can imagine she might feel the need to be particularly strict, in order to erase the private connection. Or maybe she's always like this. She's professional, no doubt about it, but she isn't especially accommodating. The hissing in my ears returns. The text messages on Jørgen's phone. Footage from security cameras in the reception of the office building where he works, showing the two of us on our way inside late in the evening, hand in hand.

"Disagreement?" Åsmund asks, frowning, as if he's trying to discern something that is far, far away. "Oh, you mean the conversation we had on the Saturday night? I mean, there was a discussion about – I can't remember what it was, vaccines, or something like that? Jørgen believed one thing, Saman something else, and things got a little heated. But it was nothing more serious than that. Nothing unpleasant. We'd had quite a bit to drink, you know how it is. It wasn't anything you'd . . ."

He pauses.

"Is that what you think? That one of us killed him?"

Ingvild doesn't answer. Instead, she says:

"Can you tell me anything about your other neighbours? What kind of relationship do you have with them?"

"Nina and Svein Sparre were already living here when we moved in," I say. "Their son is a couple of years older than our daughter – they don't go to the same school. We see the family in the garden and bump into them out in the corridor and whatnot, but that's about it. Nina is deputy head at Emma's school, so I've met with her there a couple of times. And Åsmund is on the board of the housing cooperative with her."

"Yes," Åsmund confirms.

"Saman and Jamila moved in, let's see, maybe a year and a half ago," I say. "Something like that? We don't know him very well – I mean, at least I don't – but I've got to know Jamila a bit. We've met up a couple of times, outside the house. Gone for a coffee together, things like that."

"And when you go for coffee, what do you talk about?" Ingvild asks.

I think back to our conversation earlier today, Jamila leaning over the coffee table and saying, with emphasis, *something evil lives in this neighbourhood.* And her description, *a pool of blood.*

"Oh, you know," I say. "This and that. Life, and . . . well, just everyday things. She tells me a bit about her job, I tell her about mine."

"And what do you do?"

"I work at a research centre linked to the university. We're looking at attitudes to climate change and sustainable consumption."

"Do you enjoy it?"

"Oh yes."

Is she asking me as a police officer, or as an old acquaintance? She glances at her notepad, apparently a little uninterested now, no longer so confrontational. Then she looks up, turns to Åsmund, and says:

"And you? What do you do?"

"I work with IT at the Directorate for Education and Training," he says.

"I see. And then there's Friday evening," she says, glancing down at her notepad again. "Let's see now."

She flicks through the pages, reads some notes. We wait.

"Robin tells me that you —" she glances at Åsmund — "came home with Lukas — that's your son, isn't it? — at around four-thirty, and that your daughter Emma arrived home half an hour later. Is that correct?"

"Yes," Åsmund says, his voice serious.

"And you," she says to me, "you came home a little after that?"

"Yes."

"What time?"

"I don't know. Half past five, maybe. Or a little earlier?"

I look at Åsmund, whose face instantly takes on an expression of deep concentration, a desire to help me.

"You let yourself in using the code to the lock on the building's front door?" Ingvild asks.

"Yes," I say. "That's all we use. We no longer have keys, everybody has a code they use to let themselves in."

"Is there anyone outside the household who knows your code?"

We look at each other.

"No," I say. "I'm sure there isn't."

"Not that I can think of," Åsmund says.

"So you came home after work on Friday afternoon," Ingvild says. "Did you go out again that evening?"

"No," Åsmund and I say, almost in unison.

"Are you sure?"

"Yes."

I clear my throat.

"Yes, we were home all evening. We watched a film. Well – it was half a film for me. I went to bed first, but you stayed up a little longer?"

"Just for an hour," Åsmund says apologetically, as if there's something suspicious about going to bed later than ten o'clock on a Friday night.

"And the children? Emma?"

"I checked on her before I went to bed," Åsmund says. "She was asleep."

"Do you have a ladder on the property?"

Åsmund and I look at each other.

"A ladder?" I ask.

"I think there's one behind the shed," Åsmund says. "There was an issue with some broken roof tiles a few years ago, it was used then."

Ingvild nods twice, and snaps her notepad closed.

"We are confident," she says, "that the man who was found dead in the apartment upstairs is Jørgen Tangen, although I'm sure you had already gathered as much. He hasn't been formally identified just yet – that will take a little time – but we see no reason to doubt his identity. We are also confident that he was murdered. He had a long incision across his throat, and likely bled to death over the course of a few minutes."

A pool of blood. When we were in high school, they bussed us out to a farm in Hønefoss, so we could learn about how our food was produced. The farmer took us into the pig barn, and with a certain satisfaction told us that when he was little, they sometimes slaughtered the pigs by cutting their throats, the blood spurting out. We shifted uncomfortably. Some of the girls shuddered or said "ugh". Åsmund, who can't stand the sight of blood, turned white as chalk just at the thought of it, and had to sit down outside the barn. I remember smiling a little at the spectacle of these city kids being confronted with the origins of their hot-dog sausages.

"So you're aware that this is now a murder investigation," Ingvild says. "We'll be holding a press conference this evening, and that's why we're informing the neighbours at this time. And as I'm sure you understand, this is a very serious matter."

She gives us both a weighty look, as if we're children and she's a strict aunt.

"So it's important that you tell us everything exactly as it happened. Okay?"

We nod. Ingvild digs around in the pocket of her leather jacket and pulls out a small rectangle of paper, which she sets on the table.

"This is my card. If you think of anything else, please don't hesitate to get in touch."

We nod again. The business card sits there on the table between us, smouldering, and I think – this is my ticket out of this. I have to speak to Ingvild. Tell her everything, exactly as it happened.

On her way out, Ingvild looks around and says:

"You have a nice place here."

"Thank you," I say.

"Really snug and homely. Warm."

In the hallway they put on their shoes, say their goodbyes, and leave. As the door slams shut behind them, Åsmund says:

"Jesus. Can you believe that actually happened?"

While Åsmund is using the toilet, I take a photograph of the business card. Later, I go into the bathroom myself, turn on the tap as I brush my teeth, and enter Ingvild's number into my phone. *Hi again!* I write. *There were a few things I didn't get to mention earlier. Can we speak tomorrow? Best wishes, Rikke.* I tap send as fast as I can, so there's no time for me to change my mind. Afterwards I lie down on the bathroom floor, feeling the tiles warm the underside of my body. My phone hasn't made a sound. I can see that she's read the message – beneath it, it says *Read 21.32.* Just minutes after I sent it. But she doesn't respond.

*

The answer doesn't come until the middle of the night. Of course I haven't been able to sleep. It's after midnight, and I'm floating around the house, unable to relax. I sit down at the computer intending to google Jørgen, but I don't want to, I'm afraid of what I might find. A long incision across his throat, a pool of blood. In the end, I do it anyway. Mainly find articles he's written, headlines and introductory paragraphs, and then his byline photo. I consider him. A handsome man, in his mid-forties when it was taken. Curly hair, high forehead, intense gaze. When I look at him like this, he could be anyone. Jørgen's face only truly came alive when he spoke. It isn't that he didn't look good. But it was first and foremost who he was that made him so attractive.

My phone buzzes, and I jump. I'm so ill at ease, as if constantly on the edge of my seat, ready to flee. *How's 10 o'clock tomorrow?* Ingvild asks. That's all she writes. *Yes*, I reply, *10 is good. Where should we meet?* Another half an hour passes, it's almost one in the morning, and then she answers. Gives only the name of a café. I've never heard of it, but I find it online, it's in the city centre. *Great*, I write. *See you tomorrow!* To this, she doesn't respond. I look at her terse messages. I'm unsure whether I should consider Ingvild Fredly a friend.

"Quiet weekend?" Jørgen said to me.

He came wandering up the stone path in the garden, a paper bag from an exclusive grocery store in one hand, slowing down as he approached.

"Yes," I said. "Well. As quiet as I can manage to make it. Åsmund's away, I'm alone with the kids."

We laughed.

"I get it," he said.

Over on the patio Lukas was playing, his red overalls bright against the sheet-white January snow. Dusk was already falling, but even in the dimness it was impossible not to see him among all the white.

"And you?" I asked.

"Yeah," he said. "It's a quiet one this weekend. Merete has taken Filippa on a cabin trip. I'm home alone."

He smiled broadly and caught himself doing it, as if it had suddenly occurred to him that being happy your family is away for the weekend isn't the done thing.

"Right," I said, politely looking away, to signal that I hadn't noticed his inappropriate joy. "Big plans?"

"Nah," he said. "Just work. I'm writing a book. Or at least, what I hope will become a book."

"Oh really? What's it about?"

He smiled, looked over at the red boy on the patio.

"It's about Afghanistan, actually," he said. "I'm very interested in Afghanistan."

"Wow," I said, laughing. "Afghanistan."

We stood there in silence, and it was as if Jørgen was trying to formulate an explanation, something that would express what he liked about Afghanistan, perhaps – the nature, or the people, or the food – or maybe he wanted to say something about why the country was so important in a geopolitical context. I stood still, waiting for him to tell me, but then he said:

"Come up for a glass of wine if you get lonely downstairs on your own. I promise not to give you a long lecture about Afghanistan. Well, I'll try not to, at least."

"Well, thanks," I said, laughing, and then he said goodbye and left.

The front door slammed shut behind him. As I looked at my son playing in the snow, I couldn't help but smile. He wanted me to go up to his apartment. I wouldn't, of course. But still. It was only natural to feel flattered.

His suggestion floated in and out of my consciousness all afternoon. While the kids watched TV and I made dinner. While we ate. As I brushed Lukas's teeth and put him to bed, and the whole time I lay there so quietly beside him in his narrow bed, waiting for him to fall asleep. There was probably nothing more to it. Just a glass of wine with a neighbour, a friendly chat. I'd drunk wine with other neighbours, after all – with Jamila, and even with his wife. I didn't think anything of it when Merete invited me over.

But this was different. I could tell. There was no mistaking that the invitation implied something else.

If I went up there, maybe nothing more would happen. But there was definitely something there when he asked.

Emma and I watched a film. She was messing around with her phone, hardly paying attention. When the film was over, she went straight to bed. I tidied up the kitchen and the living room. Glanced down the stairs towards her bedroom – the door was ajar – and when I could hear her calm, regular breathing coming from inside I caught myself seriously considering his offer. Should I just go on up?

Now, I should also add that Åsmund was the only person I'd ever been with. I don't know whether I told you about this, about how we met, or if he maybe told you himself. We went to the same high school. From the first year, in fact. We've been together since we were sixteen. My thirty-ninth birthday was just weeks away. If I thought it seemed sad to go through life having slept with only one person – and I did – then now was the time to do something about it.

I thought it would be something I did for my own sake. It wouldn't have anything to do with Åsmund. Yes, we'd had a few tough years, with his father dying and Lukas's early birth. But things were starting to get better. And yes, something happens after you've spent several decades together. And then you throw kids into the equation, along with high mortgage repayments and demanding jobs, the feeling of being constantly pressed for time and arguments about the division of labour at home while the laundry piles up.

But then, it's probably the same for most people, right? It wasn't about that. It was something I needed to do. Or at least, that's what I thought. Something wild, before I fully settled down. Or before it was too late.

But I remember that I felt the butterflies in my stomach as I walked up the stairs. I remember how my hand was a little shaky as I lifted it to knock on the door. Am I utterly crazy for doing this? Have I lost the ability to take life seriously? Is this what it is to be not of sound mind at the time of the crime?

He opened the door.

"You came," he said, and seemed genuinely happy, as well as a little surprised.

"Yes," I said, feeling as if I was revealing too much. "Yes, it was getting a bit boring down there on my own."

"Come on in."

He had been sitting in his study – which, as you know, is where he was found. The door to it was open.

He went to collect a wine glass from in there – it helps me work, he said. Then he went into the kitchen to find a glass for me, too. Alone in their living room, I looked around. It seemed different when she wasn't home. Less like something from a magazine – more his. The smell, the light, his clutter on the coffee table too, perhaps, his phone, a remote control, a box of snus. We sat there on the sofa, each with our glass of wine. Now we were supposed to talk. Neither of us said anything, so we both cleared our throats at the same time and began to laugh.

"You first," he said.

"No, no," I said, "it wasn't important. What were you going to say?"

He grinned.

"I was going to tell you about Afghanistan. So please, you first."

"No," I said. "Tell me about Afghanistan."

Have you read what he wrote? His book was never finished, but he published a few articles about Afghan history and politics, and if you've read them, you'll know how he writes. Taking a story and twisting it open, using it as an entry point to two hundred years of Afghan history. Writing about a family he met, some small thing they told him about their everyday lives, such as the difficulties involved in getting a pair of shoes repaired, and then seamlessly sliding into the story of how the British attempted to take control of the country without much success, how the mujahideen fought the Soviets in the eighties, and then on to the Taliban regime and the aggressive Haqqani network, speeding through the sentences in a kind of free association where you have to concentrate, hard, because the content is so rich you don't want to miss a single word.

How did one thing lead to another? Who kissed who first? Here there are things I would rather not share. Not that I wish to obstruct the investigation, but what happened affects me, too. This grief at his absence is also mine, even if I have no right to it. Some memories are private. If you must, you can ask me. I'll answer as best I can.

But what I can say is that he looked at me before we undressed. He kissed me and pulled away, stroking the side of my face with his hand, and said:

"Are you sure you want to do this?"

And in that moment, I was sure. I wasn't passive. It wasn't something that just happened. I made a choice. And so did he. It was something we wanted.

So you might ask whether it was worth it. And how good it was if so, to be worth sacrificing house and home and an intact family for, to be worth the risk. Not to mention the potential damage to the others – my husband, my children. Whether it's possible for anything to be worth such a price. But when I came home afterwards, I stood beside the kitchen table and chuckled to myself. So often I had imagined what it would be like, to be with another man, I'd envisioned it so many times that it seemed almost impossible to actually do it. All that belonged between Åsmund and me – it felt as if I'd never be able to manage it with anyone else.

And then it was so easy. Like riding a bike. You just have to do it. Take the chance.

TUESDAY

It's the kind of place that has old curiosities on the walls. Tools from earlier times and more rural regions have been hung up for decoration, in such a studied way that I catch myself wondering whether they are in fact old – and if they've even been used – or whether there are companies that produce cheap imitations for restaurants and hotels to purchase and hang on their walls. I can imagine their web store, with categories like *Norwegian rustic for eateries*.

She's running late. I, on the other hand, have deliberately arrived early. I've had too much time to think. I called work this morning and apologised profusely – I still have a migraine, have to stay home. Afterwards, I sat alone in the house as the other residents left it, listening to their creaking steps on the stairs, the goodbyes shouted to each other in the corridor, the slamming of doors, the footsteps click-clacking on the paving stones outside, and then they were gone, all of them. I've hardly slept. Åsmund left with the kids, and I had all the time in the world to plan this meeting, think about what I was going to say to Ingvild Fredly, how I was going to present myself. But I got no further than this: I should get there early. Be seated and ready when she arrives. Prove myself obliging. Of course, it's important to help the police. It's a serious matter, as she informed us yesterday evening with that admonishing gaze. As if we didn't already understand that. As if we weren't already afraid.

The rest of the morning I spent sitting in front of the computer. I'd vaguely intended to get some work done, to continue with the data storage plan for our latest project, but I couldn't manage it. I brought up the results of the previous night's Google search again instead, all Jørgen's articles. He's written many reports from the

Middle East, as well as from Russia and Afghanistan; the Central African Republic a couple of years back. But the most recent hits were about Norway. There was a series of articles Jørgen and another journalist had written for a major Norwegian newspaper, about corruption in the cleaning industry. They were behind a paywall, so I couldn't read them, but judging by their introductory paragraphs they seemed to be about both money laundering and social dumping. I saw the journalists' byline photos before the paywall stopped me. Jørgen's was the same as the one I saw yesterday evening, taken a few years ago. The name of the other journalist was Rebekka Davidsen. She looked young, perhaps just a couple of years into her thirties. Younger than me. Pretty, too, at least in the photograph.

Ingvild Fredly finally arrives at twenty past ten. She hurries in – I see her straight away and am able to follow her with my eyes as she stands there looking around, trying to find me among the other customers. The café isn't full, but between the booths and all the bric-a-brac on display it takes a moment to get an overview of the premises. There's something agreeable about seeing her this way, as if her confused search for me re-establishes the balance between us, previously disturbed by the authoritarian, straight-to-the-point investigator she was yesterday. She catches sight of me.

"I'm so glad you were able to meet me here," she says as she sits down at my table.

Now she suddenly smiles a wide smile – she doesn't hug me, but she takes my hand and shakes it heartily.

"I'm heading up to Tåsen afterwards, so I could have met you there, but I thought this would be better."

She looks about her, surveying the knick-knacks without the slightest hint of irony.

"Neutral ground," she says.

I think about the gap in the wall between our apartment and the Sparres', this feeling we have in Kastanjesvingen that everything can be overheard. I nod.

"Of course," I say. "No problem at all."

The barista comes over to our table. Ingvild orders a double espresso, and asks me what I'd like, she's buying. I order an ordinary coffee. Nobody can say that I'm demanding, at least.

"So," she says once the barista has gone. "How are you doing up there?"

"Oh, you know," I say, clearing my throat. "We're fine. All things considered."

"It must be tough," she says. "When it's so close to home. For me it's a job, but for you, when it's a neighbour . . ."

Now she's willing to talk, going on about a case she once worked, a man who had been murdered, and how his wife was left teetering on the brink of insanity. It later turned out that someone was trying to make it seem as if she was losing her mind, Ingvild said, but still, she had thought about it a lot afterwards. What it's like to have a police matter enter your life. A murder, in your very own home. But it's her job, she's received training in how to handle it, so for her it's different. I nod again. Look for a point of entry, a way to redirect the conversation. The barista arrives with our drinks; Ingvild thanks him and asks him to put the order on her account. She tears open a sachet of sugar, laboriously tips its contents into the coffee, and stirs. As she completes this ritual, she remains silent. I don't say anything either, even though I now have the chance. I simply watch her as she brings the cup to her lips and tastes the coffee, apparently considering something as she takes a sip, and then, when she seems satisfied, she puts down the cup and looks at me.

"Anyway, Rikke," she says. "You had something to tell me?"

"Yes," I say.

This is the moment. This is what I should have been thinking about at home, instead of looking at Jørgen's articles online. The opening words.

The hardest thing about it, what's making me feel so reluctant to have this conversation, is how everything will be reduced. I know that already. Once the tale is told, it will become a story about infidelity. About sex. Explaining it to others, the sensitivity that existed between Jørgen and me, will be so difficult. The significance, how important he was to me – his friendship, too. How I longed to know what he thought about everything that was discussed during lunch at work, how I might read something in the newspaper and look forward to telling him about it. How quickly he became a point of reference for me.

Last summer, many months before we initiated anything, I took to sitting on the bench under the meagre apple tree with a book in the evenings. I wanted to make the most of the garden, telling Åsmund that we ought to look at it as an extension of the apartment. One evening, Jørgen came over to me. He had a book with him, and a bottle of beer.

"Mind if I sit down?" he asked. "I promise I won't disturb you."

At first, it was awkward. I was intensely aware of him and registered his every movement, unable to concentrate on whatever I was trying to read. But he kept coming. Not every time I sat there, but now and then. I began to anticipate him. Surprisingly quickly, I'd say. So we could sit beside each other and share that effortless silence. Sometimes we would exchange a few words – I'd ask him about what he was reading, or he'd ask me what I thought about my book – but we didn't need to talk. There was a rare closeness in this wordless time we spent together.

But nobody will be interested in any of this. The depth of our friendship won't mean a thing. Everything he was to me will be reduced to sex. To the raw numbers, I imagine – how many times, how often, for how long.

And I've only just lost him. It pierces me – am I truly surprised at this grief, this misery? Did I genuinely believe that there would be a happy ending? No, I didn't. Or, I don't know. It was supposed to end with us going our separate ways. It was supposed to become a beautiful memory, something I could take with me. Something to cherish through my years as a middle-aged woman, and on into old age – that period of my life when I was young and crazy. Or at least sort of young, a little crazy. It's easy to scoff at these thoughts now. A beautiful memory? Is there anything about this that is beautiful?

But this is what I tell Ingvild. There was something real there, I say. I try to justify it. Clear my name in advance. An utterly futile exercise – to explain what I can't even explain to myself. Ingvild nods slowly as I speak. Her face is serious, but contains no condemnation; instead, her expression seems focused. One of her hands lies on the table in front of her beside her cup, and it's a fine hand, I think, just the right size, no nail polish or jewellery, serious and absolutely calm. She doesn't interrupt me and so I continue to speak, attempting to explain how it happened that I started calling him every time I was alone and saw a chance. How I ended up arranging my family life so that opportunities could present themselves. The ease with which I did these unforgivable things, when I'd never done anything wrong in my life.

I haven't got very far when Ingvild's phone, which is lying on the table between us, begins to vibrate.

"Excuse me, I should take this," she says, her first contribution to the conversation for quite some time.

She doesn't stay sitting at the table; she answers the call and says: just a moment. Then she gets up, walks alongside the bar and down a corridor I presume leads to the toilets, until I can no longer see her. I follow her with my gaze until she disappears. The barista casts a glance after her. Then he looks at me, and for an instant his eyes meet mine, before he flashes me a polite smile and goes back to his newspaper. I look towards the corridor down which Ingvild disappeared, wondering what he saw as he watched us.

It feels like an age before she comes back. I pick up my phone, scrolling aimlessly here and there. Jamila has sent me a text message, *Can we meet up today??* Everything is urgent for her. I suddenly feel no urgency at all. It's been said. The cat is out of the bag, I think, and in a flash see the tortured cats from my conversations with the neighbours, Hoffmo going to seed, the mothers at the school gorging themselves on the gory details. This thing that Jamila calls evil. Is this not how we rank these things? Aren't they more evil, the people who kill house cats, than those who cheat on their spouses? At least, the cat killers have no reason for doing what they do, they don't get anything out of their crimes, it's purely sickening. But nobody will see it like that – I feel sure of it. What is the life of a cat, compared with destroying a family?

Ingvild is gone for almost ten minutes. When she returns, she has a deep cleft in her brow. I say nothing, suddenly empty of words. She sits down in her chair, puts her phone back on the table between us and remains silent, apparently still deep in concentration about what was said on the call. Then it's as if she notices me – she clears her throat, and sort of shuffles her thoughts. She moves her empty coffee cup, sets the spoon neatly on the saucer, as if these actions also help her to clear her head.

"I have to go now," she says. "Something's come up that I need to deal with right away. We'll have to continue this conversation later."

I nod. Who am I to demand anything of her?

"But Rikke," she says. "You're going to have to tell Åsmund about this. You understand that, right?"

I shake my head, hard.

"No," I say. "No, I can't."

I think of him yesterday, in the process of making dinner for the family. *Feel free to look all you want*, he had quipped. *All this is yours.*

Ingvild clears her throat.

"Maybe I shouldn't say this," she says, "but it will likely come out over the next few days anyway, so I'll risk it. It doesn't look as if any-one broke into Kastanjesvingen 15 on Saturday night. Do you understand? The window to Jørgen Tangen's study was ajar, and there was a ladder on the grass below it. But we've analysed the soil beneath the window over and over, and there are no markings there. The ground was wet and soft – a ladder bearing the weight of a per-son would have sunk into it. So it seems unlikely that anyone made it into the apartment that way. Nor are there any windows at ground level that have been pried open or smashed in, and none of them were open. And your front door is, of course, very solid. We've received some files from the company that installed the code lock on it and we're investigating how many times it was opened that day and night, but there are no signs that anyone gained entry using force. Do you understand what I'm saying to you?"

I simply stare at her, blankly.

"It doesn't look as if some junkie made their way up from the city centre and broke into Jørgen Tangen's apartment in the middle of the night," she says. "It looks as if the person who killed him was let in or had the code to the front door."

There it is again, the shiver from when I let myself into Jørgen's apartment. That uneasy feeling that something was wrong.

"It's early days as yet," Ingvild says, gently patting my cold hand where it lies on the table before me. "But for the time being, we have to assume that those of you who live at Kastanjesvingen 15 had the greatest opportunity to do this. And what you just told me puts Åsmund under even more suspicion. Gives him a clear motive. So, if you love him, you're going to have to let him know that this is how things stand."

"But," I say, and my voice sounds high-pitched and afraid. "If I tell him, everything will be ruined."

She puts her other hand over mine, holding both my hands with hers, safe and warm.

"I understand that, Rikke," she says. "This isn't good. But you're going to have to do what you can to help your husband."

I say nothing. Think about Åsmund the way he was when I first met him, his young, open face.

"Besides," she says. "It will probably come out anyway. This will become part of the investigation now. It has to."

"But does he have to know?" I ask. "Can't it just be something you know – the police – that doesn't get broadcast to the wider world? I mean, there's a high probability that this has nothing to do with what happened to Jørgen."

Ingvild looks at me, with a weight in her eyes I don't understand at first. Then I realise. She's not convinced. She thinks Jørgen died because of what happened between him and me. Or at the very least, she's keeping it in mind as a possibility. She doesn't know Åsmund, doesn't understand that there is no way he could have slit Jørgen's throat. All Ingvild sees is the motive.

"Surely you don't think that's why," I start, my voice breaking. I'm unable to speak calmly about this, and the barista is reading his newspaper in such an affected way that I'm almost certain he's eavesdropping on us.

Ingvild straightens the spoon and coffee cup again.

"Listen to me, Rikke," she says. "Here's what I can offer you. We'll make a deal. You help me. You tell me what you started to tell me just now. Everything you know about Jørgen, your relationship from when you met him until what happened at the weekend. Okay? And everything you happen to know about his family, his job, his financial situation – everything you can think of. You assist with the investigation. So we can catch the person who did this."

I nod – yes, of course, I'll do anything.

"And if you do that, I'll do everything I can to protect your secret.

I will of course have to share it with the other investigators – and I mean, our private relationship will probably necessitate somebody else taking the lead on the case, that's only proper. But as far as possible, I'll protect what you've just told me."

"Thank you – really, thank you so much."

"But all it will do is delay having to deal with it," she says. "You understand that, don't you? One day, this is probably going to come out anyway. When the police enter the scene like this, in a criminal case, that's generally what happens. But I'm buying you some time. So you can speak to him yourself first."

"I get it. Thank you."

"And I don't know how long I'll be able to keep this a secret. The next person assigned to head up the investigation might have different priorities. You don't have all the time in the world."

"I understand," I say.

Afterwards, as I walk to my bicycle which is chained up a couple of blocks from the café, I ask myself whether I really do understand. Whether what it will mean to tell Åsmund has actually sunk in. The only thing I feel is relief at having been granted a reprieve.

I see them as I cycle up Kastanjesvingen – the TV station van, along with several other vehicles, one of them a police car. There are some people standing there too, and a man in a windcheater is leaning over our fence with a huge camera. To get past them I get off my bike and push it the rest of the way. As I reach for the gate a woman wearing a smart overcoat and scarf comes rushing towards me.

"Excuse me," she says. "Do you live here?"

"Yes," I say.

Without thinking I glance up at our house. It used to make me so happy to see it lying there, waiting for me, this perfect compromise between Åsmund's wishes and mine. But it could do with a lick of paint.

The woman in the smart overcoat is from one of the biggest TV channels in the country, she tells me, and in covering this story they'd like to hear from the neighbours.

"What this has been like for you," she says, arranging her face into sad creases in a somewhat affected way. "It must be quite extraordinary, to be living right next door when something like this happens."

We look at each other. She has a straight fringe and a pretty face, and there's something about her clothes, the cut of her coat, the length of her trousers, that communicates that she's someone in the know. It wouldn't surprise me if she lives in Tåsen herself.

"I don't really want to talk about it," I say.

"I won't ask you anything except how all this has been for you," she says. "And you can remain anonymous, if you like."

"No, thanks," I say.

I reach for the gate. It swings outwards, and holding it open and wheeling my bike through at the same time is always a little awkward. The journalist shoots out a hand, intending to help me, and a slightly embarrassing moment arises in which we attempt to come together over this task: I think you have to open it a little more, can you make it through now, the hinges are a little stiff, there, that's it. She closes the gate after me and I thank her, because of course I must.

"You're welcome," she says, smiling broadly. "And I'll be here a little while longer, if you change your mind."

At least they're waiting outside the gate. I wheel my bike up the paved path, punch in the code on the front door and open that, too, on my own this time. As the door slams shut behind me and my bicycle, Svein Sparre comes out into the stairwell.

"Hi," he says. "Out in force today, aren't they?"

"Yeah," I say. "Journalists, it seems like."

He looks over at the front door – it's closed, so it isn't as if he can see anything, but the way he stares at it you'd think he could. He's wearing his jacket, and has a bag slung over his shoulder.

"Leeches, the lot of them, if you ask me," he says. "The minute they smell blood, they come swarming."

I take a deep breath, give a brief nod. I find myself in conversation with Svein now and then, and on a couple of occasions it's been uncomfortable. He has strong opinions, which I don't share. We look at each other. His shoulders are slightly stooped. I've never realised how tall he is, tall and broad-chested.

"Now there's a profession nobody will miss if it disappears," he says, knitting his brows and glowering at the closed door. "Asking how it feels, now that one of us is dead. It's fucking ridiculous."

"Jørgen was a journalist, too," I say gently.

"Yes," he says, looking at me. "And he was no better than the rest of them. Writing column after column about insignificant breaches of the law that honest working people have committed in the struggle to just stay afloat. Have you seen the regulations? Anyone could make a misstep – it doesn't necessarily mean you're a fucking slave driver."

He clears his throat. The sound echoes through the stairwell, it's so empty in here.

"I don't exactly have the greatest respect for the work he did," Svein says, a little friendlier now. "But he was still a neighbour, and a good guy in his way. That lot out there . . . it makes me sick, the way they're carrying on. Swarming around the blood of one of their own."

I give a doubtful nod at this, unsure what to say. Jørgen had plenty to say about journalistic duty. About the importance of journalists reporting from terrible situations, how it isn't necessarily inhumane to take a photograph instead of providing emergency assistance. But this isn't a discussion I want to have. Especially not with Svein, and especially not now.

"Yes," is all I say. "Well, I think I'd better be getting on."

I wheel my bicycle past him. On the way towards the cellar door, I have a sudden impulse; I turn, and say his name. Svein turns to face me.

"The police," I say. "Did they ask you about the cabin trip you went on last summer, you guys?"

A wide, nasty smile spreads across Svein's face, splitting it in two, and I shudder at this sign of malicious pleasure – it makes me like him even less. It occurs to me that I don't really like him all that much, only I haven't thought of it in exactly these terms until now. He has his softer side, too. Can seem good-natured, kind. Nice, in his own way – generous with his cabin, taking on his fair share of the tasks around the property. But there's something mean in him. A readiness to express ill will towards those who disagree with him.

"Yes," he says, sticking his hands into his trouser pockets. "They did. And I told them – there was a, what would you call it, a *discussion* one evening. Well, the others were discussing something. I wasn't – I couldn't have cared less. But *they* were angry. Our friend Saman in particular. He was frothing at the mouth, I thought he was going to take a swing at Jørgen."

I look away. I should have known better than to ask Svein Sparre.

"Okay," I say, beginning to fiddle with the lock to the cellar door. But Svein makes no move to leave the building. I can feel his eyes on me as I undo the lock, can feel his beady eyes following my movements. I'm flustered, want only to get the door open, but my hand is shaking slightly, and the key keeps missing the hole.

"And you know," he says behind me. "He was no choirboy, either – your husband, I mean. I'm just saying. He took Saman's side, and he was raging, too. It almost makes you wonder. Yes, it does. What might be lurking deep inside a man who otherwise seems so mild-mannered when he explodes like that? Hm? I mean, I know Åsmund, but if I didn't, it would have given me pause for thought."

I get the key into the lock and twist it, pull the cellar door open. I don't want to hear about this. In no way do I trust that Svein is telling the truth. I have much more faith in Åsmund than in this poisonous snake, and yet a morsel of uncertainty attaches itself to me – I can feel it already. Could Svein be right? Even a story that is bent and twisted to fit the narrator's agenda can have a grain of truth to it. My hands tremble as I set them back on the bike's handlebars, and had I not known better, I would have said that I was afraid.

"Right," I say, setting the bicycle on the landing, ready to wheel it down.

He nods. His face smooths out again, and the ugly smile disappears. When he doesn't tense his jaw, there's something appealing about him. He was probably an attractive man when he was young, like the one his son is now on the threshold of becoming. Though, to be honest, it's hard to imagine Svein ever being young at all, that at one point he was happy and bursting with energy, looking to the future with hope.

"Well," he says. "I suppose I better go out and face the wolves. See you."

The door slams behind him, and I breathe more easily. As I lock up my bike, I realise that Svein must have passed all this on to the police. That's why they've been asking questions. They might have been taken in by him, or perhaps they figured that they would have to check out his story regardless, no matter how unreliable a source he may seem. Or might they have seen something in what he said? Something I'm struggling to catch sight of. Something that keeps slipping away from me.

When Ingvild Fredly used to hang out in our flatshare she was around thirty years old, I think as I clean up the kitchen after dinner. Maybe six or seven years older than us, and that made quite a difference back then. We were students and thought we knew everything, but she was a grown-up. She had a job and an apartment, opinions based on experience. We would question her about police work. Is it the way it is on TV, my friends and I would ask, do you have a partner? Do you play good cop, bad cop? My friend who was studying criminology and had read Foucault attempted to drag her into a conversation about how the punishment of criminals makes society itself inhumane. Ingvild patiently tried to end the discussion, but my friend wouldn't let it drop. I remember watching from the other side of the kitchen table: Ingvild's polite attempts to snuff out the conversation; the criminology student refusing to take her hints. I remember that I grinned at Ingvild and rolled my eyes, and that in return she had given me a resigned smile, along with an almost imperceptible shrug: *what can you do?* I felt I was more grown-up than the others then, thought that Ingvild and I were above them. But her smile may have been less conspiratorial than I imagined. To her, maybe I seemed just as immature as the flatshare's other residents. There was a gulf between us back then, and it must have been more tangible to her than it was to us.

On one of the evenings she was over at the apartment, one of the last, if I'm not mistaken, we were discussing an absent friend's hopeless dreams of becoming a musician. Our friend had dropped out of her course to focus on her music, and now she wanted to use her savings to record an album. The problem was that the songs she wrote were terrible, and she wasn't particularly good at guitar. Her voice was lovely – we had to give her that – but the overall package was simply not good enough, and it was agonising to see her pouring her heart and soul into a doomed project. Our moral dilemma, as her friends, was whether or not we should be honest with her. We were leaning towards not saying anything. Was it our responsibility to deprive her of these illusions, I asked rhetorically. A psychology student in her third semester believed that on one level, our friend likely understood that her dream was unrealistic, but was unconsciously protecting herself from this insight, and if so, it would be arrogant of us to try to intervene.

At this point, Ingvild seemed to wake up. How could we call ourselves friends, she asked, if we weren't willing to face the discomfort of being honest? How would our friend be able to make an informed decision if she didn't have all the necessary information? Wouldn't we want to know? We exchanged glances. Would we? Well yes, of course, one of us said. Not necessarily, said another, what about the average person's need to view their life through rose-tinted glasses – the dangers of depriving people of their illusions? Ingvild Fredly considered us. She looked as if she couldn't quite believe what she was hearing. Then her eyes glazed over, and I can still remember the feeling of having disappointed her.

Have I disappointed her now, I wonder, as I lean against the kitchen counter to look out through the window. Will she feel obliged to tell Åsmund what I told her? I take a deep breath, down into my lungs. Out there lies the garden, empty in the early dusk. The journalists are gone, and there is nobody else down on the street. I can see into the detached houses opposite; at Hoffmo's, the lights are on. The street lamps along Kastanjesvingen are already lit. No, Ingvild won't say anything to Åsmund. But she's ordered me to tell him, and I feel a blow to my stomach just at the thought of it.

I hear his steps enter the kitchen behind me. Think: I have to tell him. One day soon, whenever, any time.

"Is something going on out there?" he asks from over my shoulder.

"No," I say, looking out. "No, it's just starting to get dark, that's all."

Nina Sparre is talking a mile a minute even before she's made it into the living room. She knocked at the door – Åsmund opened it – and now she's tumbling into our apartment in a flood of words. First, she must apologise for disturbing our evening, but she has something important to share with us, and she didn't think it was right to wait until the morning; nor could she drop it in our mailbox because this information is of a *confidential nature*. Åsmund and I stare at her, perplexed. We were watching TV when she knocked, and apparently she has no time for pleasantries – she gets straight to the point. She's obtained the code-lock data from the previous week, she says, because she feels it is of *paramount importance* that all of us who reside in the building are privy to the same information as the police, and since she believes in *full transparency* in processes such as this one, she's providing all the neighbours with a copy.

"And here is yours," she says, placing a couple of sheets of paper on the table.

Åsmund and I glance at them. There are our names, jumbled together in a long list: Tangen, Karimi, Sparre and Prytz/Ellingsen. We each have one code, just one per household, so you can't see which member of each family has let themselves in, but it still gives a pretty complete picture of how life unfolds in our shared building – we can see our own and our neighbours' movements over the previous week in terrifying detail.

"Oh my God," Åsmund says. And then: "I can't believe they're allowed to give this to us."

"Oh," says Nina, "but it's only reasonable. If the police are able to get hold of it, then I should jolly well think that those of us who live here should have access to it, too. That's what I told the man at the locksmith – a very young man, couldn't have been much older than twenty. He was reluctant, but I said, now listen here, this is in fact *our* property. We're the ones who installed the lock. Since you've provided the information to the investigators, it shouldn't be any trouble for you to give it to us. It's scandalous that I had to go down there and ask for it – it should have been passed on to us as a matter of course."

Printed on the sheets of paper are the times at which we've let ourselves in, alongside the surname of the household to which each code belongs. I can just imagine Nina leaning across the counter at the locksmith's. She probably revelled in her authority as head of the housing cooperative's board, most likely threatening this, that and the other. Bullying the poor guy on duty late in the evening into releasing the data. *Our property*, she says with self-righteous exasperation, forgetting that at the same time, she's obtaining access to data about her neighbours. We're not one unit in this house, despite what she seems to believe. We're four. At least. Now it feels as if even this is beginning to crumble. Are Åsmund and I together in all this, for example? Do I want him to see how I sometimes come home during the day, when everyone but Jørgen is out? And how much openness would Jørgen have wanted? I study Nina as she speaks. It seems she expects us to be grateful.

Ingvild insinuated that the police think the crime was committed by one of us. Either that, or someone Jørgen himself let in. In addition to the third possibility, of course, which is that it was someone who was let in by one of the rest of us. What about Nina, standing there prattling on? Could it have been her? She must be a gifted actress if so. I wrap my arms around myself. You play a role for your neighbours. That's what you do. The happy spouse, the loving couple. The patient parent. You do what you can to prevent them peeking behind the curtain, because they are – if not exactly strangers – not exactly friends, either. We're all so up close and personal, it's best for all of us if we simply take each other's facades at face value. Nina often talks about Svein as a prop, as a like-minded person. Her stories are peppered with *and then I said to Svein* or *and that's what Svein says*. Their arguments, his toxic comments, her flustered scolding, what they scream at each other – this remains strictly confined to the apartment. Had it not been for the weakness in the wall behind the kitchen cabinet, we would be none the wiser, apart from the screaming. I rub my hands along my upper arms, as if I can feel a chill coming on.

The only thing the lock registers, Nina explains, is the time at which a code is entered. When you open the door from the inside you simply twist the bolt, and this information isn't stored anywhere. So, if anyone on the inside had let someone in, there would be no way of knowing. On Friday afternoon, it says that Tangen entered at 15:24. This is Jørgen, I think, coming home early so he could sit in his study undisturbed and work all evening. Ten minutes later, a Sparre lets themselves in – I would guess that this is either Nina or Simen, because Svein tends to get home later. 16:17 and 16:51 are registered to us – this is Åsmund and Lukas, and then Emma. Karimi is next at 16:54, and then it's us again at 17:25 – that's me. Then Sparre at 17:32, which must be Svein. The last entry for the evening is Karimi at 22:54. By my count, this means we were all home by then, possibly with the exception of one Sparre, if mother and son didn't arrive home together at three-thirty. At 00:14 – technically Saturday – there is another entry for Sparre – likely Simen returning home after an evening out, and then there is nothing until the following morning.

"Thank you," I say to Nina, gathering up the sheets of paper.

She's still speaking – I've interrupted her in the middle of a torrent of expository reasoning – but she takes the hint, smiles flatly, and says, "Not at all." Åsmund accompanies her to the door. Then he comes back in and rolls his eyes.

"Jesus," he says. "I could have collapsed on the floor, and she still would have kept on babbling away uninterrupted."

I leave the sheets of paper in a pile on the bookshelf. I know that I'll return to them later during the night and go through them, spying on my neighbours and my family, following the movements of Åsmund and Emma over the previous week, checking whether they came home at a time when they should have been out. Will Åsmund do the same? It's almost two weeks since I last came home to see Jørgen during the daytime, but still. All this data, I hadn't even imagined that it might exist – let alone that it would be made available to us, that it would be printed out and delivered right to our door. And I hate Nina for making this base prying into each other's private lives so easy, so irresistible.

Åsmund is emptying the dishwasher, listening to music as he does so. I'm tidying the living room, gathering up toys, folding up newspapers and piling them up on the ugly list from the locksmith's, letting them cover it. I can hear my husband out there in the kitchen, humming now and then, clattering the plates.

I could do it now – I have the opportunity. To do as Ingvild Fredly says. It's simply a matter of choosing the right moment. I pretend to consider it, as if I'm seriously contemplating going over to him, setting a hand on his shoulder and pouring it all out. Åsmund, I could say, we need to talk. There's something I have to tell you. What is it? he'll ask. And then I can just say it. It would be quick, that part. Like ripping off a plaster.

But then what? The next bit wouldn't go so quickly. I can imagine how his face will change, how he'll pull away from me, and how everything between us now – my natural permission to touch him, kiss him, put my arms around him – will vanish. The kindness I currently expect of him – asking me how I am, offering to put the leftovers in a container for me so I can take them to work the next day – that will be gone. Perhaps forever. It would take so little.

The risk was always there. I knew all this when I walked up the stairs that first time on that evening in January. I made the assessment, and I decided that it was worth it. In the kitchen, Åsmund is humming along to the music. Yes, okay, I think, I knew what I was risking, but there was something on the other side of the scale back then. I remember how I stood down here that night, before I went up to see Jørgen for the first time, thinking: Åsmund might find out, everything could be ruined. And then I thought: if I don't do this, will I regret it? Will I always think of this moment and wish that I had acted? I'll be forty next year. I've had two children, and it shows – I no longer look the way I did when I was twenty-four. I look less and less like that with every passing year. When will it be too late? When do the offers stop coming? What if this is the last time I encounter someone I could imagine saying yes to? It seemed so much easier then. So much more important, too. Isn't it true that people regret the things they don't do so much more than the things they do?

I already know that I'm not going to go over to Åsmund now. I can't. I have to be better prepared. Have to think through what I'm going to say, how I'll say it. This is one of the most important conversations of our marriage, and I do not intend to go into it unprepared. Not now that I've bought myself a couple of days by promising Ingvild that I'll tell her my most intimate secrets in exchange. Of course I'm going to use the time I have. I'll do it tomorrow. I'll spend the day planning, and then we can talk tomorrow evening, when the kids are in bed. I have one more day.

My feet no longer fit together. I try lying on my side and then my back, but it feels wrong, they bother each other, refuse to lie comfortably against each other. I separate them, putting one in front of the other, but that's wrong, too – it feels artificial. I turn over in the bed. Beside me Åsmund lies sleeping, his mouth half open and his brow faintly wrinkled, as if he fell asleep while concentrating on something difficult he wanted to say. I move my feet again. Can't seem to remember what I usually do with them. Never before has it occurred to me that this might be a problem. How have I gone to bed every single night, for decade after decade, without asking myself how I should position my feet?

In the end I get up, tiptoe over to the door and go into the living room. It's dark out there. I lean my back against the bedroom door. Try to resist the compulsion to look into the shadowy corners of the room. The person who killed Jørgen was either let in by him or lives in the building. It has to be the former – it simply cannot be the latter. There were six of us adults here. Saman and Jamila, Nina and Svein, Åsmund and me. For a terrible moment I imagine it, one or the other of us on our way into his apartment. Saman, sneaking across the upstairs landing. The broad-shouldered figure of Svein bending over Jørgen as he sits in front of his computer. Åsmund's hands around the handle of a knife. I feel dizzy, as if I'm standing before a chasm and each of these images I'm conjuring up is a step towards the edge. I stand completely still, listening. Almost expect to hear footsteps, a throat being cleared, a cup being moved. Feel my breathing quicken. What guarantee do I have that the person who murdered Jørgen isn't after me, or us? There's not a sound to be heard. Nothing but the whispering wind outside, the chestnut tree's branches scraping against the window. I'm the only one awake. I go across to the door that opens out into the corridor, check that it is locked and put on the safety chain.

I stand at the kitchen table, looking out across the empty garden. Lean my hands against the tabletop and take a deep breath. Okay, I tell myself. You have to think clearly now. You're a rational person. You're a researcher, and you've always understood that science is impersonal, apolitical. You like that it's not an ideology, but rather a method for attacking problems. And what are we always taught on methodology courses? To gather data systematically. To use logic. Premise, premise, conclusion. If a, then b; a, therefore b. Logic, dialectics. I take a deep breath. In the windowpanes I glimpse my own reflection. It's dark in here, too, so I can see only the contours of my body, the way I'm leaning over the table. Under these conditions, the mirror image could almost belong to a young woman.

That Saturday in Jørgen's apartment, I had let myself in and been overwhelmed by a sense of unease. It was almost supernatural, I might have thought, if I believed in that kind of thing, almost as if something was showing me what lay on the other side of the closed door to Jørgen's study. But that's like believing in ghosts, or that apparently random coincidences are part of a greater cosmic plan determined by how the stars were arranged at the moment you were born, one that can be read in the coffee grounds at the bottom of your cup. I reject all this. There is no cosmic plan. The positions of the heavenly bodies, or rather the earth's position in relation to them, have nothing to do with how our lives turn out. It wasn't a supernatural sixth sense that caused me to back out of Jørgen's apartment that morning – this sense of unease can be explained. It was the sum of tiny details, not enough to be noticed individually, but taken together enough to tell me that something posed a threat. I sit down in one of the kitchen chairs.

What was it that I saw up there? What was it that made me back out? I hadn't received a reply to my messages, and that worried me a little. The light in the kitchen was on – he must have been home – and yet he didn't answer. That's part of it, but there's more. I frown, looking out of the window. The outdoor lights of the houses across the street illuminate the walls. I look over at Hoffmo's house, remembering how I saw him come out in his comical tracksuit that morning. Recall him going on about the cats to Nina Sparre – *but what's the board actually* doing, *Nina, do you expect us all to sit idly by and watch our neighbourhood being destroyed?* Now his house is dark. The road is deserted, but down at the end I can see the headlights of a car, they vanish and reappear again between the bushes as the vehicle turns onto Kastanjesvingen. The clock on the oven says ten to twelve. I follow the car's headlights with my eyes.

There's something that's eluding me here. There's more to be obtained from the memory, from the few seconds I stood up there in his apartment, the closed door. The vehicle enters my field of view – it's a small white car. I try to conjure up the inside of Jørgen's study where the window was left open, probably to give the impression that someone might have got in that way, using the ladder. I don't like thinking about this – the calculated use of the ladder. Nor do I like thinking about how it was taken from behind our garden shed, as though whoever it was knew exactly where to find it. The white car stops at our gate.

Why am I unable to put my finger on it? Why am I unable to place what it was that scared me? Is it because the episode with Saman and the eggs has muddled the memory? Or is there something here that I don't *want* to remember, causing me to sabotage it myself?

Down on the street the driver's-side door is opened, and a woman gets out. She walks around the car, opens the passenger-side door, and another woman emerges. It's hard to see them clearly from a distance and in the dark, but I know who they are, almost instinctively. The driver opens the door to the back seat, and a third woman comes into view, a young woman, slender enough to be a child. The three of them stand there, looking up towards the house. The kitchen where I'm sitting is dark, so they can't see me, but I'm able to watch them.

There was something more, I think. The unanswered message, the light on in the kitchen, the fact that I let myself in – this isn't enough. There must be other things. Small things, insignificant things, things I noticed at the time, but didn't think about. I have to concentrate. I close my eyes, imagining it – I'm standing in the middle of the apartment. I look around. The piano? The bookshelf? Something that was lying on the floor? Or just something in the air? Had I not bumped into Saman just afterwards, had I not turned all my attention towards him in panic, I would have remembered it better. Without that distraction, it would have been possible for me to now reconstruct those seconds in the apartment, the thing that terrified me.

Down in the road, the three figures begin to move. The woman who was driving takes something from the boot of the car. The other woman opens our garden gate and walks through it. The young girl follows her. The woman puts an arm around the girl's shoulders, and together they begin to walk up the path. The woman pulls her daughter close to her, as if to support her, although one might wonder which of them is actually supporting the other. I catch a glimpse of her face, pale and drawn. Then I slide down onto the floor in order to be certain that they won't see me when they get close enough, and for a while I stay there with my back against the oven door. The lock on the front door clicks; I hear their steps out in the stairwell. Merete is back.

It was supposed to be a one-off. One last crazy fling. My first, too. Then I was going to settle down. The worst thing about it was that it worked – the weeks that followed were good ones. I don't know whether it was a coincidence, but Åsmund seemed to be in a better mood. Maybe it was down to me, because I became spontaneous. Made the chicken dish I know he likes so much – the one I usually only make on his birthday, and in recent years hardly even then – out of the blue, on a Wednesday. Called him one day when I was in the city for a meeting and invited him out to lunch. Kissed him every morning before he left, every evening when I got home. We started having sex more often, and we put more into it, tried things we hadn't had the energy to try since before Lukas was born. We talked, the way we did when we were young.

Do you regret it, I asked myself a few times, and I was surprised to find that, in all honesty, I had to admit that I didn't. On the contrary – I was almost glad that I'd done it. I didn't feel guilty. Maybe it had been necessary, I thought, because just look at us now. See how things are between us. I even went so far as to think that it had been good for us.

A few weeks before the evening when I first went up to Jørgen's apartment, I had met up with an old friend, Hanna – maybe you remember her? I had suggested that perhaps there were circumstances in a relationship that might justify infidelity. That in some cases maybe it could even be positive, a shot in the arm.

Hannah wasn't convinced. As a general rule, infidelity destroys relationships, rather than saving them, she said.

Even so, might it not be important to do it, I said. For oneself, personally. Haven't great men always slept around whenever they felt like it? Bjørnstjerne Bjørnson. John F. Kennedy. François Mitterrand. And, I don't know, loads of other men, too – probably most men. Haven't their wives always forgiven them? Isn't there a kind of double standard here? Shouldn't we women take for ourselves the pleasures that men have always taken for granted?

But Rikke, Hanna said. This isn't about equality. This is about trusting your partner. About taking care of the relationship, not running away when times get tough.

I backed down. Yes, of course, I said, I didn't mean for either of *us*, just hypothetically, in a theoretical relationship.

And when all was said and done, I didn't tell anyone about it. I didn't need to. It felt private. When I saw Jørgen in the stairwell or in the garden, we greeted one another as usual, smiled and nodded, asked each other how things were going, wished each other a good day. Maybe these remarks had a new weight to them, perhaps there was something charged in the little smiles we exchanged before we went our separate ways. But there was no invitation in it. It wasn't as if anyone put their hand over the other's on the gate.

Those first weeks after that Saturday in January, I honestly believed that the little spark of excitement between us would fade with time, that we would forget it. But then my mother-in-law slipped on the ice and suffered a fall.

Åsmund called me, his racing pulse audible in his voice. Mamma's in hospital, he said, I have to go there, can you pick up the kids? Of course, I said, and asked whether we should go with him. And when he said it was probably better that we just stayed home, I thought: He wants to be alone with her.

She was discharged the same evening. It turned out that she'd fractured her foot, and she was black and blue from the fall, but it wasn't serious enough to require admission. Åsmund despaired – poor little Mamma. To think that they had discharged her, couldn't they see how afraid she was? He had made dinner for her, bought her some groceries. He felt terrible about having left her, but his brother was going to stay over. Åsmund would take the next night.

Over the next few weeks, he went over to her house every day. He had to help her with everything, not just the things she was unable to do with her cast on, but all kinds of other things, too. She thanked him profusely for everything he did, he was so good at making coffee, and it was so nice that he had cleared the snow off the step, he did it much better than she ever could. Åsmund was proud and happy, oh, come on now, he said, it was no problem, just a bit of snow.

I wasn't invited. He hardly ever picked up Lukas

from kindergarten anymore, and usually came home late. At weekends he often slept over, because it was so nice for her, she feels so unsafe all alone at night. I see, I said. Fine, I said. You do what you have to do.

And then, one Friday afternoon, I bumped into Jørgen in the supermarket.

TUESDAY NIGHT

My fingers have been hammering against the keyboard. I don't become aware of this until I'm done. It's three-thirty in the morning. Several hours have passed. When I first started on the email I typed slowly, wanting to be quiet so as not to wake anyone, but something must have come over me as I wrote. It feels as if I've forgotten myself, writing as if I've been in a kind of trance, and only now, out of it again, do I feel the stiffness in my back. I must have been tensing my shoulders, sitting here hunched over on the sofa with my laptop. Utterly absorbed. I seem to recall hearing steps in the apartment above, Merete, or maybe her daughter. Åsmund coughed in his sleep once or twice, and maybe the front door opened at some point, too, but I was so deep in concentration that I hardly registered it. The message field of the email is filled with text – the whole story, from when I met Jørgen until the last time we spoke, and then the night it happened. I quickly scroll up, words and sentences jumping out at me, *breathing hot and shallow, felt as if every cell in my body was aglow,* and *I lay down in his arms.* It feels strange to be about to send this off. It doesn't feel like an email – it's more like a diary entry. Or a confession, with elements of a defence. I can already feel the shame creeping in. Will Ingvild Fredly read this with her police officer's eyes? Will she share it with her colleagues, with baby-faced Robin? Will it be appended to the case, become evidence, my innermost thoughts, my most private acts and their motives? I feel that I might come to regret this, but I don't have the strength to start over again, so I write: *So that's it, hope it might be of help. Speak soon, best wishes, Rikke,* and click send.

Surprisingly enough, I don't regret the email once it's sent. I'm relieved, it's done. No matter what, I've done my bit – nobody can accuse me of not cooperating with the police. I lean back on the sofa. Arch my upper body to stretch my lower back. It feels good to have it over and done with. Is that how I'll feel once I've spoken to Åsmund? I may well feel mostly relief after that, too, because I'm dreading it, my stomach twists just at the thought. Maybe I should write it down, give it to him. That way I won't have to see his face collapse as I say the awful words, won't have to see it change from curious and attentive to raging, hateful, hurt. Especially the latter. I can't stand the thought of hurting Åsmund. It squeezes my guts again, with such force that I have to press my hands to my belly. It's almost four o'clock in the morning. It's technically Wednesday, and by the end of today I have to have spoken to him. I just have to find the words. Practise them, think about how I want to say it. So he understands that it isn't his fault, and that it didn't mean anything. At least, that it didn't mean what he'll believe it did. And that it will never happen again – especially that. I can feel it now, all the way down to my marrow. I'm done with this. Not just because Jørgen is gone – no. The restlessness I felt within me is no longer there. It's as if I had an itch that I tried not to scratch, but I finally scratched it anyway, and it felt good, so I scratched some more, digging my nails down into the skin, scratching until I began to bleed, but now that it's slowly starting to scab over, I can't imagine ever scratching at the site of the wound again. I close my eyes. I will never do anything like this again. I'm absolutely certain of it. Oh, Åsmund, can't we just put this behind us and move on?

But before we can do that, I have to hurt him. And he will have to rage and hate me, and I will have to bear it. After that, we can be friends again. He'll forgive me, and I will do my penance. Prove to him that he can trust me. He will forgive me, won't he? He has to. He's Åsmund. We've been together since I was a child, just a few years older than Emma is now. This pinching pain in my diaphragm, it radiates out into my arms and legs, this crushing fear, worse than before, because only now does it truly dawn on me, not just as a theoretical variable, but as an actual possibility: Åsmund may leave me for good.

I stalk around the apartment, unable to sit still. It occurs to me that I should try to sleep, and I get back into bed. Try to calm myself, counting backwards from a hundred, challenging myself to think of as many cities as I can whose names start with each letter of the alphabet in an attempt to force my brain to let go. Åsmund is lying on his back, snoring. The air he inhales rumbles down his throat, it's so peculiar, that sound, nothing like any sound he makes while awake, a deep rattling that echoes in the hollows of his throat and chest. I've often been irritated by his snoring, jabbing him in the side with my sharp elbows, but now I just lie here and watch him. Imagine having to sleep alone, without him. His big, safe body, the snoring, the comical expression he makes when he's asleep, his mouth half open, as if he's about to say something. He lies at the edge of the bed, nearest the door, protecting me against potential intruders. Who will protect me if Åsmund leaves?

At twenty past five I give up. I haven't slept a wink all night, but now it's almost morning anyway. I can go out into the kitchen, put the coffee on, collect the paper and set myself up for a calm early morning at the table. I do it, too, I go out into the kitchen, but my head feels heavy and grey. There's a cotton-wool-like layer covering my larynx, as if I'm about to cry. My body is so tired, all I want is to sleep, this early morning with a coffee and the newspaper will be an immense chore from beginning to end. But I make a start on it, because what else am I to do? I put on the coffee, throw on a jacket over my nightie, stick my feet into my rubber boots and go out into the chilly, empty corridor, where my footsteps reverberate against the walls.

It's cold outside. A thick fog lies over the landscape, and I can hardly see the houses on the other side of Kastanjesvingen, even the street lamps are indistinct. The fog is grey-white, and it smells good, it's fresh out here, so my aching, heavy head clears. When I was little, I used to think of fog as fallen clouds, and that's what it feels like, as if fluffy clouds have tumbled down over Tåsen while I was in bed trying to sleep, changing our garden completely, enveloping it and covering it, transforming it into something from a fairy tale. It doesn't feel as if I'm in a city. I feel unexpectedly uplifted as I take my first steps along the path.

The mailboxes hang on a stand, just inside the fence. In the fog, I don't see it until I'm quite close. A shadow hanging beside the last mailbox, and at first I think it's something someone has lost, a hat or scarf. Then I see the outline of the head, bent at an unnatural angle. I see the shoulders – if it's possible to say that a cat has shoulders – and the little front and back legs hanging down like the arms and legs of a person, the paws limp on each side. It isn't bleeding. The body hangs from a blue nylon rope, the end of which has been fashioned into a noose, and it's as if something thumps me in the chest: it's hanging from a gallows. Worst of all is the head. The ears are sticking up like those of a live cat. Its mottled grey fur is smooth and intact, and it's so small, maybe just a kitten, which makes me want to take it in my arms and stroke its little head. But its eyes are open, like tiny glass buttons, and then there's the rope, the gallows.

It is completely silent around us, around the cat and me. I stare at it in the foggy stillness for several seconds. See every hair of the fur that covers the soft ears. And then I scream.

PART II

Cognitive dissonance

WEDNESDAY

The neighbours' summer party has always been held at the end of June, just before the summer holidays begin, but this year nothing happened until the autumn. Last year's summer party was particularly enjoyable. We decorated the apple tree and patio with paper lanterns, Jamila hung garlands over the table, and Merete brought out an electric piano and played old jazz tunes. Aretha Franklin, Miles Davis and Nina Simone: "My baby just cares for me". There was dancing on the patio. I danced with Jørgen, who was a good dancer, he held me lightly. I danced with Åsmund, too, and with both Svein and Saman. It was that kind of evening. We'd all had quite a bit to drink, and the laughter was free and easy. Svein talked about hunting – he used to set out from his cabin, he said – and Jørgen leaned forward and asked him questions. I may be wrong, but I think that was when they all agreed to take the trip together in August this year. Even Nina seemed relaxed. She told a few anecdotes from the staffroom that didn't paint the school in an entirely good light, I remember, and it was nice to see her that way, off duty for once.

But this year, we forgot all about it. Only right before the summer holidays did anyone think of it, and by then it was too late, so we arranged something early in the autumn instead. It wasn't an evening thing this time – it was colder outside and got dark earlier. It was also hard to find a day that worked for everyone, so we decided on a lunch instead. Everyone brought along two dishes for the buffet. There were no paper lanterns, no piano, but Jamila dug out the garlands from the previous year, and the food was good. I said as little as possible to Jørgen. This was around the time I was attempting to break it off with him – right before I abandoned those attempts, in fact. Åsmund was in a bad mood for some reason or other, probably something to do with his mother, because he had to leave to answer his phone a couple of times and otherwise sat with it in his hands, scrolling. When he spoke to people it looked as if he had to force himself, as if he would have preferred to sit alone with his phone, and I remember that I considered asking him to put it away. Merete seemed tired. Nina talked about the board's plans for the garden and the list of jobs she would soon be putting up in the stairwell, how much work each and every one of us would have to sign up for. Svein sat sullenly beside her, looking at his watch every couple of minutes. Filippa went inside before we had finished eating, Simen went out somewhere just afterwards, and Emma, who I permitted to go neither in nor out, sat by herself and made it unnecessarily obvious that she would very much rather be *anywhere* but where she was. Saman was reserved but pleasant. Only Jamila tried to improve the atmosphere. She fluttered from one person to the next, asking questions, telling stories, gesticulating with her hands and laughing. In the end, her spark fizzled out, too, and then we just sat there. It was a bit chilly. We all went back inside early, to our own apartments.

Now there are police officers in the garden again. Two of them are standing by the mailboxes, one of them taking photographs, the other watching. I stand at the kitchen window and watch them. It's overcast, and probably cold, but the officers seem too focused on their work to be bothered by it. A man in a windcheater is standing outside the fence with a huge camera, taking photos of them. They don't try to stop him.

While we were eating breakfast a female police officer had come to the door, asked me a couple of questions and asked me to stay inside. Somebody would come and talk to me in a little while, she said, unless I was planning on going out? I said no. I still don't know whether or not I'll bother going in to work today, I haven't had the strength to decide, but I do as the police ask, and wait. The patio lies abandoned as the police officers concentrate on the mailboxes, and I look at it, wondering why there was such a bad atmosphere at this year's neighbours' party. Was it my fault, because I was avoiding Jørgen? Was it the teenage kids, who were now too cool to join in? Or was it about whatever happened on that cabin trip, the one that the police have been asking about? It had taken place just a few weeks before the party. I feel a shudder down my spine. Could it have been something to do with the cats? Had the creepiness of the spring's grisly findings settled over us, so that we no longer felt our neighbours could be our friends if we only had the time to properly get to know them? Had we already begun to look at each other as potential psychopaths, even back then?

This morning, while Åsmund was in the shower, a worried Lukas asked me what happens to a cat once it's dead. I interpreted this as an existential question and answered accordingly – some people believe in heaven, others believe that things that die become part of nature again. I tried to be pedagogical, but I could feel myself stumbling. My hands were still shaking, there was a knot in my diaphragm, and almost incessantly the image popped up in my mind – the furry little creature, the noose. Lukas, however, was more concerned with the body itself. A boy at kindergarten had said that dead cats get thrown in the dustbin. Emma looked at me with eyes brimming with contempt, as if she couldn't believe that this was her biological lot in life – to have received half of her genetic material from me.

"Oh my God," she said. "All this commotion over a cat."

Her comment reverberated in my chest. That tiny baby animal, hanging from a blue rope.

"It was killed, Emma," I said.

"So what?" she said.

"Just . . . Just show a little respect, that's all."

"Oh my God, Mamma," she said, getting up with her bowl in her hand. "It's only, like, two days ago that you said the same yourself."

She's right, I think, as I watch a car parking down on the street, she's absolutely right. Wasn't I also full of disdain for the two mothers at the school theatre rehearsal who had discussed the matter, their faces deadly serious? When I was a child, our neighbour had a cat that occasionally had kittens, and I remember that he would put down the ones he was unable to give away. He gave them an overdose of something or other he put in their food, and then wrung their necks for good measure. There were limits to how many cats he could keep, he said when my sister and I cried. He couldn't give them away, and this was kinder than letting them starve to death in the forest. In all other respects he was the world's friendliest man – he'd let us pick the sweet plums from the trees in his garden, and said nothing when we cut across his property as we walked to school. These sensitive city people, I've thought, getting all worked up over murdered cats, but have they ever asked themselves what the chickens and the pigs they eat go through before they end up on their plates? Isn't that the height of hypocrisy? Why does the suffering of a pet carry so much more weight than that of a farm animal?

Two men step out of the car. One of them is wearing a police uniform, and I see immediately that it's Robin Pettersen. The other man is tall and thin, and wearing an all-weather jacket. The tall, thin man walks ahead, opens the gate, and obviously says something to the two officers standing beside the mailboxes because they stop what they're doing and turn to look at him.

It's absolutely true what Emma says – I have indeed said that far too much fuss has been made over the dead cats. But something changed when I saw the little body hanging there beside the mailboxes, its neck broken. Those tiny, limp paws. The little mark left by the chip in its ear which indicated that it belonged to someone — that there was a family who gave it food and shelter, who had given it a name, who would be missing it. The soft ears and the little face — it was just a kitten. The gravity of it, when a man has been murdered in the same house — the violence of it all. The gallows. Robin and the other man walk up towards our building's front door, and I think about Emma and feel a trembling at the base of my throat: how can she be taking this so lightly?

The knock is sharp and efficient. It says something about the character of the person knocking, I think, as I walk over to open the door — I can tell right away, for example, that it isn't Robin Pettersen. It's the other one, the man in the all-weather jacket. I lift off the safety chain and open the door for them.

"Hi again," Robin says, his brows lowered, head cocked to one side in sympathy. "How are things here?"

"Oh, you know," I say.

The man in the all-weather jacket clears his throat once and sticks out a long, bony hand.

"Hello," he says. "Gunnar Gundersen Dahle. Head of the investigation. Can we have a little chat?"

Brief, informative sentences. He has a firm handshake, which is brief, too. It seems as if everything is urgent for this man — maybe because things really *are* urgent right now, or perhaps he's always like this. He's thin and sinewy, with a huge moustache across his upper lip. It's the kind of moustache hipsters have, and yet you can see straight away that this man isn't one of them, he's probably had it since he was twenty years old, unfazed by the fact that moustaches were seen as tacky back then, the kind of thing girls giggled at, and which probably ruined his chances of getting lucky with them. He's the head of the investigation, which means that Ingvild has relinquished the role. Gunnar Gundersen Dahle is holding a plastic bag in one hand, and he smells of cigarette smoke.

"Come in," I say, stepping aside.

They walk into the apartment. Gundersen Dahle keeps his shoes on.

"So," he says once they've sat down. "You were out early this morning?"

"Yes," I say. "I've been sleeping badly lately."

He nods. We're sitting in the kitchen. I've offered them coffee, but the boss gave a firm no, and Robin – who actually looked as if he might have liked a cup of coffee when I asked – politely refused, too. Gundersen Dahle looks around, shooting glances here and there. It feels as if he's cataloguing our apartment, registering all the details and putting them together. As if he can read what kind of people we are from these details: the crumbs on the kitchen counter, the cupboard door hanging slightly askew on its hinges, the empty space on the wall where the previous owners' designer clock once hung.

"When did you get up?"

I shrug. I'm not even sure if I ever actually went to bed last night.

"Five-thirty, maybe."

"And then?"

"Well, I probably pottered about a bit. I wanted to get the news-paper, so I went outside, and . . . yeah."

Robin nods, his expression friendly.

"She called the police at 05:42," he says helpfully.

To this, the moustache says nothing. Instead, he asks:

"Do you always sleep badly?"

"Well," I say. "We have a four-year-old, so I sleep lightly, wake often. But this past week I've hardly slept because of . . . you know."

I cast a glance at the ceiling. Robin does the same. Gunnar Gundersen Dahle fixes me with a steady gaze, and I think: He knows.

They probably all do. It's only a matter of time until he reads the email, if he hasn't already.

"Where's Ingvild Fredly?" I ask. "Is she no longer part of the investigation?"

"She was assigned to a new case," Gundersen says. "Or rather, a development in an old case. She'll help us out as and when she can. But I'll be leading the investigation from now on."

Is there something self-satisfied in his voice? I don't know, I'm unable to read him. Ingvild will still be involved, I think. Just from the sidelines. Will they use her? Try to take advantage of our private relationship?

"So you were awake most of the night," he says. "Did you hear anything?"

"How do you mean?"

"I mean, was there anyone opening and closing doors, stomping down the stairs, that sort of thing? Movement in the building. The walls are pretty thin here, are they not?"

I think about this. Remember how I sat there on the sofa as if in an intoxicated daze as I wrote to Ingvild, how I hammered away at the keyboard without noticing the time pass. I must have written for several hours. But at some point, I'd had the impression that I'd heard a door open and close. Hadn't I? I think I looked up for a moment, wondering who was out and about in the middle of the night. But I'm not sure, perhaps it was nothing.

"I don't know," I say. "It's possible I heard a door at some point or other. But I . . . well, I was busy with something just then. I wasn't listening."

"You weren't listening?"

"I was writing an email," I say, feeling the heat flood my cheeks. "I'm not sure whether I heard anything, I can't really remember. But it's possible."

"Upstairs or downstairs?"

"I don't know."

He nods thoughtfully. I think some more. It can't have been up in Jørgen and Merete's apartment – we can hear everything up there, I would have heard somebody crossing the floor. Not to mention that they would have had to come down the stairs, which are wooden and creak under people's weight, you can hear it throughout the apartment. No, nobody came down the stairs from the first floor, so it can't have been Saman or Jamila, either. But it could have been one of the Sparres.

Gunnar Gundersen Dahle sticks his hand into the plastic bag he's brought with him, pulls something out and sets it on the table between us. It's a coil of blue nylon rope.

"Do you recognise this?" he asks me.

I look at it.

"Is that what the cat was – you know. Strung up with?"

It makes me shudder: the rope's garish shade of blue, the brutality of the whole thing.

"We believe so," he says. "Have you seen it before?"

"I don't know. Isn't that a fairly common type of rope?"

"Here on the property?"

"I don't know whether we have any rope. If we do, it must be in the shed."

He nods.

"Is the shed usually kept locked?" he asks.

I frown, trying to remember. The wall creaks for a moment, and we turn our eyes towards it, all three of us. Perhaps somebody is sitting next door, listening to us. Maybe Nina also knows about the structural weakness that allows you to hear everything that's said through the wall. No further sounds come, and the policemen turn back to me.

"I don't know," I say. "I think so. There's a padlock with a code on the door, the kind with dials where you have to put the numbers in sequence, you know."

The moustache nods. He's already aware of this, I realise.

"What's the code?" Robin asks.

"1951," I say. "The year the house was built."

A tiny smile steals across Robin's lips. Gundersen Dahle remains, of course, unmoved.

"Well," he says. "I think that's it."

They get up. I get up, too.

The person who opened and closed the front door must have come out of the Sparres' apartment, I think. Nobody came down from the first floor, and no matter how immersed I was in my email, I would have noticed if a member of my family had crossed the living room while I was sitting on the sofa and writing. But what about the fire exit in Emma's room? It leads directly from her bedroom and out into the shared area in the cellar. Would I have heard her if she went out that way? My ribs tighten around my chest. If her bedroom door was closed, she could have sneaked out so quietly that I wouldn't have heard her from the floor above. Couldn't she? Though I'm not sure why she would. I can't imagine that she had anything to do with the dead cat. But I can't rule it out, either.

"Was there something else?" asks the moustache.

"Sorry?"

"It looked as if you just thought of something."

"No," I say, a little too quickly, so that I have to attempt to soften my answer. "No, I just – we need to clean the windows. I only noticed it just now."

"Oh."

He gives me a friendly smile. He doesn't believe me.

"People often think of things later, after we've spoken," he says. "Once they've had a little time to mull things over. Give us a call if you do think of anything. Pettersen, do you have a piece of paper?"

Robin hands over his notepad, and we stand in silence for a

moment as Gundersen Dahle writes. Then he hands me a scrap of paper. *Gundersen*, it says, along with a telephone number.

"I'll do that," I say.

I hold the note between my finger and thumb, as if trying to ensure I have as little physical contact with it as possible. Gundersen looks at me. There's something in his eyes that unsettles me. Ingvild might not have been a hundred percent on my side, but I trusted her. This man – I don't know. He doesn't know whether he trusts me, either – or at least that's the impression I get. He studies me one last time.

"We'll speak again," he says. "Good morning."

When their footsteps tell me that they're safely up on the first floor, I go down into the cellar and stop outside Emma's door. She's at school, I have free rein, but I hesitate all the same. I'm not entirely sure whether I want to do this.

It's embarrassingly tidy in here. My teenage bedroom was this way, too, but Emma has taken it further, she's even more meticulous than I was. I look around, following the seductive, empty gazes of the girls on her posters. There are names printed on some of them, but they mean nothing to me, I have no idea whether they're pop stars or actors, or whether they just model clothes.

At the centre of her desktop lies her script for *The Threepenny Opera*. It's a little dog-eared, uncharacteristically so for Emma, but it's been set here all neat and tidy, parallel to the edge of the desk. I carefully lift the front page, peek inside. Flick through the script. Emma has noted down the director's instructions and underlined all her lines. A few are hers alone, but most of them she says or sings with others, as part of a kind of chorus. On the last page, she's underlined some words that don't seem to be hers, because they're marked as Peachum's: *Therefore never be too eager to combat injustice.* I frown. Why has Emma highlighted this? But just below it is a verse that everyone sings, *Combat injustice but in moderation*, so maybe she marked it by mistake. I turn over the final page. On the back cover, close to the binding, a heart has been drawn in pencil, and inside the heart: GG. Has Emma written this? I don't know – I'm unsure whether it's her handwriting. It could have been one of her friends. Messing around, perhaps. Girls can be like that at that age, I think – this is the kind of thing they find funny. I look at it.

GG? Is there a Gustav or Gaute in Emma's class? For a moment I think of Gunnar Gundersen Dahle, and it makes me giggle; the astonishing sound escapes me to bounce between the walls. I take care to put the script back exactly as I found it, parallel with the edges of the desk and right in the middle, no mess here. I turn towards the fire door.

The emergency exit was probably required by the Planning and Building Agency before the cellar could be incorporated into the apartment. Åsmund had joked about it with Emma when we moved in, look here, he said, you can sneak out to meet your boyfriends when you get older. Gross, Pappa, she had said – she was only nine at the time. Just you wait, Åsmund had said, give it a few years. The door is metal, to keep any fire on whichever side it happens to be on, I suppose, and it can only be unlocked from the inside. I twist the lock. First once, then again, as slowly as I can. It gives out the tiniest little click. I sigh, emptying my lungs of air. I would never have heard it on the floor above – no question. Or, at least, not if the door to her room was closed. I click the lock back and forth a few times, and then I try the door. It permits itself to be pushed soundlessly outwards, and the cellar opens before me. It's cold down here, cold and damp. Four bicycles stand beside each other; one of them is mine. Next to the bikes is a big white chest freezer that Svein didn't have space for and therefore put in the shared area, declaring that *everyone is welcome to use it*, before he promptly secured it with a padlock, effectively preventing the rest of us from taking him at his word. Beside the freezer is yet another door, the fire door that leads into the basement floor of the Sparre family's apartment. I stand there for a moment, and then I hear footsteps on the stairs. Before I can retreat, I see the tall body of Gundersen, and then his head, as if he has to duck to make his way in through the door frame.

"Hello again," he says. "You're down here?"

"Hi," I say. "I just wanted to check if my bike was here."

The lie slips off my tongue so easily, as if I really did come down here for this purpose.

"I see," Gundersen says. "And is it?"

"Yes," I say. "There."

He looks at it, and then his eyes roam about the room. Robin appears behind him and turns on the ceiling light. We stand there for a moment, and I think: He doesn't believe me. He doesn't believe in the slightest that I came down into the cellar to check if my bike was here, because why would I do that, and why would I do it right now? But how likely is it he would think I connected the sound I heard with Emma and wanted to check whether she could sneak out? My head feels heavy and I'm suddenly not sure, it's all too elaborate, too improbable – or might he actually draw that conclusion?

"Whose freezer is this?" he asks.

"Nina and Svein's."

"It's locked."

"Yes," I say. "The spoils of Svein's hunting trips."

"Ah," Gundersen says, and then a smile flits across his face. "A man who protects what he's shot himself."

"Something like that," I say.

But suddenly, I don't feel like smiling. Something about the context, the grotesque in it. The dead cat, Jørgen. We stand there for a moment.

"And this door leads to your apartment?" Gundersen asks, looking over my shoulder.

"Yes," I say, taking a step to the side so that he can get closer if he wishes to, but he only looks at me. "My daughter's bedroom."

He nods, as if he's thinking of something else.

"Well," he says. "We won't keep you. I just wanted to take a look at the windows down here."

For a moment the three of us look towards the two tiny cellar windows that face the garden on either side of the front step. Then Gundersen turns and says:

"Pettersen, do we have photos of these?"

"Yes," Robin says.

"See you later, then," I say, and close and lock the door behind me.

I stand there in Emma's bedroom, my breathing quick and agitated, as if I've been running.

"I see," says the young Swedish doctor. "Okay, right."

He's arranged his features into a sympathetic expression. His hairless, well-maintained hands lie one atop the other on the table, a shiny wedding band encircling his ring finger. His nails are evenly clipped, I notice, almost down to the quick, but not entirely. I can just imagine him in the bathroom in the morning – early, most likely, before the two Gore-Tex-clad children in the photograph on the noticeboard behind him and their mother have got up – sitting on the lid of the toilet with a pair of nail clippers. Imagine him saying to his wife: It's about inspiring confidence.

I – in sharp contrast – can hardly be said to inspire confidence. I wring my hands as I speak and shift my position constantly, unable to sit still. I know I appear nervous, and I am, too, although I'm not sure why, because there's nothing to indicate that this young Swedish doctor is sceptical of me. I tell him about the murder of my neighbour – go online and check if you like, I say, as if I'm expecting him not to believe me, and he holds up his manicured hands and says, no no, that won't be necessary, he believes me. Then I tell him about the headache and the sleeplessness, I didn't sleep *a wink* last night, I say, and then of course there was the incident with the cat, I tell him about that, too.

"I see," he says again.

He takes a breath, but before he can say anything further I tell him that Jørgen and I also had a special relationship, because after all this is just between us, I say, duty of confidentiality and all that, and I mean, I hope you won't have to write anything about this in my notes because you never know, computer systems can be hacked, and, well, I'd prefer this not to be written down anywhere, but we did have a relationship of sorts, you might say. So perhaps, I continue at breakneck speed, he might understand why I can't sleep at night, that I'm not doing very well, and I can't stand the thought of going into work – yes, I know that I'm not technically sick, not in a purely clinical sense, but nor am I entirely healthy, either, or at least, I'm not in any fit state to work. And he mustn't think that I'm the kind of person who goes running to the doctor all the time asking to be put on sick leave, he'll surely be able to see that from my notes anyway, if he wishes to – that I don't do that sort of thing. I'm not sure I've ever been on sick leave at all, actually, but now I'm going through a pretty tense time in my private life, yes, to be frank it's all been quite *difficult*, so I thought, if it might be possible, that I could be granted a few days off on sick leave, some time to get on top of things, and maybe also something to help me sleep.

"I see," says the doctor, taking a deep breath. "Well – it isn't easy, is it?"

"No," I say, taking a deep breath, too. "It isn't."

We sit in silence for a moment. I feel empty; all at once I don't have a single word to say. All I can think is how true his statement is. It isn't easy.

"Of course, I can write you a sick note," he says, turning to face his computer and setting his hygienic hands on the spotless keyboard. "What do you think – is a week sufficient?"

"Yes," I say. "Yes – I'm sure that's more than enough."

"Good," he says, and begins to type.

His fingers leap across the keyboard. I watch them. Remember how a colleague once told me that her cat used to watch her fingers as she typed, as if they were mice. That the cat would crouch there tracking them, often without her noticing until it pounced on her hands and stuck its claws into them.

The doctor looks up.

"Right, and then there's the issue of your sleep."

I nod, slowly. He's quiet, apparently thinking, and I act as if I'm thinking, too.

"Here's what I think," he says. "I think we should hold off on prescribing you any medication. There's always a risk with sleeping pills. It doesn't do anything to help the cause of the sleeplessness, the medication disrupts the internal sleep rhythm, and then there's the potential for addiction. So I think we should try the natural method first."

I nod again. I don't agree, but nor do I feel that I'm in any position to protest. Tiredness begins to creep over me. The natural method.

"Exercise," he says. "Every day. Preferably outdoors, so you get plenty of daylight, and well before you go to bed. No heavy meals just before bedtime. And cut out alcohol and coffee completely."

"Okay," I say.

"How do you feel about that?" he asks.

He gives me a friendly smile that seems almost smug.

"I don't know," I say.

It feels as if I'm a hundred years old, full of days.

"It really will be okay," he says. "Just wait, you'll see. Give it a couple of days. If things aren't any better after the weekend, then come back and see me and we'll reassess. Okay?"

"Okay," I say, resigned.

A pill would have been so nice. A tiny foil-covered friend I could swallow down with a glass of water before I went to bed, one that could knock me out, enable my feet to lie against each other and my tongue to fit in my mouth – that could be set like a lid over everything that's spinning in my head, so things could finally slow to a stop in there.

Yes, I could have done with a pill. Especially tonight, when I have perhaps only hours left of my marriage. Is it really too much to ask, a little sleeping pill for support on the day you're going to stake your entire relationship on telling the truth? Is there really a risk of addiction if the medicine is used in a situation this rare, so completely beyond the everyday?

But I don't have the strength to protest. I'm afraid that he'll change his mind and take back the sick note. I don't want to be the kind of person who begs their doctor for drugs, especially not this doctor, so clean and healthy, irreproachable to his core. And if I'm being honest, I'm terrified that he'll tell me what he thinks of me. Am I asking him for sympathy for the situation I find myself in? Me – who has broken my marriage vows? What does he think of people like me, this man who doesn't seem to have a single care in the world?

"Go for a run," he says, pressing my hand against his, which I'm sure he'll thoroughly wash and anti-bac the moment I'm out of his office.

"Get yourself really tired. And avoid red meat and fatty foods. Chicken with rice and salad is better. Things will get better with time, just wait and see."

Ingvild has responded to my email – I read her reply on my laptop, at home in the kitchen. *Thank you, Rikke*, she writes. *We'll speak soon. Best wishes, Ingvild.* Nothing about the cat, which I assume she must have heard about. Nothing about the fact that Gundersen has taken over her investigation. A prickle of shame runs up my spine – what on earth did I write? I was too personal. Shared too much. Private details that are nobody else's business. Why didn't I ask if I could just tell her everything in person? If Åsmund ever reads the email, it will crush him.

I lean over the computer to look out into the garden. Outside, Merete Tangen is doing some gardening. She's standing before the apple tree. In her hands she has a huge pair of loppers she's using to clip away excess branches. Strictly speaking, it's a job for the spring, but perhaps we neglected the tree this year, because it looks as if it could do with a pruning. Merete works quickly. She has strong arms, doesn't hesitate, simply hacks away, the branches falling around her. Now she squeezes the shears together at the root of a branch that is slightly too thick – it resists, and I can see it in her shoulders, the way she digs deep, it's her against the tree now, and she's going to win. She's wearing gym clothes and a woollen sweater, all in luxurious high quality. Trainers on her feet, and even those are expensive-looking, all chalk-white and feminine. I've seen her wearing them before and know that they have a tulip on the side, sewn in tiny, careful stitches. The head of the tulip is slightly downturned, it's blood red, and I think, as I often do, where did Merete buy those shoes? Beside the flower bed, over on the patio, sits Filippa. She's also wearing gardening gloves, but she doesn't seem to be doing anything. Right now, she's watching her mother battle with the obstinate branch, following her movements with her eyes.

I consider the girl. She's thin and quite short, with thick, dark-brown hair and big brown eyes. Nothing about her is affected or embellished – she doesn't use much make-up, and I've never seen her tottering around on heels that are far too high, as many of the other girls do. She doesn't swing eye-catching handbags from her shoulder and never leaves heavy clouds of perfume in her wake in the stairwell, but it's clear from the moment you see her that she's aware of how beautiful she is. She just doesn't make a big deal out of it. I realise that I usually always see her with friends, she seems to have an entire flock of them. They all speak in voices that are higher pitched than hers, draw more attention to themselves than she does, and glance at her constantly to see whether she's paying attention, what she thinks, what her opinion is. Filippa, I think, is one of those people who leads without raising their voice.

But something is different now. There's something unhealthy about her face, something pale and sunken, as if she hasn't slept, either. Her movements are slow, and a little jerky. Mine are probably the same, I think, and as I think this, it dawns on me that Filippa, more than anyone else, is grieving for Jørgen. Perhaps she and I have something in common, something we don't share with many others. But Filippa Tangen's grief is different from mine. Possibly less complicated, but deeper. A sharp, jagged pain that will probably never fully go away, and what I'm seeing is just the outline of this.

Down beside the fence, Simen Sparre comes into view. He has his school bag slung over his shoulder, and he opens the gate with slow movements. I can tell when he catches sight of Filippa because he straightens his back, as if realigning his body. Merete takes a momentary break from the branch and appears to say something to Simen, but she has her back to me, I can't see her facial expression. It does seem strange that they should be out there gardening today, when their grief is so fresh. But maybe it does them good – practical work to ease existential sorrow. Simen smiles and nods at what she says. He looks a little uncomfortable. Just as he did when I bumped into him at the school theatre rehearsal, I think. Every now and then he casts a glance towards Filippa, simultaneously nodding and smiling while responding to her mother. Filippa sits still at the edge of the patio, studying a plant she's holding in her hands. She appears to be completely lost in it, taking no notice of the boy-next-door who is trying to catch her eye.

On a telephone call just before we made an offer on the apartment, the real estate agent told us that a girl of nine or ten lived in the apartment above. Had we believed in that kind of thing, we would have thought it was a sign. A friend for Emma, Åsmund and I said to each other. After we moved in, we would occasionally arrange with Jørgen and Merete for the girls to spend time together, attempting to pair them up. Emma made friends at the new school almost immediately, a faithful gang who rang our doorbell when she asked them over, and stood there on the step fiddling with their phones as they asked whether she was home. But was Filippa one of them? She had been over a few times. She was polite, said thank you for the meal, carried her plate from the dinner table to put it in the dishwasher. I don't know when she was last here, it must be a long time ago now. I frown. I haven't ever noticed any ill will between the two girls.

Simen and Merete have finished talking; she goes back to her branch, he pads slowly up the path. He looks at Filippa. Stops beside her. She says nothing – she apparently hasn't noticed him – and continues to stare down at the plant in her hands. Finally, Simen says something. Filippa answers, but without lifting her gaze. Simen fiddles with the strap of his bag as he speaks, telling her something. His hand is trembling. His body is stiff, his face serious. Filippa turns and looks at him. I can't see her face, and it lasts for just a moment before she turns her attention to the flower bed instead. Simen walks on. I watch him as he reaches the front door and punches in the code. There's a certain set to his young, smooth forehead – the boy is pained. He's probably in love with her. It wouldn't be surprising, I'm sure half the teenage boys in the neighbourhood are. But there's something in his gaze, his wide-open eyes. Something is going on between these kids.

The front door opens, and Simen disappears inside. Out in the garden, Merete finally gets the better of the branch. She squeezes with all her might and it succumbs, hanging limply by a thread. A tug of the shears and it falls to the ground beside her white and red trainers. She straightens up, shouts something to her daughter. Filippa turns away and doesn't answer.

I lie down on the sofa, leaning my head against the armrest. Close my eyes. Perhaps I'll manage to sleep now. Fall into a deep, dreamless sleep, a peace I haven't known in many days. Wake up rested and restored in a few hours' time. I'll need it, if I'm going to talk to Åsmund. I twist my body; can't quite believe it. For almost nine months I've kept it secret, but now I'm going to tell him. Oh, Ingvild, isn't there another way out?

As I fall asleep, I remember the expression on Simen's face. It wasn't unrequited love. Or at least, it wasn't only that. His shaking hands, the stiffness in his movements. His wide-open eyes and furrowed brow. It was fear. Simen Sparre is afraid.

Something awoke in me when I saw the helpless kitten hanging by its neck. I wanted to cut it down, take it in my arms. To stroke its fur, rock it like an infant. But I mustn't get sentimental. There's nothing unusual about taking the lives of animals. In fact, almost one in every ten Norwegians is a hunter in some sense of the term, the Internet tells me. Where I grew up, the hunting parties would often come past – they parked their station wagons in the car park deep in the valley before taking out their rifles, tightening the straps of their backpacks and setting out to shoot birds or other small game. Several of the men in the village enjoyed hunting as a hobby, as did at least a couple of the women. Good people, too. Of course, there's clearly a difference between shooting an elk and killing a cat. At least if the cat belongs to someone. But in my tired head, the line begins to blur. At a neighbourhood party a few years ago, Svein told us about how he had once shot and wounded an elk, and was forced to follow the trail of blood in order to put it out of its misery. It was a female elk, and she had a calf. Custom dictates that you shoot the calf first because it will be unable to survive alone, and it would be unethical to start with the mother. But to shoot the child in front of the mother, on the other hand, is clearly fine. I've forgotten how his story ended, although I think they got the better of the elk in the end. Knowing Svein, he wouldn't have told the story if they hadn't.

But my discomfort at his story is illogical, because I eat meat – even elk – without thinking anything of it. I imagine Svein Sparre leaning over Jørgen as he sits there in front of his computer, oblivious to the fact that Svein is in the room, to the huge hunting knife in Svein's hands. Feel the knot in my diaphragm again. Surely it can't be? But somebody *did* draw a knife across Jørgen's throat. Ingvild says that those of us who live here at Kastanjesvingen 15 had a better opportunity to commit the crime than anyone else, and what do I actually know about Svein Sparre?

We've been friends on Facebook for several years, but I haven't ever thought to look at his profile until now. Once I've sat down in the living room with my laptop and logged in to investigate, I see that it isn't especially informative. He has few friends, although that doesn't necessarily mean very much. In his profile picture he's sitting aboard a boat, it's summer and he's wearing a cap and sunglasses, smiling happily towards the camera. Twelve people have liked the photo, I see. There isn't much on his wall. Birthday wishes, a photo of three dead birds lying in the heather with the comment *Today's kill!* beneath it. A newspaper article about celebrating Christmas in an inclusive way, which he's shared with the comment *Soon nothing will be allowed any more.* Only two people have liked this. A third has responded with an angry emoji.

I google his name. The first four hits are about a Sveinung Sparre from Mo i Rana, who has become a star member of the local orienteering team. Then Google encourages me to search for Svein's name in the public register of taxpayers, and I get a hit in the telephone directory, which rather redundantly informs me that Svein Sparre lives in Kastanjesvingen. The seventh hit is for a temping agency called EasyTemps. I click on it, and am taken straight to their contact page, where Svein is listed as the general manager. There's a photo of him, in a suit this time, and without sunglasses. It must be a few years old: he looks younger – thicker hair, thinner face – although he's just as broad-shouldered as ever. I navigate to the home page. *Temporary staff from EasyTemps*, it shouts in big white letters against a turquoise background, *We're here when you need us.* Below this is an image of a group of smiling people, men and women, dark-skinned and light. All of them are young and attractive, their teeth straight and glowing white, their skin smooth and obviously retouched, and something about this photograph tells me that it's a stock photo taken from some database or other, rather than an actual group photograph of EasyTemps employees.

This is as far as I've got when there's a knock at the door.

Out in the corridor, Nina is waiting for me. She's wearing her coat – perhaps on her way to work a little later than usual today – and she smiles nervously, shifts her weight from one foot to the other.

"Hello, sweetie," she says. "How are you doing?"

"Oh," I say. "Well enough."

"I heard about the cat – it must have been absolutely horrific for you. Of course, it's just a cat, and nowhere near as bad as what happened to poor Jamila on Sunday, but . . . well. It must have been awfully unpleasant all the same."

She cocks her head to one side and reaches out a small, warm hand, which she sets on my forearm.

"Especially," she says, glancing around, "when you think about . . ."

She casts a glance upwards, towards the floor on which Jørgen was found.

"Such a nasty business," she says, her eyes darting about, up and down the corridor and then into the apartment behind me. "So terribly frightening. I can hardly sleep at night, I've been so stressed out by all this."

And she really does look stressed. On the evening they found Jørgen, when we stood out in the garden, Nina had seemed almost ecstatic about what had happened. As if it gave her a sense of being relevant, at the centre of the action for once. But she exudes no such elation now.

"To think that this could happen here," Nina says, her voice weighty. "Where it's so safe. Oh, dear me, no, I never would have believed it."

She wrings her hands – I've never seen her so agitated. Not in connection with the controversy surrounding *The Threepenny Opera*, not when Hoffmo complained that the board wasn't doing enough to find the cat murderer. She casts a glance over her shoulder again, and I think: Nina really is afraid.

"I don't think any of us could have imagined that something like this would happen," I say.

She closes her eyes, shakes her head.

"It's like a bad dream," she says. "I'm almost expecting to wake up, to find it was all just a nightmare."

The code lock on the front door beeps. Nina and I stand in silence and listen, unwilling to speak when we don't know who might hear us. We glance nervously towards the door, and I feel my breathing quicken, becoming shallower. Then the mechanism clicks, the door is pushed open, and Saman comes into view.

"Hello," he says.

"Hello," we say.

We stand without speaking as he walks past, as if we're not entirely reassured, even though it's just a neighbour. This is how things are now, I think. Here, where up until last weekend everything seemed perfectly harmonious. If you ignore the incidents involving the cats, that is – and that's becoming harder and harder to do. Saman is halfway up the stairs when Nina says:

"I just hope they catch him soon. The one who did it."

She casts a long glance up the stairs.

"Whoever he is. Of course, it's impossible not to have your own ideas. There are certain people around here who seem more aggressive than others. If you know what I mean."

On the stairs above us, Saman's footsteps cease. For a moment we stand stock-still, Nina and I down here, Saman upstairs, all three of us listening, and then we hear him coming back down again. He appears on the landing.

"What did you say, Nina?" he asks.

"What did I say?" she asks innocently.

"Yes. What did you say?"

His cheeks are flushed. Nina doesn't answer.

"What kind of *ideas* are you having?" he asks, his voice hushed.

He seems to be trying to appear collected, but his jaw gives him away, the muscles vibrating under the skin. Nina looks at his shoes, and then her gaze jumps up to me, her eyes perfectly round, and she says:

"Just ideas."

Silence. Saman breathes in and out several times, and we stand there looking at each other. Then Nina can no longer restrain herself.

"It isn't just me," she says. "The police are going around asking about all kinds of strange things. About the neighbours. About what was said and done on that cabin trip. And Svein has all sorts to say about the discussion that night."

Saman glares down at her. Then he shifts his weight to the other foot, and something calm and calculating comes over him.

"I wasn't the only one who was angry," he says.

He shifts his gaze to me. His brown eyes are attractive, the kind you notice. Now they narrow, considering me as if I'm a specimen in his lab and it's his job to study my reaction.

"He was fairly worked up, too, your husband," he says. "That evening. He shouted pretty loudly."

"Åsmund?" I ask.

Nina gives a snort.

"Oh, you were there, were you?" Saman says to her, his voice sharp.

"I've heard all sorts," is Nina's haughty reply.

She casts me a knowing glance, then looks at the king begonia on the landing, her mouth closed, as if to signal that she's said all she has to say. All the air seems to go out of Saman. He emits a sigh, throws out his hands and says: "Fine." Then he turns and stamps up the last of the stairs, his footsteps thundering through the staircase's ramshackle structure. We hear the jangle of his keys upstairs, and then the apartment door slams shut.

Nina turns towards me, meaningfully raising her eyebrows.

"This isn't about . . ." she says, looking up, considering. "About *race*, or skin colour, or anything like that. Although you sometimes wonder what kind of culture people come from. But you know just how *fond* I am of Jamila, so that's not what the problem is here."

She lowers her voice. Instinctively, I lean towards her, and even as I do so I think we must look as if we're conspiring, although of course there's nobody here to witness it.

"Svein says that he was furious that night. There was something they were discussing, you know, between friends. Saman properly lost it, screaming and cursing and saying awful things. Couldn't control his anger, Svein says. Like a wild animal. And then I think of the way Jørgen was killed, how brutal it was . . ."

She shudders.

"The sheer *fury* it would take. You know what I mean."

She looks at me, seeking validation. As if it's my turn to say something, to offer up an anecdote that confirms what she's just told me. But I have nothing to say. My throat is bone dry. The apartment above us, the study where Jørgen was killed, lies there like a terrifying void, a black hole we don't want to acknowledge but that is sucking us in all the same. What happened there. The dizzying implications: are we safe in this house? And now we're behaving the way people always do when threatened – we're turning against each other.

There is silence between us for seconds that seem to last an eternity, and I already know that later I'll come up with oh-so many excuses. I was tired, I'll say, it was the lack of sleep, I'm no longer able to act in the way that I want to. Or – it all happened so quickly, before I could say anything the moment had passed. I will play down this long, viscous moment in which Nina has accused Saman and is looking to me for approval, in which I could protest, could defend him, but don't. I just didn't act quickly enough, I'll say to myself. Or could it be that I believe her? Or, at least, fear that she might be right? With Jørgen gone, there are eleven of us in the house. If you ignore the children, we're seven. Jamila and Saman, Nina and Svein, Åsmund and me. And Merete, who was in a tent far from civilisation when it happened, and who obviously didn't let herself in that night. Six suspects. Were I to hazard a guess, I would have said Svein. But I have so little to go on. It could just as easily be Saman. There aren't many of us.

"Oh, deary me, no," Nina says at last. "I just don't know what to make of it. It's simply awful to think that there's that kind of anger among us – in someone who has a code to get in and who lives right next door."

A shiver runs through us both. The lonely, cold room upstairs.

"But the police seem to be making progress," Nina says in a small voice. "They'll surely get to the bottom of it."

She looks around again, turns to face me and adds:

"It's utterly incomprehensible. I just don't know what anyone's supposed to do in a situation like this."

And in that moment, I think, she's being totally honest.

That's not what this is about, I think, as I sit before my computer, with *Saman Karimi* typed into the search field on Facebook. It isn't about suspecting someone because of their name, or their first language, or anything like that. I hear the echo of Nina's words in my own, and argue against them. This isn't about *that*. But it has to be okay to ask certain questions. I click Search.

Several profiles come up, three in Iran, two in the US, one in Australia. Nobody in Norway. I navigate to Jamila's profile, see whether Saman can be found through hers, but there's no information to be found there, either. It says that Jamila is married, but not to whom. There are no photographs of them together, and in fact there are very few private images there at all – they're photos from work, models staring impenetrably towards the camera, affectedly dishevelled, with tangled hair and artistic smiles, red eyeshadow, white eyelashes. They're wearing long skirts and stiletto heels, or skin-coloured bikinis under see-through T-shirts, and Jamila has photographed them in autumnal forests or old cabins, all of it very artsy. Not pretty, not in the way you might imagine a fashion photographer's work to be, but there's something self-confident about it all. Like Jamila's own image. You're never in any doubt that she knows what's what.

I google Saman's name. Just to have a look, I say to myself. Again, nothing but hits about others with the same name. I add Oslo, and then I get four hits that look relevant. One on the university's website, a three-year-old post about Saman presenting his doctoral thesis, with its long and incomprehensible title, full of letters and digits put together in ways that require you to be from the right circles in order to understand them. The next hit is from the employee pages of Rikshospitalet, where Saman works as a doctor of orthopaedics. On to the employee pages of the university, where he apparently has an additional post – I wasn't aware of this, but that isn't so strange, we're not very close. Then a hit on Google Scholar – an article he's written. Yet another incomprehensible title. It has been cited over 500 times, I read, feeling a stab of jealousy – my most quoted article has fewer than 200 citations. The final hit is from a page titled *From Cradle to Grave*. I frown. Click on the link. My computer takes a while to load the page, but when it does, it's blank. I scroll up and down, clicking at random. Nothing happens. Cradle. Grave. I don't know what I'm supposed to make of it, there's nothing that hints at how the page should be interpreted.

Then I search for Jamila. More fashion photographs, more expressionless models in coniferous forests and screes. Her website is a catalogue of her work, and that's pretty much all I find about her. I go back into her Facebook profile, snoop around there, and the longer it takes me to find something personal, the more brazen I become. I forget how I'm invading her private life, focused solely on finding something – I'm not sure what, something or other that shows she's more than a photographer. Way down on her wall, I find it. A woman named Shamala has written a message. *Jammie! I heard about what happened! Thinking of you.* Crying emoji. Forty people have reacted – there are hearts and thumbs and crying faces. Most of Jamila's other posts have several hundred reactions. She's liked Shamala's post herself, I see, but she hasn't commented, and nor has anyone else. The post is a year and a half old. Shamala must have written it just before Saman and Jamila moved into Kastanjesvingen.

Next up is Nina Sparre. Her profile is full of inspirational quotes and moving news stories about children making it against all odds, or strangers who are unexpectedly kind to each other. She often comments with *So beautiful!* and sometimes with advice or wisdom: *This is what happens when we dare to listen to each other!* She cares about school policy too, I see, and these posts are markedly more informative. Here, Nina writes about the consequences of lowering the age at which children start school from seven to six, and other educational reforms. She's worried about the red tape in schools; is afraid it will lead to less time for teaching. Nina is highly engaged and posts almost daily, sometimes several times a day. Her last post is from Sunday morning, the day Jørgen was found. It's an article about a single mother who couldn't afford a bicycle for her child, and how her neighbours got together to buy the boy the exact bike he had wanted. *Take care of the people around you!* Nina has written in her post. After this, nothing.

Merete's Facebook profile isn't especially active. She has many friends, and many people like what she posts, but there isn't much to look at. A few links to news items or music events or art exhibitions. Pictures of Filippa every now and then, always taken with her back to the camera. Filippa on skis in a beautiful winter landscape, Filippa sunbathing on coastal rocks. Not many comments.

I bring up Åsmund's profile. His profile picture was taken on holiday with some friends, and it's probably six or seven years old now. He has his sunglasses on his head and he's grinning broadly – he looks happy and free. I scroll through the posts and images he's shared, the things his friends have tagged him in. Try to imagine how I would interpret all this if I were his neighbour. He has a lot of friends, and they like him. He likes to watch sport on TV. He's proud of his e-bike. He cares about his job, but not too much. He dreams about going on holiday to exotic destinations, about seeing his favourite football team win the league. Is this all I'll have left of him if he turns his back on me?

Then I search for Emma. Her profile picture has a filter applied to it, with intense shadows and lots of contrast, so she's almost unrecognisable. She's pretty, but also looks as if she could be anyone. This is all I see. *This content isn't available*, says the page. I click again. Reload the page, as if that will help. Emma's account shouldn't be unavailable – not to me. We're friends on Facebook. That was a condition of her being allowed to create a profile three years ago, before she was old enough.

The unease takes hold of my body as I fish out my phone and check other platforms – I'm breathing more quickly, feel tiny twitches in my fingers. She's blocked me from Instagram and Snapchat, too. At a parents' evening at Bakkehaugen school a few months ago, Nina invited a psychologist from the local council to give a presentation about young people and the Internet. Talk with your kids about what they do online, advised the psychologist. Create profiles on the platforms they use, and follow them. Show interest in their online lives, show them that you're there for them online, just as you are every day in real life. Let them know that they can come to you. And so on. The psychologist was young, I remember – she clearly didn't have teenagers herself. I stare at the hostile piece of text on the screen. *This content isn't available*. I don't have access – Emma has blocked me.

She slams the apartment's front door, and it wakes me. I'm disoriented at first – I'm lying on the sofa, hadn't even realised that I'd fallen asleep. My body is stiff and sore, my tongue waxy.

"Hello," I say.

My voice is deep and cracked and foreign, as if another version of me rises from the depths of sleep, a night-self I don't recognise in the slightest. I have to cough and splutter and clear my throat to get rid of it.

"Mamma?" Emma asks, sticking her head around the corner from the hallway. "What are you doing here at this time?"

"What time is it?" I ask, feeling my usual voice come to the fore, my day-self slinking out of the shadows.

"Quarter past three," she says.

I sit up, stretch. Emma goes back into the hallway. I hear the bumping sound of her boots as she kicks them off against the parquet, and then she comes into the living room.

"Were you asleep?" she asks, wrinkling her brow.

"Yes," I say. "I slept so badly last night."

I yawn.

"I've been to the doctor. He's put me on sick leave, so I'll be home for a few days. You know, what with the cat and everything."

The wrinkle in her brow deepens. I swallow.

"And with what happened to Jørgen."

Her forehead smoothes out. She presses her lips together, and her face takes on the expression I occasionally see in her, one of complete superiority, as if she is quite within her rights to judge anyone who shows even the slightest form of weakness, because she, Emma, thirteen years old, refuses to be moved.

"So you're not really sick, then," she says.

"No," I say, feeling tired, not wanting to get into a discussion about it. "But the doctor thought I should stay home while I'm not sleeping properly."

We say nothing more. She goes into the kitchen. I follow her with my eyes, her slender figure in tight clothes. There is still something childish in her gait, but it's in the process of disappearing, I can see that. I wonder how much of the way she moves is calculated. I've seen them, teenage girls – they try it out. I've seen Emma and her friends, as recently as at the school play rehearsal this weekend, the way they pose for one another, sashaying around with their breasts out and bottoms swaying from side to side, making their friends laugh. It's exaggerated and silly, but not only that. They're testing themselves. Trying to see how far they can push it, while also adding elements of it into their movement patterns. They want the boys to look at them. For the boys' sake, but it's just as much for the other girls, too. They show off for one another, and what I've observed, I think, is that the other girls tend to show off for Emma in particular. Her mocking laughter – which she doles out mercilessly, and especially to the weakest among them – is enough to send them to the outer fringes of the circle. And now she's blocked me. I should have a word with her about it. I follow her into the kitchen and watch her reaching up into a cabinet, looking for something. I wonder what I should say, whether I should be interrogative or play dumb, act as if I think it's a mistake. Or whether I should confront her. I try to predict her reaction, to one option, to another.

"What are you looking for?" I ask.

She doesn't answer, just continues to rummage around in there, standing on tiptoe to reach the top shelf. She's fairly tall – she gets that from me. Åsmund and his brother are of average height, but towards the shorter end of the spectrum. They're stocky, while Emma is slim, just as I was at her age. She takes the box of O'boy chocolate powder from the cabinet and shows it to me in answer to my question, and I take it back, the thing about her calculated womanly gait, because she's about to make herself some chocolate milk after school. I sit at the kitchen table and watch as she pours the milk, measures out three spoonfuls of powder, and then stirs the mixture, the spoon tinkling gently against the sides of the glass. She returns the milk to the fridge, puts the box of chocolate powder back in the cupboard, and then hesitates for a moment before she takes a seat opposite me.

"So," I say. "How was school?"

She shrugs.

"Good."

"What did you have?"

"What do you mean?"

"What subjects did you have today?"

Another shrug.

"Norwegian, maths, English. The usual."

"Did you learn anything?"

Now she laughs. But not in the way that she laughs with Åsmund. More aloof – a laugh that's supposed to show me something.

"Mamma, seriously. You don't have to do this."

"Do what?"

"Pretend to be interested."

"I'm not pretending to be interested," I say, and think of the blocked Facebook profile and the young psychologist, *show interest in their online lives*. "You're my daughter, of course I care about what's going on in your life."

"Right," she says, rolling her eyes.

"It's important to me to know how you're doing," I say, a little too loudly.

She sighs deeply.

"Fine," she says. "But that isn't what I meant."

"What did you mean?"

"Just that you're not that interested in school and stuff. It's fine, Mamma, you don't have to be. It doesn't matter."

But I don't agree. *Show them that you're there for them online, just as you are every day in real life.*

"Am I not helping out with the school play?" I ask. "Do I not volunteer, come to parents' evenings? Don't I care about your grades?"

"Oh my God, Mamma," she says. "Name my four best friends, then."

"Saga," I start. "Thea. Carina?"

"*Carina*," Emma says condescendingly.

"Filippa?"

"Mamma," Emma says. "Filippa and I aren't actually friends."

I say:

"Have you fallen out?"

"We haven't fallen out," Emma says, hesitating a little. "We just don't get on that well. She's so conceited."

"Conceited?"

"Yeah. It's so pathetic, she thinks everybody loves her."

Emma looks at me with her clearest gaze. There's a strength in her I don't fully understand. Is she challenging me? I'm not sure why she would.

I try to imagine them at school, the two girls. Filippa, who is so beautiful, who has her mother's innate elegance. Next to her Emma is ordinary, I think – I've never thought about it in exactly this way before, but as the thought occurs to me, I realise that I've simply taken it as a given for several years already. The way I'm ordinary, when viewed next to Merete.

"Is there something going on between Simen Sparre and Filippa?" I ask.

For a hundredth of a second Emma's mouth hangs open. Then she closes it firmly, and says:

"Not that I know of."

But she's red in the face. There's something there.

"Poor girl," I say. "Just imagine, losing your father like that."

Emma says nothing. Only drinks her chocolate milk.

"And how are you doing, honey?" I say, reaching out a hand towards her and stroking her arm. "With everything that's going on here in the building?"

She looks at me.

"I'm the same as usual," she says. "I feel like it doesn't really have anything to do with me."

I nod. Withdraw my hand.

Later, as she sits in the living room with her eyes glued to her iPad, I think: What was it she said about what happened to Jørgen? I feel like it doesn't really have *anything to do with* me? Or did she put the emphasis somewhere else? I don't really feel like it has anything to do with *me*. As opposed to who? Filippa? Or was she talking about me? Surely she can't know, I think – no, she can't possibly know. Jørgen and I were careful. Not careful enough, perhaps – there was that time with the baby monitor, but she didn't see anything then, and it was just the once. She can't possibly know.

Still, there's something in the way she looks at me, this moral superiority. This calculated indifference to the murder of a neighbour – what am I to make of it?

"There's a whole load of journalists out there now," Åsmund says across the dinner table.

"Oh?" I say.

"I was stopped three times on the way in. It must be what happened to the cat."

"The kids," I say, nodding towards Lukas.

"And the police seem to have held a press conference. They've made a number of discoveries and they're interested in certain individuals in the neighbourhood, or something like that," he perseveres. "It's crazy."

He shakes his head in disbelief.

"You didn't talk to them, did you?" I ask.

"Well," he says.

"Åsmund!" I say.

"That one woman from the TV station was so young," he says, as if in his defence. "She said it was important for people to understand what it's like to live through something like this."

I think of the journalist with the fringe from a few days ago, the one who held the gate open for me and my bicycle. Didn't she say more or less the exact same thing to me?

"I didn't say anything bad," Åsmund says. "Just that we're in shock, and that we never would have believed something like this could happen here. That sort of thing."

"Right, okay. Fine," I say.

"Maybe this will be our fifteen minutes of fame?" he says, trying a smile – can we joke about this, or is it too soon?

Against my will, I do smile a little.

"Pappa," Emma says, her smile wider than mine. "I'm not sure that news reports about murders are really the best place for you."

Åsmund's grin widens, too, and I feel it like a punch to the gut. Maybe this will be our last evening as an intact family. A happy family, even. Not perfect, not without our issues. But an ordinary family. Good-natured teasing and conversations at the dinner table – isn't happiness found in the little things?

I have the words all prepared, in a way. I just have to come up with a way in, and then the rest will probably follow. Tonight, I'm going to do it – I can't delay it any longer. He'll find out regardless, that's what Ingvild said, and the longer it takes me to tell him, the worse it will be.

He's so rarely angry. I can't remember the last time I saw him direct his anger at me. I know that it's happened, of course; we've argued, like everyone else. But I'm not sure I've ever seen him truly furious. Can't imagine how he'll react to being told something like this.

"Pappa," Lukas says. "Are you going to be on TV?"

Rikke, Jamila writes, *is it true that you're the one who found the cat?* Three crying emojis follow her question, and then one with its head exploding. I sigh. While Åsmund puts Lukas to bed I sit in the living room, waiting, ready to tell him. Although it isn't entirely accurate to say that I sit, because before I know it, I'm pacing between the kitchen and living room, dreading it. There's a void from my throat all the way down to my chest and stomach, as if I have no body, as if I'm nothing but a vast, echoing chasm. If I sit still, I'll fall into it, and so I keep moving. Walk from the kitchen to the living room, picking up this and that, tidying things away here and there, before going back to the kitchen.

I don't have the energy to reply to her. I put down my phone, go back into the kitchen and wipe down the table again. Hear the creaking of our stairs. Hear his steps as he enters the living room. I take a deep breath. So now we're finally here. It's about to happen.

He's already turned on the TV when I come in.

"Hey," he says.

"Hey," I say.

My voice is almost nothing but air.

He says:

"I suppose I ought to see whether I do actually end up on the news. I've never been on TV before."

I say:

"Åsmund? Can I talk to you about something?"

"Sure," he says, turning to face me.

His round, cheerful face. But I have to watch out for sentimentality now. Mustn't start to think of him the way he was when we met, at the high school I started attending alone, knowing no-one, where I had no friends at all until the day he turned to me in science class and said: I want to be in your group. Kind Åsmund, popular Åsmund. Who saw someone on the fringes and pulled her into his circle. Because you were the prettiest girl in the class, he says to me whenever I mention this. So he wasn't exactly selfless, either. But I remember my intense relief at the fact that someone had spoken to me. And what Åsmund had shown the others in doing so – he had chosen me. Look at her, he seemed to say to them, haven't you noticed her? And then they looked at me, every last one of them. But I mustn't think of this now.

"I just wanted to say," I begin.

He looks at me, attentive. Then everything gets confused – I'm gearing myself up, ready to do it, when his gaze slides over towards the television.

"There's our house," he says.

The yellow wooden building is indeed emblazoned across the screen, as a background to the journalist with the fringe. *New developments in Tåsen murder*, states the text below the image. On TV, the house looks surprisingly small. Not quite as exclusive as it had appeared to me the first time I saw it – cosy without being overly flashy, yet still expensive and well maintained. On the screen it looks more like some miserable little dwelling at the foot of a cliff. Perhaps it's something to do with the camera's filter.

Then the image cuts to Åsmund. He, too, looks different on TV. Not smaller, exactly, but more serious. More self-important. Like a man I don't know giving a testimony that should be listened to. The journalist's questions have been cut, so it looks as if he's speaking on his own initiative.

"Well, it is disconcerting," says TV-Åsmund. "Of course it is. The children were frightened by what happened to the cat, and there's certainly something sinister about the whole thing."

The journalist's voice can be heard from somewhere off camera:

"And do you think the incident has any connection to the murder at the weekend?"

TV-Åsmund wrinkles his brow, as if thinking carefully. He looks older, I think, finding myself somewhat astonished, he looks like an adult. *Is* an adult. And not even a young adult, at that.

"Well," he says. "That's up to the police to determine, of course, but you can't help wondering. This is a very quiet, safe neighbourhood. We've lived here for a few years now, and nothing like this has ever happened before. And now two incidents, one after the other, in such a short space of time."

He looks worried. There's another cut then, to the police press conference. A woman in uniform is speaking. She speaks in a strong Nordvestland dialect, her consonants leaping and skipping out of her mouth. I've never seen her before, and from her title it seems she's far up the hierarchy, so perhaps she doesn't work out in the field. I see Gundersen to the left of the screen. He's wearing his uniform now and looks different from the way he did here this morning. More groomed. Almost attractive. He says nothing, but he plays close attention as the woman speaks.

"Crikey," Åsmund says. "My TV debut. What do you think, Rikke? Was it terrible?"

"No," I say. "No, no, it was good."

Police making neighbourhood enquiries, says the text at the bottom of the screen. This is all I have time to see before Åsmund switches off the television and turns to face me.

"There was something you wanted to say," he says.

"Yes."

I swallow. There's something odd about us, the way we're positioned. He's sitting, while I'm still standing in the middle of the room. I walk past him, take a seat on the sofa, but it feels wrong to sit down, too. I can't find anywhere to put my hands.

Now the moment is here. The TV is off, the kids are asleep. No interruptions. No excuses.

"There was something I wanted to tell you," I say.

"Yes?"

For a moment I think about when Emma used to do gymnastics; that time she hesitated for a moment in the middle of a routine, not entirely certain that she had control. Then she missed her footing and messed up the landing. The important thing is not to hesitate. Not to draw it out. To just do it, as if you're not afraid.

"Yes," I say. "You see . . ."

If you haven't already messed up the landing by hesitating, that is. I greedily grab this idea with both hands – yes, perhaps. Perhaps there's simply no hope of having this conversation now, since I've already hesitated. I want the conditions to be optimal.

"You see," I say, quickly and frantically, "I spoke to Emma today, about what happened, you know, tried to get a bit of insight into how she's doing. She was so, what's the word – so *indifferent* to the whole thing. It frightened me a little, to be honest. It's as if she doesn't care at all."

Åsmund nods slowly. I'm almost out of breath. I try to hide it. The room appears to be dancing around me. He looks at me, and there's something in his eyes now. Does he realise it now, I think, or is it just that I'm being too intense? My breathing is fast and shallow.

"You know what, Rikke?" he says. "I think it's best if we just leave Emma alone when it comes to all this. She'll react as she wants to. We have to let her do that."

There's something alien in his voice. He says the words so heavily and seriously, as if he's ordering me: leave her alone. I nod, not sure what to think.

"Right," I say, ready to agree to anything. "Okay. It just made me wonder, that's all."

He nods, too.

"Was that all it was?" he asks.

For a dizzying moment the opportunity hangs there – to say what I have to say after all, what I've decided to say, and know that I must. But then I bail – yes, I say, that was it, and Åsmund smiles and says good, and then he turns the TV back on, and I know I'll be furious at myself for this cowardice when I'm unable to sleep tonight.

We spend the rest of the evening like this, in front of the TV.

But is there something there after all? Does Åsmund look at me with curiosity every now and then, when he thinks I won't notice? On the floor above us, Merete is stomping around. Her presence towers over us, the empty study pulling me in, and we sit here and watch TV as if nothing has happened, my pulse pounding at my temples.

I devour Jørgen in huge gulps; he's mine, at least here and now, and I am ravenous. I want all of him, skin and hair. To taste him, to wolf him down into me. I run my fingers through his curls, my hands over his entire body, over the muscles of his thighs and upper arms, the smoothness of his lower back, the fine hollow at the back of his neck. Want to know everything about him – how did you get that scar on your leg, why is the nail of the little finger on your left hand cleft in two, does that mark on your earlobe mean that it was once pierced? – but I don't have the time to ask. I want to consume him. Am so greedy.

Afterwards we lie in the clean, white sheets, in the bed that fills most of the hotel room, and I turn towards him and think about how strange it is to know this intimate side of a neighbour, a person you're sort of predestined to share pleasantries with at the mailboxes. You're supposed to offer something of yourself, of course – tell a few anecdotes while weeding the same flower bed, or share dinner tips when pushing your shopping trolleys past each other in the Kiwi supermarket – but the relationship is so limited, you're neighbours, you're the father or mother of, you're those above or below. I pass a hand over Jørgen's stubborn curls and ask him what he's thinking about. He props himself up on his elbows.

"I'm thinking," he says, "that this trip to Bergen was an excellent idea."

What is rarely mentioned when these types of affairs are discussed is all the practical problems they entail. Time and space, with space being the most precarious, at least when you're neighbours. There was no dependable place where Jørgen and I could share a bed. We tried his car, and one night we sneaked into the co-working space where he rented a desk. A couple of evenings we set things up so that both Åsmund and Merete would be out at the same time, and then I went up to his place. It felt risky, even though our spouses weren't in the building, because in Kastanjesvingen the walls are paper-thin.

But meeting out somewhere was possible. We found an Italian restaurant in Enerhaugen, a place our partners would never think to go, and sat on either side of a table covered with a red-chequered tablecloth, getting to know one another. He had grown up in central Oslo, in a big apartment full of books, he said. When he was young, he messed around for a couple of years, bumming around Europe. He got drunk in Prague, was mugged in Bratislava and fell in love with an Italian backpacker he met in Athens. When his money ran out – and he meant ran out, to the point that he couldn't even afford breakfast the following day – he borrowed a few coins from his Italian girlfriend and called home to ask for more. An advance on his inheritance, he said hopefully. His mother said no, under no circumstances. He had to make his way home. The only thing she would consider paying for was a train ticket to Oslo, and even then she expected him to pay her back. So Jørgen stood at a coin-operated telephone in a back street in Athens – in the cradle of civilisation, he added with a smile – realising that his childhood was over. He borrowed the money, travelled home to Norway, and began studying the relevant subjects that would enable him to enrol at journalism college.

"Have you ever regretted it?" I asked, and he laughed and said:

"I generally regret very little."

I told him about growing up in the village on the edge of the forest. My little sister was the area's superstar, I said. She sang on TV and released albums, and her increasingly fairy-tale career demanded so much of our family – of my parents, but also of me. My job was to manage fine by myself and ask as little as possible of them. To take it with a smile when friends bought her CD and asked me if I could get it signed for them. To say *Good, thanks*, when teachers, coaches, neighbours asked me, with that idiotic smile they all wore, what it was like to be *Caroline's sister*. You'd think that it would have bothered me, I said to Jørgen, but I actually can't remember that it did. More that I sort of laughed at it, thought it was dumb. But I did choose to attend a high school on the other side of the municipality where nobody knew me, so maybe it did bother me a little after all.

"At least, I think it contributed to me falling for Åsmund," I said. "The fact that he was completely lacking in the adoration she evoked in others. When I

216

took him home to meet my family, it took him an hour and a half to ask her a single question."

Beyond this, I said little about Åsmund, told few stories about sex and love. I had no Italian backpackers to choose from. At the time, I almost felt embarrassed. Not that there's anything wrong with Åsmund. He might not be as well read as Jørgen, he doesn't write for a newspaper and has no opinions about Afghanistan, but he's a good guy. Many would say that I'm lucky. But the only thing was that the ordinary in him rubbed off on me, making me grey as a result. Had I had a few wild years in my twenties, in which I fell in love with musicians and actors and my professors, and had I slept around during those years and wandered home carefree in the early mornings, then Åsmund would have been an entirely understandable choice. Maybe I would have woken up one morning when I was around thirty and felt that I was *done with all that*, as people say, and more than that, felt a desire to *settle down*, to have *someone to share everything with*. And if I had then met Åsmund, at a party held by mutual friends, perhaps, and thought that yes, isn't this what I've been missing, isn't this friend from my youth exactly what I need? And then subsequently settled down, got married, had a couple of kids and bought an apartment in Kastanjesvingen – then Åsmund would have completed the picture, in a way. But to have chosen him so early, so young, and then to have stood by that choice? What did that say about me?

So instead, I talked about work. Told Jørgen about the ideas from my PhD thesis, about using behavioural economics, the intersection between economics and psychology, to study climate behaviour. About the findings from the survey, the experiments we were now planning.

"I'm interested in how self-contradictory we become when we talk about climate change," I said. "How in supermarkets and restaurants we ask whether the fruit is organic, but never question how environmentally friendly a mango really is when it turns up in Norway in January. It's called *cognitive dissonance*, this feeling of discomfort when there's a disparity between who we believe we are and what we do. It's uncomfortable for us, because of course we like to see ourselves as consistent – not to mention rational and moral. And so we attempt to remedy this dissonance, preferably by glossing over the situation, so that we don't have to change. It's fascinating how a little rewriting of the facts enables us to maintain that contradictory statements are simultaneously true."

"And is there any dissonance in your life?" Jørgen asked above the red-chequered tablecloth.

I smiled at him, and he added:

"I'm guessing there isn't. You seem to have most things in order."

"Well," I said. "I have gone and found myself a lover."

As soon I said this, I regretted it. The word seemed so huge, so melodramatic. Maybe it was stupid to put a name to it. It was almost four weeks since that evening in January, and the relationship was still new, untouched, and we'd never spoken about it this way. But Jørgen tilted his head, and said:

"A lover. Isn't that a good thing?"

"I don't know," I said, picking at the candlestick that stood in the middle of the table, removing wax from its edge with my fingernails. "Some people would probably call it immoral."

Jørgen smiled, showing the gap between his teeth.

"But not you?"

"No," I said, but I hesitated a little.

"You know," he said, "I've always thought there's something nice about the word. One who loves. That's something I'd like to be."

Later that evening, he told me about a trip to Bergen he would be taking the following week. He reached his hand across the red-chequered tablecloth and said, as if as a joke: Didn't you say you were going to Bergen for work that week yourself?

Well. There was, in fact, a research group at the university there that I'd been meaning to speak to. I could always contact them, I said, and try to set up a meeting.

On the airport bus into the city I'm like a kid at Christmas. I drum my hand against the seat and check my phone every few minutes, grinning so widely and unprovoked that I have to hide it from my fellow passengers, to turn to face the window and beam out of it instead, out into the unusually intense March sun, out at all these hills and fjords and bridges, the houses that cling to the mountainside. I smile right up until the bus crosses the Puddefjord and I'm actually there, almost at my destination, where he's waiting for me. I hurry along Strandkaien to the hotel in

C. Sundts gate. The young man at the check-in desk consults his computer and says that yes, the other member of my party has already arrived. I'm given a key card and wait for the lift, it can't come quickly enough, I think, I'm practically hopping from foot to foot. And when I let myself in, he's standing there, in the middle of the room, tall and beaming. Come in, he says, I've been waiting for you, and I fall into his arms.

Later, we go out to eat. Jørgen has booked a table at a restaurant on Bryggen. It's right in the city centre, not hidden away in an area where people like us seldom go, the way the restaurants we choose usually are. We hold each other's hands across the table. To everyone who sees us, we look like a couple in love. Those sitting around us probably assume that we're married. Maybe they think we're taking a weekend for ourselves, away from the kids, or perhaps they deduce that we don't have children, that we're the kind of people who would rather travel, write, research, eat breakfast in cafés and drink Amarone until three o'clock in the morning on a Thursday night, rather than change nappies and get involved with the school play.

On our way back to the hotel we walk hand in hand. We're slightly tipsy, talking over each other. On Vågsallmenningen a mariachi band is playing, and one of its members shouts something to us in broken English. At first, we don't understand him, and Jørgen stops and laughs – What did you say? The man tries in an Eastern European language, and then in English

again, *in the love*, he says, *you are . . . in the love!* Jørgen and I laugh, the man laughs, and then Jørgen
begins to ask them what they can play, no, not the old
traditional songs, "La Paloma" and "Lambada" and all
that stuff, what else? Can you play anything by the
Clash? No? The Rolling Stones? *Stones*, says the man,
yes, yes, pleased to meet you. Yes, yes, cries Jørgen,
and then all three of us laugh again, and then the band
begins to play "Sympathy for the Devil" on the accor-
dion and trumpet, the whole shebang. Jørgen takes my
hands and swings me around. We have to dance,
Rikke, he says, come on, it would be rude not to, and I
laugh so hard I can hardly stay on my feet.

And it's so easy. That's almost the worst thing about
it – that there is so little mental anguish involved. I
arrive back in Oslo one day before Jørgen so as not to
arouse suspicion, and I'm in a good mood. I've bought
sweets for the kids at the airport. When Åsmund asks
me whether it was a useful meeting I tell him the
truth – that they were pleasant and willing to collab-
orate, but that we'll have to see what happens, this
kind of thing is always so uncertain. And when he
asks me how the trip was otherwise, I say that the
research group took me out to eat at a restaurant on
Bryggen, and oh, something funny happened on the
way back to the hotel, we passed a mariachi band,
and the head of the group in Bergen made them play
"Sympathy for the Devil" by the Rolling Stones.
Åsmund laughs heartily at this, and I think, wow –
who would have thought that it would be so easy?
Whenever I've daydreamed about this kind of relationship in the past, in my more sober moments I've always

imagined that the guilt would gnaw away at me until I'd be forced to confess, so as not to go mad. But the truth is that it costs me nothing to tell Åsmund these stories. They slip from my tongue as if they are phrases I use daily, and I feel no guilt when I lie down beside him in our double bed that night.

"You smell different," he says, setting his head against my shoulder.

"Hotel soap," I say, kissing him on the forehead.

And it isn't in the least bit difficult. It's almost disappointing that it doesn't cost me more.

WEDNESDAY NIGHT

The house is no longer so quiet at night. I can hear Merete upstairs. She obviously can't sleep, either. I've hardly tried, in fact I've lost faith that it's even possible, all I ever do is lie there tossing and turning in bed. Åsmund starts snoring just minutes after his head hits the pillow, and I feel a sharp envy, as if there's only a finite amount of sleep between us and he's greedily helping himself, leaving nothing for me. I give up when the clock says one-thirty, because what's the point?

The only light I turn on in the living room is the lamp on the nesting tables beside the sofa. It provides a small, warm circle of light in the dark room. I check the security chain on the door just as anxiously as I do every night, but it's in place, apparently untouched. Then I open my laptop and log into my emails. Read what I wrote to Ingvild Fredly.

Merete not waving to me – I wrote about that. The day before we moved in, when I had stood there watching her and Jørgen out on the patio with their friends. It's true that it happened. But it's also a somewhat distorted depiction. Further down, I've described their apartment. I write about how nice it is, but between the lines hint that it's cold and impersonal. *As if all the humanness had been removed*, I write. Merete's home. Merete's fingerprints all over it. Then I write about when I went to see Jørgen up there for the first time, the evening she was away. *It seemed different when she wasn't home*, I write. *Less like something from a magazine, more his*. Otherwise, I don't say much about her, not until the end, where I write about their marriage, what it was really like. But I'm already insinuating something here. The ice-cold wife, so concerned with their facade. Sceptical towards me from the moment we met. No wonder I had no scruples about getting involved with him – that's what can be read from this. No wonder he came running to me.

What I don't mention is that for a while after the dinner at their apartment, Merete and I tried to be friends. I would sometimes go up there after the kids were in bed, on nights Jørgen was out; we spent a couple of summer evenings sitting out on the patio, drinking wine. She told me about her childhood. She was the middle of three sisters, she said, and grew up in a large apartment in Frogner. Her father was high up in the Ministry of Foreign Affairs, her mother was an opera singer. They lived in Paris for a year when she was a child, she and her sisters were fluent in both English and French and there was always music and theatre and diplomacy around the kitchen table. We were so fucking cultured, Merete said to me and laughed, but then, she was a little drunk – she hardly ever said *fuck* otherwise. She told me that she loved music, she'd played the family piano from a young age. The family's piano, I laughed, and she said yes, didn't I tell you, so damn cultured. She was a competent pianist. Better than her big sister, who had more of a sense for diplomacy than Merete. Better than her little sister, who sang more beautifully. I got the impression that there was a certain amount of competition between the sisters. Merete said that her parents expected their girls to be the best at whatever they did. She was good at playing piano, so they simply took it for granted that she would play piano at national level and preferably become world class. That's how they are, she said to me. She's never doubted that they love her. They're just unable to understand how easy it is to disappoint them when their expectations are so high.

I told her about my sister. Caroline Prytz, I said, you've probably heard of her? She won that talent contest on TV, you know, the one where she was the only child. She was already a celebrity in the tiny village where we grew up, sang the solo in the church choir when she was eight, sang the finale at the school's Christmas concert when she was nine, and then suddenly she was famous across the country. She recorded an album, and then there were concerts, a Christmas record, TV interviews, tours. Then a minor breakdown, as is only proper – all the pressure, everybody wanting a piece of her. Then a psychologist, and straight back into the studio to record yet another album. My parents were extremely careful not to treat us differently. When they praised Caroline, they always added: But Rikke does so well at school. So very, *very* well at school. So then what do you do? I smiled lopsidedly at Merete – I was probably a little drunk, too. Of course, I said, you become the best at school. I got straight As, defended my doctoral thesis before I was thirty and had a permanent research position before I turned thirty-five. Merete said: Maybe that's the better way to be. I was a child prodigy, and just look at me now. I looked at her. Yes, she was most definitely drunk, otherwise she would never have insinuated that all she had – the house, the husband, the daughter – wasn't enough for her.

Then we stopped meeting up. I don't know why. Maybe it was the same as it was for our daughters, we quite simply didn't get along all that well. Maybe she reminded me too much of my sister; perhaps I was too reminiscent of one of hers. Had anyone asked me, I would have said that our everyday lives got in the way. It wasn't that anything happened. It wasn't as if either of us withdrew. Or at least, I don't think so. Our encounters just slipped away with the sands of time, as such things do. It happened long before I started seeing her husband.

Now she crosses the floor up there. Her footsteps seem more listless than usual. Poor Merete. She's no ice queen – I'm well aware of that. Maybe it suited me to think of her that way. Not to mention to describe her that way to Ingvild Fredly.

I go into the kitchen. I have a night-time tea somewhere in the cupboard, which allegedly will make me more sleepy. The damn doctor wouldn't give me a chemical solution to the problem, so I have no choice but to resort to herbs from the supermarket. Suddenly, it occurs to me that Merete is in her kitchen, too. Maybe she's standing directly above me right now. We're the only people awake in the house.

FIRST THURSDAY

The door to Jørgen's study is closed, but I know what's in there. I look around. There's something here. Something in the air. I don't want to go over to the door, but I do it anyway, my feet acting of their own accord, steering me towards it. I press down the handle, push the door open. He isn't there. All there is to see is a pool of blood across the desk. On the windowsill, beside a pot containing a king begonia, sits a cat, licking its paws. It lifts its head, stares at me with its button eyes.

There's a hammering at the door, and I jump up into a sitting position. I'm lying on the sofa. I can't even remember having sat down here, but I must have done, probably just after the others left this morning. I have no idea what time it is, or how long I've been asleep. It's light outside, I see, and the hammering continues as if it's the work of someone possessed, and then I hear Jamila shout: Rikke, are you there?

I stagger towards the door on unsteady feet. The dream refuses to release its grasp on my body, I'm still half in it. The staring cat. Shuddering, I open the door, and there she stands in a cloud of perfume, with glossy lips, freshly washed hair, a sympathetic expression on her face. She throws her arms around my neck and says:

"Oh Rikke, honey, how *are* you?"

There is strength in her thin arms. She pulls me to her so hard that I'm almost winded, rocks me from side to side so energetically that I have to fight to maintain my footing. When she finally lets me go and looks at me, she exclaims:

"My God, you look terrible."

We sit in the kitchen. Jamila makes coffee for us, while I explain how I can't sleep, and she takes care of everything, finds the cafetière, locates the can of coffee among all the mess in our cabinets, and puts on the kettle. She speaks continuously, not even pausing for breath. She was here yesterday, she says, several times, but she couldn't get hold of me, and didn't I see that she had sent me a text?

She's heard about what happened. A police officer came to their door yesterday, his name was Gundersen, apparently, and Gundersen had asked what they had seen and heard, which was easy to answer, since neither she nor Saman had seen or heard anything at all, Jamila says. After all, we were asleep. Not that it's been all that easy to sleep lately. She's been up a lot at night, too – not last night, though, because she managed to get to sleep, and so did Saman, and so they hadn't heard anything, and that's what they told the police. The police officer who was with Gundersen told them that a dead cat had been found, and that I was the one who found it – the neighbour downstairs, he had said, but Jamila had known straight away that it must be me. She turns to me, her eyes widening.

"And then I thought, poor Rikke, she must be feeling awful right now."

I nod. I'm still half asleep, unable to take her entirely seriously. Do I feel awful? I don't know. I just want to sleep.

The coffee needs some time to brew. Jamila sets the pot on the table with a clatter, the cups jingling beside it. They're standing almost exactly where Gundersen set the coil of rope this morning, and I shudder, I don't want to touch anything that's been in contact with it. What does she want from me?

Jamila says:

"Surely there can't be any doubt that there's a connection here. Between the dead cat and what happened to Jørgen?"

I swallow. My throat is thick and sluggish. What time is it, I wonder, but Jamila is sitting in such a way that I can't see the clock on the oven's display behind her.

Two such brutal incidents on the same property, she says, and not even a week between them. Of course, the incidents are entirely different, because the cat murder, no matter how gruesome it might be, doesn't come close to the murder of a human being – of course that should go without saying – but then again these types of incidents happen extremely rarely. And there's something disturbing about it, there's a warning in the cat killings, about what exists within people. She pushes down the plunger of the cafetière as she adds: I'm actually quite shocked.

I'm about to protest: they're not *that* rare, I want to say – after all, dead cats were being found long before anything happened to Jørgen. But then I don't bother. I'm drained of all energy when it comes to this subject. So I simply nod. The coffee does me good; my throat opens.

"But anyway," Jamila says. "I've been doing a bit of searching online, and I found some stuff Jørgen wrote."

She takes some printouts from the leather handbag she's hung on the back of her chair, spreading them out over the kitchen table so that they almost cover the tabletop. They mainly appear to be newspaper articles. In several of them, I see Jørgen's byline photograph beaming at me, that broad smile with the crooked front tooth, and I can hardly bear to look at him, have to turn away.

"Now where is it," Jamila says, searching among the sheets of paper. "Yes – look at this!"

She snatches one of them up and reads.

"*Oslo-based cleaning company gives foreign workers slave contracts.*

That's the headline, it's a piece about Baltic workers in the cleaning industry being forced to work under conditions that are in total violation of the Working Environment Act. Let's see here. Yes. *'Krzysztof' explains that the workers live together in an empty apartment block in Grønland. 'At most, there's been forty of us here,' Krzysztof says. He requested that we not use his real name due to fear of reprisals.'*

She looks at me over the sheet of paper.

"Fear of reprisals," she says again with emphasis, and continues.

"The industry is lucrative and poorly regulated. So few supervisory inspections are performed to ensure the workers receive proper treatment that, in reality, this almost constitutes an exemption for breaches of the law. 'Krzysztof' and the other workers are left with just a hundred kroner a day after the deduction of their living expenses, and that's only on the days they are offered work. But to complain would be futile. The contracts are signed in their homeland, their boss retains their passports, and the workers are clearly afraid of what they and their families may be subjected to should they try to demand more. 'Krzysztof' makes it clear that he is taking a significant risk by speaking to us."

Jamila puts down the piece of paper. I nod. I've seen the article before. I remember the young female journalist Jørgen wrote it with – what was her name again? The one that was so blonde and pretty.

"These people are afraid, Rikke," Jamila says. "In several places here it says that they're scared of what the men behind these schemes will do. I've underlined them all, look."

She pushes the sheets of paper across the table to me. I see hectic blue lines and circles scattered throughout the text, exclamation and question marks in the margin, a few sections marked with a highlighter. My gaze travels towards the byline. Rebekka Davidsen. Just as blonde, just as pretty, smiling just as self-confidently.

"Jørgen writes articles about crimes committed by dangerous

people," Jamila says. "And then he's found murdered in his own home. That is, he becomes the victim of a crime himself – committed by a dangerous person."

"Yes," I say. "But the police seem to think someone who lives here in the building did it."

"Here in the building?" Jamila says, frowning. "No, I don't think so."

I quickly think back to what Ingvild told me in the café. Did she tell me that in confidence? Was it something I could share? I don't remember, I'm in such a daze.

"I just think – all this with the front door," I say. "Nina showed us the lists. And it doesn't look as if anyone broke in, although of course it could have been someone he let in himself."

Jamila thinks about this. Her defined, neatly plucked eyebrows seem like two graceful worms making their way towards each other. I look at her, take a sip of my coffee. Why is she really here? What's the point of this investigation of hers? Is it not a little over-enthusiastic?

"Yes," she says. "I'm sure that's more likely. Because who here in the building would be capable of something like this?"

We look at each other, and the silence – albeit a brief one – is uncomfortable, as if we've only just thought to suspect each other. I take another sip, hiding my face behind my cup so that she won't see the scepticism in my expression. Wouldn't that be the best way to hide, in fact, if you yourself were involved? To play the morally irre-proachable detective, even gathering evidence against others? And isn't she almost too keen to direct any suspicion away from Kastanjesvingen? I smile as best I can. Feel hot in the cheeks. But Jamila is unmoved, her thoughts already running ahead. Her brows straighten out again, taking on their usual positions in her face, and then she looks so young again, so innocent.

"There's one more thing, Rikke," she says, her voice serious. "I've gone back and forth over whether or not I should tell you this, because, you know, I don't want to speak ill of the dead. But I think it might be necessary. If it helps us get to the bottom of this, then so be it. That's the most important thing in the long run, don't you think? That they catch the guy? But the thing is . . . I think . . ."

She looks around, as if to make sure we're alone.

"I think he was having an affair."

Something rises from my stomach, moving up into my chest. I take a breath. Try to act normal. I'm acutely aware of how intensely she's studying me. Jamila wants a reaction, I can see that – she wants shock and disbelief, but I've completely lost my grip on myself and I'm unable to perform.

"My goodness," is all I say.

"I know," she says. "I heard something several times, when Merete was away. High-heeled shoes and female laughter, and then the sound of . . . well, you know. It's unmistakable."

This hits me right in the chest, rips me open. I can't remember what I was wearing on the times I went up there, but one thing I do know for sure: I've never gone up to see him in high-heeled shoes.

"There's a kind of fault in the wall between our kitchen and theirs," she says, unmoved by the fact that I'm starting to gasp for breath. "In the cabinet where the boiler is. If we open the cupboard door, we can hear what they're saying. Of course, this isn't something I make a habit of, it isn't nice to spy on people, but one time, when I heard a woman in there, I thought I ought to check, you know? So I opened the cupboard door and listened. And he was speaking to a woman with a sort of husky, sexy laugh – you know the kind I mean? A bit like Janis Joplin. They were talking about someone they both knew, and then she said: But I haven't come here to talk about work. And then I heard Jørgen say: Okay – so what did you come here for? And then they laughed. And then a few moments later I heard them getting down to it. And it *definitely* wasn't Merete's voice, let's just put it that way. Besides, it was during the Easter holiday. Merete and Filippa had gone to the mountains with Merete's parents, so I *knew* they weren't there."

This stings like salt in the open wound: Jørgen had asked whether I'd be around during Easter; he'd have a few days alone. But sadly I was going away.

Jamila says:

"So you can understand why I don't like him. He can be as compassionate as he likes in all this –" she throws out her hands, gesturing at the articles that lie spread across the table – "but if he's cheating on his wife, he's a creep in my book. Infidelity – that's a betrayal."

I look down into my coffee cup in an attempt to dull the blow. He and I never spoke about whether we were also seeing other people. It never occurred to me to ask him about it, quite simply because I couldn't believe that I wasn't enough for him. Easter fell right after our first trip to Bergen. I'd had such an incredible time with him. Had believed he felt the same.

"Maybe they were having problems," I say, my voice weak. "He and Merete."

"Problems," Jamila splutters. "Everybody has problems. Don't Saman and I have problems? Don't you and Åsmund? But solving your problems by running into the arms of someone else? No. If you've promised to stand by someone, you've promised. You solve your problems there."

She slams her hand against the tabletop, making the coffee cups jump.

"And not by going to bed with somebody else. I mean, if it's no longer possible to make the marriage work, I can understand that, of course. But you have to end it first. You don't just hop into bed with somebody else while you're still married. You still have to show your partner a little respect."

I have nothing to say. But Jamila doesn't exactly seem to be waiting for me to chip in, anyway.

"I made it crystal clear to Saman," she says, "from day one. Be dissatisfied with me, argue with me, shout at me, but don't ever go behind my back, I told him. That's the least you can expect from a partner."

I take a breath, inhaling deep, deep down into my lungs. She looks at me, and then her face changes. Her furious expression evaporates, and she places a small, cold hand over mine. Squeezes until it hurts.

"Oh Rikke, I'm sorry – I'm getting carried away," she says. "You had a shock yesterday, you poor thing. I didn't mean to turn up with all this now – I just wanted to tell you. But we can talk more later."

Her hands gather up the sheets of paper. She sweeps them into a pile and stuffs the entire bundle back into her handbag as she gets up.

"But what I think is important about this," she says, "I mean, about the woman who was in there with him. Or *women* . . .'

The wound in my chest burns again, enough to almost make me collapse. Visits from women in high heels. And then I think: This Rebekka Davidsen. Does she have a husky, sexy laugh?

"It means there's a motive there," Jamila says. "Right? Infidelity leads to a whole load of possible whys and wherefores. It gives Merete a motive, too – that's obvious. But she was deep in the forest when Jørgen was murdered, with no car. And then there's Nina's lists, which show that she never let herself in. But what about the other women? Who are they? Was one of them jealous, or did they grow to hate him because he refused to leave Merete? Or maybe one of them is married – and in that case, what did her husband think of Jørgen? You see?"

I nod, speechless. I feel like a wax dummy, can't wait to get her out of the house. Her eyes narrow, as if she's weighing things up, pondering the consequences of what she's just said. Jamila isn't stupid, I think. She might have heard us. Not me, not my voice – or at least I don't think so, because then she would never have come to me like this. But she might have heard something else. The crackling of my baby monitor, or something else, perhaps — what do I know? Something she hasn't yet understood the significance of . . . but it might suddenly dawn on her.

Then she smiles at me.

"Anyway, I just wanted to tell you," she says, hugging me. "But we can speak more tomorrow. And try to get some rest, sweetie — you really do look exhausted."

I hear the clicking of her boot heels echo throughout the stairwell and up onto the first floor.

Just how hypocritical is it possible to be, I think. The T-banen rattles past Ullevål Stadium, slowing as it approaches the station. On the platform, school students stand in small clusters – they probably have a free period, so they're heading into the city to hang out there. They're noisy as they board the train, chattering intensely in high, piercing voices, their laughter cutting the air to shreds. I'm seasick with fatigue. Just sitting upright and maintaining my balance is an effort. How very appropriate, I think – the cheat has become the cheated. And how ironic: when it comes down to it, I'm unable to simply shrug and accept that it was just a brief, meaningless fling, as I hope my husband will when I finally tell him. Nothing in me is ready to say: Well, you're the one who went to bed with a married man, what did you expect? Yes – I'm a hypocrite. There's an ache in my chest, and I turn my face away from the prattling students, unable to bear their enthusiasm.

It isn't as if I loved Jørgen. It wasn't that I wanted us to be together. The possibility of us both leaving our spouses and starting a new life together was never mentioned. And to be honest, had he suggested it, I would have said no. I'm almost certain of that. I've never wanted to leave Åsmund. That wasn't what it was about.

In March, Jørgen spent a week in Afghanistan researching his book, and when he came home, he had a gift for me: a pale blue pashmina scarf with a pink embroidered border, finely woven and of the very best quality, he assured me. He had bought it in a store that belonged to the father of one of his sources, someone he had known for years. I was ridiculously happy to receive it and had worn it all spring. Even indoors, especially at work, where I would throw it around my shoulders instead of a sweater. I might sit in my office, reading an article on my computer, and set the soft fabric to my cheek. Imagined how he had walked around the store searching for just the right gift for me, and then caught sight of it, thinking: This will be perfect for Rikke. Perhaps he even imagined it around my naked neck. Sometimes I would put my nose to it, try to smell him over my own perfume. And so I have to ask myself, as the T-banen pulls into Majorstuen station, stopping alongside the platform and opening the doors to let the irritating, babbling schoolkids pour out like marbles from a bag: Is this something I often do with gifts? Had I been given a pashmina scarf by a friend, or my sister, or by Åsmund, would I have imagined how it was bought? Would I have conjured up an image of Åsmund rummaging around in a store to find me something? Would I have sniffed it, in an attempt to catch the scent of him?

Around that time, excitement would shiver through me whenever my telephone beeped – because maybe it was Jørgen. If I heard his footsteps on the stairs, I would find some excuse to go out just then – to collect the newspaper, check the mail, take out the rubbish – just so that I could see him, perhaps exchange a few words with him. Early in the summer there had been the end-of-term celebration at the girls' primary school, and all afternoon in the schoolyard I had felt his presence physically. For every moment of those few hours I knew exactly where he was; made sure I could see him out of the corner of my eye throughout the gathering's entire duration. I acted, to put it simply, the way people in love do.

But apparently it wasn't like that for Jørgen. To him, I was just one among many. A colleague here, a neighbour there. Oh yes – Jørgen appears to have been doing very well for himself. Family life and bachelorhood in one, without having to choose.

But this is also unfair. I know very well that it wasn't that simple.

There was a darkness in Jørgen, a space nobody was permitted to access. When he told me about Sarajevo, I was offered a peek inside. Other times, I could only glimpse the contours of it. There were things within Jørgen that he struggled with. But I don't want to see these nuances now, don't want to try to understand. I exit the T-banen with hard steps, marching up into the daylight, hurrying down the street. Fuck you, Jørgen Tangen. *One who loves*, he said to me early in our relationship at the Italian restaurant, *that's something I'd like to be*. But it was just lies, I see that now. Nowhere in who he was, the way he acted, do I see intentions of loving – not me, nor anyone else, either. And what hurts the most is that it's all so laughably simple: I thought we'd found each other through an irresistible and almost fatal attraction. But all of that was just what I projected on to us. He offered nothing but hollow compliments and flattery designed to get women into bed, and this realisation twists within me. It makes the whole thing seem so cheap.

"You're in luck," says the cheery young man with the Stavanger dialect from behind the reception desk. "She's in her office. Just a moment, I'll give her a call."

I smile weakly. Glance around as I wait. I don't know what I expected from the reception of a newspaper's offices – glass surfaces and cutting-edge design, perhaps, or dusty open-plan spaces with people running back and forth between the desks and discussing things, the way I've seen them do in films. This reception is anonymous. It could just as easily be a dentist's waiting room.

"Yes, there's someone here to see you," the receptionist says into the phone. "Somebody who'd like to talk about Jørgen Tangen. Let's see – Rikke Prytz. Yes, okay."

He hands me a small sticker with my name and a code on it.

"She'll be down in just a minute," he says, and I nod.

In a glass cabinet on the wall stands a small bronze sculpture of a dog balancing a ball on its nose. I lean forward to look at it. It's exceptionally ugly, and I wonder what made someone want to display it here. Maybe it symbolises something. Perhaps the dog is a guard dog, and the ball the world.

I have no plan for this meeting, I simply came here on impulse. Just wanted to see Rebekka Davidsen, to talk to her, form an impression. I gave Jørgen's name to the receptionist thinking there was a greater chance she would see me if she was aware that I knew him, but I have no idea what to ask her, what I want her to tell me. And she's a journalist. What if she wants to ask *me* something? What do I have to say to her?

There's a ding from the lift, and then she walks out.

"Hi," she says, smiling, holding out her hand, and when I give her mine, limp and heavy and listless, she squeezes it hard.

She says her name. I say mine.

"Let's go take a seat in the cafeteria," she says, beckoning for me to follow.

She walks with quick steps; her figure is small and neat. She's curled her blonde hair the way they do on TV – it looks radiant in her byline photograph, but as I walk after her now, I can see how stiff it is, just how much she's sprayed on it to force the style to stick. She's wearing jeans and a blazer, relaxed but simultaneously fashion conscious, and she's thinner than me. Younger, too.

We stop at a coffee machine. Rebekka takes two cups, asks me whether I'd like anything in mine, and makes small talk as the coffee pours, yes, the building is starting to look a little tired, but management have opposed extensive renovations, especially now, you know, restructuring within the industry and a decrease in the number of people buying paper newspapers with everything now online, and so on. Uncertain times, but what can you do? Let the building fall into disrepair?

Yes, she's cute, I think as she speaks, feeling a stab to my chest. Pretty, even. She knows it herself, and leans on it a little too heavily, but she's clearly attractive, no question about it. This colleague from Easter, the one with the sexy laugh – is it her? Rebekka is wearing flat shoes, but she's short, so maybe she compensates with high heels when she wants to look her best. She hands me a cup, and we sit down at a table.

"So," Rebekka says.

"So," I say.

"Jørgen Tangen."

"Yes."

Something guarded crosses her face, then disappears again. She sighs deeply.

244

"It's so fucking sad, what happened," she says. "I just can't believe it. It's as if I'm still waiting for him to come wandering into the office at any moment."

She looks over at the door we came through, as if that's where she expects him to enter. I turn towards it, too.

"We were supposed to have a meeting today," she says, almost to herself. "At one o'clock."

I glance at my watch. Not that it matters.

"Who are you?" she asks. "I mean, who are you to him?"

"I'm his neighbour," I say mechanically. "We live in the apartment below him."

"Oh," says Rebekka, her eyes lighting up a little. "Were you there when – you know, when it happened?"

"Yes."

She tilts her head a little, and for a moment I think she's about to question me, the way the journalist Åsmund spoke to did: *How does it feel to live right next door to a crime scene?* But she only says that it must have been awful.

"Yes, it is," I say. "And so I just wanted, I mean, I saw that you'd written articles with him, and then I was just passing by, and so I thought . . ."

I swallow. Rebekka looks at me, she's listening: yes, what did I think?

"I thought," I say, "I'd like to hear how things were between you. I mean, did you know him well?"

I can't decide whether her voice suggests a laugh like Janis Joplin's. *I haven't come here to talk about work.* Has Rebekka been in our building? Been let in the front door to hurry up the stairs in her high heels, been welcomed by him?

She hesitates.

"Well enough, I suppose. Not especially well outside of work, but we did often work together. He took me under his wing when I was new, taught me the tricks of the trade. Who you should work with, who you should steer well clear of, you know? We worked on the slave contract story that was published in March, it caused quite a bit of debate. I was on the news to talk about it – maybe you saw it?"

I didn't, but I nod anyway, hoping Rebekka won't ask me what I thought of what she said.

"Got the SKUP award for journalism, too," she says, and a small, self-satisfied smile plays at the corners of her mouth.

"Congratulations," I say mechanically, and she catches herself, looks a little embarrassed.

On the hand that holds her coffee cup I see a wedding ring.

"So, yes, I'd say I knew him well in a work context. I liked him. Smart guy, very knowledgeable. Although maybe a little, well, how should I put it?"

She looks at me, seeming to weigh her words.

"Keen on the ladies, if you know what I mean?"

This pierces my chest, a thousand knives.

"Yes," I say.

"He tried it on with me once," she says, turning her wedding ring between two fingers. "Nothing creepy though, nothing metoo-worthy or anything like that. It was all a bit too obvious, the kind of thing that makes you think, Christ, does anyone honestly fall for that? It was more comical than anything else."

I smile stiffly.

"But it was fine," Rebekka says. "I said no and that was that, he took it well. And he was great to work with. Did his fair share, but without sticking his elbows out too far. You know, this industry can be funny like that."

Here she laughs. It seems she's being self-deprecating, or that she's trying to show me she isn't afraid, that she can laugh things off. I know nothing about what it's like to work in journalism, and I haven't exactly asked her, either. There's something forced about that laughter. Perhaps something about her friendliness, too. Maybe she's secretly irritated at me, for coming here and wasting her time.

"That article the two of you wrote," I say. "About the slave contracts. Was there anyone who, I don't know, got angry with you for it? You know, threatening? Anything like that?"

I hear myself say this, as if I'm sitting at the next table and watching. These are Jamila's words, not mine, because I don't have any confidence in this theory. I'm just recycling Jamila's points to have something to say. But the effect it has on Rebekka Davidsen is immediate – you'd think I'd just pulled out a gun. Her eyes widen, and she leans back a little in her chair, her face now frozen.

"Why do you ask?" she says.

I don't know. More than anything else, I'm asking to justify my visit, so I say:

"The police were wondering. And of course, you have to ask. Was there anyone who might have had something against Jørgen?"

A few seconds pass. Rebekka's eyes flit hectically about the room. I sit there, numb. Ever since Ingvild Fredly told me about the unsuccessful attempt to make it look like a break-in – the ladder under Jørgen's open window, which hadn't been used – I've thought that he must have been killed by someone he knew. Someone he himself let in. Possibly a neighbour. And while he was prepared to take a significant risk for an important interview, surely not even Jørgen would let in the head of a semi-criminal organisation he had exposed in an article, should such a person come knocking.

But Rebekka is afraid. She looks down at her hands, which lie flat against the tabletop. Her fingers are short and stubby, I think. Not long and slender like Merete's, but probably strong. Working hands. She's bitten her nails down to the quick.

"I've become a little jumpy," she says with a sigh. "That's just how things have ended up after that story. There are significant financial interests involved, y'know? If it only costs you a few measly thousand kroner to keep these workers in the country, and you can hire out the workforce for a return of up to eighty per cent in pure profit, almost risk-free, you're bound to be a bit miffed if a couple of journalists come along and expose your business idea. These people have rigged up an entire enterprise on this premise – that the authorities simply don't care about breaches of the legislation governing their industry. There's a lot of money to lose. Not to mention that they now might end up prosecuted for it – to make an example out of them, if nothing else."

She moistens her lips with her tongue. Leans forward, as if she's in work mode now. I imagine her presenting these arguments to her bosses, or on the evening news. But there's still a faint quiver in her voice.

"We're working on a new story," she says. "That's what we were supposed to have a meeting about today. It's similar to the last one, but about the temping industry this time. There's a whole load of slave contracts there, too. In addition to money laundering and corruption. We've come pretty far already. I'm following the corruption lead, while Jørgen is following the contracts. Was following."

A shudder runs through the both of us.

"Okay," I say. "That was actually all I wanted to ask."

She puts on a smile. This seems to be something she does often – a winning smile that she pulls out on such occasions, but it's a little ragged around the edges.

"I hope you're all doing okay, you and the rest of the neighbours," she says. "Jesus, it's just awful, the whole thing. I did think that maybe we ought to send someone up there, do a story on it, but, you know . . ."

She smiles uncomfortably. It's clear that nothing could be less appealing to her. We get up, and I follow her across to a sink, where we leave our cups.

"Maybe I'll get in touch," she says. "If we do decide to run that story."

248

"Of course," I say.

After all, I can't exactly refuse, not after everything she's told me. She glances at the name badge I was given at reception, which I've stuck to my jacket.

"Prytz," she says. "Are you related to Caroline Prytz?"

"Only distantly," I say.

"Cool," she says. "I liked her last album. The electronica style suits her voice."

We walk out into the reception area, and she accompanies me to the door.

"I have to go out and buy a packet of cigarettes," she says, digging around in her handbag. "I'd actually quit, but all this with Jørgen has knocked me for six."

Out of the handbag she pulls a scarf. It's a light blue pashmina, finely woven, with a pink embroidered border. The thousand knives slice my flesh. Rebekka Davidsen flashes me a friendly smile.

"Thanks for the chat, Rikke Prytz. Maybe we'll see each other again soon."

Christ, does anyone honestly fall for that, Rebekka had said. More than anything else, his advances had been comical. I'm almost alone in the T-banen carriage on the way back. No school pupils, just a few lonely passengers: an old woman, a man with a newspaper. Rebekka had wound the pashmina scarf about her neck, a scarf bought in Afghanistan. Unless, that is, he was lying about that too. Maybe he just bought it here in Oslo.

But he didn't lie, I think. He didn't make me any promises. I never asked how many of those scarves he had, how many other people he was seeing. And it doesn't necessarily mean anything, the fact that he bought her a gift. They'd just published a series of articles, won that prize. Maybe he just wanted to be nice. In my mind's eye I see Rebekka Davidsen's stiffly sprayed curls. Try to believe it, that it means nothing. Let my eyelids slide closed. It feels as if I could fall asleep right here and now, resting my head against the windowpane. That I could close my eyes and damn the consequences. Just let the world hammer away out there, do what it will.

In the bar in London, there had been a seriousness about him. It was hard for him to talk about Sarajevo – in fact, he didn't want to talk about it, I'm almost certain of that. I don't know whether he told anyone else about it, his colleagues or friends, or even Merete. Why did he mention it to me? Did I mean something special to him after all – was there something between us that made him feel safe, able to tell me about it? Or was there something in the situation, something I didn't pick up on, that made it absolutely necessary? Maybe it was true that he wanted to be one who loves, I think, maybe he knew that he lacked the capacity for love that most of us have. To really stand by someone through thick and thin, to forsake all others, to make it work. To do those little or not-so-little things to make the other person happy. Perhaps he quite simply wasn't capable of it.

I imagine him, under that car in a suburb in a country at war. He thought he was going to die. But he didn't. He was given his life as a gift, he said, everything after that day would be a bonus. So he went home and continued his life, travelled to new cities in more countries at war. Met a woman, got married, then divorced. Met another, got married again, had a daughter. Met new women constantly. This was the way he lived his bonus life. Was this something he chose? Was this the way he wanted to live?

In fact, I remember when they were awarded the SKUP prize. It was just a few weeks before we left for London together, and on the evening he told me about Sarajevo I had ordered champagne at the restaurant. We have to celebrate, I had said. Maybe I was a little drunk. Jørgen half smiled at my enthusiasm. The prize didn't seem to make much of an impression on him. When we'd had half a glass of champagne each, I said:

"Oh, come on, be happy about it!"

He shrugged. Later, when we sat in the armchairs, just before he told me about Sarajevo, he said that he could never feel happy about something like being awarded a prize. That he knew it was a great honour, but that there were in fact very few things in life that genuinely filled him with joy.

"Don't be so childish," I said. "That's the kind of thing Emma might say!"

I was definitely tipsy by this point. A little cross, too. Didn't *I* fill him with joy? But maybe nobody did – I'm able to appreciate that now. Perhaps that was Jørgen's misfortune, this inability to appreciate the kinds of things the rest of us enjoy. An award, a smile. An evening spent hand in hand with the one you love.

So maybe that's how it was after all – I wanted to be his one and only. I wanted to be better than Merete: cooler, smarter. Did I not think, deep down, that whatever ailed their relationship was about her? Did I not believe that I could offer him something she couldn't? No, I think, looking out of the dirty train window. That wasn't what it was about. But I don't quite manage to convince myself. Wasn't that why I talked about my job so much – to show him something, perhaps? How competent I am. That I'm the kind of person people listen to. Didn't I adorn myself with my career precisely because I knew Merete would fall short on that front? Didn't I try to show him that I'm better than her? No, no, *no*. The man with the newspaper turns his head, casts a glance in my direction. I may well have forgotten myself and said that last one out loud. I attempt a smile. He turns back to his newspaper, making himself deaf and impregnable, the way you do when shielding yourself against the insane. I lean my head against the window. If only I could sleep.

Only when I get off the train at Tåsen does it occur to me that something Rebekka Davidsen said has been buzzing around in my mind since we said our goodbyes outside the newspaper's offices. Their new story was going to be about temping agencies. And I must have been pretty dazed from my lack of sleep to not have immediately connected this piece of information with the fact that Svein Sparre runs a temping agency.

I see her too late. She's striding up Blåsbortveien at a brisk pace, and by the time I catch sight of her she's already seen me. She fishes her phone from the pocket of the neat little bumbag that hangs across her training jacket, taps the screen a few times, and has the phone back in the bag when we're still ten metres apart.

"Hello," says Lea's mother, the housewife from upper Tåsen, smiling with her brilliant-white teeth.

"Hi," I say.

I smile – of course, I have to. I can still feel Saturday's rehearsal for the school play in my chest, the conversation about the dead cats. Me clumsily attempting to play the whole thing down, she taking offence.

"How's it going?" she asks.

"Oh, you know," I say. "Fine."

I can't say *good*, I realise that, but at the same time I can't be finding all this too difficult, either. I can just imagine her leaning towards another mother from the school – at a parents' meeting, at yoga, or on the street, just like this, and saying: I bumped into Rikke Prytz earlier today – Emma's mother, you know, in eighth grade, they live directly below Jørgen and Merete Tangen – and she seemed *completely* out of it.

She considers me. Huge sunglasses with mirrored lenses cover her eyes, and when I try to make eye contact with her, all I can see is myself. Maybe it's just my imagination, but I'm sure I can see the sleepless nights in my face, even in the tiny, curved reflections offered up by her glasses.

"Dreadful what happened to Jørgen," she says.

I concur, and we stand there nodding at this for a little while. I wonder what she knows. Is it public knowledge, the fact that nobody broke in? Has Nina blabbed to everyone – are those of us in the building now suspected by the entire neighbourhood?

"I heard they found a cat down by your place, too," she says. "Yesterday? Somebody even said you were the one who found it."

I nod. Of course, it must have been Nina. Usually, these mothers don't pay her much attention – she must have been beside herself to find she finally possesses the kind of information they're hungry for.

"How horrible," the housewife says.

"Yes. It was."

She takes the sunglasses from her nose, and now I can see her eyes. They're a kind of cold, grey-blue Nordic colour, like the sea in overcast weather. She's a few years older than me, although this isn't easy to see just from looking at us. From the bumbag she pulls a leather glasses case. She opens it and snatches up a polishing cloth, which she rubs across the sunglasses' lenses with confident movements, looking down at her hands as she says:

"So it seems it was a little dramatic after all, this thing with the cats? Doesn't it?"

She glances up at me. I know what I have to do, there's no way round it. I take a deep breath. I would have so preferred not to have to do this.

"Yes," I say. "It seems it was more significant than I thought. Maybe I took too light a view of the whole thing."

"It sounds terrible," she says.

She sounds genuine, I have to give her that, at least. Because she could have rubbed it in, let me really feel how much of a fool I'd made of myself.

"Yes," I say.

"You know," she says. "There's a connection between violence against animals and violence against humans. Many psychopaths torture animals when they're young."

All at once, the weight of the cat murders feels overwhelming. I want to lie down on the ground, weep for the dead creatures.

"And a man murdered in the same house," she says. "In such a – and excuse me for saying this – in such a *brutal* way."

She gazes off into the distance. On the other side of the street, big trampolines can be seen sticking up over the fences.

"To think that there's a psychopath on the loose in Tåsen," she says, as if to herself, sounding astonished. "Maybe it's even someone we know."

It's as if I can see Svein's shadow – see it slinking up the stairs to tower over Jørgen's door. Only now do I notice how quiet it is here.

"But anyway," I say, forcing a change of subject. "How's everything going with the school play? You're the head of the school activities group, aren't you?"

"It's been postponed," she says. "Hasn't Emma told you? The premiere will be in the spring instead."

In my head I quickly rewind through the past few mornings, the last few dinners at home, the four of us around the table. Has it been mentioned, without me remembering? Or has Emma kept this from me?

"We're sending out an email to the parents this afternoon," she says, taking her sunglasses from the bumbag again. "It was the right thing to do. Filippa Tangen has a central part, as you know, and I can't imagine she'll be in a fit state to perform as things are now. And besides, the piece is about a criminal who murders people with a knife. It felt a little inappropriate, all things considered. But maybe it's just as well. After all, it was a little strange, the whole thing with the dancers. Gard opposed the rewrites, and you can't deny that it's a little peculiar when a grown man thinks it's fine to direct teenage girls dressed up as prostitutes. Don't you think?"

"Yes," I say.

Gard. I think of his ungainly appearance: the heavy fringe, the horn-rimmed glasses. His deep, powerful voice. Emma, who all of a sudden became interested in theatre. Surely she doesn't have a crush on him? He's in his early twenties, so young to me, but old to her, a grown-up. I think back to the discussion about the dancers, how Gard had argued his case. What did he say, specifically? And – an unpleasant thought – why was it so important to him? Was it about artistic freedom, about being faithful to the text and depicting the hard truths of life honestly? Or was he getting something out of it? But I don't want to go down this road. I close my eyes. It's just the local rumour mill doing its thing.

"Unofficially, of course," Lea's mother says, raising a suggestive eyebrow. "The official reason that the play is being postponed is consideration for Filippa and Merete. And for the neighbourhood, you might say."

We stand there in silence for a moment, and then she says:

"You know, I knew the people who lived in your apartment before you moved in. Inga is a friend of a friend. She says there was always something that wasn't quite right in that house. Something to do with Jørgen and Merete. Of course, they seem nice and totally normal when you meet them, but she always had the feeling that there was something off there."

Now the cars can be heard in Maridalsveien, but only faintly, in the distance, because although the city is close this area is curiously shielded from the sounds and smells that emanate from it. I remember the couple who owned the apartment before us very well – her in particular. I remember that at the handover meeting she demonstrated how everything in the apartment worked – this is how you turn on the induction hob, here's the fuse box. Did I not think that there was something a little condescending about her manner? I remember mentioning it to Åsmund afterwards.

"Well," says the housewife. "I suppose I'd better be getting home. You take care of yourselves down there."

256

She taps her phone, and when I say goodbye, music is presumably already streaming into her ears, so she doesn't hear me. I watch her hurry away at speed-walking pace, back straight, arms against her sides as if she's jogging, her pointy elbows sticking out behind her.

You have to be allowed to make mistakes, I think as I march home. You have to be allowed to change your opinion about whether something is dangerous or not as more information becomes available. This is what's wrong with our society – we're expected to stick to our guns, to never go back on anything said or done but persistently claim we've *always said* this, that or the other. And not least, it's our fucking *emotions* we expect to lead us. There's a truth in feelings that rational argument simply glances off. If someone is afraid, they have *a right* to be afraid. God help those who attempt to challenge this fear, who try to say that in the light of this or that perhaps it isn't so dangerous after all, because then you're being *disrespectful*, you're being cold and cynical; everything other than self-sacrificing sympathy must be shut down. I slam the garden gate closed after me. Why should I feel as if I had to offer the house-wife an apology?

Of course, the story about the cats looks different now that we know a man has been murdered. Of course, that changes everything. But when we spoke about it back at the school rehearsal, nobody knew that Jørgen was lying dead in his study. And she has the cheek to say that something wasn't quite right with Jørgen and Merete – now, just days after his death. While I have to stand there and be reprimanded by her, all because of some offhand comment about dead cats. I take a deep breath, try to calm down. After all, I *agree* with her. I saw the cat hanging from its neck there beside the mailboxes, and the seriousness of the situation settled over me. I admit it. I was wrong.

In the stairwell hangs Nina's list of tasks. I let myself into the apartment, thinking: She's quite something, is Nina. She's left that hanging there, even after there's been a murder in the building.

At home, I clear the kitchen counter with quick, savage movements. Am I simply angry at the housewife, I think, for the disrespect she's shown Jørgen? Or is he the one I'm angry at? The stream of women making their way up the stairs to his apartment when Merete was out, it burns my cheeks, twists in my chest. But I can't get myself all wound up about it, because what did I expect? Maybe the comment about Gard has kindled my sense of unease. Her malicious insinuation – which I regard myself as above believing – has it crept in and taken root in my mind after all?

I sit down at the kitchen table, drum my fingers against the tabletop. It's an ordinary Thursday, the middle of the day, quiet out in the street. On the other side of the road Hoffmo comes out onto the veranda with a tarpaulin, which he starts to pull over his garden furniture. He's preparing for the long winter. He's probably done this every autumn for the past forty years, and yet there's still something clumsy about his movements. I look away, not wanting him to see me. By now he must know that it was me who found the cat, and I imagine he must be eager to talk to me about it, get all the details. Maybe even discuss how we might go about catching the perpetrator. But I have so little to say about it. I feel no bloodlust, no violent indignation. Just a deep, dark sadness, the dead kitten with the soft fur.

On the patio outside I see Filippa's gardening gloves from yesterday. There they were, mother and daughter, just days after Jørgen was gone, helping out with the communal tasks. Nina can't possibly have nagged them about it, surely not even she is that insensitive. But her list still hangs on the wall. We're supposed to enter our names on it, next to each task we've completed, and note the number of hours it took. So that we all do an equal share, Nina says. In a couple of weeks she'll come knocking on the door and complain that Åsmund and I have only spent five hours *in total* on the communal tasks, while others have done far more, and not to nag, but can't we spare a weekend, make an effort, to ensure things stay *fair*? Talk about doing whatever you like, I think. Gossiping to the mothers at the school about the kinds of things people say in their own home, and *still* acting as if she has the moral high ground. Running the housing cooperative as if it were hers alone – as if she's the one who makes the decisions about the areas we share. Putting in the gigantic front door against significant opposition, because that's the way *she* wanted it. And then she demands that we be her obedient subjects, painting and tiling and lugging stones in accordance with her instructions.

And isn't it this way with other things, too? The list of who accessed the code lock is undoubtedly meant to be confidential, in which case it's downright illegal for her to even have it in her possession, never mind hand it out all over the place. And what about the freezer she and Svein keep in the cellar? Not in their private storeroom, oh no, because they didn't have enough space, so now it's right in the middle of the shared area, where they felt it was appropriate to put it. Isn't *that* a breach of the housing cooperative's regulations, I think, and I know, I'm being petty, I'm being just as bad as them or worse, but it feels so good, so wonderfully energising to have an outlet for this painful, hard lump that has been stuck in my chest since Jamila's visit this morning. I can't give Jørgen a piece of my mind, he's dead, and besides, he never promised me any form of fidelity. To the housewife I have no choice but to bow and scrape, but this I *can* be furious about, here I'm perfectly within my rights. I'm entitled to be furious with Svein, too, but I'm a little afraid of him, he's so huge, so angry and uncompromising – but Nina I can take. I can tip a little of my rage over her – better than that, I can counter her pedantic nitpicking with a bit of my own, take her on home ground. Look at that freezer, I can say. Is *that* really allowed? Remind me again, Nina, what does it say in the regulations about storing private property in the shared areas in the loft and cellar? Oh, right, so we can all use it, can we, ah-ha, I see, but then tell me something, what's that hanging there – yes, there, just next to the handle? Well, maybe I'm the Queen of Sheba, Nina, or maybe that's a fucking *padlock*? So tell me, how are the rest of us supposed to use the goddamn freezer, then?

They've probably locked it with a separate code, too – I'd bet on it. Not the shared code to the shed outside, but one they've kept to themselves, which effectively prevents the rest of us from accessing the freezer. Fucking Svein, spraying his toxic hints all around him – to me, and probably to Saman and Jamila, too, not to mention the police. Svein, who disliked Jørgen's journalism, and who also runs a temping agency.

I stop myself, let my fingers lie calm against the tabletop. Do I really mean it? Do I really intend to go down into the cellar again? At the end of the day, am I no better than Jamila – am I going to play amateur detective, too? Or worse – is it just plain nosiness?

No, I think. That's not what this is about. It has to be okay to check the lock. If he insists on putting the freezer there, I'm well within my rights to try to open it. The cellar belongs to all of us. I can say that I have something I need to store there. The freezer will be locked, the code will be one I don't know, and I can hurry over to their place as soon I hear Nina come through the door, before Svein gets home – go hammer on their apartment door and ask her to please remove that damn colossus from our *shared* cellar. And then I might mention this thing about the temping agency to the police, because why not? Svein is out there mouthing off about Saman and Åsmund – why should I be any better?

*

The air down there is damp, heavy. In the walls there are huge brown spiders, they hide in the nooks and crannies, building nests, scurrying away if you move something. The freezer has been set against the wall, below one of the windows. It's a huge white slab and it gives out a constant buzzing sound, low and intoning. Just below the lid there's a small orange light, and next to the handle is a metal mount that holds a combination padlock. I set the code to 1951 – the year the house was built. I'm convinced that it won't work, but the lock clicks. I feel it release in my hand, the hard metal loop letting go of its base to become loose and yielding.

Down in the freezer lie the deep-frozen remains of the animals unlucky enough to have crossed paths with Svein and his hunting party. Most of them have been filleted – one plastic bag white with frost even has a label on it that says *Elk burgers 2017* – but I can also see a Ziploc bag that contains an entire hoof. I consider it, and the leg to which it is attached, cut mid-calf, the pelt still in place. It's too small to belong to an elk, I think, it must be from a reindeer or roe. It's covered in frost, both the fur and the hoof – the freezer must be really cold. I open another bag, which contains frozen pieces of meat, hard as bone.

All the way at the bottom lies a slightly bigger plastic bag, white and thin, the kind people use as rubbish bags in large institutions like schools. Something about it is different from the other bags. The size of it, but also its type. I find the opening, peek inside. Within it is another bag, in which the contents are wrapped. I fold this aside.

The first thing I see is the ears. They're pointed, the fur full of rime. Then I see another set of ears. And yet another. The bodies are stiff with frost. There are three of them. I open the bag a little further, as if I can't quite believe it, and see a nose, whiskers that have frozen against the fur of the animal's face. A red felt collar, with a little medallion hanging from it. I drop the bag the instant I stare into the empty, frozen cat's eyes.

Jørgen and I fuck in silence. We suppress all sounds, nothing but the tiniest sigh escaping us now and then. Above us is the skylight of their converted loft, because after a fair bit of back and forth we've discovered this is the best place to be if we have to meet at home. Next door to this room is Merete and Jørgen's bedroom, and we don't want to go there. Their daughter's bedroom is also up here, and of course that's not an option, while down on the first floor it's possible for anyone standing in the building opposite to see into the apartment. The loft room isn't ideal, but we make it work. In the corner, where the sloping roof meets the wall, Jørgen and Merete have set an old box mattress without legs. It was formerly used by Filippa and her friends as a sofa – some gigantic IKEA cushions persist as remnants of that time – but Filippa has since retreated to her room and now the mattress is mainly used by guests. They call it "the daybed". The first time he mentioned it I thought it was ridiculous, but over time I've come to think of it as an appropriate name, considering the activities we subject it to.

The silence is a necessity – I don't object, but it does make the whole thing more mechanical. As if it's a compulsion, a set of movements we have to go through to reach a goal that seems somewhat unclear once you've taken passion out of the equation. It reminds me of TV recordings of dancers going through their routines without any musical accompaniment. Which isn't to say that I get nothing out of it. I press my nose against Jørgen's neck, sniffing in the smell of him, something warm and spiced I can't place. He breathes heavily, rhythmically. Like this, I think, it's just fucking, nothing more. I don't know whether there's anything wrong in that. But then the baby monitor crackles.

On the floor beside the daybed the little black speaker lights up in angry orange. Merete and Filippa are at a cabin with Merete's parents; Åsmund is at his mother's, but my children are asleep down in the cellar. I've put the other monitor out in the hallway between their bedrooms and opened Lukas's door, thinking that I'll be able to hear, should anything happen. Jørgen and I freeze, look at the monitor. It's silent. We look at each other. Just as I'm about to say something to take the edge off the panic, it crackles again, hissing with static, and then I hear Emma's voice:

"Mamma?"

In a single leap I'm on my feet, gathering up my clothes and pulling them on – there's no time to put on my bra so I simply pull my sweater straight down over my head. With the baby monitor in my hand, I run down the stairs from the loft into the living room, past the grand piano. In the hallway I stuff my feet into my shoes and run out, as quietly as I can, down the steps and into my apartment.

She's standing in the middle of the living room, barefoot and in her nightie. Her eyes are narrow and sleepy.

"Mamma?"

"Emma, honey," I say, rushing over to her. "Is everything alright?"

I pull her to me, pressing her against my body. She's limp in my arms, doesn't hug me back. When I let go to look at her, her eyes have widened.

"Where were you?" she asks.

It's the kind of moment where you have mere seconds to decide what you're going to say, how honest you're going to be. When misjudgements can easily arise because the assessment is so complex, and you have to make it quick as a flash. There isn't time to weigh up the pros and cons. You have to act on gut instinct, and whatever else you might say about it, it does have a built-in tendency to pull us towards whatever is most comfortable.

"Upstairs," I say. "I just went upstairs for a little while. To see Jamila. Have a cup of coffee."

She says nothing, just looks at me. Later, I'll think: Could she smell the wine on me? Or even worse, could she smell him? And in this house, where you can hear everything the neighbours do, did she hear my steps in the apartment directly above? Does she understand that I'm lying? Or was she unable to tell which direction my steps came from, was she tired and disoriented because she'd just woken from a nightmare and couldn't find me?

"Is something wrong, sweetie?" I ask, combing my hands through her hair.

As if she's a small child. As if I'm a warm and friendly mother, ready to comfort her.

"I just went up to see Jamila – she sent me a message

and asked me over. The two of you were asleep, and I was here all alone. Surely that hasn't upset you?"

I hug her again, feeling my heart beating fast and hard. I'm nervous, almost frantic.

"No," Emma says.

But she doesn't look at me when she says it.

That's the last time I take the baby monitor upstairs. I fume at Jørgen afterwards – do you know what could have happened, are you aware of just how close that was? We can't carry on like this, what on earth are we doing? It tears at me, the thought of what Emma might have realised, what she might think, I almost can't stand to think about it. This has to stop, I say to Jørgen, we can't do this anymore, realising in a dizzying surge what's at stake here, my life as I know it, everything and everyone I care about. We can't do this. It's over. That was the last time.

But I'm in too deep. A couple of weeks pass, and then we meet again. We arrange our trip to London. If I'm going to sleep with you, I tell him, it has to be on foreign soil. On the flight over I fidget, intertwining my fingers – I'm flying alone, of course, so nobody will suspect anything, and once again I feel alight with anticipation. Is this some kind of compulsion after all? I ask myself. I lean my head against the cold window. Take comfort in the fact that I'm at least done with the daybed.

FRIDAY

Gundersen leans over the kitchen table and grabs the coffee pot, perfectly at ease. I've set it there along with two cups and was just about to serve him, but he beats me to it. He fills his cup to the brim, puts down the pot and takes a slurp.

"Ah," he says with relish.

He's one of those people who needs stimulants, I think, as if his tobacco-stained fingers and the smell of smoke that oozes from him to fill the room hadn't told me this already. I wonder what kind of relationship he has with alcohol, whether he drinks a lot or is excruciatingly careful about how much he consumes.

"Would you like one?" he says as he sets down his cup, and without waiting for an answer he fills the other one, also to the brim.

"Yes, thanks," I say pointlessly when he's halfway through the ritual.

He sets the cup down in front of me. It's so full I have to take a few sips before I can drink from it properly. The coffee is hot, and I burn my tongue; my throat stings, too. I put down the cup and wipe my mouth, trying not to notice the pain, which, after all, will pass soon enough.

"So," he says.

"So," I say.

We look at each other.

"So you went down into the cellar and opened the Sparre family's deep freezer."

"Yes," I say with a sigh. "Yes, and I'm not entirely sure why. I just . . . I thought of it after we spoke. That was why I decided to go down there that day."

"Thought of what after we spoke?"

"The freezer. That Svein had just put it there, and, well . . ."

I stop. I can't say anything about Emma, about the fire door that leads out of her room. How I was checking to see what sound it makes, and that I realised she could have sneaked out during the night without me noticing. I can't implicate her. Nor can I talk about my rage, because if I don't explain what Jamila and Rebekka told me about all Jørgen's women, the whole thing would seem so petty.

"He said that we could all use it," I say instead. "And yet it was locked. And had they chosen to use a different code – not the one we use for the shed – then of course it would be impossible for the rest of us to use it, so yes, I thought I ought to check."

Gundersen looks at me. This is a technique, I realise that. It's something that journalists also resort to occasionally, I've seen Jørgen do it: when you meet a statement with silence, the person speaking feels that she has to say more, to explain or elaborate. I know this, and yet I'm still unable to resist.

"It wasn't as if I thought I was going to find dead cats in there," I say. "I just . . . I just find all this so disconcerting, that there's someone in our building who . . ."

I only managed to get a few hours' sleep last night, too, and it shows. I'm finding it hard to collect my thoughts, and I'm unable to come up with a plausible explanation as to why I checked the freezer. I'm also convinced that Nina might be sitting in her kitchen next door and listening – or Svein, or their son. I feel the unease creeping in at the thought of bumping into them after all this business with the freezer, of having to look Nina in the eye once she knows that I've been snooping through her belongings. And then there's the unease that creeps around my middle to settle in my stomach. Why were there frozen cats in their freezer anyway? Svein's towering figure in Jørgen's study that night, this mental image I've seen in my mind's eyes so many times that it's starting to feel like a memory.

Gundersen says:

"Just help me out a little bit here, Rikke, because I find this hard to understand. We have a conversation upstairs – you, me and Pettersen. We talk about the cat you found, I show you the rope from the tool shed, and you tell me that you were awake and didn't hear anything, but that maybe you heard a door open and close at some point. Correct?"

"Yes."

"Then we say goodbye, and you go down into the cellar. To check on your bike."

He gives me a long look.

"Well," I begin, and then I say nothing further.

"Well what?" he asks.

I take a deep breath. I don't know how to explain it. At work I'm good at this, I build arguments, theorise about people's feelings, explain errors of thought and apparently irrational acts with arguments taken from behavioural theory, economics and psychology, quote Richard Thaler and Daniel Kahneman, and end with a conclusion so convincing that those listening have no choice but to agree.

Right now, I'm just not capable of it. Although I know that I have to appear trustworthy, that I have to avoid directing suspicion at my daughter, at all costs. I heave a deep sigh and take another sip from my cup. When I put it down, I see a coffee-coloured stripe that divides it lengthwise, coffee that has run down after my last sip to hit the tabletop and form a ring.

"It was the fire door," I say. "I just wanted to check whether anyone could have got in through it."

"If anyone could have got *in*?"

His tone gives him away, I think, as an icy feeling begins to spread upwards from my belly. He's already figured out that I went down there to see whether anyone in my family could have left the apartment that way.

"Yes," I say, my voice frail. "There might be a murderer here in the building."

Gundersen says:

"So, okay, you went down to see whether anyone could come *in* the fire door. Did you check the lock on the outside?"

"Yes."

"So can they?"

"Can they what?"

"Can anyone get in that way?"

For a moment my mind is blank. Then I say:

"I don't know. I was interrupted. You came along."

He nods slowly. Gives me another of his long looks, but continues:

"I came along, we spoke, and then we went our separate ways. You went back into your apartment, if I remember correctly?"

"Yes."

"And then?"

"Then I went to the doctor," I say. "I was put on sick leave because, well, because I've been a little out of sorts after all this. I can't sleep at night, and . . ."

Is it strange to have asked for a sick note? But he must have read Fredly's email by now. He *knows*. Surely he understands the effect this is having on me? It's as if there's something there, a thought, but then it's gone, and I stare solemnly into space as Gundersen considers me.

"I'm sorry," I say. "I'm so tired, I've hardly slept since it happened. It's hard to concentrate."

He nods. He's waiting, I realise, because he doesn't pick up the thread, just looks at me.

"And yesterday I took a trip into the city," I continue. "I came home on the T-banen, sat here at the kitchen table and looked out at the mailboxes, and then I thought . . ."

"Yes?"

"Then I thought, for fuck's sake, what is that massive freezer even doing there? I thought of it when we were down there on Tuesday morning. The lock. That perhaps I ought to just check."

"And so you tried the code, and when it worked, you dug down to the bottom of the freezer?"

"Yes."

"Seems a little overenthusiastic?"

"The bag was different."

"What did you think it was?"

"I don't know. More hunting meat. Or who knows? I just opened it."

He nods, slowly.

"I can't explain it any better than that," I say. "It's just the kind of thing you do, you know, the sort of stupid thing you don't think you'll ever have to admit to anyone. You eavesdrop on your neighbour, you look in the bathroom cabinet when staying over with friends, you take a peek in a cupboard or open a drawer, it's, I don't know – it's *curiosity*. But you don't think you're going to find something that means you'll have to call the police."

My voice is too desperate. I don't quite have control over my tone and facial expressions, or even over what I'm saying.

Gundersen says:

"And how does Åsmund usually sleep?"

"What do you mean?"

"I mean, on an ordinary night, how does your husband sleep? Is he a deep or a light sleeper?"

"I don't know," I say. "Just average, I think."

"And you?"

"Light. Sometimes Lukas cries out, and I have to go down to him during the night."

"And if Åsmund wakes during the night, do you wake too?" he

asks. "Say that he gets up to go to the bathroom, for example – do you wake up then?"

"He doesn't usually go to the bathroom," I say. "He generally sleeps straight through. But yes, if anything happens, I wake up. Like if a phone buzzes, or something."

"Hm."

A little too late I understand what he's doing, the purpose of these questions. His sudden shifts in the conversation distract me, and I'm exhausted, so I don't have the mental agility to follow him as quickly as I should.

"Remember, we have a young child," I say. "So we probably sleep lighter than most – both of us. I mean, Åsmund wakes up, too, if Lukas cries out. It's just that I'm the one who tends to wake up first. I'm usually already on my feet by the time Åsmund's awake. But every time I get up during the night, he wakes up, too."

Gundersen studies me. I curse myself for not having been one step ahead here. Åsmund is my alibi, and vice versa. If one of us had gone out to kill Jørgen that night, the other one would have woken up.

"So if you went up to see Jørgen Tangen," Gundersen says. "On a – what would you call it? – a nocturnal *visit*. Did Åsmund wake up then?"

"I never went up to see Jørgen when Åsmund was home," I say, lowering my voice, acutely aware of the neighbours on the other side of the wall – and all the other neighbours, too, for that matter, as if the very house itself is listening. "Both Merete and Åsmund had to be away, that was the deal."

"But not the kids?"

"Filippa was usually with her mother," I say. "My kids slept several floors below us. I put on the baby monitor. As I wrote to Ingvild."

Gundersen takes a slurp from his coffee cup, apparently finishing off the dregs. As he drinks, I see that there is no stain on the table

274

where his cup has stood, that he has lifted it and set it down with absolute precision.

"How has Jørgen's death affected you?" he asks.

"What do you mean?"

"I mean just that: how has it affected you? Are you sad, are you angry, perhaps a little relieved?"

"Relieved?"

"You wanted out of it, didn't you?"

I sit there, silent. How much have I actually cried over Jørgen since Sunday? I wept despairingly on the bathroom floor the night I learned of his death, but since then? It's true that I was unable to stop seeing him. We ended it a couple of times, but we always slipped back into our old ways, and afterwards I asked myself why I couldn't just stop seeing him, if that was what I really wanted. But it was so hard. We were neighbours. Resisting the desire to go up there was easy if it came over me when I was feeling good, or even when I was just okay or a little down. But when things got difficult down here, when something happened that Åsmund and I struggled to handle, the walk up the stairs seemed such a short one. Jørgen was so accessible, and in order to have really ended it I would have had to resist the impulse to seek him out – not just now and then, but all the time, including in my weakest moments. I can easily understand why dry alcoholics can't have a bottle of wine in the house. And even though I'm grieving for Jørgen – because I am – there's no escaping the fact that there is also relief. The bottle of wine is gone; I no longer have to think about it.

But I daren't tell Gundersen all this, so I simply say:

"I'm devastated."

This isn't a lie, either.

"Well," he says. "I won't keep you any longer. I'll probably talk to you again at some point over the next few days, so we'll see each other again soon."

"I was just wondering," I say once we've got up. "The cats I found?"

"Yes?"

"Are they . . . ? I mean, are they the ones that were reported missing?"

We stand opposite each other at the kitchen table.

"It isn't usual to perform a post-mortem on a cat," Gundersen says slowly. "And unfortunately, cases of animal abuse have to be fairly large-scale before they're properly investigated. But the cat you found beside the mailboxes was sent to the Norwegian School of Veterinary Science. And the veterinarian who examined it says that until quite recently, it had been frozen. That is, it had been dead for a while. And it didn't die by hanging, so to speak."

I remain beside the kitchen table, let him show himself out. Hear his quick footsteps out in the corridor. A door slams, perhaps the door to the cellar, but the stairs that lead down there are concrete, making footsteps difficult to hear from inside the apartment. I just stay standing there. Everything around me feels unreal. It's as if I'm only half awake. As if part of me is dreaming all this.

It's Filippa who opens the door – this is something I wasn't expecting. I'm standing there, steeling myself, ready to meet her mother, utterly unprepared for an encounter with the daughter.

"Hi," she says.

"Hi," I say.

We look at each other. She makes no move to go get Merete. The responsibility for the situation, in all its weight, settles over me. She's a child who has lost her father. I'm an adult. There's nothing I can say to ease her grief, to comfort her or make it better, and yet I have to try.

"Oh sweetheart, how very sad this is," I say.

Although I can't say that I know her well, I can see that there's something different about her, the thing I could sense when I saw her in the garden. She's paler, harder. Her gaze seems turned inwards, even as she's looking at me.

She stands there for an insufferably long time, and I don't know what to do – should I go, should I ask her to let me in, should I call for Merete? But then she takes a step to one side.

"Come in," she says in a tired voice. "Mamma's in the kitchen."

She turns and goes. I just listen to her footsteps as they make their way up the stairs to the loft.

The apartment is rough around the edges. A couple of cups stand on the table beside the creamy-white sofa, the wrapper of a chocolate bar between them, half turned inside out. The sofa cushions have slipped down a little, nobody has bothered to straighten them up. I walk slowly through the living room. Without wanting to I turn my head towards the study, our building's open wound. Feel a tightening in my stomach, but fortunately the door is closed.

The last time I was up here – if you disregard that Saturday when I let myself in, and I intend to – I was here to see Jørgen. It was a morning a couple of weeks ago. I'd cycled home during my lunch break, he was working from home, Merete was out. I was feeling a certain resentment towards the whole thing, as if these meetings were a task I had to get out the way. We lay on a rug on the floor up in the loft room because I had developed a distaste for the daybed, and when Jørgen pointed it out afterwards as we lay beside each other on the floor – you know, he said, we would have been much more comfortable on the daybed – I got irritated with him.

"Go lie on the fucking daybed by yourself, then," I said.

Have we become that kind of couple, I thought afterwards as I cycled back to work, the kind that picks at each other all the time? Has reality caught up with us, even here, in this forbidden relationship where time ceases to exist?

Jørgen didn't answer me. He got up and walked naked over to the record player. He had an entire collection of LPs up there – he always bought vinyl because he thought the sound was so much better. I began to put my clothes back on, knowing without needing to turn around how he was selecting a record, teasing it with the greatest of care out of its sleeve to hold it between his flattened palms, so that his fingertips wouldn't touch the grooves. A nimble baseline filled the loft, a rockabilly version of "Susie Q".

"This is the kind of music my dad listens to," I said.

Jørgen smiled at me.

"I've always liked this song," he said, and hummed along. "You know why?"

"The complex poetry of the lyrics," I suggested. I was in a bad mood.

Jørgen didn't seem to notice. He pulled on his trousers and looked out of the loft window, across the neighbourhood. Turned to face me.

"This is the way a man of few words would express love," he said. "Someone who doesn't understand the language of the emotions that people use, someone who's unable to articulate what he feels for his woman. But who maybe loves her just as deeply, all the same."

I laughed, a little reluctantly. He grinned, showing all the straight teeth that surrounded his crooked front tooth. I can still remember the first time I noticed that tooth, in the stairwell once, long before we began seeing each other like this.

Before I left, he had pushed my hair behind my ear.

"My Rikke," he said. "You go out there and show them who's boss."

As I cycled back to work, I thought as usual about how I had to end it, how it was enough now, this had to be the last time. But I didn't believe it, and that realisation filled me with sadness.

Merete is sitting at the kitchen table. She has a newspaper open in front of her, her phone lying beside it, and a big cup of tea next to that. As I come in, she turns her head.

"Hi," she says.

Is she surprised? Did she not think I'd come?

"Hi," I say. "I mean, I'm so sorry. How are you both doing?"

"Oh," she says. "I don't know. It's . . ."

She falls quiet for a moment, stares out of the window. Their kitchen is like ours, but since it's one floor up, the view is better. They're sort of level with Bakkehaugen up here, raised above the other houses on the street.

"I don't think it's really sunk in," she says to the sky outside. "It feels like he's just popped out somewhere."

She's pale, I think, looks tired. And yet she's still so beautiful, yes, almost even more so than usual. As if it suits her, this grief.

"I'm sure it will take time," I say listlessly, because what in all the world am I supposed to say?

It feels wrong to be here. As if I'm intruding on something, stomping around in a place I have no right to be.

"Yes."

For a moment it looks as if she's about to cry, but then she swallows and gets up. She goes over to the kitchen counter, turns her back to me and says:

"Sit down. I'll make us some coffee."

"There's no need," I say.

"No," she says. "I need one."

I sit down, there's nothing else for it. I'll just have to drink up quickly.

"How's Filippa doing?" I ask once the coffee is ground and tipped into the pot.

"Well," Merete says. "I don't know. It varies from one day to the next. Maybe she's still in shock. She doesn't say very much."

She sets the pot on the hob and comes over to the table. She moves like a ballet dancer, with steps so light and soft they're hardly audible.

"I don't really know what to do with her."

She runs her hands through her hair, rubs her temples. Everything is an effort, it seems, and yet there's nothing resigned about her. No, I think, Merete will get through this. Come out the other side even stronger, perhaps. As for her daughter, I don't know – she's been dealt a wound that will never fully heal. We can hear her walking around up in her bedroom, directly above the kitchen.

"It isn't strange if she's struggling," I say.

"No," Merete says. "It isn't."

"Is she back at school?"

"For the most part. Hasn't Emma told you?"

Just then, some simple guitar chords can be heard above us. Acoustic guitar, nothing rowdy, but played at a dangerously high volume because we can feel it reverberating all the way down here. A riff I know, immediately followed by male voices in harmony, the intro to an old Simon & Garfunkel song. My father had it on CD when I was a kid – I borrowed it and played it on my Discman. I'd set the player beside my pillow and lie in bed and listen.

"This is how it is," Merete says.

"Simon & Garfunkel blaring out at maximum volume," I say. "That's not something you hear every day."

A small smile ripples across Merete's lips.

"No," she says. "It's really not."

I give a half smile in return, unsure whether it's appropriate. Merete can be funny, I realise now. She has a good sense of humour, she's intelligent.

"Jørgen used to sing those songs to her as lullabies when she was little," she says. "I don't know. I think it's probably healthy for her to have an outlet. At least she's in touch with her pain this way. Better that than suppressing it."

I nod. Simon & Garfunkel bellow out their harmonies upstairs.

The coffee cups are in the third cupboard I open. I put on an act, pretending as if I don't know where to find things in this kitchen, thinking that if I go straight to the right cabinet it will reveal that I've been here many times before. I detest this devious streak in myself, but I have no other choice. I pour a cup for her and one for me, just a little coffee in each, and set them on the table between us.

Upstairs, Simon & Garfunkel become quieter. I wonder what the purpose of this ritual was, whether there was something Filippa wanted to demonstrate by it. To Merete, or perhaps to me. I feel so transparent. Here I come, one of the forbidden women of the man Merete and Filippa have lost, ostensibly to express my condolences.

I'm fake through and through, and I'm not sure how well I'm managing to hide it.

"I hope you're looking out for yourselves," Merete says over her cup.

"What was that?"

"You have to look out for yourselves. The police seem to think it could be one of the neighbours."

Now she holds my gaze, and there's something intense about it, it only lasts a moment but there's definitely something happening here. Then she looks out of the window. Did I imagine it? Am I projecting my own guilt on to her? Does she trust me? Do I trust her? But she was away that night. She didn't use her code to the front door.

"And this thing with the cats," she says.

I, on the other hand – I was here. And Merete knows that. For all she knows, it could be me.

"Yes," I say. "The two of you should be careful, too."

"Yes."

She looks at me again, calmer now. She doesn't seem afraid. We hear Filippa walk from the record player into her room, hear the door slam shut.

"If there's anything I can do, just let me know," I say.

As if I haven't done enough already.

"Thank you," Merete says tonelessly.

She accompanies me to the door. Neither of us look towards the study, but I see that she notices the cups and chocolate wrapper on the coffee table.

As I'm putting on my shoes, she says:

"Rikke? It was really kind of you to come."

I straighten up. We stand facing each other, me a head taller than her, and she takes hold of my arms.

"If you mean it, that I should just let you know if I need help, well then I think . . . Maybe Filippa could come down to your place for a few hours every now and then?"

"Of course," I say.

"And at some point, maybe we could have a glass of wine again? It's been so long, but we did used to do that sometimes."

"Of course," I say. "That would be nice."

It feels as if I could collapse into her arms. Anything she wants, I will do it – all she asks me for, I will provide. I no longer have a will of my own, she can take over completely and I'll be happy to let her.

Only when I'm out on the stairs do I feel the weight of her suggestion. That we be friends. Meet up and chat, make snacks, pour wine. I feel it in my body, that not only have I betrayed Åsmund, but I've betrayed her, too. And the black, wounded eyes of her daughter. One day it will come out anyway, Ingvild Fredly said. Soon they'll know, and they'll hate me.

The smell of rain and moss oozes up from the forest floor to mix with the fresh, wet air I pull deep into my lungs in sporadic breaths. The pines stretch their heavy branches towards me from either side of the path, and I like this, the sight of the forest and the rough surface of the trail, where roots and rocks stick up out of the earth so that I have to concentrate on not missing my footing as I move at speed. It doesn't leave me much space to think. Perhaps it was exactly this state he thought I needed, the Swedish doctor who believes the cure for sleeplessness lies in diet and exercise, five a day and cardio. It feels good to run, I have to give him that. The walls of the yellow house in Kastanjesvingen are starting to close in on me, but here I can move freely. Maybe I'll sleep better if I run more. Perhaps all my problems – Jørgen, Åsmund, the cats, Emma – will seem small and unimportant if only I run fast enough.

I push myself. Feel my heart. Feel it in my throat, which is becoming sore. Feel the lactic acid starting to build up in my thighs. It's too much. The trick is to stop before it gets this far. To push, but without exceeding your tolerance level. Then you can keep going for longer, train your endurance. That's my sport – not the sprints, but the long-distance stretches. But my head clears when I really push myself, when the landscape rushes past me. I'm not sure if it's true that you can run from your thoughts – I suspect that it isn't, because it sounds too simple – but nobody can accuse me of not trying. If only the doctor could see me now. Soles hammering against the forest floor, a foot here and a foot there, I jump over stones, leap aside to avoid gnarled roots, dodging pitfalls but splashing through puddles, the water spraying up my calves. I move faster and faster, giving it my all, feeling invincible, and just when I think that anything is within my power, that I can do anything, change the facts, turn negative to positive, I set my foot against a rock that turns out not to be as flat as it appears. The unexpected slope of it throws me off balance, I hit it with full force and at top speed, and I fall, my knee crashing into the stone so that pain flashes along the neural pathways to my brain.

The sobs come in fits and starts. I cry like a child with a grazed knee, in jolts, since I'm out of breath. It's hard and sharp, the pain of kneecap against rock. One of my hands is bleeding, too, the one I threw out to break my fall. I sit on the wet forest floor. When my breathing calms, I also stop crying. I pull up the leg of my running tights, investigate the knee. There isn't much to see there – it's red, but no worse than if I had just rubbed it with my hands. It will turn blue, of course, and then yellow and purple, but as yet I have no wound to point to that can justify this pain.

I hobble slowly down the path to the Brekkekrysset crossing. I've run a long way, it'll take an eternity to limp back. I'll be freezing by the time I get home, I can already feel my wet tights, that my jacket is too thin once I'm unable to keep up a decent tempo. The sweat dries on my body and turns cold. It takes twenty minutes for the bus to arrive.

From Blåsbortveien and over to Kastanjesvingen, I walk slowly. The pain changes in character, becoming less sharp, more fuzzy, gnawing, I'll be able to feel it for many days to come. Down the road, where Kastanjesvingen begins, a figure is walking in my direction. He's bearded, burly, slow on his feet, and yet striding energetically, as if he hasn't yet got used to the fact that age now prevents his body from keeping up with his mind.

"Prytz," he shouts when there are forty metres between us. "Something's afoot. The police are everywhere again up there. Just like on Sunday."

I stop. My shoulders stoop immediately and something pierces my stomach. Who is it this time?

"Three police cars in the road," Hoffmo shouts. "And the garden and house are swarming with police. Is everything okay, Prytz?"

"What's happened?" I whisper, doing the sums in my head. Åsmund is at work, Lukas is at kindergarten, and Emma – Emma is at school.

Isn't she? No, with her I never know for sure, she's blocked me, hides things. Perhaps she goes out when I think she's asleep, I don't know, I have no control. Oh God, don't let it be one of mine, let it be something else entirely, something that concerns somebody else.

Hoffmo scratches his head.

"They've taken Simen Sparre," he says. "Looks like they arrested him, the young kid. I saw it from my garden. Two police officers led him out, one on either side. They put him in a police car and drove off. Took his computer, too, and that wasn't all. Are you sure everything's alright, Prytz? You look a little pale."

Simen Sparre held the door open for us on the day we moved in. He must have been around thirteen at the time. He had a side-parting and a blonde fringe, greeted us politely.

"I'll try not to make too much noise," he'd said playfully, and he was handsome when his smile lit up his face.

Even back then I'd thought he possessed the kind of beauty that wouldn't come into its own until he grew up. That as a teenager he probably felt unattractive – too short, skin too blemished, too shy. But he would grow into himself.

What more do I know about him? I've heard him in the cellar every now and then, his bedroom is right next door to Lukas's. Sometimes he has friends over – you can hear their voices, rough and deep, the way the voices of young boys are when they haven't quite got used to their adult vocal cords. Occasionally they put on music – in our apartment only the beat of the song is audible. Too faint to determine exactly what type of music it is – dance or house, rock or pop? In much the same way, I can't quite categorise Simen himself, or at least not using any of the labels that existed when I was in high school: nerd, jock, stoner, loner. Popular, average, or unpopular. I'd guess average. Something about the way he dresses, how he carries himself. But he has a certain charisma.

When his parents argue, we never hear him. When they shout at each other next door, there's never a peep to be heard from Simen. I've often thought about it. Where does he go when the ugly fights break out? Does he go down into his room? Does he go out, to see friends, or does he wander the streets? Or does he just stay right there, put on his headphones, and shut them out that way? And is it even possible to shut them out? I've never heard them address him when they're screaming at each other.

The tenderness in his eyes as he approached Filippa Tangen in the garden, the way his gaze hung on her, the way he tiptoed nervously, apparently desperate to speak to her. The way she turned away from him. The pain in his face afterwards, that first unrequited love. His fear, too. Oh Simen, Simen, what have you done?

Bakkehaugen secondary school stands on a gentle slope. The entrance is surrounded by large chestnut trees – they must be hundreds of years old. The architect did a good job situating the buildings in relation to them, so that as you approach the school you have the impression that it lies at the centre of a grove of beautiful, venerable trees. Later, when you enter the schoolyard, you see that this isn't true – there are only three of them, two at the entrance and one in the schoolyard. But the illusion is there initially, and in a sense, this reflects what Tåsen is best at: giving a certain impression.

There aren't many students outside. It's ten to three, and most of them are probably just about to finish their lessons for the day. A couple of other mothers are on their way into the schoolyard – we nod to each other, but nobody says anything. One of them, a woman in a camel-coloured coat, the mother of a boy in Emma's class, looks as if she's afraid that I might speak to her. This wounds me, at first – has our house become so toxic that nobody wants to have anything to do with us anymore? Then I realise that I'm still wearing my sweaty, dirty training clothes, that I have mud on my knees and hands, and perhaps on my face, and that I'm limping. It's quite possible I shouldn't have come here. The impulse was to collect Emma, bring her home before anyone was able to get hold of her, but of course I understand that she's thirteen years old, and that everything I do reflects on her.

In the schoolyard I look around. I can't remember Emma's timetable, don't know where I can expect to find her, and would prefer not to have to enter the building. The mother in the camel-coloured coat disappears through the double glass doors of the main entrance, and for a while I consider following her, but then I cast the thought aside, because where would I go once I was inside? And limping around, no less, like the hunchback of Notre Dame. I shuffle across to the chestnut tree instead, lean my back against it and look around. The basketball nets, the benches. The enclosed walkway leading to the sports hall. This is where Emma spends her days. In this school-yard, her dramas play out. Filippa and Emma, each with their own clique, the looks they send each other. I can almost hear Emma saying to her friends, *Oh my God, she's just so conceited*. What does Filippa say about Emma? She's quieter than my daughter, less confident in wielding her power, but hardly more gentle. Something sinks within me. I'd prefer not to have to see all these teenagers. The kids of the housewife and her friends, all Emma's friends and enemies. I don't want to be seen by them, especially not now, all cold and sweaty and dirty, about to lose my grip. I just want to pick up my daughter. If I stay here, there'll be no avoiding them, so I hurry across to the sports hall and go in.

Inside it smells of sawdust, sweat and coffee. The stage curtains for *The Threepenny Opera* hang heavily along the walls, I walk straight into them as I walk into the hall. They're attached to a ceiling rig, forming a dark ring around the space. In here I could find myself a hidden corner, I think, a gap between the wall and the curtain. I could lie down and fall asleep. I consider this, in all seriousness. Then I hear someone rummaging around in there. I push the curtain aside and look into the hall. Gard is standing just in front of the stage. The rows of seats have been broken up, and many of the chairs that were set out for the audience have already been removed, but the first row is still intact, and he's digging around in two cardboard boxes placed towards the middle.

"Hello," I say.

He looks up.

"Oh, hi."

His gaze is unfocused when he looks at me – I'm not sure whether this is because he doesn't remember me, or because he's thinking of something else. I remember what the housewife said, about how it's strange that a man of his age would want to have teenage girls play prostitutes. All the teenage girls, or just one in particular? I look at his hands, which are surprisingly strong, considering the slightness of his body. Could he have put them on her? Is there any possibility? Emma is a child, but is that just as clear to others as it is to me? Might he have seen something else? The thought makes my head so light and blank that I feel faint, as if I'll hit the floor if I pursue it.

"Rikke," I say. "I'm Emma's mum."

Not the tiniest hint will escape me. If he blushes ever so slightly, if his eyes flick away for just a hundredth of a second, I'll notice it. But nothing of the sort happens, he only gives a brief nod, and if her name does stir anything in him it's impossible to tell from the outside. His horn-rimmed glasses are pushed up into his hair, his chin is stubbly and he looks tired. It seems strange that girls would find him attractive. But he looks different now. The skin beneath his eyes is puffy, and he's pale. He moves slowly. Behind him, on the stage, is a wooden construction, a crate with a post stuck in it. Out from the post sticks a beam, and from the beam hangs a rope, and I recognise it from the rough sketches: it's the scaffold where Mack the Knife is hanged. At least somebody has had the foresight to wind the rope with its noose around the beam. At least the rope isn't made of blue nylon.

"Tidying up?" I ask.

"Winding down is probably more like it," he says. "They're dismantling the stage this evening. I'm just trying to save the props."

In his hands he holds Mack the Knife's hat. It's an old-fashioned fedora, with a broad brim and ribbon. An authentic one from the fifties, I remember, provided by a mother in the costume group who holds a senior position at the opera house.

"I heard the play has been postponed," I say, taking a few steps towards him into the hall.

"Postponed," he snorts, looking up at me. "Do you think I believe that? They already wanted to shut us down back in the autumn, because of all this business over the whores. The head and the Parent-Teacher Association and the school activities group. And her – Nina Sparre. We wouldn't have lasted a day beyond the first angry email if some of the parents hadn't started talking about freedom of speech."

His hand flies up towards his head and hits his glasses. It seems he's forgotten that he put them there, because he jumps. They slide towards his forehead, and he catches them, just before they fall off his face and onto the floor.

"Everybody at this school thinks they're so progressive," he says. "Before the summer, they thought it was so fun to be putting on Brecht, so *courageous* to choose something critical of society. But the minute they encounter opposition, they falter. Fucking Nina, with all her monologues and on-the-one-hand-but-on-the-other-hand, but oh, I mustn't think that *she's* against it, it's the school and the PTA and blah blah blah."

He fixes me with his gaze. His eyes are little a bloodshot, and he's so young. Maybe this is his first job. I almost wonder whether he might have been crying.

"You know what your problem is?" he says, raising his voice, almost shouting now. "It's that none of you are honest enough to tell it like it is. Instead, people get forced out. You mustn't do it like that – but oh no, not like that, either. That's the way things are done around here, until you finally find yourself standing there with nothing but the realisation that you no longer have a job."

It looks as if he's about to say something more, but the school bell interrupts him, ringing in hard thrusts. Like an alarm, I think. He slings the hat into the cardboard box in front of him so that it falls across the other items that lie inside it, a couple of manuscripts and the false engagement ring Mack the Knife gives to Polly Peachum. For a moment I think he's about to burst into tears. I want to withdraw, look away and leave him alone, but I'm so unspeakably tired. It's as if I don't have the strength to move, or even turn my head. So I just stand there, staring, as he falls to pieces. The school bell stops ringing. Gard pulls himself together.

"When it came down to it," he says, his voice thick, "nobody defended the play. All those parents who had written emails about how important it was before, you know? After Filippa's father died, they were silent, all of them. The school is just shutting us down. As if the death was our fault. The decision was made without anyone even asking me. And none of you – not a single one – protested."

I don't meet his eyes. Instead, I look down at his hands. They're white, with black hair on them. What does Emma see when she looks at them?

He rubs them over his eyes, hiding his face, and when he removes them again, he's calmer. There's something young and unmarred about him. I wonder how he'll look back on this unsuccessful production in five or ten years' time: as a lesson, an experience he needed, or as the first of many blows to his idealism.

"Rumour has it that the police have arrested someone connected to the play," he says tiredly. "Apparently, some subversive videos have been posted online. And you know, the piece has a communistic sting. *What is the murder of a man to the employment of a man?* So now they have all they need. A murderer, some tortured cats, and me giving incendiary material to kids. As if *that's* the problem. These kids watch YouTube sitting on the edge of their beds at night, and their parents think they'll be damaged by Bertolt Brecht?"

He looks at me with hard eyes.

"The world your children live in – you wouldn't believe it. What they see online. What they share, how they talk to each other. You'd be quite shocked, all of you, if you knew what they say when you're not around."

This I believe, without question. I'm about to say something, ask for details. What do they do? What is it I wouldn't believe, can he be more specific? But then Gard grabs the box on the chair in front of him and snatches it up.

"Well," he says. "There's no point in delaying the inevitable."

He sets the box down on the edge of the stage, then swings up there himself. He picks up the box and straightens his back, standing before the gallows, and looks down at me.

"Would you say hi to Merete from me?" he asks. "And Filippa?"

It's hard to judge whether he's being genuine, or whether there's a certain bitterness beneath this request. But I nod. Gard turns and disappears into the wings. Behind the curtains I hear a door slam shut behind him.

She isn't home when I let myself in. It's now long after the final bell rang, and I've gone into her room, found her timetable and confirmed that yes, that was her last class for the day. I'm in the kitchen. I'd like to just sit here and wait for her but I'm unable to stay still. What if Simen didn't act alone, what if he had a friend? You'd be shocked, all of you, Gard had said, if you knew what they say when you're not around. The kid who was playing Peachum, who spoke to Simen at the rehearsal on Saturday, who performed with such sensitivity when he declaimed his defence of harming others: *I'm no criminal, I'm just a poor man, Brown*. I pace the length of the kitchen, back and forth. Yes, he's young and impulsive, this friend of Simen's, and something about him hints at a potential for recklessness, a willingness to commit violence. If he wanted to get in the front door, Simen could have opened it. I glance out of the window, looking for Emma, picturing it: Peachum following her as she walks home from school, passing her up where Kastanjesvingen branches off Bakkehaugsveien. Asking her to come over, or worse, grabbing her by the arm, pulling her after him. Dumping her in a garden, covering her with leaves and branches. I imagine how I will sit here and wait, wonder how long it will take for me to finally take out the scrap of paper with Gundersen's number on it. Then a search party and a thorough investigation of the gardens using dogs, and then later, deep into the night, Robin Pettersen standing at our door with those apologetic eyes: I'm sorry, but I have some very sad news. This friend of Simen could have killed Jørgen, I think. If Simen let him in, it wouldn't have shown up on the list from the locksmith. Simen could even have given him the code. Yes, maybe Peachum let himself in using the Sparre family's code that night. Simen could have told him about the spare key. Taken the ladder from the shed and put it under Jørgen's window as a diversion.

Not to mention Gard – he's been to the house several times, gone up to Merete's place to talk with her. Maybe she gave him the code? He was furious just now, and who knows what he might be capable of? What if Jørgen had some dirt on him? Something about the young girls who were going to play prostitutes in the school play, perhaps. Filippa, who got the lead role as promised, or Emma, who might have fallen for him.

The moment she touches the door handle I leap up, and pain shoots out from my knee and up to my brain again. I limp towards the hallway, there to meet her before she's even had a chance to close the door behind her. She has her schoolbag on her back and her jacket on. Her long blonde hair is styled over one shoulder, but it's got tangled, the long day and the wind have messed it up, the strands of hair rubbing against the shoulder strap of her bag all the way home. She looks at me.

"What is it?" she asks.

She has this impatient look, as if the world owes her, needs to pull itself together. I'm aching to ask her about Gard, what she thinks about him, whether anything has happened between them.

"Why have you blocked me on Facebook?" I ask instead.

She doesn't answer right away. Her eyes have a calculated calm to them, as if she's the adult and I'm the child, and I'm so afraid I could scream at her – slap her, even.

"Why are you asking about that?" she says eventually.

"That was the deal," I say, already too loud, too shrill. "Don't you remember? That was the condition of you being allowed on social media. It was totally fine by me, I said, absolutely fine, no problem, as long as you let me follow you."

No words are forthcoming. Her bag hangs over one shoulder and she's stuck her hands into her pockets, taking on a sort of holding position, as if she thinks she just has to ride out my rant.

"It's not that I want to watch over everything you do online," I continue, and now something snaps, now I'm shouting. "But Emma – I'm your mother! I'm doing this to protect you!"

"By looking at what I post on Facebook?"

"There's a murderer out there! Somebody has murdered your neighbour!"

"I know that," she says.

Calmly, as if it bores her. But a slight uncertainty has crept into her otherwise smug expression. Yes, I can see it – she's afraid, too. I double down.

"The police have arrested someone," I say. "Did you know that?"

"No," she says. "Who?"

"You don't know?"

Somewhere, deep inside, I'm enjoying this. To have her attention, absolute and undivided. To have the upper hand.

"Who is it?" Emma asks again.

"Simen Sparre."

Something flits across her features. For a moment it's as if the face she shows the world is just a thin veneer that could be scraped away, revealing the blood and seething anxiety just beneath. It lasts for a few hundredths of a second, and then it's gone. She sniffs, and says:

"Simen Sparre? No, I don't think so."

"Well," I say, taking her words as a challenge to my authority. "The police certainly seem to think so. They took him away this afternoon."

This nameless, rebellious impulse flutters over her again, it's like a tic, like something that just happens, something she has no control over.

"Simen cares about the environment," she says firmly. "Simen has morals. He has a YouTube channel."

"He has what?"

She takes a deep breath then puffs out her cheeks, as if I'm so ridiculously naive, and it's so exhausting that it always falls to her to explain just how the world works.

Simen's face is frozen in a strange expression in the still image on the iPad. His eyes are half closed, his mouth open, the lips slightly curled, he's obviously about to say something. Beneath the triangular icon that will set the video playing, it says: *Green Gonzo Explains: Life in the Goldfish Bowl*. I have my finger poised, ready, but feel a sudden reluctance to tap the screen.

"How do you know about this?" I ask Emma.

"Mamma," she says, getting up from the sofa, "everybody at school knows about it."

I hear her footsteps disappear down the stairs.

He has 109 subscribers and has posted 17 videos. I tap play. Simen's face comes to life on the screen. His eyes open and he grins, leaning towards the camera.

"Hello," he says, "and welcome to the goldfish bowl. I'm Green Gonzo, and I'm going to show you why we just can't seem to get anything done to fix the big problems in the world, and – spoiler alert! – it's because people are so fucking *stupid*. So yeah, that's what we're going to talk about today."

He takes a deep breath and laughs. Part of me thinks: God, he's so childish, a little boy playing TV presenter. Another part of me is watching in terror, thinking: What *is* this?

The subject of the video is climate change. Simen is apparently disappointed in his parents' generation's lack of willingness to solve the climate crisis. He thinks we're hypocrites.

"Air traffic is just increasing and increasing," he says, "and it isn't as if we don't know that we have to fly less, and it isn't as if nobody has told us that we shouldn't drive everywhere or buy new clothes all the time or suck up all the fucking oil that's in the seabed. But we do it anyway, and this, all this, is about the self-delusion in what I call the *goldfish bowl*."

At this point he leans back in his chair for a moment, appears self-satisfied. Behind him I can see the cold stone wall of the cellar, and I shudder and think: He's sitting right next door to my little miracle baby. Lukas might have been asleep in his bed on the other side of the wall while Simen was filming this.

The goldfish bowl, Simen believes, can best be illustrated by the well-off, well-educated neighbourhood in which he himself lives.

"All my neighbours here *believe* all the right things. Politically-correct-o-rama, know what I mean? So of course everybody is extremely environmentally conscious. They put it in their Facebook profiles – go check it out. But I'm asking you, yes, *you* watching this video: What do you think happens when summer comes around, and there's a wine tasting happening in Tuscany and a safari in Botswana? Do you think these people go on a camping holiday in Elverum instead?"

Here he leans back and guffaws, you can see his Adam's apple vibrating in his throat. Something in his message reminds me of my own research, the way that I've explained it to my neighbours – including his parents, most likely: the intersection between attitudes and behaviour, cognitive dissonance.

"I call this neighbourhood the goldfish bowl because it's small, and because no ideas come in from the outside. Get it? We're talking *classic* echo chamber. And it's precisely this hypocrisy we're going to expose in these videos. So stay tuned, okay? See yaaaaaaaaa."

The video ends with him looking for the off button on his computer, you can see his eyes focusing on something on the screen for a moment, and then the image freezes.

The next video is about microplastics. You get the impression that Simen has read up on things a little more by this point because he's more serious now, sticking to a kind of script and serving up statistics. There's something neat about this video, a hint of the youth column of a national newspaper about it. The third video he's made with a friend, and it's rather long. Aside from a bit about the environment at the beginning, they mostly talk about a computer game they obviously both play. The fourth one is about the bees dying. In this video, Simen is more crass, angrier. I now feel the tiniest bit struck by his critique. Realise that I've sat there at dinner parties talking about how people are destroying the planet, feeling I had a right to do so because of my work, and the more guilt-stricken my listeners have seemed, the better I've felt. When we ate dinner with Jørgen and Merete, Jørgen had asked me about my job, and I felt so high and mighty as I went on about my research project which *thematises over-consumption* in order to *acquire knowledge about effective interventions*. To save the environment – simple as that. Did I not say all this, amiably and soberly to Jørgen, as I felt Merete's eyes on me and thought: And what are *you* doing with *your* life? What do *you* have to show for yourself that will measure up to this?

In the eleventh video, Simen launches a serious attack on hypocrisy. The people in the goldfish bowl think nothing of taxing or making life more difficult for others, he says, as long as it doesn't affect them personally. And then he moves on to animals. Claims that the eradication of animal species we see today is equivalent to a mass extinction. The loss of 800 species has been linked to human activity, but the real figure is likely far higher. One million species are at risk – like the white rhinoceros. The last male in the northern subspecies died just a few weeks ago. There was the odd mention in the newspapers, and he saw a Facebook post here and there with crying faces and hearts, but where is the despair? Where is the rage? A story about a disease that affected Norwegian house cats cultivated far more engagement than the one about the rhinoceros, the newspapers wrote article upon article about it, all of them shared and liked and commented on, and since Facebook's algorithms are steered by engagement, the rhinoceros story was shoved far down into the pit of collective oversight. Here, Simen's eyes are big and round.

"After all," he says, "who cares about the white rhinoceros? What people care about is their fucking pets. Dogs and cats – then people take an interest. Despite the fact that we have so many house cats that they exist at the expense of natural fauna, all these well-fed pets killing small nesting birds. If those fucking cats were facing a mass extinction, *then* you'd see people taking action."

I imagine the furry baby animal hanging by its neck beside the mailboxes. Is this what Simen is talking about? Quick as a flash, I copy the link and send it to Jamila.

I'm halfway through video fourteen when Åsmund and Lukas arrive home.

"What are you doing?" Åsmund asks, coming over to peer down at the iPad.

"It's Simen Sparre's YouTube channel," I say. "Emma showed me."

"Oh," Åsmund says. "And what does he make videos about? Cargo trousers? How you absolutely *shouldn't* shave?"

"Can I watch *Ninjago*?" Lukas asks, groping for the iPad, which I have to lift out of his reach.

I buy him off with a box of raisins he immediately empties across the coffee table, and while he's busy with that, I follow Åsmund into the kitchen.

"They've arrested him. Simen."

"Simen?" Åsmund asks. "You mean the most virtuous teenage boy this side of the Sølvguttene boys' choir?"

"Yes."

Åsmund wrinkles his brow.

"No," he says. "No, that sounds way too far-fetched. They've arrested him for murdering Jørgen?"

"Yes, it seems so."

"Why in the world would he want to kill Jørgen?"

"I don't know," I say. "He has this YouTube channel. Emma showed me, I've just been looking at it. And, well. It's pretty crazy, quite a bit of it. He has some wild ideas."

For a while we stand there in silence. Åsmund empties the bag of shopping while I stand there passively and watch him. Then he says:

302

"No, I'm sorry, but I just can't believe it. I'm sure the police know what they're doing, but this . . . he's just a kid, Rikke."

Just a kid, I think, as I sit on the bathroom floor behind the locked door, scrolling through Green Gonzo's channel on my phone. How old are the students behind the school shootings in the US? How old were the kids who joined ISIS? I agree that Simen Sparre seems harmless, but what do we actually know about what people are capable of? Jamila has countered my link with another, the one to video fifteen, where, nine minutes and four seconds in, Simen encourages his subscribers to take to the streets to wake people up – using any means necessary.

I undress, get into the shower. As the hot water closes around me, I think: Let's just say that the police are right. Let's say that Simen Sparre killed Jørgen. Because he wanted to wake people up, and Jørgen was as good a candidate as any. Maybe Jørgen's article about temping agencies is a threat to Svein, and Simen knew about it? Or maybe he heard the high-heeled shoes on the stairs when Merete and Filippa were away – this, too, can be seen as a form of hypocrisy. And don't the clicking heels on the stairs also constitute a betrayal of Filippa?

Let's say that Simen had decided to kill someone in the goldfish bowl in order to wake up the general public, and that he selected Jørgen as his victim. In that case, I think, squeezing shower gel from the bottle that stands in the small basket that hangs from the fitting, Jørgen's death would no longer have anything to do with me. At least not directly. And then there'd be no need to say anything to Åsmund. I quickly rinse my hair, step out of the shower and wrap myself in a towel. Perhaps it's as simple as that. Maybe all this is over now.

Åsmund is sitting at the kitchen table fiddling with his phone when I come out. There's a pan on the hob; he's presumably waiting for the water to boil. I approach him from behind, put my arms around him and press my face against the warm skin of his neck. Close my eyes, inhale the scent of him. He's used the same after-shave since high school – it smells pleasant and fresh, like the forest after the rain, and it reminds me of being young, of being so happy because you've found the one you love. It's home for me, I think – this smell is the essence of home. It doesn't matter what kind of house we live in, where it is. This – Åsmund and my children – is my home.

"Wowzers," he says. "Have I done something special without realising it?"

"No," I say, my lips against the skin of his throat. "I just felt like hugging you."

With my head leaning against him, I feel just how tired I am. Perhaps I might even manage to sleep tonight.

The road out to Strandkaien appeared different this time. I pulled my suitcase after me, it was heavy and bumped over the cobblestones and the cracks in the pavement. And it was raining. The reception was as I remembered it, and when I said the name on the booking, the young receptionist, hardly distinguishable from the previous one, said that Jørgen was already there. I took the key and pulled my heavy suitcase after me towards the lift.

When I opened the door to the hotel room he came towards me, smiling, and I hugged him and rested my face against his shirt, ran my fingers through his curls, thinking that despite everything it had become familiar, this – he gave me the feeling of coming home. And I so wished that he didn't, because then everything would have been so much easier.

There was no mariachi band that played for us this time. Instead, the smell of fried food hung heavily over Torgallmenningen – it was pervasive, impossible to escape. We walked slowly back to the hotel after the meal, hand in hand. It was June, but the air was cold because of the rain, the sky a shade of grey that failed to disclose whether it was spring or autumn. We didn't say much. One or the other of us would make the occasional observation, but all attempts at conversation died on the spot, as if we were both unspeakably tired.

Back at the hotel I dug my nails into his upper arms, pulling him towards me as if I would drown if I didn't hold onto him with all my might, and made love to him with an intensity I suspected was pure desperation. Afterwards, he took a small bottle of wine from the minibar and poured it into plastic glasses. We sat in the bed, each with our own duvet around us, and he said:

"Okay. Tell me what's bothering you."

"It's nothing special," I said. "Nothing new, anyway."

"You look as if you're about to go to pieces."

Out on the street we could hear a ruckus – students on their way into the city, hollering at each other, drunk and teeming, the night open before them. I took a deep breath. I had no idea how I was going to say it.

Jørgen hadn't wanted children, he had told me. He had suspected early on that he just wasn't the fatherly type, and even though he loved his daughter – of course he did – there was no escaping the fact that, in a sense, he had been right. There was so much he was expected to have an opinion on. Winter boots and school subject choices and packed lunches and sleep hygiene, grades and homework and friendship dramas and recreational activities. He had told Merete, in no uncertain terms, that he didn't think he was the type who could drop everything for another person. That he couldn't, for example, imagine saying no if his boss asked him to cover a conflict in a war-ravaged area. That he couldn't prioritise what it would mean for a child if something should happen to him. Merete said okay. Of course, the child would still have her, she said – she wasn't going off to cover any war. That had been the deal, Jørgen told me. He didn't want to get married and start a family. Merete thought that he was just afraid of change. Perhaps she had believed things would be different once the child arrived, but they weren't, or at least not in the way she had imagined. She was the one who wanted to let go of her career. She said, quite unambiguously, that it didn't matter to her, and anyway, she didn't know whether she was good enough to be the very best in her field; the competition was cut-throat, all the elbows so sharp, and that wasn't the kind of life she wanted to lead. It didn't matter to her if he was the main bread-winner, if she worked part-time and took on the main responsibilities at home.

"I was willing to end it," Jørgen said to me. "I loved her, but I was willing to take the consequences of my eccentricities. She wanted a child, and I thought she deserved to have one with somebody who wanted the same thing. I left her, but she cried down the phone and asked me to come back. Said that she would do all the work, that I wouldn't need to change. And I was stupid enough to believe her."

He didn't blame Merete, he said. She had believed that it would be possible for them to live that way. Sure, it was a little naive, but on the other hand he had been just as naive himself. They had entered into a compromise that obviously wouldn't hold, and they should have understood that, the both of them. But she blamed him. All the time, Jørgen said. For every-thing he didn't do. For everything he was clueless about, or took no interest in. And, as time passed, for everything he was. But they made it work, in a way, finding an arrangement they could live with until Filippa was old enough for them to leave each other.

"If we ever do," Jørgen said. "Sometimes I wonder whether we've taken root."

He didn't want to leave Merete, at least not now. He had made certain promises, thought he owed her something. She took care of their daughter, and he supported them – that was his duty. But he felt no guilt about his extramarital indiscretions.

It wasn't like that for me. I loved Åsmund. It wasn't promises that bound us together, and I didn't blame him for anything. I lived with him because I wanted to. When Jørgen spoke about his relationship, I would listen with horror. Several times I had shuffled close to Åsmund during the night to set my cheek against his back, in gratitude at the fact that we didn't detest each other that way.

And I did feel guilty. And now, I felt the weight of this guilt. It squeezed around my chest whenever Åsmund came to me with his humdrum declarations of love. When a childhood friend left his wife for a younger woman, Åsmund uncomprehendingly shook his head – what was he thinking? As for me, I was forever putting forward new accusations against my own behaviour, knowing that this could continue no longer. I had to let Jørgen go. It was something I should have done a long time ago.

He understood, he said, as we sat there under the duvets in the hotel room. It was different for him, but he understood that it wasn't right for me.

"I don't want to make you unhappy, either," he said as I cried.

Afterwards, we slept together for the last time. The following day I travelled home alone, and that was that. When Åsmund asked how the trip had been, it gnawed at my chest, and although I felt relieved that it was over, I was – if admittedly a little late – half crushed by my guilty conscience. At least I had managed to draw a line under it.

SECOND FRIDAY NIGHT

The Sparres leave Kastanjesvingen in the middle of the night. Under cover of darkness, so late that they're certain not to bump into anyone, they pack up their things. I've somehow managed to fall asleep, but I wake to the sound of rummaging around on the other side of the wall, and I'm instantly on high alert. Throat tight and hands clammy, I hurry barefoot out into the kitchen, kneel down beside the cupboard that houses the boiler and open the door.

At first, I hear only footsteps, things being moved. My clammy fingers tap the emergency number for the police into my phone. I hold my finger above the button, ready to call. But then I hear Svein's voice.

"Do you want to take these?" he says in a loud whisper.

"No," Nina replies.

Or at least I think it's her. Her voice is different, hoarse and small, drained of its usual energy. Empty, somehow.

They carry on for a quarter of an hour, and then Svein says:

"Well. I think that's it."

She doesn't answer. A few seconds pass, and he says:

"Oh, but honey. Come on now."

She's sobbing. I carefully push the cupboard door closed. This is private, not mine to overhear.

They leave a short time after that. From the darkness of the kitchen, I watch their shadows walk down the paved path without them seeing me. They each carry their own bag. Svein opens the gate. Nina stops down there, turns, and looks up at the house. Svein sets down his bag, puts his arms around her. She leans her head against his shoulder. They stand like this for a while, these two parents, and it breaks my heart.

The police held a press conference late yesterday evening, I think. I turn on the news and see the policewoman with the Nordvestland dialect, the same solemn face. *Police apprehend suspect in Tåsen murder*, it says in huge black letters beneath her image, although it seems the policewoman herself is doing everything she can to downplay the whole thing. The person in custody is a suspect, she says, but she cannot say with any certainty that they are close to solving the Tåsen murder. They have made interesting findings, which have heightened suspicion towards this person. No, she cannot say anything about these findings. No, she does not wish to speculate as to when the murder will be solved. For the whole time she's speaking, the black letters at the bottom of the screen scream that somebody has been arrested and that the case is approaching a resolution – in a manner fundamentally at odds with what she's saying, as if the TV channel is flat out ignoring her careful bureaucratic language and saying to its viewers: But we all know what this really means, don't we? All the newspapers are covering the case. One has interviewed its own so-called legal expert, an ageing journalist, from what I gather, who has reported on legal proceedings for so many years that they've deemed him worthy of this title purely on the basis of his staying power. He claims that the arrest indicates that the case has moved into a critical phase; states that it isn't uncommon for the police to now keep their cards close to their chest. Another newspaper has found the YouTube channel and writes, in a way that hardly conceals his identity for anyone who has seen one of the videos, that the person who has been apprehended has published several videos with extreme content, in which he urges viewers to save the climate through *partly violent means*. The back of my head begins to ache. I have this exhausted feeling of a woollen blanket being wrapped around my head, close and heavy, smothering my access to oxygen so that I can no longer see or think or breathe properly. I sit there on the sofa, lean my head back against the wall and close my eyes. I'm too restless to sleep, I know that, there's no point in going to bed now. I curse the healthy-to-his-core doctor who maintained such a tight grip on his medication. What I wouldn't give for a pill that could take the edge off all this, knock me out.

And now, of course, the case is moving away from me. Simen Sparre has created videos in which he encourages violence, the newspaper writes, although part of me doubts just how seriously we should take any of them. They've arrested him. The police know what they're doing. They're probably in possession of compelling evidence that they're currently unable to share with the general public. All will become clear in time. And it has nothing to do with me. Not with creeping up the stairs in my bare feet, not with weekends spent away under the pretence of work, nor with text messages sent late in the evening. I squeeze my eyes shut. At the end of the day, none of this had anything to do with Jørgen's death. A crazy seventeen-year-old, on the other hand – madness right next door. Not the kind we overheard when we opened the door to the boiler cupboard, but another, quieter madness. When it comes to that sort of thing, there's nothing that can be done. You can't protect yourself against everything. The potential for violence exists in every family, in every area and social stratum, and no matter how you might scrape together to be able to afford an apartment in the right neighbourhood, you can't buy yourself out of the risk of living right next door to someone dangerous, lethal.

In the dream I'm in Jørgen's apartment. I'm standing in the middle of the living room. The door to his study is ajar, it's dark inside, and

I'm pulled towards it, even though I'm doing my best to resist, because I know what awaits me in there.

Then I'm standing in the study. Jørgen lies across the computer keyboard, all I can see is the back of his head. There isn't any blood around him – it looks as if he's sleeping – but I know that isn't the case. As I'm about to touch his shoulder, I sense that someone else is in the room. Somebody is standing behind me in the dark. I know this, even though I can't hear anything, and I understand that my life is in danger.

The next moment, I'm out on the lawn. I'm breathing heavily, terrified. I can see through the wall, can see the door opening up in Jørgen's apartment, and I know that they're coming. Realise that it's someone I know – yes, I know who this is – and I say to myself: *But this means, but this means.* I look up at the house. Someone is coming, no name is mentioned, but I know who it is.

At the crack of dawn, I wake on the sofa. My back aches, my shoulders are stiff, and I'm shivering so much that my teeth are chattering. My knee hurts. I fumble for my phone and see that it's six o'clock. I automatically open the browser and update the last page I looked at. It takes a moment, but then the morning's newspaper headline appears: *Tåsen murder suspect released.*

PART III

Hello, darkness

SECOND SATURDAY

The policewoman looks tired. To compensate for this, she's put on some deep-red lipstick. It's another press conference, and this time the entire fourth estate is in attendance. No matter which channel I turn to, no matter which newspaper I open, the same image of her is the main story. Tired and serious, I think – she assures us that they're working hard, day after day; the truth will out in the end.

"The seventeen-year-old arrested yesterday has today been released," she says as the light from camera flashes flickers across her face. "He continues to be a witness, but we would like to emphasise that he is no longer a suspect in the Tåsen murder case. He is, however, central to an unrelated matter regarding animal cruelty, and the Assistant Chief of Police will be filing charges later today."

"Rikke," Åsmund says to me, exaggeratedly raising his eyebrows. "The kids."

But I'm unstoppable. Unable to take my eyes from the screen.

"Is this about the cat killings in the same neighbourhood?" asks a journalist from somewhere off-screen.

"I'm unable to answer that," the policewoman says.

Lukas has taken out all his dinosaurs. He's sitting on the living-room floor, arranging them on the rug. He says nothing. Åsmund gives me a look.

An online newspaper has managed to get hold of a photograph of Simen. His eyes are blacked out, but you can still see his mouth and nose. He's standing against a backdrop with a pattern of blue waves, the kind school photographers often use. He's smiling. Wearing a hoodie. You can see a few pimples on his chin. I wonder what I would have thought of him were I a stranger, how I would have viewed this photo had I never met him. Would I see a child? Or would I see the scum of society, someone with a seething anger building there behind his acne, who hates the girls who don't want him, the boys who think they're better than him, and this neighbourhood that breeds the kind of success he believes is beyond his reach?

A suspect in an unrelated matter. The paws of the little cat hanging limply beside its body, its head bowed, the neck bent at an unnatural angle. I'm unable to rid myself of this image. I'm so tired. All I want is to lie down, to sleep for a hundred years.

To compensate, I go the extra mile when preparing breakfast. I make banana pancakes and set out several different types of jam. I grind coffee beans. Simen could still be a suspect, I think – at least unofficially. They probably need pretty solid evidence in order to be able to hold him for any length of time, and the fact that they don't have this doesn't mean he didn't do it. And there are so many other possibilities, besides. Svein Sparre, who wanted to protect his temping agency, and who may have egged the others on, encouraging them to argue on the cabin trip so he could later shift the blame onto Saman or Åsmund. The construction industry villains who Rebekka Davidsen fears. The rejected husbands whom Jamila suspects. I can feel the conviction that this doesn't concern us coming apart at the seams – my dream, the shadow that was so familiar – but I vehemently hold on to it all the same, pushing it ahead of me as I whisk eggs and fry pancakes. Nobody can say that I don't do nice things for my family.

I shout that it's ready, and Lukas comes running.

"Pancakes!" he cheers.

Åsmund strolls in after him.

"This looks lovely," he says, but he looks tired, or expectant, perhaps.

322

He isn't quite as excited as I had hoped he would be. I feel the panic sneaking in, what if it isn't Simen, what if we become suspects again? Then I'll have to tell Åsmund anyway. What if he leaves me? But I mustn't start doubting everything now. It will all work out, all of this.

"I thought we could enjoy ourselves a little today," I said.

Lukas clambers up onto his Tripp Trapp chair.

"Can I have?" he shouts, holding out his little child's hand. The green plaster around his index finger is dirty at the edges.

"We have to wait for Emma," I say.

"I'm not sure Emma will want to join us," Åsmund says.

"What do you mean?" I ask.

"She's not feeling well, apparently. Says she wants to be alone."

I lean a hand against the kitchen counter. *This content isn't available.* Emma, shutting me out. These pancakes I've made – for them, for her. I feel it building in me, first in my chest, before it shoots out into my arms and up into my face, tightening my jaw. I collect myself. Tell myself I'll be cordial.

"Oh, we can't be like that," I say. "We're eating together. It's Saturday."

"Rikke," Åsmund says, in a voice that sounds as if he's already blaming me for what's to come.

I take the stairs two at a time, hammer at her bedroom door. She doesn't answer, and I hammer again.

"Emma," I shout. "It's breakfast."

No answer.

"Emma! Open up."

Silence.

"Emma, I'm coming in."

Something moves behind the door then. I hear a groan, rustling, and then heavy, slow steps towards the door.

She has the duvet around her shoulders, held together with a hand at her neck, so she looks like a turtle with a shell. Her head and pyjama-covered legs are sticking out, but otherwise she's all duvet. Her hair is dishevelled, and mascara is smudged around her eyes, which are puffy – from sleep or crying, it's hard to say. Her cheeks are red from the warmth of her bed. Just as they were when they were tiny, both my children, red and hot in their baby cheeks when they woke up.

"I was sleeping," she says.

Her voice is raspy, but she doesn't fool me – she wasn't asleep, this is far too affected.

"We're having breakfast," I say, friendlier now. "Why don't you come up and eat with us?"

Like an invitation. Just to be nice, just to give her something to eat, and just as importantly, to ensure that she's seen, heard, acknowledged.

Emma says:

"It's Saturday. I'm going back to bed."

"Oh honey, come on up and eat with us."

I reach out a hand to stroke her cheek, and she jerks back. My hand remains hanging there between us, she looks at it, and there's something in her eyes, terror or disgust, as if the worst thing she can think of is this sign of affection from me.

"Emma, what is it?"

I mean to be gentle, curious. But I have so little control over myself. I'm no longer able to present myself in the way I intend.

"There *isn't* anything," she says, but her voice isn't especially convincing.

"Obviously there is," I say. "You blocked me on Facebook, you don't want to eat with us, I only tried to touch your cheek, and . . ."

"Can't you just leave me alone?" she shrieks.

It erupts from her so suddenly. There is a wildness in this scream that I didn't see coming, and I jump. Take a step back, as if I'm afraid of her.

"I don't want to eat with you, I don't want to sit with you, you can just shove all of it!"

"But Emma . . ."

"Go away!"

She slams the door in my face.

She went through a phase of angry outbursts as a child. At first, she was so calm and sober-minded – determined, but predictable – and then, when she turned three, the outbursts began. She would lie on the floor and howl because I sliced her bread wrong. Didn't want to put on that sweater, nor that one either, and screamed at me, DON'T WANT IT, her face like a single great hole as tears sprang from her eyes. I stood there with the two sweaters, one in each hand, and I had no idea where the rage had come from or how to deal with the hot-tempered child before me. At the clinic, they said that I should give it time. That's just how they are at that age, said the nurse, be consistent, but friendly. I took this on board, tried to be consistent above all else. Emma would not be allowed to choose what she ate or wore, or when she went to bed – I would be the adult. I said no, you're wearing *this* sweater, and she howled even more, turned bright red in the face, NO, NO, NO, she shouted. She lashed out at me. I got angry – you're not allowed to hit me, I shouted, you do not do that. I was more forceful, shoved her arms into the sweater. She stiffened, resisting, locking her elbows and spreading her fingers so I had to tug the sweater over them. It was difficult, and I may have been heavy-handed. She screamed, furious, no more words, just a roar. She kicked me. Hit, bit, pulled.

I don't remember how long it lasted, whether it was a few weeks or months. I remember only these battles with her, and the white-hot, glowing rage within myself – she will not win, I'll show her.

*

I throw open the door. She's halfway across the room, still with the turtle shell around her, and she turns as I come in, mouth half open in surprise because this has never happened before, me coming into her room after she's closed the door. I stride over to her, grab her by the arm – it's so thin and small there under the duvet – and I say:

"You're coming to eat with us, do you understand?"

"I don't want to," Emma howls.

I tighten my grip, drag her out with me. Feel the same white-hot rage, my jaw tightening, my teeth sinking into my upper lip – she will not win. I refuse to let go, dragging her by her scrawny chicken arm. She doesn't exactly resist, but nor does she walk of her own accord, I have to lug her up the stairs. Her turtle shell opens, the duvet falling from her shoulders and dragging after us along the floor, she's in her pyjamas, screaming at me.

"Mamma, have you gone completely psycho?"

Is she angry? Is she afraid? Am I scaring her? I'm unable to stop, I'm so furious – I'm her mother, she has to do as I say. I don't know how long any of us will last, but for now certain things will stand: she will sit with us, and we will eat the fucking pancakes. I haul her into the kitchen.

"Sit down," I shout, the way you bark a command.

I can feel Åsmund and Lukas staring at us, but I don't look at them. I let go of Emma's arm and move to sit down, but this is where she sees her chance. She turns, pulling the duvet with her, and runs out into the living room. I turn and run after her, but she's faster. The lock to the bathroom door clicks into place; I pull on the handle, but it's no use. I can hear her sobbing in there, the sound loud and wild.

"Emma," I shout. "Emma, let me in. Open the door. I'm sorry. I didn't mean to. Honey, can't you just open the door?"

She doesn't answer, but the crying subsides. She turns on the tap, and then that's all I can hear. Perhaps a quieter sobbing underneath it, it's hard to tell. I shout to her again – Emma, honey, can you please just let me in? I want to comfort her now, although of course she doesn't know that, but it is in fact what I want. She's my child. She shouldn't be permitted to decide everything for herself, but she shouldn't be alone and upset, either. I knock on the door again, please come out, Emma. I have no idea what she wants but I'm desperate to make it up to her, to hug her and ask her forgiveness.

Then I feel hand on my shoulder. Åsmund, his face tense and closed.

"That's enough, Rikke," he says.

On his Tripp Trapp chair in the kitchen, Lukas sits and looks at us with marble-round eyes. He doesn't say a word.

"Now let's eat," Åsmund says calmly.

Jamila sweeps into the kitchen as I'm clearing the table. We have eaten in silence, Emma is still in the bathroom, and now we're moving soundlessly in here, slowly, too, as if the air is made of cotton wool, as if each movement encounters resistance, making it an effort to lift an arm or move a leg. But Jamila cuts through. She click-clacks in on her pointy stiletto-heeled boots and grabs hold of me with her thin, strong hands.

"Simen Sparre has posted another video."

"Oh," I say dully, and when I'm not sufficiently shocked Jamila squeezes my upper arms a little harder – it hurts, she's pinching me, in fact.

"He uploaded it ten minutes ago. I've just seen it – we could watch it together."

"We can put it on the TV," I say lamely.

It doesn't matter what's in the video, I think – what's it to us? Jamila pulls me after her, into the living room. Åsmund looks a little put out – he's installed Lukas on the floor with his dinosaurs and has just sat down on the sofa with his phone – but at the same time he's far too polite to say a word against a guest, no matter how invasive she might be. He picks up Lukas and the dinosaurs and goes down to Lukas's bedroom. Jamila fiddles with the remote controls, first one, then the other, impatiently pressing the buttons with her fingertips beneath their acrylic nails – she can't get the TV to work, so she throws the remotes at me. Just then, the lock on the bathroom door clicks. I turn and see Emma hurry out and disappear down the stairs, still with her turtle shell around her, so all I can see of her is her feet and her blonde ponytail.

"Emma," I say listlessly, but she doesn't stop, and nor do I expect her to.

I'm about to say something about this to Jamila but she doesn't seem to have noticed, she's staring impatiently at the remote controls – don't I intend to do something? Slowly, I press the right buttons and the screen illuminates. Down in the cellar I hear a door open and close.

Jamila clicks on the YouTube icon and searches for Green Gonzo. In the top video we can see a still image of Simen Sparre, sitting in what appears to be a smart, well-furnished office. There's a bookshelf behind him, and light falls across him from a window that must be located somewhere to the left of the desk at which he's sitting. This isn't the cellar room next door to Lukas's bedroom. Nor is it any other room in Nina and Svein's apartment. Something about the furniture, the light. He's somewhere else.

An explanation, it says under the still image – this is the video's title. No adjectives, I notice, and he doesn't use the name Green Gonzo. The brief text exudes a kind of seriousness, or perhaps self-confidence – as does the office behind him. Simen has taken his YouTube channel up a notch, out of the cellar and into the public realm. Beneath the title are the number of views and reactions. The video was posted 14 minutes ago and has already been watched almost 300 times. It appears that Green Gonzo now has more than 2,000 subscribers. Jamila is one of them, I think, and then it dawns on me: All of Tåsen is following him now. All the neighbours. Everyone at school. The parents of his friends, out of fear and disgust. And the media, of course, so they can be the first to break the story, to write about whatever he posts next. Jamila presses play, and Simen comes to life.

"As you've probably heard," Simen says, looking into the camera, "I was arrested yesterday, in connection with something that's happened in my neighbourhood."

Here he casts a glance to the side, as if there's someone sitting there who might give him instructions. His face is serious and exhibits none of the tomfoolery of his previous videos.

"A murder case," he says, and clears his throat.

He looks down at the desk in front of him, and then into the camera.

"Firstly, I'd like to say that I have nothing at all to do with that case. It's affected a neighbouring family whose members I regard as my friends, and I feel very sad for them. Of course, I would *never* think to hurt another person."

He casts another glance just to the right of the camera. He's wearing a dark shirt and his hair is combed into a side-parting, and something about him looks so tidy, so grown-up. In front of him he has a few sheets of paper that he occasionally looks down at. There's something insecure about him, something a little afraid. He's nervous, I think. One of his hands is trembling slightly. But his voice is calm.

"The police have released me, and they emphasise that I am not suspected of the murder of my neighbour. I am, however, a suspect in some cases of animal cruelty, and this is what I would like to explain in this video."

He steals a glance at his sheets of paper and looks up again, his gaze determined, fixed.

"Firstly, I would like to apologise."

For a moment I think of the execution scene in *The Threepenny Opera*, Mack the Knife begging for his life in the sports hall of Bakkehaugen school. I now see what it is that's so attractive about Simen. In addition to his handsomely shaped lips and strong jaw he has such large eyes, so clear and genuine. Eyes that will soon make girls weak at the knees. Maybe. If all this can be put right, that is.

"I would like to apologise to the families who owned the cats. I feel awful."

Here he swallows, falling silent for two unbearable seconds. Then he straightens his back.

"I would first like to emphasise that the cats did not suffer a slow, painful death. It's important for me to let people know that. They died in their sleep, of an overdose. This was never about cruelty to animals. It was about putting on a show to make people see. And I would never have done what I did had I not believed that I could achieve something significant by it, something that might benefit the neighbourhood, and maybe even the world."

He looks directly into the camera, straight at us.

"In my opinion, the climate crisis is clearly the biggest threat we currently face as a species, and we are not doing nearly enough to counter it. Newspaper articles and protests don't seem to be waking people up, and this is very frustrating. So I thought that the best way to rouse people would be to hit them through something they're already invested in."

Here he again looks over at the person or people sitting off camera, as if to check that they're paying attention. It seems they are. So are Jamila and I. His speech is a little pretentious, but there's also something authentic and sincere about it. Yes, Simen Sparre is going to get through this just fine.

"The . . . bestial aspects of the cat killings were intended to shock, and I can promise the families that the animals did not suffer. I thought that the ends justified the means, but I see now that they didn't. I stand by my motivation, which was to shake my neighbourhood out of the collective trance their consumerism has put them in. But I deeply regret the method I chose. I'm terribly sorry for the pain I've caused the families who the cats belonged to, and especially . . ."

He stops here, looks down.

"Especially the children in those families."

Simen pushes his sheets of paper aside. He looks at us, his

expression serious, and then he glances to the side again, before with a small nod he signals that he's done. Immediately afterwards, the screen turns black.

Jamila turns and looks at me.

"Simen Sparre," she says.

"Yes."

There's nothing more to say. I'm not sure what to make of the performance we've just witnessed. I still don't understand the boy. It's as if a few pieces are missing, or perhaps it's that my tired brain can't quite put them all together. Jamila starts to give me her opinion – she thinks he appeared sympathetic, despite what he's done, which she of course finds reprehensible. As she speaks, I hear the door downstairs open and close again. Then a stamping on the stairs, its intensity and rhythm such that I know it's her well before her head appears above the top step.

"Emma," I shout, getting up.

But by the time I reach her she's already in the hallway, putting on her shoes.

"What do you want?" she says without straightening up.

This was probably meant to seem indifferent, but she's unable to pull it off – she's angry, afraid. When she stands, I see that the skin around her eyes is flushed and swollen. It gives her a foreign appearance, she doesn't look like herself.

"Can't we talk about it, please?" I say.

I want to say I'm sorry, want to put my arms around her, pull her close, but I can't quite do it – something in my body resists touching her. She straightens up, looks at me. We're almost the same height now.

"You want to talk?" she says, her voice husky and hard. "Fine. Shall we talk about Jørgen, then? I thought maybe you didn't want to, but if you do, please, go right ahead."

The air between us vibrates. My eyes flit randomly around her face in an attempt to find clues – what exactly is she saying, what is it she means? This opening of hers is like a landmine she's laid on the floor between us – it might explode if we so much as approach it and so we must tiptoe cautiously around it, watch our every move in order to prevent it blowing up, taking everything with it. I take a cautious step to one side. Say her name. Feel my voice become thin and full of air. There is total silence. We look at each other, and she's asking me about something with her eyes, wants me to say it, her hard jaw quivering.

"Rikke!" cries Jamila from the living room.

I turn my head in her direction, just for millisecond, but when I turn back Emma is taking her jacket from the hook.

"Fine," she says, still facing the wall. "That's just what I thought."

"Wait," I say, and set a hand on her arm.

She waits, ready to listen to me, and for a moment I feel the pull of her landmine – to just stamp on it, say something about what happened and let the chips fall where they may. But I can't. Too much is at stake.

"Where are you going?" I ask instead.

She takes a deep breath. For a moment it looks as if she's about to cry.

"Out. I don't know. To Saga's place."

"Will you be long?"

"Mamma," she says, and now she really is on the verge of tears. "Can't you just leave me alone?"

After she's gone, I stand there looking at the door she closed behind her. Hear the bang of the front door out there. I'm powerless. Perhaps the landmine went off after all, and there are shards of it sticking in the walls, in my skin, in my chest. I hold my breath. I can still save this. Can still rewrite it, *talk about Jørgen*, she said, it could have meant anything at all. I think of her standing there in her nightie, when she called out to me over the baby monitor.

"Rikke," Jamila shouts impatiently from the living room.

And I know that I have to go in there. That I have to continue to play this role, listen to Jamila play detective, yield to her so she'll fail to figure it out. Even now, in this position, I have to ask myself what Jamila might have heard of what Emma said. It's so base, so calculating, but I have no other choice. Or maybe I should just lay all my cards on the table for Jamila, let her think what she wants? For a moment it's almost as if I'm asleep, as if I can see the figure from my dream. As if I can now put a face to it, and it isn't the face of a criminal kingpin from Jørgen's article, it's no longer Rebekka Davidsen with her blonde locks, or Svein, or Saman. It's Jamila, with her designer jeans and that uncompromising gaze – all or nothing. It's Emma, barefoot in her nightdress, her jaw hard and a knife in her hand. It's me.

"Rikke!" she shouts again.

"Yes," I say dully.

I'm not even sure whether I actually say it. I look at my hands, look at the door, and see Emma standing there in her nightie, staring at me.

Jamila shouts:

"Simen says he wasn't the one who strung up the last cat."

Later, I sit in the kitchen. I'm not entirely sure why, or how I got here. Jamila has gone. I stare at my hands again. Remember how I came down from Jørgen's apartment that night when Emma had called out to me over the baby monitor, when she asked me where I'd been and I'd had just seconds to decide what I was going to say.

Something must have woken her. After the cry over the baby monitor, she went up into the living room. She must have heard me coming down the stairs from the first floor, but did she hear me crossing the floor of the apartment above her? Did she know that Filippa and Merete were away, and did she – just a child – did she understand, even if only partly, what my visit to Jørgen's apartment meant? What have I been doing, I ask myself, what on earth was I thinking? What kind of person does something like that? I'm sorry, I say quietly, out loud into the room, I'm sorry, I'm sorry, I'm sorry. There's nothing else to say, and it's rather late, even for that. I say it again, louder now, but nobody's home. Or are they? Emma is out, but Åsmund must be here, he and Lukas. I try to pull myself together, holding on tight to the first and best thing that occurs to me: What was it Jamila said? What was it Simen Sparre had said? And then I go into the living room and find the iPad.

A journalist from one of the newspapers has obviously got hold of Simen on the telephone, and since then the story has spread from this one newspaper to every other media channel at lightning speed. A news broadcast on one of the major TV stations reports that the young environmental activist who was arrested in connection with the Tåsen murder, and later released, has posted a video on YouTube in which he explains himself. The young activist has since told such-and-such newspaper that he takes no responsibility for the killing of the last cat that was found. The TV channel has taken the quotation from the newspaper and presents it in its entirety with graphics around it as the TV journalist speaks incessantly, analysing and drawing conclusions.

Journalist: Why did you kill a cat just a few days after a person was found murdered in your building?

17-year-old: I didn't.

Journalist: It wasn't you who killed the last cat that was found?

17-year-old: I mean . . . I may have killed it earlier and put it in the freezer. But it wasn't me who hung it beside the mailboxes. I was out that night, and I slept over at a friend's place. And I would never have done something like that after someone in our building had been found dead.

With slow fingers I tap the link to the newspaper that did the original interview with Simen. It's the first story I encounter on their website, divided across several articles with different editorial angles: the case itself, an interview with a legal expert who has something to say about the significance of the boy's statement, an opinion piece about the Green Gonzo phenomenon by an expert in social media, and an argumentative op-ed penned by the newspaper's editor: *Why we have chosen to reveal the details of the 17-year-old's YouTube channel.* At the very bottom of the last article is a link to Simen's explanatory video. It has now been watched more than 3,000 times.

The baby animal with its broken neck. And the others, those I found in the freezer, the one with the deep-frozen felt collar. I close my eyes. For a moment I hover between sleep and waking, and I'm aware of the dream beginning. I'm standing beside the mailboxes in the mist. I see Simen – he's fiddling with a piece of blue rope, trying

337

to hang something up, but it isn't a cat, not this time, it's a person, a thin girl with long blonde hair, wearing a nightgown. I reach out my hand towards her, about to lift the fringe that covers her face to see whether it's really her.

Åsmund shakes my shoulder.

"Are you nodding off?"

"Where's Emma?" I ask him.

"I think she went out. I was downstairs with Lukas."

"She shouldn't be out alone," I say. "It isn't safe here."

"Surely it's not *that* bad," he says. "And anyway, what are we supposed to do – force her to stay in here with us?"

"Anything could happen out there. Just out in the stairwell. Out by the mailboxes. Simen Sparre was out there, Emma was in her nightie. Did you see?"

"When was this?" Åsmund asks.

"Was she dressed when she went out?" I ask.

A furrow I've never seen before appears in Åsmund's forehead.

"Why would Simen want to hang Emma beside the mailboxes?" I ask.

"Rikke," he says. "I think you need to relax."

And now there's something new in his voice, something friendly and calm, and yet disquieting, because he's never spoken to me using this tone before, the way you speak to someone who is entirely out of it, someone who's suffering from severe dementia, or who is experiencing a psychotic episode. This carer's voice. Intended to soothe, but I hear the worry beneath it, see the fold of skin at his brow. I take several deep breaths. All the way down into my belly. I can feel how he's watching me as I do this, and so say to myself: Pull yourself together, calm down. I am, after all, an adult. I have a high-powered job, I publish more research papers than most. I should be able to calm my breathing.

"I've hardly slept this week," I say, and then I begin to shake.

Åsmund puts his arms around me, and I lean my head against his shoulder, take in the scent of him.

"I know," he mumbles. "I think I have one of Mamma's prescriptions in a drawer at work. If you like, I can pick it up on Monday and bring you a pack of sleeping pills."

I close my eyes. Just to be able to sleep. To be knocked out. To not have to dream. To simply rest, for many, many hours.

"Yes," I say, straightening up. "Maybe."

We sit beside each other for a while, completely still. My breathing calms; the furrow in Åsmund's brow disappears. Eventually, I say:

"I'm sorry about all that just now."

"Oh," Åsmund says. "I'm sure it'll blow over. Just give her some time to vent."

"It's just that she screamed at me. And I was so out of it because I haven't slept, and I can't stop thinking about Simen Sparre and the cats."

I stop to take a breath.

"It's no longer safe here," I say. "I mean, God – both people and animals are dying right outside our door. And she would rather go out there than stay in here, with us."

Åsmund places a hand on my arm, as if to comfort me, but there's something in his eyes, something he wants to tell me.

"What is it?" I ask him.

He doesn't answer; looks away. For a moment I think: He knows. Then I think: He's the one who did it, in some strange way or other I haven't been able to see through just yet – *he's* the one who killed Jørgen. And then I can no longer stand it – what is it, I shout, just say it – and if he thinks I'm crazy now, it'll be perfectly understandable.

"She's in love with him," Åsmund says quietly. "Emma is in love with Simen."

"What?"

"Hadn't you noticed?"

I hadn't. The thought hasn't even occurred to me.

"Haven't you seen the way she carries on when he's around?" Åsmund says. "The way she gets all dressed up before the play rehearsals because he turns up there every now and then? The way she hung around the garden this summer, hoping he might come out?"

I'm speechless. I didn't see it. I didn't even notice her hanging around the garden. I've clearly been far too wrapped up in my own love affair. Not only have I forgotten that I have a husband, but I've forgotten my children, too.

As I stand in the shower, I think of the heart written in Emma's script. GG. I lean my head against the tiled wall and think: Green Gonzo. There he is, hidden on the story's last page.

Åsmund is sitting on the sofa with his phone, as he usually does. He's stretched out his legs across the chaise longue, slinging one across the other, but his eyes are glued to the phone. He's wearing that empty expression he gets when he's bewitched by it, his mouth half open, eyes fixed on the screen.

I sit down beside him, in my bathrobe and with a towel around my wet hair, and for once he sets the phone aside.

"Do you think she was the one who strung up the last cat?" I ask him.

"The last cat?"

I tell him about what Simen had said to the journalist who called him, broadcast to every TV screen in the country. His denial. Credible enough – especially considering the fear I saw on his face in the garden on Wednesday, because it must have terrified him out of his wits to realise that someone had undertaken an act that bore his signature. His alibi, too, which Emma may have known about. She might have thought that she was doing it for him. Drawing suspicion away from him, now that our building was at the centre of a murder investigation, by doing this one night when he was demonstrably elsewhere. Or she may have done it to show him something. That she's here, perhaps – that she sees what he does, and that she likes him. The fire door downstairs, which makes it so easy for her to sneak out. How accessible the deep freezer has been for her. And the clicking sound of the front door I thought I heard that night.

"Hm," Åsmund says, looking tired and worried. "I don't know. It doesn't seem like her to do something like that, but who knows anything these days? It could be."

"I can't believe it," I say.

"Me neither," Åsmund says, and then we sit this way again, silent beside each other.

I can say it now. We're alone, it's calm. This silence between us – it's an opportunity. To just get it done. A column of stress shoots up from my stomach – is it really about to happen, right now?

"Rikke," Åsmund says. "I think it's best that we don't say anything about this to Emma. Don't you?"

"I don't know," I say.

"We need her to trust us right now," he says.

There's an earnestness to his voice that I don't often hear.

"This is serious," I say.

"And that's precisely why. And we shouldn't speak about this to anyone else. Not to the police, not to Jamila, not to anyone. And not to her. I mean, we'll have to talk to her about it at some point – of course we will. But not now. What she needs from us, right now, is our support. To know that we're there. That we trust her. That we won't go storming into her room accusing her of things. You see what I mean?"

I nod slowly, rocking my head back and forth.

The fact that Emma wasn't wanted at first has often gnawed at me. Of course I love her, and I have done ever since she was a baby. But I wasn't filled with joy when the midwife laid her in my arms. And although I took pleasure in her first steps and the first time she said Mamma, although I felt so warm and proud when the kindergarten staff said that she was advanced for her age in learning this, that or the other, there was so much else that demanded my attention. I had a child, and yet I still wanted to complete my doctorate within the usual time frame. I wanted to show that I could have a family and rise through the ranks as quickly as anyone else – that's how smart I was, how competent, hard-working, determined. And I praised her independence above all. Emma could dress herself when she was three; she made her own packed lunches at seven.

We've never had problems with her at kindergarten or at school. When she cried at night, afraid of the dark, she allowed herself to be convinced to sleep alone in her room all the same – she endured the fear until it passed, because I insisted. She received so little of the care and intense attention that fell to her brother. That's how it was for me, too, I think – I too was the self-motivated big sister with the younger sibling who demanded so much; the one who claimed her place in the family by being the best at demanding nothing at all. Of course I tell my daughter that I love her, of course she knows that. But there is no escaping the fact that her little brother, my miracle baby, with all his check-ups and doctor's appointments, receives something from me that I never gave to her.

Luckily, she had Åsmund. Fortunately, he's cheered her on wholeheartedly, thrown her into the air as she squealed with delight, hugged her tight and said that she's the best girl from here to the South Pole, because she's his. He's never used this against me, not even when we argue – and he could have done. And so now, as he offers up such a clear opinion – when he says, with a firmness he doesn't often use, that we must now handle Emma just *so*, and says this not as a request or a suggestion, but as a clear instruction – do I have the right to do anything but agree?

So I consent. Yes, okay. We won't say anything. He smiles. Strokes my cheek.

"That's great, honey," he says to me, and something in me collapses under this benevolence.

Look what a good girl I am. See how I conform to his wishes, how I pack away my madness and become sober-minded and reasonable, how I do as he asks. I trust his judgement. Isn't this generosity, this effort I'm now making, worth something as a counterbalance to what I have to tell him?

"I was at the police station yesterday," Åsmund says. "Did I tell you?"

The column rises from my belly again.

"No," I say, and then: "What did they want?"

"Just to talk. It was the new guy who's handling the case, the one with the moustache – Gundersen, or whatever his name is – who asked me to come in."

"To talk about what?"

My voice is so thin and small. They can't have told him about my email. We couldn't have sat here like this, had he known. But still. They called him in. And he went. Without saying anything to me first – nobody gave me the opportunity to confess at the eleventh hour. It's as if the seriousness of Ingvild Fredly's prompt only truly dawns on me now. As if, up until this moment, I have been waiting for it to become even more critical, even more necessary that I tell him. But it never will, and I understand that now. There will never be a now-or-never moment. I simply have to do it. And now is as good a time as any.

"Oh, I don't know," Åsmund says. "Much of the same. Our relationships with the neighbours, everything we know about them. And they're still going on about that cabin trip we went on in August, us guys."

I *will* do it now – it's what I want. I'm about to do it, the words are on my tongue, but then I'm distracted by this new thing that pops up at the very outskirts of my field of vision: the cabin trip.

"Why are they so obsessed with that?" I ask. "Jamila says that they asked Saman about it, too."

Åsmund shrugs.

"I don't know. Nothing in particular happened. They asked about the discussion we had on Saturday evening, but I mean, it was just a discussion. Something about the anti-vaxx movement and how it should be handled, medical competence versus freedom of speech. Maybe things got a little heated, the way they do sometimes, but it was no worse than that. We were all friends again afterwards. I really don't understand what they're getting at."

Now he smiles at me, disheartened.

"It feels as if there's something they're looking for, and I mean, I'd like to give it to them. I just don't know what it is. I've told them absolutely everything I remember from that night. And, you know, we'd all had a bit to drink."

"So what kind of things were they asking?"

Do I really care about this? Or am I attempting to spin out our conversation, prolonging it on purpose to get out of the other one?

"Just that," he says. "What we talked about, who said what, how I perceived the others, blah blah blah."

"And what did you say?"

"I said that Jørgen said freedom of speech is important, even when the speech is idiotic. He got a little pompous, actually, started quoting Voltaire, stuff like that. But we were all a bit tipsy. And then Saman said that was the most ridiculous thing he'd ever heard – there are children literally dying of diseases we had practically eradicated, just because their parents read something on some blog. And then Jørgen said maybe so, but didn't Saman think that people will die in a world where freedom of speech is suppressed? And so it went on. I listened, supported Saman for the most part, but I was nowhere near as wound up as he was. And Svein sat there half asleep in the corner, as far as I remember. I think he was the most drunk."

"Saman says that you were pretty vocal, too," I say, without looking at him.

"Does he?" Åsmund asks. "Well, maybe I said more than I remember. There are nuances from that night that are little fuzzy, to put it mildly."

He looks at me and smiles, and for the first time I see his smile and think: Is he telling me the truth? Is he covering something up?

"So is Saman going around talking about that night?" he asks.

Is there something a little wary in his voice?

"He mentioned it in the stairwell once," I say. "I don't know why, it wasn't as if I asked about it."

I think of Saman, furious, leaning over the railing: *He was fairly worked up too, your husband*. And then there was Svein Sparre, who said Åsmund was no choirboy. Åsmund shrugs again.

"All the neighbours have become a little paranoid," he says. "That's what this situation has done to us – every last one. I hope they catch someone soon, so we can put it all behind us."

He sets his feet on the floor, leans his weight over them. If I'm going to say something, I have to do it now. There's a ringing in my ears. Every time I put it off, I make it worse.

"But we agree, right?" he says as he gets up. "We're not going to say anything about this to Emma. Right now, we'll just be as supportive as we possibly can be. We'll deal with the rest later."

"Yes," I say lamely, watching another opportunity slip away. I'm unable to muster the strength to grab it.

"And who knows," Åsmund says as he crosses the living-room floor, making his way towards the kitchen. "Maybe she'll come to us of her own accord. Stranger things have happened."

That afternoon, the police call.

"Gundersen here," he says when I pick up. "Are you able to come down to the station for a little chat just now?"

"Well," I say.

Lukas is drawing; Åsmund is working in the garden.

"I'll just have to check if my husband can watch the kids," I say.

"Good," says Gundersen.

He waits. I'm expected to check right away, I realise. I open the kitchen window. Åsmund is standing over by the patio, raking the lawn, and I call out to him.

"The police want me to go down to the station. Can I go? You can watch Lukas?"

He straightens up.

"Sure," he says. "Of course."

"I can come down there now," I say to Gundersen.

He says good, he'll send a car, it will be there any minute. He'll wait for me in reception at the police station. There's something compelling about this man, I think. He asks whether I'm able to come in, and yet it doesn't feel as if I can say no. It's uncomfortable, has certain implications that I would prefer not to think about. On the lawn, Åsmund stands with the rake in his hands, watching me. His eyebrows are pulled down, his forehead furrowed, as if this fills him with the same unease that's pounding within me.

Gundersen meets me in reception, as promised. He's energetic, taking my hand in his thin, bony one and squeezing it hard as he thanks

347

me for coming in at such short notice – they're working round the clock now, I must understand; the first week of an investigation is always the most important, so there's no time to lose. As he speaks, he waves me through some plastic gateways, a security system he himself navigates using a card. He signals wordlessly to a man behind a glass wall, asking him to press the right buttons so that I can enter, all while continuing to speak. Were I in the right mood, I might have found this impressive.

Luckily, he doesn't show me into anything resembling an interrogation room, as I'd expected. We walk up and down a considerable number of corridors, and then he suddenly opens a door and ushers me into an office. His office, apparently. It contains a desk, a bookcase and a couple of chairs.

"Sorry about the mess," he says, tidying away a few piles of paper from the desktop.

He doesn't really seem all that apologetic. I look around. The office is small – it screams of public funding and efficient utilisation of space, and it's true that it is markedly messy. The desk is overflowing with paperwork, newspapers, grey envelopes, and I count at least three half-full coffee cups. Half hidden under some sheets of paper that appear to be printouts from an online newspaper lies a pale-blue packet with the logo of a loose tobacco manufacturer on it. On the wall hangs a watercolour in diluted blues and pale yellows, in a gold-coloured frame that is covered in dust. Over the back of the office chair hangs a shabby all-weather jacket. Something about its faded colours tells me that it has been worn almost every day for at least a decade. The air smells of cold coffee, and something a little sour I can't place.

"So," he says, taking a seat in the desk chair and leaning back in it, so that the plastic gives out a screech. "Please, sit. Mind if I use this?"

He waves a Dictaphone around, and I nod wordlessly. I choose one of the two chairs that stand before the desk, wooden chairs upholstered in woollen fabric – these too bear the obvious stamp of a governmental agency. There we sit, each on our own side of the desk. Gundersen looks at me. He smiles, and almost appears friendly.

"How are you all doing?" he asks. "Up there in Kastanjesvingen?"

"Oh, fine," I say.

I take a deep breath, filling my lungs. It feels as if the oxygen spreads through my circulatory system in an instant, with intense efficiency, giving nourishment to my exhausted body. When I let the breath out again, it's as if I've collapsed.

"Must be tough, though?" he asks. "I can't exactly say I blame you – it's no surprise. You're right in the middle of it."

There is a palpable strength to him. On all the previous occasions I've spoken to him, I've vehemently wished that Ingvild Fredly could take his place. But now, as he shows me this unexpected concern, I think that were he on my side, it would feel wonderful. I could lean back and rest, simply wait for him to solve the case for me. Trust that everything would be well.

"I've hardly slept since it happened," I say. "It's been a week now. Well, almost a week."

"When did the trouble sleeping start?"

I think back.

"Sunday, I think. No, Monday."

"You slept well before then? Because didn't you . . . Just a minute."

His hands search through the papers on the desk to fish a new bundle from an envelope. His fingers are long, yellowed at the tips by the tobacco he uses, and now he flicks quickly through the sheets of paper.

"Yes, here," he says. "Didn't you write to Fredly about this – here's what I was wondering about. That is, about the night it happened, last Friday night. Yes, here it is. You said you slept unusually heavily?"

"I don't know," I say.

"*The night it happened there was an unease in me as I slept*," Gundersen reads, his eyes fixed on the sheet of paper. "*And yet I slept deeply. When I woke, it felt as if I'd been in a coma. As if I'd been far away for many hours.*"

He looks up.

"Unease and a deep sleep at the same time."

"Yes," I say, frowning, trying to remember. "Yes, I wrote that, I remember, but I can't quite imagine . . . But yes, it must be right. I remember that morning. I woke very early. The others were asleep. And Lukas had come into our bed without me realising it."

He nods, and for a moment it's quiet between us.

"What?" I ask.

He shrugs, gives me a half smile.

"Everything is potentially of significance," he says. "And of course, that was the night it happened. Had you slept poorly that night, you might have heard something."

"Yes," I said. "But I slept well."

"So well that you wouldn't have been woken by a noise?"

"I don't know. Yes, probably."

In his half smile, something stirs. Yesterday, as he sat in our kitchen drinking coffee, it dawned on me that Åsmund and I are each other's alibi. To claim anything other than that I slept undisturbed is to put Åsmund in danger.

"As I said, I sleep very lightly," I say. "I wake up the moment someone moves."

And at the same time, this tiny doubt, this entirely absurd fear: If I really did sleep so heavily that night, would I have woken up if Åsmund went out?

"Hm," Gundersen says, and nods. "But that night, you didn't wake up when your son came into your room?"

"I mean," I say, "I probably forgot. It often happens. It was an entirely normal night. Apart from the fact that I was feeling uneasy, but I think that was to do with a dream, a nightmare."

"Hm," he says again.

He leafs through his papers. I feel a blush of shame creep along my neck and up into my cheeks – there he sits, reading what I wrote to Ingvild. This confession I deposited in the kitty to buy myself some time. If that is in fact what I've done.

Gundersen puts down the sheets of paper.

"Did you enjoy being with Jørgen?" he asks.

The question surprises me.

"I don't know," I say. "To be perfectly honest. In the beginning I'm sure I did. There was something that attracted me to him, something that made me do all this."

I gesture towards the printout he's holding, as if that's what's really responsible.

"But towards the end, I wanted it to be over. I mean, not that I wanted him dead or anything. Absolutely not – I was crushed. I still am. I don't know . . ."

And then it bubbles up in me, this entire week. I sob over Gundersen's desk, bursting into tears that are surprising in their ferocity. My entire body shudders, wracked by jolts. As if something has possessed me, shaking me like a rag doll. Gundersen hands me a serviette – it's one of those hard, rough ones that can be found in dispensers in public toilets, paper towels to dry your hands on. It scrapes my face as I rub it against my eyes and nose. Something about this sobbing reminds me of the storms I remember from when I was small, the sudden downpours that washed over the valley, threatening clouds that had built up over time but didn't reveal their violence until they were right above us. And then they would suddenly pass, the sky would clear, and in the forest it smelled fresh and good, and no matter how you sat you ended up with a wet bottom, marks on your knees.

"I'm sorry," I say once it's over.

I wipe my eyes, the paper towel scratching the thin skin below them.

Gundersen doesn't say anything. He considers me, but not in an unfriendly way. More as if he's just waiting for me to finish. He understands, I think, he knows this weeping. Perhaps better than I do myself.

I say:

"I can't cry for Jørgen. I have to keep up the mask. It's so exhausting."

"You cared about him," Gundersen says neutrally.

"Yes. But I wanted out. After all, I came to realise what I was risking. In the beginning it was probably, I don't know, almost like a kind of drug. But after a while . . . the high wore off, so to speak."

He says:

"You wrote to Fredly that you tried to end it. You write: *This has to stop, I say to Jørgen, we can't do this anymore.*"

"Yes. I tried several times. I'm not blaming him, the fault was just as much mine. Maybe it was because we were neighbours. He was there all the time. Sooner or later it always became too hard to resist."

It's quiet for a moment. Gundersen narrows his eyes, as if pondering what I've just said. I'm about to continue, taking a breath, but then he beats me to it.

"Does Åsmund know about it, do you think?"

"No," I say. "No, I'm sure of it."

"How come?"

I take another breath. Why am I sure? Because I know him – Åsmund is so transparent. But I can't say that.

"There's no way he could have found out," I say. "We were that careful."

"But you write that maybe Emma knows."

Emma in her nightie, and my own nightmarish image from earlier this morning, the child in a nightgown with a knife in her hand.

"No," I say. "She doesn't know. But it may be that she suspects something, or – I don't know. Not *that*, exactly. But something."

He nods again, but slower this time. Not because he agrees, necessarily, but as if he's signalling that he hears what I'm saying, that he's considering it. My throat tightens; it becomes hard to breathe. Now I'm implicating my own daughter. Now he thinks that Emma knows, that Emma did it. This is a new low, even for me.

"Listen," I say. "This isn't about my family. Neither of them would have done this. Åsmund faints just at the sight of blood, and Emma – Emma is a child, for fuck's sake!"

My voice is high-pitched, terrified. The tiny click I heard that night, the footsteps that may have belonged to Emma, heading out of the fire door, to the dead cats in the freezer. This is something I *do* suspect she did, perhaps to prove something to a boy she likes. Gundersen doesn't acknowledge my protest. It's as if he hasn't heard me.

"But does he suspect anything?" he asks. "Åsmund?"

"No," I say firmly. "I would have noticed."

The slow, doubtful nodding starts up again. My breathing is quick and shallow – what have I written, what have I done?

"On the morning Jørgen was found," Gundersen says. "Did you see anything then? Or did anything happen?"

"No," I say, breathing a little easier. "It was a sunny day. I saw Hoffmo out on his front step – you know, the retired military guy who lives across the road? It was quiet up in Jørgen's apartment. Nothing unusual."

"And the rest of the day? Did you ever go up there?"

I take a breath.

"What do you mean?"

"I mean," Gundersen says, "were you at any point up in Jørgen's apartment on Saturday last week?"

One of those moments again, just seconds in which to make a choice.

"No," I say. "I knocked at his door. He'd invited me up there, but nobody answered, so I went back downstairs again."

"And you didn't go in?"

Is there something more to this question? He's looking at me with clear, open eyes. It's impossible to read this man.

"No," I say. "When he didn't open the door, I went back downstairs."

"Did you speak to any of the other neighbours that day?"

"Saman came out while I was knocking," I say, feeling my heart squeeze blood up into my face. "I said that I needed some eggs, and he gave me two. You know – it was an excuse."

And so it's come to this, I think – I'm now lying to the police. I know that I should be honest here, that this is risky. But everything I say, everything I've written, seems to drag me further and further into all this. And not just me. My family, too. My husband, my children. To say that I went in there now seems impossible – that I was there that Saturday, standing in the middle of Jørgen's living room, before I backed out again. I can just imagine Gundersen nodding cautiously: I see, excuse me for a moment. Can just imagine him leaving only to return with a couple of colleagues, and someone saying: I'm afraid we're going to have to detain you. And the newspaper headlines: *New suspect apprehended in connection with Tåsen murder*; and in the tabloids: *Neighbour suspected of sex murder*. I imagine Jamila, startled by the online newspapers on her smart little MacBook. Imagine Åsmund, wide-eyed and gaping-mouthed in front of the TV – Åsmund, who cannot understand how this can be happening. And my children. Emma in her turtle shell. Lukas asking Åsmund: Is Mamma in prison now?

Gundersen sets down the printout of my email among the clutter on the desk and leans back in his chair again. He puts one leg over the other, ankle balanced against knee. Sits with his legs wide apart, just as he probably always does.

"So what do you think?" he asks. "Just between you and me. What do you think happened?"

I swallow.

"Did you know that Jørgen was writing an exposé about the temping industry?"

Gundersen looks at me. Narrows his eyes, concentrating.

"Was he now?" he says.

"Svein Sparre runs a temping agency," I say. "And Svein didn't like Jørgen. Although I'm not sure if that was why, or whether he disliked him for some other reason. And that cabin trip."

"What about it?" Gundersen asks.

There's not a trace of eagerness in his expression. Not a hint of the fact that he's been asking around, digging for information about the trip, for days.

"There was a disagreement there," I say. "I understand that you've been asking about it. And I mean, I wasn't there, and from what Åsmund says it was mainly Saman and Jørgen who were arguing, but I think . . . It was Svein's cabin. And Svein says . . ."

I interrupt myself. I can hear how I sound, how petty it is to point the finger at someone else. Just how eager I am to do it, too. I think of Svein putting his arms around Nina's shoulders outside the house last night. All they've gone through over the past few days.

"I don't know," I say. "I honestly can't imagine any of us going into Jørgen's study and slitting his throat. Not Simen, not his father, not anyone. I don't know what would make a person do something like that."

Something glitters deep in Gundersen's grey, impenetrable eyes.

"Hate," he says. "Fear. Money. Losing face. You'd be surprised what people are capable of. People like you and me. Or the pleasant neighbour you exchange a few friendly words with. We see repeat

355

offenders, of course – the ones with a record who kill to avoid being put away again, or for the money, or what have you. But I've also seen cases that make me wonder."

For a moment it seems as if he's following a train of thought. He stops speaking and stares at the pale watercolour as if he can see straight through it, into something important that lies behind it. Then he catches himself, turns to face me, and smiles his half smile again.

"People say that this or that individual wouldn't hurt a fly," he says. "And I say: Given the opportunity and a strong enough motive, we could all become murderers. If someone posed a threat to your child's life, wouldn't you kill them? It's easier to think that murder is something that relates to just a few of us. Those who live in a certain area of the city, for example, those who use drugs and steal, and who associate with others who use drugs and steal. The kind of people the police keep an eye on, or at least *should* keep an eye on. And all the rest of us have to do is steer well clear. But I no longer think like that. No. That much I've learned, at least. But – well. I shan't keep you any longer. Do you think you can find your way out?"

I'm not sure I can, but I nod all the same. And five minutes later I'm standing outside the police station, as the low autumn sun paints the city dark red.

At least I had managed to draw a line under it. But after the summer, we slipped back into our old ways. There was a major conflict at work, and Åsmund didn't have the energy to listen to me go on about it. He was spending a lot of time out at his mother's place again, there were some trees that bordered on her neighbour's property that needed pruning; her house needed a fresh coat of paint. I'm sure you'll be fine, he said to me with narrow, tired eyes as I described the problem to him, you're so good at sorting out those kinds of things. And one evening, when I was home alone attempting to answer a toxic email from a colleague as my children slept, I sent Jørgen a message.

I don't mean to put the blame on Åsmund here, Ingvild. I take full responsibility. I was the one who went running back to him. I can't even blame Jørgen, because he asked me several times whether I was sure that was what I wanted. I don't really know what to say, I just felt so desperate for a break from reality. I cycled home from work at around eleven-thirty, let myself in and ran up the stairs to him, and when we lay on the floor beside that goddamned daybed, I felt a kind of relief, a kind of eradication of everything else. As if Jørgen could still offer me sanctuary.

It didn't work as well as it had previously – that's obvious. But to go from having a space in your everyday life where you can breathe, to not having it . . . I don't know how to explain it. It's like being a dry alcoholic, standing in the middle of all the shit that life can throw at you, all the arguing and stress and the grey monotony of the weekdays as they come tumbling towards you, one after the other, and being forced to bear it all without opening a beer or having a drink. And not just now, but forever. To never again be able to pour yourself a little glass of something to take the edge off. I'm not saying that it's impossible. I'm not saying that I wouldn't have managed it in the end. But I relapsed. Maybe I would have continued to do so, over and over again.

The last time I was up there, he stroked my cheek before I left. Show them who's boss, he said, and that was the very last thing he said to me.

The night it happened, there was an unease in me as I slept. And yet I slept deeply. When I woke, it felt as if I'd been in a coma. As if I'd been far away for many hours. We spend almost a third of our lives asleep – did you know that? And yet we often have no idea what we dream about.

SECOND SUNDAY

The garden lies abandoned in the dusk. I'm standing outside in nothing but my underwear, but I'm not cold. All the windows are illuminated. I see no people, but I know that they're there, in the house. They're inside, all of them, and once again I'm filled with this deep understanding that something terrible is about to happen.

I open my mouth, ready to call out to them, to Emma and Lukas, to Åsmund. But no matter how hard I scream, not a sound emerges from my throat. And now I see a shadow up in Jørgen and Merete's apartment. It's familiar. I know who it is. I start to run – I have to go inside, warn the others – but no matter how hard I try, I can barely move. In the lit windows I see the shadow leave Jørgen and Merete's apartment, then walk downstairs and open the door to ours. I give it my all, screaming at the top of my lungs, trying as hard as I can to run, and the next moment I'm awake. I'm lying in bed, every muscle in my body tensed. I blink. My throat is hoarse and sore, but my cheeks are dry, and beside me sleeps Åsmund, undisturbed.

The pain grinds with every step I take. The idea was to run gently, without overloading my injured knee. Just do a little route around Voldsløkka, sticking to level ground. But despite warming up with a brisk walk I can feel it in every step, it gets worse the more weight I put on it, and I realise that it's useless, I'm unable to conquer this physical weakness. I stop in the middle of the gravel path. A man in his forties, wearing tracksuit bottoms and a yellow hi-vis jacket, swooshes past me. Over on the rugby pitch some players are jogging around and throwing passes to each other. Two mothers with push-chairs come towards me at a slow pace – they're so deep in conversation they hardly see me until they're forced to divert their pushchairs to either side of me at the last minute. I stand stock-still. There's nothing to do but go home, but the idea is off-putting. I have no plan B, however, so I simply stand there.

In the end, I manage to pull myself together. I shuffle slowly towards the end of the park and take the little path between the trees and out to Maridalsveien. The pain still gnaws at me with every step, although I can at least manage a slow walk now. Or a limp is probably more like it.

Out on the road, I stop. Cars drive past, and a bus slows before the roundabout – it's busy here, even though it's a Sunday. I turn my head towards the bus stop. Standing there is Saman. The instant I see him, he sees me, and we nod to each other. I haven't seen him since that day on the stairs, but I recognise this encounter as an opportunity.

"Take a seat," he says, and I obediently lower myself onto the bench inside the bus shelter.

He crouches down on his haunches beside me and lifts my leg.

"How did you injure it?"

"I was jogging in the forest," I say. "I was pushing myself a little too hard, and then I fell. It's a few days since it happened."

"Hm."

He wears his doctor's expression as he studies my leg, lifting it slightly here, bending it a little there, asking me if it hurts when he twists it like this, when I bend it like that. I answer. We've slipped into a new relationship – doctor and patient. The bus shelter has become a doctor's surgery, and the strangest thing is that it doesn't seem strange at all, that it costs me nothing to accept this.

"You haven't sprained it," he says. "It's likely just bruised. It seems a little swollen where you hit the rock, but that isn't unusual. Give it a couple of weeks, but if it's still painful after that you should go see your doctor."

"Okay," I say. "Thank you."

He gets up and sits beside me on the bench, the improvised doctor's surgery dissolving around us as he does so. But perhaps something of it still hangs in the air, because I hardly know him and yet somehow still feel able to say:

"Saman? There's something I'd like to ask you about."

He nods at this – I can ask, I'm to understand – and as I look for the words, he turns his head and says:

"It's about Jamila, isn't it?"

When I say nothing further, he says:

"I thought you might be wondering. The way she's been beating down your door, armed with her printouts and all kinds of theories."

He sighs deeply. Suddenly seems like a much older man.

"I've known Jamila since she was a child, so I've always known that she's like this. Both her mother and her little brother have bipolar disorder. I've read up on it – the disease has a strong genetic component. It's the most hereditary of all the mental illnesses, did you know that? But Jamila doesn't have it; she's never been diagnosed as bipolar."

This last thing he says firmly, as if it's important. Something he's holding on to, hard.

"A friend of mine who's a psychiatrist mentioned something called cyclothymia. A less severe variant, if you will. The lows are not quite so low, the highs not quite so high. So I think, if she were to be diagnosed with anything . . . cyclothymia."

He takes a deep breath. Further down the hill at Nydalen we hear the bus accelerating. We don't have much time, and this wasn't what I wanted to ask him about, but I can't interrupt. I think of Jamila in my kitchen, all the sheets of paper spread across the table, the sections of articles highlighted and strewn with exclamation marks, all the patterns she saw in them. The air of intensity about her when she stopped by earlier. Her impatience; the way she squeezed my arm.

Saman was a friend of her older brother; he met Jamila while visiting the family and fell completely in love with her when he was just sixteen. There's never been anyone but her. Her intensity was attractive – she had passion, was full of life and colour. Her brother had said to Saman: If you choose her, you have to accept her as she is. If you leave her because of this, I'll beat the living daylights out of you. Saman promised. Took this vow – given to a brother who knew exactly what it involved – seriously. He still does. He'll stand by her, steadfast, always.

"For the most part, it poses no problem," he says. "In her day-to-day life, she's basically fine. She uses her intense experiences in what she does. Have you seen her photographs? It's hard to separate this, this instability – the seriousness with which she views everything – from the rest of her. Or maybe that's not right. Maybe it *is* her. It doesn't matter. She's strong. She knows how to use it."

The bus slows down and stops, opening its doors, but Saman makes no move to get up.

"The problem," he says, "is when dramatic things happen. Jamila is so susceptible to life events. Two years ago, she became pregnant, and we thought . . ."

He interrupts himself and looks at the bus, which closes its doors, pulls away from the bus stop and disappears down Maridalsveien.

"When she had a miscarriage, she fell into a depression. A so-called reactive one, triggered by stress. It happens sometimes, and isn't necessarily connected to her genetic vulnerability, but I thought . . . Let's just say she fell down a very deep hole. I was afraid she was going to take her own life. She was admitted to hospital for a brief period, and when she came out, we wanted to make a fresh start. We bought the apartment in Kastanjesvingen. Decided we would wait before trying to get pregnant again, so she'd have time to get properly back on her feet. And now . . ."

He smiles at me, and there's something infinitely sad in it.

"We had just started talking about trying again. And then all this happened with Jørgen. And then, of course, Jamila had to be the one to find him."

I nod. I didn't know all this, but I understand.

"I've been wondering whether we ought to take a holiday," he says. "Get away for a few weeks while the investigation is ongoing. A bit of distance from it all. Come back when they've caught the guy. Maybe it would help."

I nod again, slowly.

"Yes," I say. "But that's not what I was wondering about."

He turns to face me. His beard is dark, his eyebrows attractively shaped and coal-black. The way he's currently sitting, his face is in shadow.

In the distance I hear the next bus pull into the stop down by the river.

"It was about the cabin trip," I say. "When we were on the stairs that day, with Nina, you know? You said that Åsmund was angrier than you?"

Saman looks over at the green apartment blocks on the other side of the road, and for a moment we're both utterly still. Then he says:

"There's something you learn, when you're a Norwegian with an Iranian name, an Iranian appearance. And that's that you don't have the same right to be angry as everyone else. To show your anger – no matter how understandable it might be. If someone dents your car, throws rubbish into your garden, if . . . I don't know, anything at all. If it happens to someone like Jørgen, or Åsmund, then everyone understands. But I get angry, and people immediately think I'm a fundamentalist. I mean, shit. I'm from Iran. My family were among the first to flee when Khomeini came to power. Do people not understand that I – of all people – dislike that kind of literalism, that kind of conservative interpretation of religion? But if I raise my voice just the tiniest bit, that's what they see. Yes – I let myself get wound up during that discussion at the cabin. But I'm a doctor. I see the consequences of vaccine hesitancy. Jørgen was talking about freedom of speech, and of course he was more than welcome to do so, but he couldn't just expect that nobody would argue against him."

Another bus stops in front of us; a couple of schoolgirls get off. Saman still makes no move to get up. As the bus pulls away, he turns to face me.

"Åsmund was angrier than me," he says. "He shouted. I raised my

366

voice, but I'd say that I stuck to a lower volume than he did. I'd had much less to drink. But when the police came to speak to me, that's what they'd heard – that I was so very angry. Svein Sparre will have told them that – guaranteed. He was shit-faced, half asleep with one cheek against the tabletop, but apparently he was awake enough to know that I was raging. It was a discussion, no more than that, but interpreting it from his hangover *of course* that's what he says – that I was furious."

Saman sighs deeply, puffing out his cheeks. We sit there for a little while, and it's completely quiet, no cars, no buses. It's sunny and fairly warm, the kind of day when it feels as if winter is far away. I say:

"Where are you headed?"

He smiles, a little shyly.

"I'm on my way to record a podcast, believe it or not. A thing with a couple of childhood friends. One of them is a comedian, the other has a PhD in philosophy. The idea is that the comedian will ask some questions – what's the meaning of life, what is death, what is love. That sort of thing. And then we'll answer. The philosopher from his discipline, and me from mine. We've made one episode so far, but we haven't put it out there yet. *From Cradle to Grave*, we've called it. I don't know, it's probably all a bit dumb."

I smile. There it is – the title I found on the website. That's all it was. Saman looks down at his trainers and grins. He looks like a hipster, I think – the beard, the clothes, even the brown leather shoulder bag. The trainers, which are bright white and expensive.

"It sounds cool," I say.

"We'll see."

Another red bus comes into view before the roundabout, and he says:

"I probably ought to get this one."

He sets his hands on his thighs and gets up.

"Saman," I say. "You know that Saturday? With the eggs?"

He turns to face me.

"When I was knocking on Jørgen's door."

He nods, slowly.

"Did you mention . . . I mean, have you told Jamila about it?"

"No," he says. "I thought it was probably best not to."

The bus pulls into the lay-by, stops and opens its doors. Once he's stepped aboard, Saman turns to me and waves. I stay sitting on the bench until the bus has disappeared, and for the first time in many days it feels as if my breath can flow a little more freely through me.

This will have to do for my exercise for today, I think, as I drag the rake across the lawn, its tines pulling up the brown leaves that cover the grass. The sun is high and hot in the sky, and if I can just get rid of these old leaves now, the conditions will be optimal for the lawn to turn nice and green again after the winter. Åsmund did a little yesterday, but now I'm on a roll, ready to finish the job. Make the garden nice for us. He'll see, I think, when he gets home from visiting his mother this afternoon – he'll see just how nice it is here. How I'm taking care of what we have. Building our home. Maintaining it as necessary.

Merete is sitting on the front step with a newspaper and a cup of coffee, her face angled towards the sun. We've exchanged a few words – not many, but I'm acutely aware of her as I rake. I wonder whether she's following my movements with her eyes, but she doesn't appear to be. She glances down at the newspaper every now and then, but otherwise keeps her eyes closed. Filippa and Emma are sitting at the table on the patio, leaning over a box Filippa has been given – by a relative, is the impression I get, likely someone pained by the darkness in her eyes and all the desperate playing of Simon & Garfunkel on repeat. In the box is a small radio-controlled drone. The girls seem to have set aside their rivalry and are now sitting beside one another, constructing the drone together – no, that goes there, says the one; oh my God, so many screws, says the other. Lukas has given up his attempts to get them to let him join in. He's settled down with a few toy cars on the bench under the apple tree to make a motorway.

This is precisely how things should be when Åsmund gets home,

I think, and feel it twist in my guts: Before I tell him everything. *This* is the image that must be projected on to his retinas as he tries to sleep tonight – his wife maintaining his home, looking after the kids. Just look at what we have. Surely Åsmund can't throw all this away? My mistake is not insignificant, but how much is he willing to sacrifice in order to punish me? Tonight, I'll speak to him, and this time I've decided, come what may. All I can do now is try to facilitate his choice. Gently nudge him in the direction of staying with us regardless, in spite of everything.

"Like that, maybe," Emma says.

"No, wait," Filippa says, and I hear their laughter from across the lawn.

Are they friends now? I think. Is that how it's worked out, in the end? Merete flaps her newspaper. Lukas is speaking to his cars in a low, serious voice.

"Hallo, Prytz!" comes a shout from somewhere down the road.

There's Hoffmo, in his comical tracksuit with the long white stripe down each leg. I lift the rake and go over to the fence.

"Well, would you look at that!" I say. "Ready for the last run of the week?"

"Of course. Healthy body, healthy mind – that's the key, Prytz. And you're keeping up with the gardening?"

"Of course – you have to do your bit."

"Oh yes, true enough."

I lean on the shaft of the rake. He says:

"And you found some more dead cats, I understand?"

"Yes," I say.

I let my gaze wander down Kastanjesvingen, towards a fissure in the asphalt in the middle of the road.

"Yup, I heard about how you went down into the cellar and opened that freezer. Good thinking, Prytz."

I say nothing, simply smile politely. Don't want to get into it.

"And it turned out to be the young Sparre boy," Hoffmo says, shaking his head. "A sad state of affairs."

"Yes," I say. "It was surprising."

"You know," Hoffmo says, "I always thought there was something truly harrowing about those murders."

That's the word he uses. *Murders.* I lean on the rake, looking down the road at the crack in the asphalt.

"Nope, Nina wasn't exactly on the ball there," Hoffmo says pensively. "And now, of course, one might wonder why. But it can't have been easy – she is his mother, after all."

A magpie is hopping around just beside the crack, looking for food at the edge of the road. We stand and watch it, both of us. I can feel Hoffmo's presence next to me.

"Well," he says. "Justice has been done. And they'll likely go easy on him in the courts. After all, he's just a kid."

There's something overbearing about Hoffmo, something upright and proud that's often resulted in me thinking of him as a gym teacher – up the wall bars, no dilly-dallying! But he spent his working life in the military, I know that. It's hard to imagine him in that profession, maybe in uniform, perhaps in command of others. I actually know very little about what it involved, what he did in the army.

"He's younger than those who show up for their compulsory military service," I say, and then: "Have you ever worked with them?"

"No," Hoffmo says.

"But you were in the Armed Forces, weren't you?"

"Oh yes," he says. "But I worked in intelligence."

The magpie approaches the crack in the road, and I wonder how brittle the asphalt is. Just how much would it take to make the damage worse? Is the bird able to hack pieces loose, make a great channel down the length of our road?

"Intelligence?" I say. "What — surveillance, that sort of thing?"

He doesn't answer. The bird stops before the crack. It bends down, cautiously pecking at something with its beak. I turn back to Hoffmo.

"No, not me," he says. "Data analysis. Office job."

But he doesn't look at me. There's something there.

"That's a shame," I say. "A bit of surveillance might have come in handy just now, here in the street."

Hoffmo doesn't answer. Down the road, a neighbour is walking in our direction with his dog on a lead. Bolívar, the dog is called — it's a huge St Bernard, a little too big, it seems, for this tiny cul-de-sac. We watch Bolívar and his owner. I weigh up their distance from the bird. How long will it take before they reach it, before Bolívar begins to bark and it has to flee?

"Did you get hold of those cameras at work, then?" I ask. "The ones you put up in connection with the vandalism that time?"

"I got a few tips from an old colleague," he says. "If that's what you mean. It would have worked, too, if only the good lawyer Hove down at the end there hadn't interfered. Said it was illegal to film on public land. As if I wanted to go around snooping on people. Let me tell you, Prytz — I have zero interest in that. Talk to the boys in charge of surveillance in the Intelligence Battalion, and you'll hear all about how sick they are of dirty secrets. Who's carrying on with who, who's a closet drinker, who peeps on his neighbour's wife. It's the same everywhere. That kind of thing doesn't interest me in the least."

Now I'm the one who looks away. I fix my gaze on the bird, as yet still unsuspecting of the good-natured St Bernard. Hoffmo lives directly opposite our apartment building. He might have seen things. Not anything downright incriminating, but little things. He might have seen me through the upstairs windows. Put two and two together, drawn conclusions from his observations.

"No," Hoffmo says. "I do not concern myself with that sort of thing. But finding the hooligans who destroy our common property? Putting a stop to such detestable behaviour?"

Just then, the bird notices the dog. To my surprise it doesn't startle, but simply hops a few metres out of the road and flutters up to settle on Hoffmo's gatepost. Bolívar sniffs at the crack in the asphalt a little, then lumbers on. The magpie remains sitting there, looking at the dog, and then it turns its gaze on us. For a moment we have eye contact, the bird and me.

"Well," Hoffmo says. "He said it wasn't allowed, the good lawyer – and what do I know, he's the one who surely knows the law. But the tone he took with me – I thought that was uncalled for. We have to be allowed to react when the neighbourhood is being attacked in that way – you have to be able to take action. It's a matter of doing one's duty. Or at least, that's what I think. My wife thought I was being too stubborn. I let it go, for the sake of domestic peace. You have to do your bit for domestic peace, too, Prytz – that's another kind of duty."

He smiles at me, a wide, good-natured smile. I take a breath and am about to agree, leave it at that. But then the magpie takes off from the gatepost, flying low over the asphalt and across our garden, between Lukas and the girls, past Merete. I follow it with my eyes until it disappears behind the house, and I glimpse the contours of something, fumble for it the way I'm trained to, the way I do at work, building hypotheses, testing them.

"There was something that occurred to me about the cats," I say. "All that business was . . . well, I mean, it was much worse than the vandalism that time. When you think about it."

"Maybe so," Hoffmo says.

I turn my gaze from the road and look up into his bearded face with its broad jaw, the little eyes beneath the bushy eyebrows. There's something intelligent in them, I think. Something it's easy to overlook when he's mumbling and grumbling.

"So wouldn't it be all the more pressing to do something now?" I say. "When the neighbourhood is being subjected to far more vicious attacks, if you will."

"That may well be."

"And yet you didn't do anything? You didn't set up any cameras this time, you did nothing to defend yourself?"

Hoffmo looks at me, narrowing his eyes. For a moment we're completely silent, and it's as if he expects me to take a step back into safety and say something disarming – oh well, this stuff isn't easy, and by the way does he have any tips as to what we should do with the lawn? It's as if he's simply waiting for my retreat. I lean on the shaft of the rake. Feel more awake, sharper, than I have done in several days.

"Or maybe you did," I say.

"I do not break the law," Hoffmo says calmly. "I promised that lawyer that I would do no more of that sort of thing. I didn't agree, but I made a promise. No cameras on public property. And I'm a man of my word, Prytz."

"But what about private property?" I say. "Your property, for instance?"

We turn, both of us, to look towards his garden. The metal trellis-work fence that surrounds it, neatly painted, without the slightest hint of rust.

"Well," Hoffmo says. "I never made any promises about my own property, did I?"

He found a loophole. And he probably felt extremely smug about it, too, after being forced to apologise to the lawyer.

"Oh yes," he says, surveying the road as if it belongs to him. "It's quite possible to obey the law and still use your head. When they found the first cat, the one in Godalsparken, I said to my wife – mark my words, this won't be the last. And something like that in my own backyard – I quite simply refused to accept it. So I set up the two cameras I had left after the vandalism debacle. On my property, of course. And why shouldn't I? Surely a man is entitled to do as he wishes in his own garden. Even my wife was on board with it."

He takes a deep breath and holds it for a moment, his chest puffed up like a cockerel's, before he exhales with a sigh.

"Well. Then you lot across the road became the next victims. It's a shame you didn't set up some cameras yourselves. If all the neighbours had clubbed together, we could have caught him ages ago."

Behind me I hear Lukas talking to himself, the way he does when he plays alone, telling stories in such a low voice that nobody can hear what they're about. On the patio, the girls are snickering about something. Am I relieved that Hoffmo wasn't filming our mailboxes that night? I imagine the grainy video footage, Emma in her night-dress coming out of our big black door with a deep-frozen animal corpse and a coil of nylon rope.

"So where are the cameras?" I ask him.

"Oh," he says. "One in the drive, facing the garden. Another on the fence, facing the front door."

"Is only your property visible in the frame?" I ask him.

"Have you become a lawyer too now, Prytz?" he asks.

I don't respond. I look at his garden, where it runs parallel to Kastanjesvingen, separated from the road by the fence of thin metal threads, all loosely woven together. Slowly, I say:

"Is it possible that you might be able to see part of the road in the footage? From the camera in the drive, perhaps?"

"Have I secretly been filming the street, you mean?"

"No, no," I say. "Not intentionally. But surely something like that could happen entirely of its own accord? Almost by chance – the camera just ended up positioned that way, without it being anyone's fault?"

Hoffmo purses his lips, considers his driveway.

"It's certainly a possibility," he says. "Of course, I've done nothing of the sort on purpose. I presume you understand that. But that part of the road might have been filmed unintentionally. Yes, that's possible. But regardless, you'd hardly be able to see anything but asphalt. If that did turn out to be the case, I mean. Your property isn't in the shot, and the Sparre boy must have come out of the cellar."

I stare at his gatepost, feel my breath coming quick and light.

"But if it *is* the case that you can see a bit of the road," I say. "Then might we be able to see if someone came walking up Kastanjesvingen on the night Jørgen was murdered?"

For a moment the air is completely still. There are no cars to be heard, no bicycles, no children playing. Then the two girls on the patio laugh again. Behind me, I hear Merete rustling her newspaper.

"I'm not sure," he says slowly. "But yes, it's a possibility."

"It might be worth taking a look?" I say lightly.

Part of me expects him to refuse, in a friendly way – no, it's too much. But then he gives a languid nod.

"Yes," he says thoughtfully. "It's certainly worth taking a look. Care to join me, Prytz?"

I hesitate, shifting my weight from one foot to the other. I'm not sure whether it's a good idea for me to get more wrapped up in this than I already am. But the lure of being able to test my hypothesis overpowers me, my curiosity to see what might be found on that footage. The sliver of doubt, too – what if I see something I don't want to see, what if Emma was caught on camera? I can't imagine it, but I can't be sure. But then I think that no matter what, it will be better to know. Hoffmo likes me, he won't be unreasonable, and since we've come this far, we may as well just get it over with.

"Emma," I shout over my shoulder. "I'm just going over to

Hoffmo's to take a look at something for a moment – can you keep an eye on Lukas for me, please?"

Both girls are peering intently into the box on the table, as if they're looking for a specific part. Merete casts a glance in our direction over the top of her newspaper.

"Sure," Emma answers, without looking up.

Inside Herr and Fru Hoffmo's house, everything is covered in pine panelling – walls, floor and ceiling. And in order to truly complete the look, they've furnished the hallway with three huge pine cabinets. There's something anachronistic about the whole thing, a nod to thirty years ago when Tåsen was just one of Oslo's ordinary suburbs and the Hoffmos bought themselves a house and moved in with their three small children. For a moment, I almost wish we had lived here back then. Fru Hoffmo peeks out from the kitchen and lights up when she sees me – oh, how lovely, she says, shall I put on some coffee, perhaps?

"No thanks," Hoffmo says self-importantly. "There's something we have to get to the bottom of."

"Not for me, thank you," I say, returning her friendly smile.

They seem so happy, the two of them, and I realise that I've thought this several times before. He with his ideas and flights of fancy; she looking out for these whims with anticipation – what on earth is he up to this time? – secure in the knowledge that he'll listen to her if she puts her foot down.

Hoffmo hastens up the stairs, and I follow him. On the pine walls of the staircase hang photographs of the couple's three children, as babies, at school age, and later as young adults. At the top hang images of all three as adults, smiling at the camera on their respective wedding days. The stairs follow the family's evolution. But we have no time to stop and look, Hoffmo and I. He shows me into a room. It probably used to be one of the children's bedrooms, but now it acts as a kind of catch-all hobby room. It's furnished with bookcases – also in pine – and an old-fashioned armchair, in addition to a desk finished in smooth veneer. On the floor in the corner, tucked beneath the lowest part of the sloping roof, stands a rowing machine.

Hoffmo sits down in front of the computer and turns it on. I remain standing, positioning myself beside him. The window before us faces away from Kastanjesvingen, towards Bakkehaugen. The Hoffmos have made sensible choices, I think, made themselves a stable home, lived good lives. They haven't redecorated, but why should they? The computer creaks and labours, and Hoffmo looks at it with a furrowed brow, as if his concentration might rub off on the machine if only he frowns hard enough. They haven't replaced their computer in a long time, either. I glance quickly at my watch – this might take some time, and I had planned to be standing there in the garden when Åsmund gets home, but it should still be a while before he's back. The desktop appears on the screen. Hoffmo moves his fingers. His hand rests heavily over the mouse; he finds the right icon and clicks. The screen is then filled by an image of his garden in autumnal sunlight, just as it is now. On the right-hand side, a strip of Kastanjesvingen is visible. I lean forward. It's more than a strip. Perhaps a third of the road.

"Well, would you look at that," Hoffmo says. He gives me an anxious smile.

"Where's the saved footage?" I ask.

At least it isn't possible to see our garden, I think. If Emma did leave the house, the footage wouldn't show it. Hoffmo's huge paw manoeuvres the mouse – he's clumsy, but he knows what he's doing. He finds the right tab; adjusts a few settings.

"Let's see," he says. "When did it happen again?"

"Friday night," I say breathlessly. "Or the early hours of Saturday morning, just over a week ago."

He finds the right day – the recording is still saved on his computer. A line with a marker below the image allows him to fast-forward, drag us up to midnight. On the screen, his garden lies empty in the dark. The road beside it is deserted, but light enough, thanks to the street lamps. The image is grainy, but we can clearly see the gatepost where Hoffmo's house number hangs. The timestamp at the bottom of the screen states 00:13.14, and counts the seconds: 15, 16, 17. We stare. Nothing happens.

"Maybe we should fast forward," I say after a couple of minutes.

Hoffmo says nothing, so I take this as an authorisation. I lean over the keyboard again, find the right key. The playback increases in speed, but not too much. I have my hand against the back of Hoffmo's chair. The pads of my first two fingers tap impatiently against it.

At around 00:30 some shadows appear. Hoffmo stops the film. They approach the camera, and then we see a pair of shoes with huge soles and go-faster stripes, the kind teenage boys wear.

"How about that?" Hoffmo says, folding his hands across his stomach.

"It could just be one of the neighbours," I say.

"We don't know that for certain," he says, noting the time on a sheet of paper on the desk.

More time passes. A car drives by, we glimpse its tyres in the image. Hoffmo makes another note. I'm starting to have my doubts about this project, because what did I expect to find? I'm no longer able to see what kind of conclusive evidence we'll be able to get from this. As Hoffmo continues to scroll through the footage, I sense the futile nature of what we're trying to do: my hypothesis, which seemed so clear to me out in the garden, will result in no more than the shrug of a shoulder – none of us will be any the wiser. On the screen the timestamp says 02:00, and then 02:30.

"Do we know anything about when it was supposed to have happened?" Hoffmo asks.

"Sometime during the night, at least," I say. "If we get to six o'clock, I think that will be too late."

Down on the ground floor I can hear Fru Hoffmo pottering around. It wouldn't surprise me if she's making coffee for us anyway, she's just that kind of person.

"Well, not much is happening here," Hoffmo says as the time-stamp approaches three.

"Presumably someone could have walked down the other side of the street?" I say.

"True," he says.

Three o'clock. Hoffmo takes a deep breath. And then a tiny light appears at the very edge of the screen.

"What's that?" I ask.

Hoffmo pauses the film. For a moment the light vibrates there, and then Hoffmo plays the video at normal speed. The light approaches. Behind it is a shadow, as if it belongs to a car, but it isn't, it's something smaller, something with just one light. Then it disappears out of the frame, and the street lies in darkness again.

"Rewind," I say.

He taps a few keys. The light appears again. It's a vehicle, I think. Something about the motion, the speed at which it moves.

"A motorcycle?" Hoffmo suggests.

"Maybe."

We play it yet again. I pause the footage, but it doesn't tell us anything. All we can see is the light and a kind of box behind it. Then something else behind that, but it's too dark, and the light facing the camera makes it difficult to discern what's in the background. Hoffmo notes the time on his notepad.

"Well, we should probably give this to the police," he mutters. "Not that I think they'll do anything with it."

The film continues to zip past on the screen. I'm about to say that I should probably get going. My hypothesis missed the mark; there's no point wasting any more time. But then we see something. Just a shadow at the top of the frame, and then something moving.

"Was there something there?" I ask, and Hoffmo pauses the video before playing it back at normal speed.

The movement is quick, over in a moment, but we rewind, set the film playing again, and after a couple of attempts Hoffmo manages to pause the film at the right moment.

It's a foot. It's at the very edge of the frame, hardly visible, but with the video paused like this, we can see it clearly. It's wearing a white trainer, small and feminine below a slim ankle. A figure has been embroidered on to the side of the shoe. The angle makes it difficult to see exactly what it depicts, but it doesn't matter, because I already know. I know exactly where I've seen that shoe before.

That summer's day when I first saw her, on the patio outside the house with her husband and her friends, she looked so content. Jørgen lifted her braid and set it gently down the centre of her back; she turned to him and smiled. This is an image I've returned to – they seemed so in love. Nothing about the situation indicated that they were disappointed in one another, that they blamed each other for how their lives had turned out.

But Merete didn't wave to me when she saw me. She simply stood there and studied me. I had felt so ashamed of my staring, but later I thought: That was also a curious thing to do, to just stand there like that. I was the new neighbour – you would have thought that she would have wanted, if not to come into the apartment and say hello, at the very least to wave. To smile, acknowledge that I was there. That she had seen me and understood who I was. Welcome to the neighbourhood – that sort of thing.

Once, in an entirely different context, after a heated discussion at a parents' evening at Emma's school, I told Åsmund that Merete is the type who bites when threatened.

I rush down the stairs as fast as I can, taking the Hoffmos' evolution in reverse. Shout to Hoffmo over my shoulder that he has to call the police and ask them to go straight to Merete Tangen's apartment – it's her shoe, her foot, probably also her stolen cargo bike. He has to do it, because I don't have time. My heart pounds painful and hot in my chest: the three kids out there on the lawn. The two girls building the drone; the little boy playing with his toy cars. Merete and her newspaper. And what might Merete have heard of what Hoffmo said, how much might she guess that I now understand? What kind of threat do I pose to her? I have to find the two that are mine and take them with me. Get them home and lock the door. Make a fortress of our apartment. Call Åsmund, get him to come home. I'm like a sheepdog, all I can think is that I have to gather my flock.

Downstairs Fru Hoffmo comes towards me with a tray – sure enough, she's overridden all instructions and made coffee for us anyway. I brush past her, she says something to me, but I don't hear what. I have only one goal, and the heavy pulse in my chest reminds me with every beat: this is urgent. This thing that has permeated the marrow of my every bone since Sunday: I've been living right next door to a dangerous person. I've made my mistakes, but I will protect my children – in this I will not fail. I stuff my feet into my shoes, leave my jacket, practically throw the door open and storm out and across the road.

I can already see the two girls from Hoffmo's garden. They seem to have put the drone together now, but they haven't managed to get it to fly. Emma is holding it in her hands, Filippa the remote control, and they're chatting. Merete is gone. Lukas, too – he's no longer sitting on the bench under the apple tree.

I fly through the gate towards them; both girls turn to look at me. Emma is about to say something, but before she manages it, I shout:

"Where's Lukas?"

"He's inside," Emma says. "With Merete."

I bound over to her, grab her arm and drag her after me; she just manages to thrust the drone at her friend. Filippa only looks at me, and there's something heavy in her eyes, as if she's far older than her thirteen years.

"Mamma, what is it?" Emma asks as I haul her after me.

There's nothing coquettish about her now, she isn't trying

anything on. Is simply asking me as a child – Mamma, what is going on?

"We have to go inside," I say.

I continue to hold her by the arm, as if she were a criminal. I don't turn towards Filippa, who is probably watching us go. I enter our code at the front door, drag Emma into the stairwell with me, and unlock the door to the apartment.

"Stay here," I say. I'm being brusque, but perhaps she can hear the panic that's boiling up just beneath the surface, because she doesn't protest. "I'm going upstairs to get Lukas."

Emma has those big, scared eyes – those of the child with the fear of the dark, the fear I forced her to learn to live with.

"What's happening?" she asks me.

She's on the verge of tears. Had I the time, I would curse myself for all that I've thought about her, for wondering what she's capable of. She's still a child, her tough attitude a shell against the world, but it isn't especially solid – prod it, and it crumbles.

"Emma," I say, putting my hands on her shoulders. "Listen to me. You lock the door after me. You put on the safety chain. You let nobody in other than Pappa or me. *No-one*. Understand?"

Her eyes are shining, but she nods. She's listening, she'll do as I say. As I run up the stairs to the first floor I hear the click of our door, the rattling of the safety chain.

This is a green home, proclaims their doormat. I take a deep breath. I lift my hand, and knock.

"Rikke," she says. "How nice. Do come in."

Her smile is measured, as it often is. Merete isn't the kind of person to show enthusiasm without good cause. I'm breathing quickly and shallowly, trying to get control of myself. I don't want to appear alarmed; don't want to seem afraid or desperate. Just want to come across as normal.

"I just came to get Lukas," I say. "Is he here?"

"He's here," she confirms. "But why don't you come in for a minute."

My eyes flit around the hallway. Beside her boots are his shoes, the tiny trainers we bought this spring, dirty along the edges from the mud in the garden, worn at the toes from him braking on his scooter. On a hook, beside her parka, hangs his little down jacket.

"We're actually quite busy," I say.

I overcompensate, smile too widely.

"Oh, come on," she says. "What's the big rush? You have time for a coffee."

She moves aside. I swallow. I have no other choice. I step across the threshold.

I register nothing of the interior this time. Form no opinion on whether the living room is messy or tidy, fail to read Merete's state of mind from the arrangement of the objects she surrounds herself with. My mind is filled with just one thing: to find my boy. To the extent that I do look around, it's to search for traces of him. Has she brought out the Lego, are there pieces here and there? Has she set out a small plate with slices of bread spread with liver pâté, and has Lukas left the crust, as he usually does? Can I see any sign that he's here, that everything is as it should be? But I find no sign, and nothing else registers with me.

"Sit down," she says once we enter the kitchen.

I scan the room for clues: a glass of milk, a sweater, anything at all.

"Where is he?" I ask.

I try to speak in a neutral tone – I'm a mother just wondering where my child is, as if the whole thing is a question of logistics. Merete must not catch on that I know. Should she realise this, I'll be a threat to her, and she has my child. I have to act as if nothing is out of the ordinary, but I already know that I'm failing, that there's something thin and desperate in my voice that I'm unable to camouflage.

"He's here," she says calmly.

She screws together the espresso pot, sets it on the hob. Takes out cups, and hands me one with a smile. I try to smile back. Pull up the corners of my mouth, hope that they'll stay there. Could she have overheard something, sitting there on the front step? Did she hear what Hoffmo and I said about the cameras? I try to calculate: how far away is the small, paved path, how easily does the sound travel on a quiet Sunday morning, just how loudly were we speaking?

"So how are things?" she asks.

"Good," I say thinly. "And you?"

"Well."

She throws out her arms.

"We're managing. It's sad, of course. Especially for Filippa. But there's a sense of peace about the whole thing, too. It's just the two of us now. Us girls. I'm sure we'll be okay."

The coffee has boiled; she lifts the pot and pours coal-black coffee into our white cups. Then she sits down, takes a sip. I take one, too.

My hands are trembling, so I have to hold the cup between them, press them against it for support. Has Hoffmo called the police? I asked him to, but I didn't wait for an answer. Did he hear me shouting for him to call? Does he understand just how serious this is?

"It hasn't exactly been easy with Jørgen," she says. "Although I'm sure you must have realised that. He and I have had, how would you put it? Different expectations of our marriage."

She laughs a little. Mostly to herself, is the impression I get. Her laughter is hard, ragged. What if Hoffmo hasn't called? Just how good can the hearing of a man over seventy be? What if nobody is on their way here to help me?

"Expectations – that's a good word for it," she says. "As if it was only a matter of clarifying a few things. But anyway. You can't imagine how it's been. Åsmund is an entirely different type of person, you can't possibly understand. Jørgen could be so ruthless, so inconsiderate. Is everything okay, Rikke? You look a little pale."

"Yes," I say.

There's not a sound in the building. Here, where you can hear even the tiniest movement. His voice, even when he talks quietly to himself, as he does when he plays. His quick footsteps, on the way to get a new Lego figure, on the way in here because he's heard me speaking. Is he here at all? But his jacket, the little shoes. It tears at me, I can hardly swallow, something wants to come up through my throat. I daren't think about what it means, this silence.

"You know," she says. "I'm not even angry at you. Although you probably think I am – that's what I would have thought, if I were you. But in all honesty, it means nothing. Well, not nothing. But there's been so many rounds of it. So many others."

She gives me a look, her brows lowered, and something expressive comes over them as she says:

"Did you know that? That there were other women? That you weren't the only one?"

No voice remains within me. It's as if I'm floating away. My body is tense; stiff and quaking. There's nothing to be done. It means nothing if she knows. It's absolutely immaterial to me whether or not everyone knows, whether every sordid detail is made public. I just want my child.

I nod.

"It isn't as if he hid it all that well, either. An idiot would have known. Text messages at all hours of the day, and the way he guarded his phone. He'd go into his study and close the door to take the calls. So pathetic. I've found two dirty wine glasses in the dishwasher on the days I've returned home from a trip – sometimes one of them would even have lipstick on it. He didn't even bother to hide it from me. That's the worst thing. He probably told you that I promised him I'd take care of Filippa alone. Didn't he? That I pressured him into having a child, promised he wouldn't need to adjust his lifestyle in the slightest. I bet he made out that he was some kind of saint, too. Did he tell you that he tried to leave me, but then I came running after him with all kinds of promises?"

"Where is Lukas?" I say, and my voice is hoarse and rusty.

"It's all just lies," she says. "Yes, I made some promises, but goddammit, so did he. He called *me*, once it was over. *He* begged to come back. I asked him to stay, that's true, but he was the one who got in touch first."

She takes a breath. In the distance, I can hear sirens. Perhaps it's just an ambulance out on Maridalsveien. But maybe not.

"To be honest, I don't regret giving up my career. I bet he told you I'm bitter about that, but really I'm not. I'm glad not to have to travel two hundred and fifty days a year, that I don't work five nights a week. But, of course, it cost me. And then there was Jørgen, who expected not to have to give up anything."

She smiles. It looks like a grimace, as if she's decided to stretch out her lips.

"So there you have it," she says. "What we agreed on fifteen years ago couldn't be renegotiated. And of course, I was young and in love. And then that's how you are – willing to agree to anything in order to have a child with the one you love."

She looks past me, out of the window.

"It's been no sacrifice for me to stay home with Filippa," she says firmly. "Not in that way. But surely I was within my rights to expect something from him, too. And then, of course, there was the money."

The sirens disappear again, and my heart sinks – have I been abandoned?

"Eight piano students a week and the odd performance doesn't provide much of an income," she says. "Nowhere near enough for an apartment in Tåsen, had I chosen to leave him. With what I would have been left with after the apartment was sold, and what the bank would give me as a mortgage, buying anything in this area would have been out of the question. And likely anything anywhere nearby. I would have had to move far away. And what would I do in the countryside? What would Filippa do? The only thing I truly hate Jørgen for is this: that I was dependent on him for my financial survival. You probably think this is about jealousy, don't you? In fact, it's quite simple. He died, and we inherit all he owned. And once we own this apartment, we can continue our lives."

Now the sirens can be heard again outside. I'm not sure whether it's wishful thinking, but it sounds as if they're getting closer.

"He destroyed our marriage," she says, and now her voice is trembling a little, there's something agitated in it that she doesn't quite manage to hide. "He neglected me, humiliated me. Carried on however he wanted – with one of my childhood friends, with our neighbour. In spite of everything, I was prepared to try and make it work. *He* was the one who made it insufferable."

The sirens are approaching – I'm sure of it now. My breath quickens again.

390

"Then I thought: if he wants to piss all over everything we have, if he wants to use me, leave his family in the lurch – then I'll use him back. A divorce wasn't possible, it would crush me, force me to move, impoverish me. And that was his fault – he chose to make the marriage intolerable. And since he had so clearly shown that he cared nothing for us, I didn't think it was unreasonable to expect that Filippa and I should continue to live as we had done, after the family was finally broken up."

Blue light flickers on the kitchen cabinets behind her. She takes a deep breath, and then we hear the slamming of a car door outside.

"Well," she says. "There was apparently something I hadn't thought of. From now on, we'll just have to do the best we can, Rikke. But I'm not angry at you. Or maybe I am now, just a little. But I don't hate you, not the way I hate him."

The front door slams; they're in the stairwell. Then we hear their boots on the stairs.

"Where is Lukas?" I say. I have almost no voice left.

There's a hammering at the door.

"Is there anyone in there?" shouts a man's voice. "Open up!"

Merete gets up. She takes a deep breath, as if steeling herself for what is to come. Then she turns towards the hallway, and leaves. It's as if she's gliding along – like a concert pianist stepping out onto the stage. Halfway across the room she turns to me.

"You'll find him in the loft."

I run from the kitchen, past Merete as she heads towards whatever awaits her behind the apartment's front door, storming past the closed door to the study and bounding up the stairs, taking the steps three at a time.

I see him while I'm still on the stairs. His little body is lying on the floor, beside the daybed. There is no Lego around him, nothing there but him, unmoving against the rug. I scream, in a way I had no idea I was capable of – it comes from my belly, a primal scream, an echo of thousands of years of evolution, of foremothers discovering the bodies of their children. When I see him lying there on his side, one little hand half open beside his head, the dirty green plaster wound around his index finger, I know instinctively that I will never be done with this moment. That the rest of my life will be spent processing it.

The hundredths of a second pass so slowly. I'm about to cast myself over him, lift his lifeless body in my arms and think, as I sometimes do, that he is so light – he's the entire world to me, and yet he weighs nothing.

Then his chest rises. The tiniest groan escapes from between his lips. The sob I have suppressed during those long minutes in Merete's kitchen finally escapes me and he turns around, pulling his little hand with the plaster on it into him, turning over onto his stomach and lifting his head. My scream has woken him.

In the next moment I'm beside him – I throw myself up the last few stairs and onto the floor. Pull him onto my lap. He curls against my body with sleepy movements and whimpers, frightened by my state of panic. But I hold him so tight, so, so tight in my arms; I press my nose into his dishevelled hair, feeling his warm, living body against mine. I'm sitting this way as the police come storming up the stairs. Collapsed here on the loft floor, crying in hard, jerking sobs, as I press my miracle child to me.

There's a different kind of quiet in the house this evening. The police have taken her in. They have spoken to me and made notes, asked me to come in for further questioning tomorrow. Filippa is being taken care of, or at least I have to assume that she is. The apartment upstairs is empty. Silent, but in a good way. The Sparre family are still away, and it doesn't seem as if Saman and Jamila are around – maybe they've decided to take that holiday. But we're here, all four of us. In our apartment it is warm and cosy; here, everyone is home.

Lukas is sleeping. I've bathed him, combed his hair so that it lies flat against his skull. I've cleaned the invisible wound on his index finger and put a new plaster on it, brushed his teeth and got him into a clean pair of pyjamas. Read him as many bedtime stories as he wanted. Lay beside him and held him, felt him wriggling, comforted him every time he's begun to cry: there, there, my little one.

"Don't leave," he said, and I've promised – no, darling, of course I won't leave.

He can ask me for anything at all. I'm so grateful, so absolutely and inconceivably grateful that I still have him.

I don't leave the room until he's fallen asleep, keeping the light on above all his dinosaurs. Leave the door ajar, so I'll hear him – at the slightest whimper, I'll come running. It's my job to look after him, and in this I will never fail.

Before I go upstairs, I knock on Emma's bedroom door. Come in, says a voice from inside. She's sitting on her bed, watching a TV series on her iPad. I've given her permission to bring it down here into her room. Tonight, nothing is forbidden.

"Is everything okay?" I ask her.

"Yeah," she says. "How about you?"

And I'm so happy that she asks, and that there's not a trace of sarcasm in it, not a hint of toxicity. She's simply wondering – am I okay?

"Yes, honey," I say. "Everything's fine."

"Is Lukas asleep?"

"Yes."

"Good."

That's all we say, but as I head up the stairs, I think about just how grateful I am for this, too. I promise myself that I'll do better with her. Be a role model. And far more patient. Ask her more questions, but not in that inquisitorial way. Listen when she answers.

Åsmund is in the kitchen – I can hear him humming to himself up there. I take a breath. I know what I have to do.

He's standing with his back to me, washing up the saucepan from dinner. I look at him. He's been mine for more than half my life. We know each other inside and out. I clear my throat, and he turns.

"Åsmund," I say. "There's something I have to tell you."

SECOND THURSDAY

The grouting between the tiles of the bathroom floor begins to crumble; I'm scrubbing it too hard. When the steel wool failed to penetrate the joints between the ceramic tiles I found an unused toothbrush, and that's what I'm using now. It does the job, gets into the spaces where bigger cleaning implements are forced to admit defeat. I'm going to clean every square millimetre of grouting in this room, a room in which both the floor and walls are tiled. It's one hell of a job, but I refuse to give up. If I'm being honest, I'm happy to have this disgusting task to occupy me.

"Look after yourself," my friend said.

I was already going at it with the steel-wool sponge when she was here just a few hours ago. She had popped by to pick up the kids, to take them to the cinema and McDonald's, so I can have a little time to myself. Treat yourself to some self-care, she said. Watch a film, read a book. Go for a run. Book a massage – why not? But I didn't hear her. All I wanted was to clean the bathroom. I went through the entire apartment on Monday, scrubbing all the floors, wiping up dust. Tried to take it easy on Tuesday, attend to the kids – Emma, who says nothing, and Lukas, who keeps asking where Pappa is and when he's coming home. I've tried to keep my answers vague, to be a dependable caregiver they can lean on, but things began to unravel, I couldn't take it. When is Pappa coming home, Lukas asked several times, and in the end I started to cry. And so, to avoid going to pieces in front of them, I began to clean the kitchen instead. Yesterday I emptied all the cabinets, sorted through the packets and tins of food, threw out anything that was out of date and wiped the shelves, cleaning right into the corners, into all the cracks where grains of sugar and tiny seeds get stuck. Then I put back the items that are still edible; sorted the spice rack alphabetically. Scrubbed the inside of the oven. Today, it's the bathroom's turn. I've cleaned it again – all the cabinets, all the shelves. I've scrubbed the toilet. But I couldn't quite get the grime out from between the tiles, so now I've taken drastic measures. Nobody will be able to complain about my work once I'm done. Although I can see that I'm going too far – now that the grouting is flaking off. I'm destroying it. But it's all the same to me. The most important thing is that it's clean.

I said this to my friend. Or some of it, at least. It has to be clean, I said. I have to get rid of the dirt, I said.

"Rikke," she said. "It *is* clean."

"Not clean enough."

She said:

"I think you need to put down that sponge now. I think you need to relax a little."

But I didn't agree.

This is the fourth day. I've not heard a word. I don't know what that means, and so I clean. It's meaningful work, physical and simple, it serves a clear purpose. Although maybe not this scrubbing with the toothbrush. That's a little excessive, I'll admit it. But I can't give up now.

Ingvild Fredly was here the other day, while the kids were at school and kindergarten. I'm on sick leave. The doctor eventually coughed up a prescription for some sleeping pills, so I can sleep at night, but it doesn't help – I'm still just as tired when I wake up. Ingvild sat on the kitchen chair and watched as I emptied the cupboards. She said:

"You did the right thing."

She said:

"Give him time."

She said:

"This will all work out for the best, one way or another."

But I didn't want to listen to her. I had no patience for these words of comfort. I don't know what they mean. There's only one way in which this can all work out for the best. And I don't want to be comforted – especially not by her. I told her as much.

"It won't," I said. "What the fuck do you know? All I know is that I have to clean this house, that it's my job. You can't help me, so what are you doing here?"

"Maybe I should go," she said, and it was the only sensible thing to pass her lips.

Sometimes, as I'm scrubbing, I cry. Other times, I just work. I've done what I had to do. Admittedly, a little late, taking no pleasure in it and without any sense of moral satisfaction, but still. The work of the guilty conscience is done. My work, on the other hand, has only just begun.

The bathroom floor is calling me. I get down on my knees, scouring and shoving the toothbrush between the tiles, so hard that its bristles splay out. Åsmund is a neurotic brusher, he brushes his teeth far too hard – all his toothbrushes look this way. When I thought about this earlier today, I cried, but now I'm all out of tears. I just clean. Work mechanically. Self-care, my friend said. I don't really know what that is. A penance, perhaps. Or an attempt to make amends.

Out in the hallway, I hear the apartment's front door open and close. It's him, I think, and sit up, listening. Or maybe it's them, my friend and the kids. Maybe Emma dug her heels in and refused to see the film, which, true enough, was selected for its appropriateness for her little brother's age group. Maybe Lukas dissolved into tears in the cinema foyer, maybe my friend had no other choice but to pick him up off the floor and carry him home. I get up. My knees are stiff and painful; my injured knee in particular, but the other has begun to hurt, too. I stagger out into the living room, the tooth-brush clutched in my hand.

He's standing in the middle of the living room. He looks like a stranger, pale and tired. His face is thinner, and he's both older and younger at the same time, as if his wrinkles have smoothed out while the stress has simultaneously become entrenched in his features, marking them indelibly. He's been crying. Of course he's been crying. Åsmund cries at weddings and christenings, he can't help himself. I stop. I just stand there, too.

He says:

"Hi."

I say:

"Hi."

He says:

"What are you doing with the toothbrush?"

"Cleaning."

"Oh."

The house is quiet, all that can be heard is the autumn wind outside.

"Are you coming home?" I ask.

He says:

"You have no idea how this has been for me, Rikke."

I shake my head. He's right – I have no idea.

"You can't do this to me. Do you understand? This hurts – so damn much."

He looks around him. Examines our walls.

"I won't be able to stand this a second time. I hope you know that. This can never happen again."

I nod. Oh, he doesn't know, he can't possibly understand just how certain I am of precisely that. I'll never do anything of the sort again. But I'm unable to say it. So I just nod, feeling the imprint of those little words, too – *a second time*. The promise of another chance.

"Because if you do it again," he says, and then his voice breaks.

I drop the toothbrush to the floor and run across to him. Set my cheek against his shoulder and breathe in the scent of him, the way it smelled in his childhood bedroom back home in Haslum, where we would sit with the old travel TV his parents had given us blaring at full volume, so they wouldn't hear us when we had sex.

"Are you coming home?" I whisper.

"Yes," he says, his voice thick with tears. "I suppose I am. I don't know where else I would go."

PART IV

Just a poor man

LAST DAY

The ventilation system is about to buckle under the heat. There's a grille in the ceiling with a temperature dial next to it, and although I've turned it as low as it goes, the sweat is dripping off me. Outside, it's quiet. I look down towards the river from where I'm sitting, and there's almost no-one there, the odd pair of tourists, some young people with beach towels and baskets, on their way to sit in the park or visit the bathing spot at Nydalen. A couple with a pushchair. Most people are probably on holiday, either abroad or at a cabin somewhere. Those who are left have probably gone to the coast or out to the islands. Our offices are virtually empty, and for the past few days it's been just the two of us: a PhD candidate who will soon be submitting his thesis, and me. I say hello to the PhD student whenever I see him; he smiles at me with a pained expression, then goes back to whatever he's doing.

On the windowsill, a small fly is buzzing. I'm not sure how it got in – the ventilation system is entirely dependent on us not opening the windows, a fact the HR officer has emphasised ad nauseam, and which is adhered to because she comes down so hard on the people who break this rule that the rest of us have realised it isn't worth it. Perhaps it followed me in when I let myself in the door. I watch it, roving here and there, butting the windowpane at one location before gathering itself and trying again a little further along. I try to establish whether there's anything systematic to its movements, if it's working to cover as large an area as possible, or simply throwing itself back and forth in panic.

I'm supposed to be working. I have some documents open on my computer, but it's so hard to concentrate in the heat. We're not going away this year. The new house cost a lot, much more than what we got from the sale of the apartment in Kastanjesvingen, so we're staying home. Åsmund and I are taking it in turns to work, and we do nice things as a family. Three weeks in July were set aside for me to work, and I told my colleagues just how much I was going to get done during this time. The office will be practically empty, I said, no meetings, no new assignments suddenly popping up, no interruptions. At the beginning of June there seemed no limit to what I could achieve.

We moved into the new house just before Christmas. Of course, it wasn't possible for us to keep living in Kastanjesvingen; neither Åsmund nor I would have been able to stand it. And anyway, it was only a matter of time before the story of my relationship with Jørgen got out. It would spread across the neighbourhood – the housewife and her cronies would ensure that everybody ended up talking about it – and I already knew how I would be depicted, the sheer glee with which I would be condemned. I didn't want Emma to have to face that at school. You could almost say that we fled. For two unbearable months we lived with Åsmund's mother while we waited to move into the house we now live in. Perhaps she finally grew tired of us, too, because since we moved into the new house, we've heard far less from her than I would have imagined.

Our apartment was put up for sale towards the end of October, once we had already set up camp at my mother-in-law's. The bank had warned us that the murder case might make the sale difficult, but the enthusiastic real estate agent we hired wasn't the least bit discouraged.

"Oh, don't you worry," she said as we showed her around the empty rooms. "This apartment is going to sell, no problem at all. I sold a similar one over in the garden city area a few weeks ago, and it went for a record sum."

"Are you sure?" I said. "I mean, our neighbour was murdered on the floor above."

410

We were standing in the kitchen, and she was admiring the view of the garden through the long row of windows. Then she turned and looked at me.

"Oh, trust me," she said, giving me her most cocksure, lipsticked smile. "This is Tåsen. A murder will have no impact on the property's value. Or at least, not when you have three bedrooms and access to a garden."

She was right, too. The apartment sold for half a million kroner over the asking price.

Our new house is an older detached property in Bærum, just beside the forest, a short drive from my mother-in-law's house. The estate is fairly large, and the houses are like boxes, but it's not so bad. We've lived there for six months now, and we've got used to it. Put down roots, you might say. Lukas goes to the kindergarten on the estate. Emma made an impact at the local secondary school right from the start, and by the time the New Year came around I would see a small group of girls wearing fitted down jackets and carrying designer bags waiting faithfully for her beside our garage every morning. We had promised our old neighbours that we'd come over for coffee, but we put off visiting Tåsen. Jamila sent me a message, and I answered politely, but suggested no date. Said we were busy, that there was so much going on with the move, but sure, after things had quietened down. Then they, too, must have learned of my role in the lead-up to the murder, because I received no further invitations to decline. Emma showed an impressive ability to put the irrelevant behind her. From the day she started at the new school, I heard not a peep about the friends she had left behind, and nobody in the household has ever mentioned Simen Sparre. Åsmund and I never asked Emma about the last dead cat, despite having agreed once or twice that we should. It no longer seemed relevant. It was so far-fetched, in a way, hard to imagine that it had happened at all. I even went so far as to wonder whether I might have dreamed the circumstantial evidence I'd believed I had – made it up. We rarely spoke about the old neighbourhood. Rarely thought of it, either. The only thing that did pop up in my consciousness at regular intervals was Filippa Tangen. The darkness in her eyes was hard to forget. But I imagined that this memory, like so many others, would also fade away with time. We started a new life. It was surprisingly easy.

The air lies hot and dense beyond the window. I sit here, sensing that the ventilation system is losing its battle against the elements, almost completely alone at my workplace. It's impossible to concentrate – my thoughts become viscous, my work tasks meaningless. At home, Åsmund is probably in the garden; it'll soon be time to go and buy groceries for dinner. And tomorrow work will be just as empty, and nobody will ask me what I've done. I have no deadlines hanging over me. And then I think: Screw it, what's the point?

The hasp of the window is stuck fast – I've obviously taken the HR officer seriously, because the window can't have been opened in months, maybe years. I really have to force it, shoving it with my shoulder, to make the window swing out. The little fly, confused, lumbers out into the great unknown. The heat from outside hits me in the face, but at least I've given the tiny creature an escape route. I close the window, pack up my things and walk towards the door. Out in the corridor I wave to the hard-working PhD student, who glances up and gives me his forced smile. In the lift down to the exit I ask myself whether the fly would in fact have been better off here in the building, where the temperature is tolerable and the bin containing the remnants of lunch is only emptied once a week. I wonder how long it will survive out there.

*

In the square in front of the building, the heat is still. I no longer have a bicycle here – it's at the T-banen station out in Bærum – but I stop nevertheless. The air shimmers above the asphalt in front of me. I stand there and study it, a phenomenon seen relatively rarely here in the north, and as I stare, a figure appears in my field of view. She's pushing a bicycle with thin tyres, and has broad, bare shoulders; her cycling shorts are tight around her strong thighs. On her head, over thick hair that hangs in sweaty tufts, she has a cycle helmet – it makes her look like a mushroom. She lifts a hand and waves, and then comes towards me. I just stand there, watching, I can't quite believe it, but when she stops in front of me and takes off her helmet, I see that it is indeed her. Here, right outside my office.

"This helmet is the worst," she says in her deep, unwavering Nord-land dialect. "I feel like an idiot wearing it, but my partner insists. *Safety first*, you know."

"Ingvild," I say. "What are you doing here?"

"Just out for a bike ride," she says.

She leans forward and gives me a hug. I lean into her and see tiny drops of sweat across the freckles on her shoulders.

"Given up the motorbike?" I ask, and she rolls her eyes.

"Apparently, it's healthier to cycle," she says. "My partner insists on that, too. I don't know – a bus almost knocked me flying at a crossing earlier today. If I'd been on my motorbike, that never would have happened. But what can you do? Everyone's supposed to be getting into cycling these days. And you?"

"I take the T-banen," I say.

"I suppose you must do," she says. "You moved, didn't you?"

"Yes. We live out in Bærum. Bought a house there after all, in the end."

She smiles at this, and I remember something I noticed back when Ingvild was seeing my friend: the way she would get this glint in her eye every now and then, which told you she'd seen right through you.

413

"It's much better than I feared," I say, just a little too quickly. "You know how I wasn't exactly keen on it – I mean, I'm sure I wrote quite a bit about it in my email, but it's actually quite nice. Green. And you realise it isn't *that* far from the city, once you live there."

Ingvild gives me a quick wink, and as she congratulates us on the new house, she seems absolutely sincere. I tell her that I'll be working for most of the summer. She nods, she's going to be in in the city quite a bit herself, she says, and then we stand there and look around us.

"Which way are you going?" she asks me. "Maybe we can walk together for a bit?"

"I can walk up to Nydalen," I suggest. "Take the train from there."

"Great," she says. "I prefer pushing this thing anyway. That way at least I don't have to wear the helmet."

We walk the short stretch down to the river in silence. Ingvild Fredly handles her bicycle with hard, jerky movements – she lacks the gentle touch that comes with experience, once you've pushed your bicycle so much that it's become a part of you, and you know instinctively how the wheel will react to a kerb or a change in incline. The path beside the river is largely empty, and we can walk side by side without creating problems – there's nobody who needs to get past us.

"So," Ingvild says. "The sentence was passed a few weeks ago."

"Yes," I say. "I heard."

"Twelve years," she says. "It isn't much. She'll be out in ten."

I nod. In spite of everything, I had shuddered when I read this. Merete will be in prison for the next decade. When Filippa experiences her first relationship, starts going out to parties and frequenting nightclubs until the early hours – when she starts sixth-form college, takes part in the traditional school-leavers' activities, moves away from home, sits her first university exam. All this Merete will have to observe from a distance. Then I had another thought: Jørgen won't be able to experience any of it. Merete deprived him of that opportunity, deprived him of life itself, so why do I feel sympathy for her?

I dreaded the approaching court case. My name was not released, and we no longer lived in Tåsen where people knew it was me, but it put a certain amount of strain on me all the same. Prior to giving my testimony, I followed the court case through the press. It received massive coverage. One newspaper had even run a live blog, so you could follow the proceedings almost minute by minute.

Merete made a good impression, I thought. And although the press had depicted her as a calculating ice queen prior to the hearing, their characterisation of her seemed to soften somewhat after she made her statement. The journalist writing the live blog seemed to like her. Merete explained that her marriage had been difficult from the start. Jørgen's infidelity had been extensive and omnipresent, something the defence lawyer dryly noted would be established through the submission of *huge volumes of evidence*. Later, Jørgen was demonstrated to have had relationships with four women, myself included. Two of the relationships had ended many years ago. To me, this appeared somewhat modest considering what the defence had promised, but the court didn't seem to see it that way, and the prosecution didn't do much to add nuance to this depiction of Jørgen as a notorious Casanova. Merete described how she had attempted to make the marriage work, first by trying to be enough for him, and when this failed, by doing her best to accept that this was just the way he was. Why didn't you leave him, the defence lawyer asked, and to this Merete replied with emotion that she only wished she'd been able to, but her financial situation would have made it impossible for her to provide for both herself and her daughter alone. The understanding between them was that he earned the money and she ran the household, and this arrangement had made it impossible for her to break it off. Or at least, not without losing everything she had. Which suited Jørgen just fine, she said. The story she had told me in the kitchen on the day that I had feared for the life of my son had been adjusted and finely honed into the defence she had settled on: he had used her, she was the victim.

On the weekend she and Filippa had gone camping, she told the court, she had decided to confront him. The plan was to return in the middle of the night and catch him red-handed. She had hidden the family's cargo bike there for this purpose, and at around two o'clock in the morning she got up, put on a head torch, walked the thirty minutes it took from the campsite down to the car park, found the bicycle and cycled into Tåsen. She parked the bike some distance away, down the street beyond Hoffmo's fence, before walking across to the house and ringing the doorbell. Jørgen buzzed her in from the apartment. He was alone, so her plan had effectively failed, but they ended up in an ugly fight nevertheless. She confronted him with what she knew. Choked with tears, Merete told the court about the evidence she presented to Jørgen: text messages she had read, packets of condoms she had found in his suitcase. The wine glasses with lipstick on them also made an appearance here. Once, she had even found a bra that wasn't hers. Jørgen admitted to being unfaithful, but denied it was a problem. He believed that he had every right to do as he wished. If she had a problem with it, Jørgen said, then she could simply leave him.

"But, of course, I couldn't," Merete said. "He had made sure of that."

Furthermore, Merete explained that after they had been arguing for a while, Jørgen had declared the discussion over and gone into his study. Merete was beside herself, felt she'd been trampled on – she could see no way out. And so, when she opened the door to the study and saw that he lay sleeping over his keyboard – and it dawned on her that not only did he not care about how much pain he was causing her, but that their argument was of such little importance to him that he had fallen asleep right in the middle of it – she went into the kitchen and found the sharpest knife they had.

The court spent quite a lot of time over this point. Merete claimed that she had acted in anger. No matter how terrible things were between them, she said, she would never have been able to do something like that with malice aforethought. If for no other reason, then for the pain Jørgen's dramatic death, and her own crime, would inflict upon their daughter. The most important thing in her life was Filippa's well-being. No – she had come back into the city solely to catch him in the act; she had planned nothing more than a confrontation. But when he had fallen asleep, fifteen years of exploitation and humiliation had surged up in her, leaving her desperate. The prosecution claimed that the murder was premeditated, because otherwise why would she have pretended that the cargo bike had been stolen, stored it in a warehouse for months, travelled up to Skar to hide it there, and then ensured that someone dropped her and Filippa off in the forest? Merete reasoned that she did all this because she needed Jørgen to believe that she had no way of getting home, so that he would feel safe enough to invite one of his lovers over. She seemed strong, I thought. Elicited compassion, without ever losing her dignity.

Part of me expected the press to crucify her when she cited her unhappy lot in life. Could people really be expected to feel *so* sorry for her, I imagined them asking, just because she wouldn't have been able to afford to keep living in Tåsen? But to my surprise, they didn't seem to see it this way. Quotations from Merete's defence appeared in an op-ed in one of the leading newspapers, written by a fairly young, fairly high-profile female academic whose appearance was not unlike Rebekka Davidsen's. I found myself wondering what Jørgen would have had to say about the article. *This is how women continue to be affected by the financial inequalities between the genders,* wrote the academic. *Not because breaking free is a physical impossibility, but because it requires that we give up the lives we lead in the process.* The piece encountered opposition, but not much, considering that it was defending murder, and the criticism that did come was quiet and sober, and never critical of Merete's motives. Instead, it seemed that plenty of people saw Merete as the archetype of the strong, proud woman – she who has endured so much for so long, and who had finally had enough.

*

Then it was my turn. Before I was due to testify, I called the court and was able to speak to the public prosecutor. Her instructions were that I answer as honestly as possible. There was nothing to fear if I told the truth, she said, but I still hardly slept the night before. That morning I sat in the window of my new living room and looked out across all the blue and white bird-box houses that lay scattered about the little valley in which we live, where people lay sleeping in their bedrooms, right next door to their neighbours, and wished that I could change places with any one of them.

The prosecution would question me first, and they would want to know the gory details of my relationship with Jørgen. The email I sent to Fredly had been submitted as evidence, so I gave a brief explanation as to what it contained. Predictably, the questions from the defence lawyer ended up being about the sex, how often, for how long, how many times, but I felt strangely isolated from the whole thing, answering dryly and neutrally, estimating as best I could. Finally, I was asked about that Sunday up at Merete's apartment, and then it was over, and I could go home.

I bumped into Jamila during the recess – she would be testifying after me. She didn't hug me, only took my hand, and her grip was limp and disinterested. Her mouth was a straight line in her face, and she didn't look me in the eyes. She was wearing a fitted black sweater, which clearly showed the bump at her belly. I didn't see Saman, but he may well have been there with her.

Åsmund testified, too, although I didn't follow his testimony on the live blog. If at all possible, I wanted to avoid hearing him talk about how hard it had all been for him. The entire Sparre family would also testify, but that would be later – after I'd given my statement, any interest I'd had in the case melted away. I saw the headlines every now and then, but I no longer clicked through to read the articles. Our part in the whole thing was over. We would close this chapter of our lives.

The sentence was passed just a few weeks ago, and this I did read about in the newspaper. I felt an inexplicable stab of sympathy for Merete, but said nothing of it to Åsmund. Simply set the newspaper aside and thought: Very well, then. The article said she wasn't expected to appeal, and for that I was glad. As far as I understood, Filippa had been permanently placed with a close relative, probably one of Merete's sisters. I acted as if I was considering contacting her, to apologise for what I had done and to express my sympathies, but this was only for show – I actually never doubted, now that the court proceedings would soon be concluded, that I would put the whole matter behind me for good.

"It's probably for the best," I say to Ingvild. "The case is closed. And isn't that good for – I don't know – your statistics?"

"Yes," she says. "Well – for Gundersen's statistics. But yes. Of course, the most important thing is to identify the guilty party, get them sentenced. You know, carry out our duty to society."

"Yes."

We walk on for a while without saying anything. There's more – I can sense it. Fredly has something she wants to tell me, but I don't particularly want to hear it. I walk silently beside her and hope that she'll decide not to say anything after all. I should have taken the bus instead, shouldn't have offered to walk with her.

"It's just," she says. "There are certain things that don't add up in that case. Just little things, but they irritate me."

"Oh," I say, and hope that will be it.

"Two things in particular have been bugging me," she continues. "The first is that cargo bike. Or, in fact, everything Merete did that night. Do you remember?"

"Yes."

"She pretended that the bike was stolen, found a place to store it and kept it hidden there for months," Ingvild says. "A few days before the trip with her sister and her daughter, she drove up to Skar, fetched the bike and hid it in the forest in some bushes. Then she arranged for her brother-in-law to drive them out there, agreed for Jørgen to pick them up, and made it very clear to anyone who asked that they had no way of getting home from the forest. On the night of Jørgen's death, she retrieved the bike from the bushes and rode it home using the motor – that is, all the way from Skar to

Tåsen – parked somewhere down the road, went in, killed her husband, rode the bike all the way back, hid it, and went back to her
tent again. And we're supposed to believe that her sister and her
daughter slept undisturbed and didn't notice that she was gone for a
couple of hours – that's a whole other story. But anyway. She did all
this, went all out. Planned it all so carefully. Why in all the world
would she do that?"

"To catch him red-handed," I say lamely. "Isn't that what she
said?"

"Apparently so," Ingvild says, and she's excited now, an agitated
red flush has appeared in her sweaty cheeks. "But she also says that
Jørgen wasn't particularly careful about hiding his infidelities – the
lipstick marks on the wine glasses and condoms in the toiletry bag
and whatever else there was. If we take that into consideration, it
seems she could have just said she was going to a cabin for the weekend, stayed over with a friend and then driven back home and
checked. Right? If he cheated in such an overt way, this painstaking
plan seems totally unnecessary."

Her bike lurches to one side; she tugs it back on course with a
brisk movement.

"The only benefit I see to sleeping in a tent out in the forest,
apparently without access to transport into the city, is this: there
would be no trace of her. Nobody would know that she'd been to
Tåsen that night. If necessary, she could prove that she wasn't there."

"So you think it was premeditated?" I ask. "Is that what you're
saying?"

"I'm just saying that I don't believe she did all this just to catch
Jørgen in the act. These laborious preparations make much more
sense if you imagine she was planning a murder."

When I was interviewed on the day of Merete's arrest, I told
police that I suspected that Merete had planned to murder Jørgen
in order to inherit the apartment. But later, I wasn't so sure. After

all, she hadn't said this straight out. My head had been spinning around Lukas the entire time she was speaking – where was he, what had happened, why couldn't I hear him? – and when I've since gone through the conversation in my mind, I can't remember that she ever said, in as many words, that she killed him. She spoke about the inheritance, but whether in terms of a lucky consequence of Jørgen's death or as a motive for murder, I'm not sure. In later interviews, Gundersen pushed me – what words did she use, what did she say, exactly? I said that I wasn't sure. I meant this, in a way, but doubtless also thought that I was making amends in some way by permitting my uncertainty to benefit her. If it truly was the case that she planned it, they would surely find other evidence. When they didn't, I became unsure myself. Maybe the story she told the court was true? Who was I to say otherwise?

We pass a group of friends in their twenties who have spread blankets over the grass and set themselves up with disposable grills and bottles of beer. They're speaking animatedly about something, and one laughs, ringing and uncontrolled – he's so young that he hasn't learned to restrain his laughter just yet, though perhaps he's just drunk. Ingvild pays them no attention. She wrinkles her brow.

"It's also strange," she says, "that everybody slept so well that night. Filippa and Merete's sister in the tent, and Jørgen – Jørgen is supposed to have fallen asleep in front of his computer, in the middle of an argument. We found traces of benzodiazepines in his blood – sedatives that can be used to treat anxiety or insomnia. Jørgen had been prescribed such medication – he had traumatic memories that gave him trouble sleeping, his GP says. But to take sleeping medication and then sit at your computer? And to take quite a significant dose of it, at that? By the time suspicion turned to Merete a week had already passed, so there was no point in testing the daughter and the sister. But I've wondered about it. I really have."

"Do you think she gave them sleeping pills?" I ask.

Ingvild casts a quick glance at me.

"Maybe," she says. "But she denies it, and I'll probably never be able to find out if she's telling the truth."

We walk under a bridge, feeling its shadow reduce the sun's heat a little, and then, when we've emerged on the other side, Ingvild says:

"And then there's the other thing – the code lock on the front door. I understand that Nina Sparre managed to wrangle a copy of the data out of the locksmith's and handed it out to everyone, so you've probably heard that nobody let themselves in after half past midnight that night."

"Yes."

"Merete says that she rang the doorbell and that Jørgen let her in. And that's a little strange, if you ask me, considering the great lengths she went to in order to be able to surprise him. She had the code, after all. Why not just let herself in? I'm not sure whether you heard, but the defence dug up a psychologist who testified in court that people can both want something and not want it at the same time. Merete claims that she wanted to confront Jørgen, but that she didn't want to walk in on him and his lover having sex, and well, what do I know, maybe that's possible. But it also seems a little far-fetched. Couldn't she have just shouted out to them once she was inside the apartment? That would have reduced the chance of any lover hiding or managing to sneak away, too. But no – Merete buzzes Jørgen on the intercom instead, and he answers. And I've inter-viewed her about this myself, Rikke, so I've heard her say that he said yes, who is it, and she said, it's me, can you let me in? I mean – it's the middle of the night, things are not good between them, and she offers no explanation as to why she's ringing the doorbell and potentially waking him instead of entering the code. So why didn't she just let herself in? A far more believable reason than that she wanted to warn him, I think, is that she knew the information about which codes were entered would be stored, and she wanted to ensure she left behind nothing that might prove she was there that night.

"But Jørgen let her in?" I say. "Wouldn't he have been suspicious if what you say is true?"

"Yes, maybe," Ingvild says. "To tell you the truth, Rikke, I can't help thinking that this would have been much easier if Merete had had somebody on the inside. If there was a person inside the building, who let her in. A neighbour, perhaps. This other person might even have ensured that Jørgen took the sleeping pills while Merete was still out in the forest."

My breathing begins to slow. It's as if the heat subsides, too; my hands become numb. Ingvild and I walk calmly beside each other, this is just an ordinary summer's afternoon, and yet it's as if everything hangs in the balance as I turn to her and say:

"Who are you thinking of?"

"I can't say any more than that," Ingvild says coolly. "But I have an idea, of course. Although it isn't something I can prove."

"But you're thinking of a specific person?"

"Perhaps," she says.

"Who then?"

We walk below another bridge. We're almost in Nydalen now, I can already hear the children's laughter from the bathing area. This must be where they are, the families who haven't left the city. It won't be long until we reach the train station.

Ingvild says:

"I can't give you a name when I don't know for sure. And the term of appeal ran out yesterday. The case is therefore closed, as far as the public is concerned."

So this was not by chance, I think – of course it wasn't some incredible stroke of luck that we met on the street just now. That I just happened to bump into Ingvild Fredly right outside the building where I work, ready for a conversation, the day after the sentence became legally binding.

"Is it me?"

Now she stops. We turn to face each other, and there's something ice-cold in the hot air. We look at each other.

"No, Rikke," Ingvild says.

Her voice is calm, her gaze firm, and we stand there like this, facing one another. There isn't the tiniest drop of sweat left on her now. She has freckles down her throat, a smattering of them across her face, too. She looks much less powerful wearing cycling gear than she does when she's in uniform, and yet I don't doubt that she's a police officer, not for a single moment.

"No," she says again, starting to walk. "No, why would you get involved? And I don't think you would have gone up into his apartment that Saturday had you known he was dead."

"Oh," I say.

I don't think my blush will be noticeable in the heat, but on any other day I'm sure it would have been.

"Saman saw you," she says, casting a sidelong glance at me. "But you can relax, Merete had sent a ton of messages that morning, perhaps to reinforce the fact that he was already dead. You had sent him one, too. And he had fallen asleep in front of a Skype call with an academic at a university in Chennai. The academic had tried to call him back several times that night, as well as the following morning. No – if you had been involved, I think you would have acted with a little more cunning that day. Although of course, one never really knows. And it was a little suspicious that you denied it."

"I was so afraid that you would suspect me," I say. "Oh God, it was so stupid. But just . . . it was him, Gundersen. Had it been you who asked me, things would have been different."

On the other side of the river we can see them now, the families. The small, pasty bodies of children clambering in and out of the water. The beach balls, cooler bags and bicycles.

"Well," Fredly says. "Here we are. I guess you're heading into the T-banen?"

"Yes," I say. "I guess I am."

She unhooks her helmet from the bike's handlebars.

"This thing is so much less stylish than a motorbike helmet," she sighs. "But you know what they say."

"Safety first," I mumble.

She grins.

"Exactly."

She slings one leg over the bike, preparing to leave. Then she looks at me, just a quick glance out of the corner of her eye, before I catch a glint there. She looks down at her handlebars, adjusts them.

"By the way," she says. "Åsmund knew about you and Jørgen. Did he mention it?"

"What did you say?"

My voice sounds strange, as if it's coming from far off in the distance. As if I'm standing twenty metres away, watching us. Two women: one on a bicycle, one in a summer dress, as if I'm watching us on a TV screen. What is the one in the summer dress saying? Maybe I should look for the remote control, turn up the volume.

"Yes," Fredly says. "Gundersen told him. He brought Åsmund in for questioning one day that week and told him what you had written in your email. He was devastated. Or at least, he said he was. And then he asked Gundersen not to tell you that he knew. Something to do with hearing it from you – or seeing whether you'd come clean yourself."

"What?" I ask again.

As if there's something wrong with my hearing. As if that's the problem, that I can't hear what Ingvild is saying.

"Well, it wasn't exactly important to the investigation how you sorted things out between you. Not at that point, at least, so Gundersen didn't confront you with it. And then the video footage from Rikard Hoffmo turned up, and after that it no longer mattered. But yes. I thought it would be good for you to know. As a kind of friendly favour."

There's something in the smile she gives me that I can't quite interpret – is it humour, or is it concern? Is she worried for me? Then she hops up onto her bike.

"Speak soon, Rikke. Get home safe."

The T-banen has almost made it out to the city limits when it dawns on me – the thing I noticed that Saturday up in Jørgen's apartment. When I stood in the hallway overwhelmed by a reluctance to go in. The door to Jørgen's study was closed, and I had stopped, feeling that something was wrong in the apartment. There was something in the air, I had thought then. And when I think back now, I can almost smell the scent that stole through the rooms. Wet moss. The smell of the forest where I grew up. The aftershave Åsmund has used every single day for as long as I've known him.

THE LAST EVENING

The bright afternoon sun filters into the living room; as I come downstairs from the children's rooms I see the stripes it creates. It's so quiet here. Most of the neighbours are on holiday. In the living room, I stop – out on the veranda sits Åsmund. He's presumably looking at his phone, all I can see is the back of his head above the back of the garden chair. I stand there for a moment. He's facing away from me, hasn't yet noticed that I've come down. I could change my mind. Go back upstairs again, fill the bathtub with cold water and take a bath. Go get my bike and cycle out into the forest, find a small lake to swim in. Walk soundlessly up the stairs to my bedroom, lie down with a book and stay there. I don't have to do this. But at the same time, I know that I must. Out there sits my husband. We've eaten dinner together; I've put Lukas to bed. He's waiting for me. But still I stand here, watching the light from the low sun fall across the parquet of the living-room floor, rectangular designs of light and shadow.

"Hey," he says, without turning around.

I go across to him and he hands me a bottle of beer – he's brought one out for me and put it next to his on the little table between the chairs. It's still cold, I can see the condensation on the brown glass.

"Thanks," I say.

"Isn't this lovely?" he says once I've sat down. "Just being able to sit like this in the evenings? On our own private terrace?"

"Mm."

"I'm so pleased we managed to get the grill to work. It was good, don't you think?"

"It was."

He laughs.

"Now we're going to have to have a barbecue every single day until October, Rikke – *that's* how happy I am with that grill."

I attempt a smile, turning up the corners of my mouth. I've smiled so many times in my life – it's usually easy. He's looking at me, I notice from the corner of my eye, but our chairs are turned to face what we call "the view". Our house is situated on the top of a hill, opposite another that together with ours creates a kind of valley. We look out over the rows of small terraced houses further down the hill, in their groups of four, with a poorer view than the one we have from up here. At the bottom of the not-quite-valley runs a road, which passes a football pitch and a kindergarten before it curves around a petrol station. On the other side of it, the forest begins. The tops of dark spruces form a jagged line that follows the curve of the hill crest. Åsmund turns to face the view again, and so here we sit.

"I bumped into Ingvild Fredly today," I say to the forest across the valley.

"Did you?" he says.

"Yes."

He says nothing further. A little time passes. Far away, we hear a girl laughing.

"She was on a pushbike," I say.

"Crikey," he says.

"We had a little chat."

"Oh really?"

Is there something guarded about the way he's acting? I don't know, and I daren't turn to face him. So I'm speaking to the trees across the valley when I say:

"About the court case. A bit about the investigation, too."

"Hm."

It's so quiet. I cast a sidelong glance at Åsmund. He's leaning back in the garden chair, a man on his own private terrace. I can't even tell if he's listening to me.

"She said that you knew about Jørgen and me," I say. "She said the detective – you know, Gundersen – told you about it one day that week, before they arrested Merete. And then she implied that you already knew."

He doesn't answer. We sit there for a while, and then I turn to him.

"Is that true?"

He looks at me. His face is completely neutral. His mouth is closed, his eyes focused, as if he's concentrating on taking this all in. I count the seconds, the way I did when I was a child and saw lightning strike: one Mississippi, two Mississippi.

"What is it you're asking me, Rikke?" he says.

His voice is calm, and something in it chills me. There's something calculating there. Something I've never heard from him before.

"When did you find out about Jørgen and me?"

I pose this question without actually deciding to do so. My voice is thin and strange. It feels as if I'm asking about something else entirely, something utterly banal. He takes a deep breath. Leans back in the chair. Looks out across the valley.

"I realised on that cabin trip," he says finally. "We were sitting around the table drinking, and then Jørgen told a story about how he was in Bergen and got chatting to a mariachi band he convinced to play 'Sympathy for the Devil'."

"Oh," I say quietly.

Åsmund takes a breath.

"I was raging," he says. "Started bawling at him. Found an idiotic reason, some point of discussion that was going around the table right then, and just flew off the handle at him. If we hadn't been so drunk, the others probably would have thought that it was fucking weird, that level of anger."

I nod, slowly. Realise that I didn't believe Saman when he told me that Åsmund was the angriest of them all. Svein, of course, thought Saman had been the most aggressive, and Jørgen never mentioned the incident to me.

"But it was obvious," Åsmund says, something quivering in his voice beneath the frosty calm. "Once I started looking for signs, they weren't so hard to see. You were supposedly going out to meet a friend one evening, and then the next day the same friend posted a photo from her cabin on Facebook. You'd go out, and then ten minutes later he would go out, too. Loads of things like that."

He turned to face me.

"When I tried checking your phone, you'd changed your pass-code. And you never change the codes on anything, Rikke. In the end, I managed to sneak a look when you were in the shower – you'd just been using it, so it wasn't locked. And then I had incontrovert-ible proof, as it were."

"Why didn't you say anything?" I whisper.

"You don't think I wanted to?" he says. "I wanted to scream at you, *what the fuck are you doing?* But it was the text messages. The tone you took in them, as if you were writing to someone you loved. I was afraid you'd fallen in love with him. So I asked Merete. I came home one day when all the neighbours were at work, went up and knocked on the door, and told her what I'd found. She fell to pieces. Said that Jørgen had been carrying on like that for years. That it had happened so many times – including with one of her childhood friends a few years earlier. Merete thought that as long as it hap-pened with someone who wasn't too close, she could live with it. What he did when he was away for work was one thing, but she hated the thought of it being someone they had to socialise with. That all this was going on at home, in her own house, where her daughter lived. That Filippa might walk in on you, find out. Merete said Jørgen was like that – he seduced people. Seemed so open, a free spirit, all that shit. She said people bought it. Especially women. And she said that from the moment she first saw you, she'd known you were just the type he'd go after."

I think of Merete when I saw her out on the patio that day before we moved in. When I stood in the window and waved to her. When she stood on the lawn and stared at me, without returning my greeting.

Åsmund says:

"I understood that he had seduced you. We'd been going through a bit of a rough patch, you and me, after Pappa died. All the stuff with Mamma, and all the worries about Lukas's health. I wasn't there for you as much as I should have been. Didn't talk to you enough about what had happened. Maybe I didn't listen all that much, either. So then I thought – I was the one who let it happen."

Now there are tears in his eyes, and he says:

"I couldn't lose you, Rikke. Do you remember the time I was out drink-driving with my friends? When we were in that accident?"

"That was in high school," I say.

"I thought you were going to leave me. And I wouldn't have blamed you if you had – fuck, I thought, what an idiot I've been. You deserved so much better. But then you stayed with me. In a way, I thought this thing with Jørgen was the same. That Jørgen was your accident, and now it was my turn to forgive you for being stupid."

"But that was so long ago," I say weakly, as if in protest.

"Well, it meant a lot to me," he says in self-defence.

We sit in silence, for a long time. This is also an opportunity to let it go, right here, I think. It's still possible to go up to the bathroom, fill the tub with cold water. But then I say:

"Ingvild Fredly thinks Merete might have had an accomplice."

I say this firmly, but I can hear only too well how childish it sounds. The statement hangs in the air between us, above the little table and the bottles of ever warmer beer. As if this sentence is a physical thing we now have to respond to, deal with.

It hangs there for some time. My breath is audible and frantic, as if I'm running for my life. I turn my head and look at him. He's sitting there observing the view, calm, his mouth closed. Then he turns to face me. There are no tears in his eyes now.

"Rikke," he says, and his voice is foreign, high-pitched and unpleasant. "Are you sure you want to ask me about this?"

Am I? I no longer recognise him. My mouth is dry, but I don't want to reach for the beer on the table. It's as if I'm acting against my own will when I speak. As if I really want to say, no, you know what, I'm not so sure after all, maybe we should just let it lie – and then I'll go upstairs and take that bath instead. It's almost a compulsion when I say:

"I slept so deeply that night. So unusually deeply. I didn't even hear Lukas come in. If you had got up, would I have heard you?"

He says:

"No. You wouldn't."

That same high-pitched, unfamiliar voice. I want to stop, but I can't, it's as if my body continues of its own volition.

"I felt tired as soon as we'd started drinking the wine that night," I say. "I couldn't even stay awake to finish watching the film. Fredly said that Jørgen had a sedative in his blood. Benzo-something-or-other."

Åsmund says:

"So what are you saying?"

"You drugged me," I say, not even aware that I've thought this until the words come out of my mouth. "You and I were each other's alibis, and as long as I'd been asleep all night, you could say the same was true for you. But I was unconscious. And while I was asleep, you went upstairs. Maybe you gave him a glass of wine, or

436

maybe you asked him to taste something or other you'd brought along, I don't know. But you gave him the sedative. And you were up in his apartment that night – in fact I know that for certain. Then you came back downstairs, washed and tidied everything up. And then all you had to do was wait. She turned up at the agreed time, you let her in. Of course, she was the one to do it – you can't stand the sight of blood, you couldn't have done it. But you made sure that he was asleep by the time she went upstairs. He had collapsed in front of his computer. All she needed to do was pull the knife across his throat – quick and easy, no resistance – and then leave again. All you had to do was let her in, and then go and lie back down in bed, beside me."

Blood is pounding at my temples. I'm out of breath after all this, still can't comprehend that I've actually said it. He sits there, stock-still. Thinking. Then he turns to me, and in a grave voice says:

"Jørgen Tangen was not a good person. He led you astray. I didn't want to lose you. And Merete wanted to be free."

The words crash to the floor between us. I can feel the reverberations in the chairs in which we sit. Think of Filippa out in the garden with her mother, shrouded in a grief that it's obvious – just from looking at her – will be with her for the rest of her life.

"They could have suspected me," I say, my voice trembling now. "Did you think about that? I went up to see Jørgen that Saturday – you didn't know that, but I did. The police could easily have thought that I was the one who did it. They might have suspected somebody else, someone who was innocent. What would you have done then? What if they had thought it was Emma?"

"If they had suspected either of you," he says calmly, "then I would have come forward. That's something I was prepared to do. Merete and I agreed we wouldn't implicate each other. If one of us was caught, they'd take the fall alone. It was a risk. But we thought it was such a small one. We were willing to take it."

437

My breathing is too shallow, the air isn't getting down into my lungs properly, I can feel it. I try to take a deep breath, down into my belly, but instantly feel dizzy. The panic is about to overwhelm me. I simply cannot believe it – not only what he's done, but also that he's talking about it like this. Jørgen Tangen was not a good person. It was a risk he was willing to take. This is Åsmund's defence, his version of how he's not a criminal, he's just a poor man. This cowardly, pointless justification for causing someone's death.

"She was the one who needed him dead," Åsmund says, slowly and earnestly, as if speaking to a child. "And she was the one who did it. All I did was facilitate it. And I did it for your sake, Rikke. So that you would have the opportunity to make things right. So that you wouldn't slip away from me."

Sparking flashes are starting to appear at the edges of my vision, and I try to concentrate on breathing evenly, calmly. Did Åsmund buy Merete's sob story, her tale of suffering? But no, that isn't what he's saying, that isn't what I hear. The defence is too well-practised, too certain. All he did was facilitate it, he claims, and yet I can see his fingerprints all over this ghastly affair. He got a lift home with Svein after that cabin trip, had the time to plant a convenient memory of the previous night's discussion in the mind of the driver – one that confirmed prejudices that Svein already had, no doubt. He was on the board of the housing cooperative, so he knew all the details about how an entry log was kept by the locksmith's. He sought out Merete, told her about Jørgen and me. I can just imagine it. He lets her vent, and when she's done, he says: But you know, there is *something* we could do about this. Merete pays the price, and he walks free. And now he lives with us, in the big house in Bærum he's always wanted, close to his mother and far from Tåsen, with Jørgen out of the picture for good. My vision swims.

"Excuse me," I say.

As I get up I become light-headed; for a moment everything turns

438

black and I'm afraid I'm about to collapse, but I grip the back of the chair and use it for support. I have to stay on my feet. I have to go inside. Just need to take a little break, throw cold water on my face. Just have to think clearly.

I fumble for the veranda door. And there, in the doorway, stands Emma.

She's already put on her nightie; her hair hangs messily around her face. She's staring at me, and something moves in her eyes, something I already know I'll never be able to make right.

The door was ajar. I didn't close it after me when I came out onto the veranda. Didn't think to ensure that she wouldn't be able to hear us before I confronted Åsmund. Didn't protect her – failed yet again. Behind me, I hear Åsmund's chair creak. I lift a hand, wanting to stroke the hair away from her face, but I hesitate. My hand remains hanging in the air between us. And before he reaches us, I just have time to think that now, yes now, everything will come undone.

HELENE FLOOD is a psychologist who lives in Oslo with her husband and two children. *The Therapist*, her first adult novel, was the winner of Norway's Best Crime Debut Prize and Iceland's award for Best Translated Crime Novel. Film rights have been sold, as well as translation rights in twenty-eight languages.

ALISON MCCULLOUGH is a Norwegian-to-English translator based in Stavanger, Norway. Previous translations include *The Therapist* by Helene Flood, *The Wolf Age* by Tore Skeie and *Lean Your Loneliness Slowly Against Mine* by Klara Hveberg, which was longlisted for the PEN Translation Prize 2022.